PRAISE FOR THE SPLIT WORLDS

"Newman brings an intriguing mix of modern world, Victorian/Regency England, and faery in her Split Worlds series, and this third volume brings a strong resolution to the conflicts between the worlds established in the first two volumes."

—*Locus* **magazine**

"A modern fantasy that playfully mixes magic and interesting characters into an intriguing mystery."

—*Kirkus Reviews*

"Newman renders the Split Worlds with verve and an infectious sense of fun, and presents in Cathy a strong and personable heroine."

—*The Guardian*

"Emma Newman has built a modern fantasy world with such élan and authority her ideas of why and how the seemingly irrational world of Fairy works should be stolen by every other writer in the field. Her characters are complex and troubled, courageous at times and foolhardy. This book of wonders is first rate."

—**Bill Willingham, Eisner Award winner, and creator of** *Fables*

"Emma Newman has created a reflection of Bath that reminds one that charming is not safe. *Between Two Thorns* shows the darkness beneath the glamour of the social Season. Learning to be a young lady has never seemed so dangerous."

—**Mary Robinette Kowal, Hugo Award winner,**
and author of *Glamour in Glass*

"With a feather-light touch, Emma Newman has crafted a very English fantasy, one brilliantly realised and quite delightful, weaving magic, mystery and parallel worlds together with ease. Newman may well be one of our brightest stars, *The Split Worlds: Between Two Thorns* is just the beginning of a remarkable jou"

—**Adam Christopher, author of** *Empi*

"*Between Two Thorns* is magical, exciting, and clever. It manages to conjure a world that feels completely natural but also mysterious, sometimes dangerous, sometimes funny, combining several different kinds of urban fantasy into one story, and capturing a lovely sense of modern Britishness that is reminiscent of other fantastic British fantasy. I'm eagerly awaiting the sequel!"

—Fantasy Faction

"I'm actually very glad this is the beginning of a series because I want more of this world, more of these characters and more of this insanity. Newman has created a great complex universe that seems to have a million different stories embedded into its walls. In a world full of supernatural and urban fantasy books, *Between Two Thorns* stands out as the start of a uniquely developed series that deserves everyone's full attention."

—Mandroid

"This novel draws you in from the very first, tempting you with magical creatures set against present day Bath. I tried only reading one chapter just to test the writing style, etc but found myself, a few hours later, having read a vast amount of the book … It sits beautifully within my favourite type of fantasy novel, fairy tale within the present day."

—SF Crowsnest

"An enchanting novel from Emma Newman, an urban fantasy that has no sign of tattooed women in leather pants. A headstrong scion and an investigator discover dark doings in the outwardly genteel world of Bath's secret mirror city."

—SF Signal

"*Between Two Thorns* really was an unalloyed pleasure to read and it's hard to write a review for it that isn't just gushing … Newman has created a unique blend of urban, historical, and crime fantasy clothed in a Regency veneer. *Between Two Thorns* is delicious, engrossing, and enchanting and, so far, my debut of the year."

—A Fantastical Librarian

a little knowledge

THE **SPLIT WORLDS**
BOOK FOUR

EMMA NEWMAN

DIVERSIONBOOKS

Also by Emma Newman

The Split Worlds Series
Between Two Thorns
Any Other Name
All is Fair

Diversion Books
A Division of Diversion Publishing Corp.
443 Park Avenue South, Suite 1008
New York, New York 10016
www.DiversionBooks.com

This is a work of fiction. Names, characters, places and incidents either are the
product of the author's imagination or are used fictitiously. Any resemblance to
actual persons, living or dead, events or locales is entirely coincidental.

For more information, email info@diversionbooks.com

First Diversion Books edition August 2016.
Print ISBN: 978-1-68230-291-0
eBook ISBN: 978-1-68230-290-3

For the lady who LARPs, she of the flaming sword,
who took a dream that had died and made it live again.

1

Cathy listened to the argument, weighed its merit, and considered her response carefully, as the Duchess of Londinium should. "This is bullshit."

That also summarised most of what Cathy had discovered about being Duchess of Londinium. She'd had high hopes—once she'd overcome the sheer dread of having such high status—that the title of Duchess would confer upon her enough power to really make a difference in Fae-touched Society. In reality, the only power Cathy had was confined to areas in which she had no interest whatsoever.

What was the use of setting Londinium fashion when she didn't give a stuff about necklines and fabrics and whether things should have lace trims or not? What was the point of being the woman all the others looked to for social cues when they were lost on her in the first place? Cathy still cringed at the memory of the first soirée they'd held at the Tower; one of the Buttercup ladies had fainted because she hadn't eaten. Appalled, Cathy had discovered that none of the female guests had gone near the feast laid out for them because she, as Duchess, hadn't yet had the first bite. Having the power to dictate when all of the women in the room could start eating was the tragic pinnacle of her influence. She should have known that only the Duke would have any real power.

Everyone kept telling her how influential and important the Duchess was, but whenever Cathy tried to pin down exactly *how* she could wield that influence and importance, it was all vague comments and shrugs. Margritte Tulipa, who had been Duchess for less than an hour and frankly, still should have been, had tried to explain it to her. Apparently, it was all about presenting an image of stability and strength whilst indicating who was in favour and who was not. Margritte had patiently described the subtleties of whom Cathy should look at or talk to in different situations and how to respond, but it was like another language. Theoretically, it was to help the ladies in the Londinium Court know who was worth speaking to and who wasn't. Cathy couldn't for the life of her fathom why that would be so. Surely they could make up their own minds!

It didn't help that at social events she just wanted to sneak off and read a book, like she had as a child. Although Cathy understood that wasn't possible anymore, it was too much of a leap to suddenly acquire all the social delicacy and insight now required of her. Cathy had the delicacy and insight of a cat with its head stuck in a box moving backwards to try and escape it, and she knew it.

Even in the library Will had created for her, with three women she loved and respected, Cathy felt impotent. No one was listening to her. She didn't want to stamp her foot and shout "Who's Duchess?" in a shrill voice, but it was sorely tempting as the argument circled again and again.

Margritte's eyes, round as pennies, were fixed on Cathy. "This is the best compromise we can reach. I think it's too early, but if you're determined to go into the Court and be controversial, this is the best we can agree on."

"I'm not determined to be controversial," Cathy said. "I'm determined to make some bloody changes, and setting up a women's court is the wrong way to go! We should have the right to speak in the Londinium Court just like the men do. A crappy girl version reinforces the idea that women have to have something separate and special."

"Who said this new court would be a 'crappy girl version'?" Margritte asked.

"No one, but it's obvious that's what it will be."

"Is it?" Margritte pressed. "I was hoping it would be a space where women can gather with the sole purpose of discussing matters of import without fearing male censorship. Forgive me, Cathy, but I thought that was what we all agreed was sorely needed here."

Cathy looked at Natasha Rainer, her former governess, for support. This was the woman who had taught her about the suffragists and Peterloo, the single most influential person in her life. Natasha's lips were pressed in a tight, thin line, as if she were using them like a dam to hold back a torrent. She still didn't have the confidence to argue passionately against Margritte, no matter how many times she agreed with Cathy when they were in private. Cathy suspected that Natasha hadn't fully recovered from the years of being cursed to forget who she was. Thanks to Sam she had been restored, but that time as a brainwashed scullery maid had scarred her.

Frustrated, Cathy looked to Charlotte Persificola-Viola. Surely she would understand? Charlotte had marched as a suffragette in Mundanus; how could she think that anything less than full equality in the right to speak would be acceptable? Charlotte's perfect brow was furrowed between her eyes as she met Cathy's gaze. "I agree with Margritte. You've already put some noses out of joint. Anything you say is going to be scrutinised. Why not wait just a few more weeks? Let them get used to the idea of an active Duchess, and then make the announcement."

Unbelievable. Had her friend forgotten the years of being trapped in her own body, turned into nothing more than an animated doll to sing her husband's praises? If it hadn't been for her and Sam, Charlotte would still be that! "How can you say that after all you've been through?"

"That's exactly the reason why I think you should be cautious!"

"But Will isn't like your husband!" Cathy said. "He's supporting us." Will knew she wanted change in Society and could have shut their meetings down weeks ago. Unlike Charlotte's husband, the odious Bertrand Viola, Will could cope with her having opinions of her own. "He's not going to do anything like that to me."

"There are other men that would, without your husband's knowledge," Margritte said. "Just because he's the Duke of Londinium, it doesn't mean he can protect you every moment of every day, not when so many have access to powerful magic."

That made Cathy pause. That git from the Agency, Bennet, had managed to curse her without anyone else finding out, and blackmail her as well. She hadn't seen him since Will found out and had him taken away. She pushed the thought aside. The Londinium Court would gather in less than an hour, and they were still arguing. "I'm not going to let the fear of men trying to silence me—with violence or magic—stop me from doing what I need to do."

Cathy went to the fireplace. She felt safe in her library but it didn't make their discussions—or the decisions she had to make—any easier. Leaning against the mantelpiece, her back to them, she tried to hold on to the positives.

None of these women would be with her, discussing how to change Nether Society with such passion, if it hadn't been for her and Will. None of the staff in her household would have rights and wages without her efforts. Even now, over a hundred people were enjoying freedom after decades of imprisonment in a mundane asylum because of her actions.

It wasn't enough.

A mere fortnight ago, Cathy had stood up in front of the Londinium Court and announced that there were going to be changes. She'd said that her being able to speak at the Court as Duchess, instead of only the Duke having a voice, was only the beginning. Filled with the drive to finally make a difference, she'd offered all of the women there the opportunity to approach her with anything they wished to discuss, as a fundamental right of all female Londinium residents. Thinking it wasn't enough, judging by the silent stares, she'd added that should any of those concerns be ones that affected Londinium or be as a result of residency in the city, she would raise them with the Duke.

That had elicited a ripple through the crowd, one that had pleased her at the time. *At last,* she'd thought, *a woman has finally had the chance to speak in the Londinium Court and be heard.*

But when they returned home, Will had made her aware of just how far she'd apparently overstepped the mark.

"You've just told every man in that room that his wife can bend my ear without having to go through him."

She shrugged. "So? That's a good thing. Any one of those women may have concerns—valid concerns—that are just dismissed by their husbands because they've voiced them. Why should their husband be the sole judge of their merit?"

"Cathy, you've just stood up in front of that court and told everyone there that you place your own ability to judge what should reach the Duke's ear above that of every man in that room."

"Oh, come on. That's not what I meant."

"That's how they feel about it."

"I don't give a shit about how they feel. I give a shit about how those women are silenced."

His voice dropped then, sinking into the cold anger that she still hadn't got used to. "Perhaps you could muster a care about the fact that I didn't agree to it, and the fact that all of those men now see you as a problem."

They'd argued late into the night. It was still frosty between them the next morning, and Cathy had barely seen him since. Being a duke was demanding, it seemed, and while she missed the times they were together and not arguing, she couldn't deny the fact she was relieved to be left to her own devices.

As frustrating and hollow as being Duchess was proving to be, Cathy hadn't been idle. There was the pamphlet she'd created with Natasha. Just the thought of it made her smile. It contained everything she felt a woman should know about her own body, the rights for women that had been fought for and won in mundane England, and thoughts on how women living in the Nether were held back by not having the same opportunities as the men. Above all else, Cathy hoped it would educate, empower, and inspire the women in the Great Families, making them want more than the intellectually and emotionally impoverished existence they were permitted.

Natasha had agreed that keeping it secret from Charlotte, Margritte, and Will would give them plausible deniability—critical when a Truth Charm could be used by anyone opposed to the true education of women, which amounted to the majority of people in Society. Over a dozen letters from concerned women in Londinium had been sent to her, complaining about how they'd found their daughters reading facts about sex, contraception, and what life is like for women in Mundanus. Cathy wanted to frame every single one after highlighting the most hysterical terms. *Dangerous, disgusting,* and *damaging* were the three that appeared the most. She wanted to get a T-shirt printed with those words on it and wear it to the next Court with a pair of jeans.

Cathy was proud of what she'd written. Natasha had edited it, typed it on a computer in Mundanus, and arranged its printing and distribution via her network of secret feminists, some of whom Cathy had already met at the bookshop in Bath. People had tried to use magical means to trace the author to someone in Society and had failed, thanks to the involvement of the computer and printers. By the time furious husbands and fathers were casting their Charms on any copy, it had been passed between so many hands that it was impossible to determine even a source of the distribution, exactly as she and Natasha had planned it.

And it had done more than just upset people. Charlotte's daughter, Emmeline, told her the pamphlet's impact was evident at the end-of-season ball in Aquae Sulis just a few days ago. Young women were fired up, speaking in hushed whispers and passing the pamphlet between each other at great risk. Some had even arrived at the ball dressed as men! Even though the Censor of Aquae Sulis had laughed it all off as just the fun of a masquerade ball, traditionally more raucous and daring than most, Cathy knew there was more to it. Surely this was the beginning of something?

So why did she feel like she was getting absolutely nowhere?

"This court for Londinium women just doesn't feel like a step forwards," Cathy said with a sigh.

"I feel the same way," Natasha said. "But we have to consider every man in that room hostile to any sort of equality. While I don't relish the idea of a separate court, I can't help but think that the majority of women need a social space in which they're encouraged to raise issues and debate without fear of reprisal."

"And my hope would be that it would give the gentlemen time to grow accustomed to the idea that women may hold and discuss opinions in topics outside of the domestic sphere," Margritte said. "In time, we could hold formal debates and invite a speaker from the women's court to present an opinion to—"

"Urgh!" Cathy rounded on them. "No! This isn't the way to do this! The men will automatically disregard anything the women's court proposes or raises and it will just entrench everyone on opposing sides."

"Then what do you suggest?" Margritte asked.

"During a discussion I could ask a woman to speak, just like Will invites the gentlemen to share their thoughts on any topic."

"Oh, no, Cathy," Charlotte said, appalled. "No lady would dare speak up and you would be left looking a complete fool!"

"We aren't the only ones who feel this way," Cathy said, thinking of her sister-in-law, Lucy. "Maybe we should have some faith in them." She'd wanted to involve Lucy more, but the others had vetoed it most forcefully. The wife of the Marquis of Westminster simply couldn't be trusted; her husband's job was to neutralise any threats to the Dukedom and stability of Society. Everything they had done and planned to do could easily be interpreted as such. Hell, threatening the stability of Society was what she wanted to do most.

"It's too much of a risk," Charlotte said. "I know you think me cowardly, but I can't be seen to do anything like that in public. I daren't risk my husband realising the curse he put on me is broken. Women offering an opinion risk being cursed into silence too."

"Which is exactly why we need to encourage a separate court," Margritte said. "To give women the confidence to speak—"

A knock on the door stopped her from saying any more. Cathy listened to the rhythm. "It's Will," she said to Margritte, who had already stood, ready to dash to the mirror and make her escape to her hiding place in Jorvic.

Cathy turned the key and admitted Will. Carter, her bodyguard, gave her a polite nod before she closed the door and locked it again.

"Good evening," Will said with a warm smile. The slight blush that crept across Charlotte's cheeks didn't escape Cathy's notice. If her handsome husband was aware of the effect he had on some women, he never showed it.

Margritte curtsied and returned to her seat as Natasha and Charlotte greeted him politely.

"I trust you're ready, my love?" Will asked with a smile. There was no hint of their previous argument. Cathy marvelled at how different he was from the other men of Nether Society. Yes, he'd been angry with her, but he hadn't put an end to these meetings and was still willing to support change. Whether they would ever agree on how to achieve that was another matter.

"We were just discussing a potential court for the women of Londinium," Cathy said.

"Oh, yes," Will glanced at Margritte as if he knew of it already. "And are you going to announce it this evening?"

Cathy frowned. "I don't think it's a good idea."

"Why not? Margritte and I discussed it at length earlier this week."

Will was helping to keep Margritte safely hidden away from his brother. As far as the rest of Oxenford and those in the know in the other Nether cities were concerned, she was still locked in the tower in the reflection of Oxford Castle. They must have discussed it when he delivered the Shadow Charms.

"I think it will be less controversial than your first statement to the court," Will continued. "I've smoothed the feathers you ruffled and made sure no one got the wrong idea."

"And what idea would that be?" Cathy asked, folding her arms.

"That you want to encourage wives to go behind their husbands' backs."

Cathy suspected Margritte had deliberately gone behind *her* back to persuade Will to support the idea before their meeting.

Will misinterpreted her scowl. "Don't worry. We can discuss the best way for you to announce this court for women in the carriage on the way to the tower. I think if you put it to the room in a certain way, no one will be concerned."

"Don't you mean 'if I tread carefully around the men's feelings, none of them will try to stop me'?"

Will leaned forwards and kissed her forehead. "Darling, there's no need to be so prickly about this. It's just good diplomacy."

Cathy sucked in a breath, feeling her latent rage rise up at the way he was managing her. So often lately she felt as if Will treated her like a feverish child, one to keep quiet and soothed with a cold compress, lest she work herself up too much. This wasn't the time to make a scene, though. She had to pace herself and work out a way to bring him round, without showing the others how strained things were between them. Bloody hell, was this what Margritte had meant when she'd said that being Duchess was about presenting an image?

"Now, if you'll excuse us, ladies," Will said, "we have a court to prepare for."

Cathy kissed them each on the cheek. "Be careful," Natasha whispered in her ear.

Sod being careful, Cathy thought as she left. *Since when did that achieve anything?*

• • •

Max looked out onto the city of Bath as he waited for Rupert, the former Sorcerer of Mercia. The gargoyle was next to him, its paws on the windowsill, the soul chain around its neck clunking against the wood. Max scanned the rooftops and streets, his eyes drawn to the various statues he knew so well and the buildings reflected in the Nether. The trees were swaying in the cold January wind and innocents had their scarves wrapped tight as they hurried from place to place. They had been without protection for over a fortnight now—longer if he included the time since the Bath Chapter had been destroyed—and it wouldn't be long before the Fae-touched of Aquae Sulis began to suspect that they weren't being policed as tightly as usual.

"Not sure about this," the gargoyle's gravelly voice echoed in the empty room. "A Chapter should be in the Nether. Not Mundanus."

They were on the top floor of Cambridge House, in the centre of the city. There was a lift, which helped, as it was six stories up, and lots of windows. Aside from an old desk lamp and a waste-paper basket, the huge room was empty. It was a long way from the large building reflected into the Nether with a portcullis, towers, and cloisters that he'd been trained in. That was a bizarre building, created from anchors in several mundane properties, and used to be filled with people. He'd never heard of a Chapter in Mundanus, but everything was different now.

Max leaned against the window frame to take the weight off his aching leg. The damp winter weather seemed to make the old wounds grumble as much as the gargoyle. "The Sorcerer of Albion thinks this is the way forwards. 'Evolution,' he called it."

"Evolution? My stone arse. He hasn't got a clue about what he's doing. Hang on. 'Sorcerer of Albion'? When did Rupert start calling himself that?"

"Three days ago."

"Not true, though, is it?" The gargoyle fixed its stone eyes on Max. "He's the last *official* Sorcerer of the Heptarchy, but there's another sorcerer in Albion."

The "other sorcerer" was more than that; she was a woman capable of wielding a hybrid magic, somehow merging Fae and sorcerous arts. Rupert still doubted that such a combination was even possible. There was no doubting that she had murdered six Sorcerers, all of the staff in their Chapters, and dozens of Arbiters across the country. As far as Max knew, the only Arbiters left were the most corrupt in England: the Camden Chapter, Kingdom of Essex. He'd watched one of their Arbiters, Faulkner, drink tea whilst an innocent was being Charmed and kidnapped mere metres away. They were a Chapter in name only.

Max thought it likely that the mysterious Sorceress had another

Chapter in her pocket somewhere, or some Arbiters left over from another, ready to do her bidding and kill anyone close to springing her plans early. Surely by now her plan had almost reached fruition; she had succeeded in destroying the Chapters that protected innocents across the country, and had murdered the Sorcerers that presided over them, too.

They didn't even know what the ultimate plan was; they had a theory that the Sorceress was the sister of the former Sorcerer of Essex and that was all. Why she had killed so many was beyond him. The gargoyle had suggested it was for power. The power to do what?

All was not lost, Max reminded himself. Despite the Sorceress's best efforts, he and the gargoyle had managed to save Rupert, but not his home or the Arbiters and staff in the Chapters under his control throughout Mercia. There had been three, the largest one in Oxford, with minor Chapters in Cirencester and Cheltenham. The Sorceress thought Rupert was dead, which was the only advantage they had. As the gargoyle had pointed out several times over the past two weeks, it wasn't much of an advantage at all.

The gargoyle made a noise somewhere between a groan and despondent whine, resting its head on the windowsill. With Max's soul housed inside it, he assumed it was feeling the weight of their situation. The only survivor from Ekstrand's household was his librarian, Petra. While she was an incredibly capable woman, she still wasn't over the Sorcerer's death. There was Rupert—a homeless Sorcerer in hiding—himself, and the gargoyle.

Max was the only Arbiter left with any sense of duty, the only one who still wanted to protect the innocents from the Fae and their puppets.

"And we're not exactly a shining example," the gargoyle said, sharing his thoughts. "Corrupted by Titanium, soul walking around in an animated gargoyle, walks with a limp. This country is going to the dogs, no doubt about it." When Max didn't reply, it waved its muzzle at his bad leg. "We're not going to tell the Sorcerer about the Titanium in that gammy leg of yours, are we?"

Max shook his head. "He has enough to work on at the moment. And it hasn't been a problem so far."

"So far," the gargoyle muttered. "Let's face it. We're screwed."

Max didn't disagree. He'd had plans to establish a new chapter, but never having been involved with the running of his home Chapter, he had very little idea of what was involved. He knew fieldwork, nothing more. Dozens of people used to support his work, giving him briefings on changes in Mundanus, tracking criminal activity so trends could be observed over hundreds of years, and keeping meticulous records on breaches of the Split Worlds Treaty. How could he train someone to do all that?

And there was the simple issue of staff recruitment. The researchers he'd known had been people exposed to Fae magic or rescued from Exilium, those who could no longer be called innocents. They were taken in, debriefed, and trained, he knew that much. But the gulf between knowing the broad strokes of how it worked and the details of finding, caring for, and training such people was beyond him. Even if someone else cared for them in a practical way, Max had no idea what skills the training would need to cover. Only now did he appreciate just how complex a machine the previous Bath Chapter had been. But by the time he had arrived there, the Bath Chapter had existed for a thousand years or so. Surely the beginning had been just as difficult for them?

The lift bell dinged in the hallway just off the office. The gargoyle scampered off to the bathroom as Max went into the hallway, the click of his walking stick echoing with each step.

The doors slid open and Rupert stepped out, a young woman following him. She was in her early twenties, with dark brown hair and eyes. She wore her hair in a messy ponytail and was dressed in jeans, walking boots, and a thick padded jacket. As soon as she stepped out of the lift she dumped her huge rucksack with audible relief.

"Max, you're here, awesome," Rupert said, pulling off his gloves and woolly hat. "Bloody cold out there." He turned to the girl. "Kay, this is Max. He sort of works for me. Max, this is Kay Hyde, from Oxford. She's our first recruit."

Kay hung back for a moment, staring at Max, probably trying to work out why he seemed wrong. He was used to this reaction from strangers. Living without a soul tended to make an Arbiter unpleasant to look at and to be around. She lurched forward after a few seconds, as if remembering her manners, and extended her hand to him. He shook it quickly and let go, noting her shudder.

"First recruit? Which family took her? How long ago?"

"Eh?" Rupert looked momentarily confused and then realised what Max was talking about. "Oh! She hasn't been taken by anyone. I knew her at Oxford. Best brain in the city if you ask me. Got a first at Trinity in English Lit, but let's face it, any sod can do that." He smirked at her and she jabbed him in the ribs.

"Piss off! I worked bloody hard for that."

"And she is the fucking bomb when it comes to riddles, wordplay, and linguistic sneaky sneakster stuff. Near eidetic memory and descended from Edward Hyde, no less." When Max failed to give any response to that, he added, "Grandfather of Queen Anne and bloody clever bloke to boot."

Max frowned. "Queen Anne was a puppet of the Tulipas."

"That's ancient history," Rupert said, shrugging off his coat. "No worries on that front."

Kay went to the doorway into the office space. "Nice. Oh wow, what a great view!"

Max went to Rupert's side as she went across the room to the window. Max moved round to the other side of the partition separating the area containing the lifts from the main office space, lowering his voice after Rupert had followed him. "Sir, am I to understand she is still innocent?"

"I can't speak for her universal innocence; we're just friends, but assuming you mean the Fae or their puppets, yes, she's never been entangled with them. Oh, tell a lie, she met one visiting Oxford— Freddy Persificola-Viola. What an arsehole he was. She gave him a tour of the city at my request. But nothing dodgy happened.

Trust me, I watched every minute she was with him and tested her afterwards too."

"This is…I don't understand."

"I've given her a job. She's fresh out of uni, bright as a button, and quick to learn. We've just got to get her up to speed on all the Fae shit and we're golden."

"When were you planning to do that?"

"After we've got a kettle and mugs. Brain-breaking should only happen over tea, Max, we're not fucking savages."

"Should I keep the gargoyle in the bathroom until then?"

Rupert nodded. "Probably a good idea. Just make sure he isn't in the ladies' loo. Don't want her to die of a heart attack when she goes for a slash." He clapped Max on the shoulder. "Don't worry, Max m'boy. This is a good thing! Kay's awesome. We'll be up and running in no time."

"I'm not worried," Max said as Rupert went back into the main office space. He was incapable of any emotion.

"You can see so much from here," Kay said to Rupert. "Office is a bit on the empty side, though."

"That's one of the first things I need your help with," Rupert said, going to stand next to her. "We don't need much to start off with—a few desks, chairs…computers….A kettle, tea, and coffee are priority."

"Okay, give me a company card and I'll get it sorted."

"Oh. Yeah…" Rupert patted his pockets. "Only got cash."

"I saw something in the paper on the way here, actually," Kay said and jogged back to her backpack. She returned with a local paper. "Crap crossword. I did it in less than five minutes. But it's only the local rag, I suppose."

She sat on the floor and began thumbing through the pages as images of a toilet brush appeared in Max's mind. The gargoyle was getting bored. That was never a good thing.

"Here we go. A local office is closing down and auctioning off all their stuff this afternoon. We could probably get most of what we need in one go."

Rupert shrugged. "Whatever you think is best. You're office manager."

"I am? You realise we haven't had the interview yet?"

"Interview? Oh, no need for that. You're hired."

"For what, exactly?"

Rupert grinned. "Kitting out the office first. Then I'll tell you about the rest once we can make a cuppa."

"Kettles are on sale at the shop down the road," Kay said, flipping over a page to point to an advert. "What do you think, Max? Like the look of that one?"

He looked at the picture she was pointing at and nodded, even though he felt nothing about the kettles at all. Then a picture above the advert caught his eye, one of a collection of workers standing in front of a large brick chimney in the courtyard of a foundry that Max recognised, taken at the turn of the century. The chimney looked dark grey in the photograph, but Max knew the bricks had been a deep red, and he could even recall the smell of the smoke which used to sink down into the courtyard on cold, still days. The men were dressed in their working clothes, with grubby shirts and neckerchiefs worn to soak up the grime and sweat. All were smiling for the camera, all faded into the background save one.

Max looked into the eyes of his father, standing in the middle of the group, thumbs tucked into his belt loops and looking very happy. There were the wrinkles at the corners of his eyes that used to gather the dirt from the foundry over his shift, until it looked like they'd been drawn on with a pencil by the time he returned home. He'd disappeared, along with several of his co-workers, when Max was ten years old.

All Max could recall about the disappearance was looking for his father near the foundry, hoping to find him and bring him home. Max knew that an Arbiter had found him as he searched for his dad and took him to the Chapter but he couldn't remember why. Nor could he recall whether the reason his father went missing was the same reason why the Arbiter thought he—an innocent ten-year-old boy—should be taken. Why could he remember the smell of the smoke from that chimney, but not the night his mundane life ended and his journey to becoming an Arbiter began?

A crash from the bathroom made Kay yelp. "Is someone else here?"

"Just a cleaner," Rupert said. "Let's get some food and then go to the auction. They'll be gone by the time we get back. Right, Max?"

Max pulled his gaze from the photograph. "Yes, sir." He scanned the article's title. *Bath's Troubled History and the Missing Rebels of Yesteryear.* "I may not be here when you get back. I need to look into something." He picked up the newspaper. "May I keep this, Miss Hyde?" When she nodded he folded it up and tucked it into the inside pocket of his overcoat. Max had never discovered what happened to his father, nor why the Arbiter was there that night. Before seeing that photo it hadn't even occurred to him that there were questions he wanted to ask. Now that there were, it was time to find some answers.

2

Will couldn't help thinking that his life would have been so much easier if he'd been married to someone as politically astute as Margritte. What he had thought would be a short briefing on how Cathy should present the idea of the Ladies' Court had turned into an argument, when all he was trying to do was help her avoid conflict.

When he'd discussed the idea with Margritte, a Ladies' Court had seemed an obvious way forward, something progressive enough to channel Cathy's energy and keep her more strident behaviour away from the attention of the gentlemen of the court. The way Cathy talked about it now, anyone would think it was some patriarchal conspiracy to undermine...something or other. He'd lost track.

Amazingly, he was starting to see Margritte as a valued friend—even though less than a month before she'd sought his destruction. Will didn't mind helping her to stay safe—far from it. He felt it was his duty now and part of his penance for killing her husband. Though he still lived with the guilt, he couldn't dwell on the past. The strange, infuriating, and spirited woman he'd fallen in love with was making more than enough trouble to keep him occupied.

Cathy wanted too much too soon and refused to be patient. Will tried to remember that she was under the influence of Poppy's magic, that damned third wish that she'd made before they'd married. It was supposedly a wish for her to reach her true potential, but ever since he'd learned Poppy was convinced it would be destructive, the thought of it had haunted Will. Surely Poppy's magic was driving her to this recklessness? He was of a mind to mention it to Lord Iris should it worsen. Perhaps he could lift it from her. Not that she'd want that. And even if he could bring himself to ask that Lord Iron for help, he knew the magic in their wedding ring and the curse his family had put on her would be broken too. Unacceptable. He needed a more subtle solution than that blundering fool.

"Darling," Will said, leaning forwards to take her hands as she paused for breath. "I understand that you have doubts. But surely you agree that a Ladies' Court would at least be a step towards more significant change?" He didn't say it was the only step he was willing to allow for now.

By the time they arrived, she seemed to be ready to make the announcement in the way he'd recommended.

Will stroked the back of Cathy's gloved hand as the carriage passed through the outer gates of the Tower. She was always more highly strung before any meeting of the Londinium Court, behaving more like a prisoner heading for the gallows.

For him, every visit to the Tower was invigorating. His ancestor—his namesake—had ruled over the mundanes from the anchor property, the first reflected into the Nether by Lord Iris, from which the rest of Londinium grew. The Irises were in ascendance, memories of the Rosa rule that had lasted for hundreds of years were fading fast, and the name of *William* Reticulata-Iris meant something at last.

To think, only a few months ago he'd been drinking cocktails on a Mediterranean beach, dreading his return home. The Grand Tour had given him a taste of freedom and life without his father breathing down his neck, watching for imperfection. In Mundanus he'd been a wealthy playboy, dawdling from place to place with his best friend, enjoying everything life under that gloriously blue sky had to offer. He'd made the most of it, knowing that he would have to fight for every scrap of pleasure once he was back in the Nether. As a mere second son, nothing would be handed to him on a plate. He was nothing but a spare to the heir of the Aquae Sulis Irises. A handsome boy who hadn't drawn anyone's attention before he'd left for his Grand Tour.

All his life, his brother Nathaniel had told him he'd never amount to anything, and his sister Imogen had seen him as nothing more than a child to torment. Will couldn't help but smile to himself. Everyone had underestimated him, from the Rosas to the Tulipas, and now he was Duke of Londinium. He was never going to let anyone take this from him.

The way the guards outside the entrance to the Tower straightened as the carriage pulled up, how the page ran to lower the step and open the door, how they all bowed when he emerged—all the tiny things drove home the fact that he was more than anyone had ever thought he would be. Will loved the way his arrival cast a ripple ahead of him, from the way the pages announced his presence with loud voices up each level of the Tower, to the sound of the residents of Londinium hurrying into the main chamber to ready themselves for his and Cathy's entrance.

But none of it was as satisfying as the hush that descended over the Court after their names were announced at the door by the Head Yeoman, and the way all of the residents and guests in the city bowed and curtsied as he and Cathy walked to the thrones. It wasn't long ago that he'd been seeking to impress them. Now all they wanted was to impress him.

There were none in the Court that gave him serious concern. All could see which way the wind was blowing and how it was wiser to support him than grumble. Besides, no one else was even close to being strong enough to take the throne from him—aside from the Viola, perhaps.

Bertrand Persificola-Viola, free of the social disaster of an older brother now that Freddy was dead, was proving to be every bit the ally he had hoped for. Will had worked hard to keep Bertrand happy, and to reassure him that the Duchess had no plans to undermine his authority over his wife or any other man's over theirs. It was clear that Bertrand was unimpressed by her, though. One comment from a new Duchess in unusual circumstances could be overlooked, but a second would be seen as a sign of a husband too weak to control her.

Despite the tense journey there, Cathy played her part well whilst the main business of the Court was carried out. Announcements given by Will and his Marquis, Tom Rhoeas-Papaver, were met with quiet approval. He and Tom had spent that afternoon making sure that only the most innocuous matters would be discussed that evening. Tom had counselled him to not let Cathy speak at the Court, but admitted how hard that would be to enforce without the use of offensive Charms. "Strange that she be so keen to talk now she's Duchess," he'd said in Will's study. "In the past you could barely get her to string a sentence together in front of other people."

"Life in Mundanus changed her," Will had said.

Tom paused at the door then, his eyes shadowed by a frown. "It seems so."

Will felt sorry for Tom. When he should have been travelling the world, tasting the delights of Mundanus before establishing his own family, Tom had been desperately hunting for his runaway sister. Whilst Will had been rolling in the surf with his Sicilian lover, Tom had been going from town to town, casting Seeker Charms and fearing that Cathy was dead. What a burden he'd shouldered, only to be married off to an American Poppy before he'd had a taste of real freedom. Will supposed the Papavers needed the money for Cathy's dowry—and perhaps to pay for all the Charms Tom had used to find Cathy—and as Tom's hunt had aged him just enough for marriage, it was deemed unnecessary to give him a Grand Tour.

At least he was proving himself to be a capable Marquis. What Tom lacked in worldliness he made up for in bookish leanings, and he had a remarkable memory for details. His wife, Lucy, was nice enough too, and mercifully had excellent social skills with a warmth that counterbalanced Tom's stiff aloofness. Even though they were all young, Will felt sure he could make this Dukedom work. He had to. His Patroon, Sir Iris, had made it very clear that the family expected him to hold Londinium indefinitely. He had every intention of doing so.

Tom was finishing his summary of business and the room felt calm. Will looked at Cathy, who was staring down at her gloves intently. He could tell she was shaking from the way her earrings sparkled, catching the sprite light with each tremble. She was wearing a new gown, one that looked different but he couldn't work out exactly how. He gave her hand a reassuring squeeze and she looked at him, her eyes bright blue against the flush of her cheeks.

"Just remember what we discussed in the carriage," Will whispered to her. "And when it's done, we'll return home and celebrate."

A flicker of concern crossed her features, as if she feared something, and then Tom announced that the Duchess was to speak.

Will studied the men's faces in the crowd as she stood. Most were too socially skilled and intelligent to betray any doubts about the Duchess being permitted to address the Court again. One of the Buttercups rolled his eyes at a Wisteria who failed to hide a smile behind a handkerchief before Will noticed it. When the Wisteria noticed his attention on him, any sign of disrespect vanished from his features and he was a model attentive listener.

Cathy cleared her throat. "My husband and I have been in close discussion regarding the Court of Londinium," she began. Good, thought Will, she remembered the opening line signalling to the gentlemen that she was about to say something he endorsed. Even that line alone had been something she'd resisted. "And we have agreed that the city could benefit from a formal court for the daughters and wives of Londinium. As Duchess, I plan to establish this new salon as a space where women of this city can come together to discuss the issues of the day…" she paused and Will tensed, fearing she was about to go off-script. "…in an…effort to keep conversations with our husbands and fathers free of any idle speculation and questions."

Will breathed out. Good. It wasn't how she, Margritte, or any of the others saw the court, but the careful phrasing was designed to nip any male fears in the bud. As he had told Cathy repeatedly in the carriage, it didn't matter whether it was the spirit of the exercise or not. What mattered was not getting anyone's backs up before she had a chance to establish it. Once it existed, she could mould it into something of merit.

Will scanned the room. The women looked surprised and uncertain, as did the majority of their husbands.

"Has this ever been done before, your Grace?" one of the Wisterias asked from the back of the room.

"No. It would be a first," Cathy replied. "Londinium should lead the way in all things and we're already a city that favours debate and the more intellectual arts."

Good, Will thought. *Keep it up, Cathy.*

"I beg your pardon," the Wisteria continued, "but could you be kind enough to explain how this…salon differs from any of the countless events that the ladies of the city participate in?"

A pause. She was thinking first, that was a good sign. "The ladies of this city enjoy a full social calendar, it's true. However, a formal salon that encourages better communication regardless of family, social status, or even the size of one's drawing room is a world apart from a patchwork of conversations shared over tea."

"Some sort of egalitarian effort, is it?" the Wisteria said. "You mentioned 'regardless of social status'."

Cathy smiled. "I am very aware that there are some ladies who are invited to discuss issues of the day more often than others. I believe that every lady has the right to participate in these conversations, for the betterment of herself and her understanding of the issues we face as a city. A formal salon would grant this."

The muscles in Will's back knotted. *Careful*, he thought. Any talk of rights for women was akin to lighting a touch-paper.

"They'll probably talk about sewing," said the Buttercup who had already irritated Will. "It might sound noble but that's all it will be. Embroidery and clothes."

He watched Cathy's jaw clench but mercifully, she ignored the comment.

"Will there be a men-only court too, your Grace?" one of the Peonias asked.

"I beg your pardon?"

Surely Cathy had heard that?

"I asked, your Grace, if there are plans to start a court for gentlemen only. If the ladies are to enjoy such a privilege, surely the gentlemen of Londinium shouldn't be denied it either?"

"You have got to be joking!" Cathy laughed incredulously.

"I assure you, madam, I ask in all seriousness. Why shouldn't the gentlemen of Londinium be given the same privilege?"

Will watched her fists clench and realised his own were gripping the arms of the throne.

"Oh, let me think," Cathy began in exactly the tone of voice that meant a storm was on the way. "I know I'm only a feeble-minded woman, so please do forgive me if I have misunderstood, but I thought the gentlemen would be satisfied with the right to own property, to have an income independent of his spouse—even of his family, should he choose to develop it—and the freedom to go where he chooses, be it in the Nether or Mundanus. And seeing as the gentlemen of Londinium can enjoy Black's as a male-only club, I had assumed that the need to spend time in the company of men would be satisfied. Am I to understand that you feel underprivileged, sir? Disadvantaged in some way? Pray tell us all why you feel it would be unfair for women to have one new opportunity when so much is denied us."

The Peonia's cheeks flushed red. "Pray tell *us*, madam, why you feel the women of Londinium require such a formal salon. Surely with their carefree lives, there is little of merit to discuss? Nothing that would require a formal court."

"You can't think of a single reason why women may need a place where they can voice an opinion without the judgement of men? Are you not demonstrating that need yourself? But then I suppose, if you think women are nothing more than decorative objects without a single thought of merit between their ears, this need would be mystifying."

Will forced his expression to remain neutral. He couldn't let any of them see how angry her thoughtless behaviour was making him feel. It was one thing for her to speak this way in the privacy of their own home, but to do so in front of Londinium?

"You are most forthright with your opinions, your Grace," Bertrand Persificola-Viola said. "I beg you to release our friend from the jaws of your sharp wit."

"You make it sound as if he is a victim, sir," Cathy said. "Surely a man cannot be wounded by the opinion and passion of a mere woman?"

The corner of Bertrand's mouth twitched, as if he were as much amused by her as insulted. No doubt he would make his opinion on the Duchess known very soon, and Will knew he would need careful handling again.

Cathy sat back on her throne, cheeks flushed, still shaking.

"As ever, gentlemen," Will said, eager to close the proceedings, "you know that I and the Marquis are available at any time to discuss your needs and concerns regarding life in Londinium. The Duchess and I bid you good night."

He offered his hand to Cathy, who rested hers upon it, and they stepped down from the dais. The assembled parted ahead of them, bowing as they passed, until they reached the doors that were opened by two of Will's men dressed as pages. Even before the doors closed behind them an uproar of commentary and speculation filled the throne room.

"Not a word," he whispered to Cathy, and steered her towards the stairs as he struggled to contain all the things he wanted to shout at her. When he was certain no one had left the court to pursue a private conversation, he let go of her hand. "You were rather harsh with the Peonia, Cathy."

"I merely corrected him. If my brother had done the same, you wouldn't have batted an eyelid."

"You humiliated him with your sarcasm."

"He deserved it. Sexist b—"

He grabbed her hand and pulled her to a stop. "You have to be more careful than that," he whispered. "I thought after the last time you'd have learned, but what you did in there was ten times worse!"

Her eyes flashed and she twisted her wrist from his grip. "I was holding myself back! Believe me, I could have said much more."

"You shouldn't have taken that tone with him."

She took a step up one of the stairs, putting air between them.

"Will, you're not about to prove the need for this new court by siding with those idiots, are you?"

"I'm not siding with anyone! I have every right to discuss your behaviour. I am the Duke and I am the one who will have to answer for your little display in there."

"Just stop and listen to yourself! My behaviour? My 'little display'? I'm a grown woman who expressed an opinion and took a bloody idiot down a peg or two. If you can't handle that, you're no better than the rest of them."

Will drew in a deep breath, using it to cool the anger in his chest. This wasn't the time or the place to have another row with Cathy. But before he could say anything, a door opened on the floor above and there were footsteps on the stairs. One of the pages rounded the corner and stopped.

"Begging your pardon, your Grace, but Sir Iris has requested your presence immediately."

Will's stomach dropped into his shoes. Neither the Patroon nor his wife had been at the Court. How had it got back to him so quickly? "Thank you, I'll be with you in a moment." He looked at Cathy. "Go home. Do not talk to anyone about this until I return. This conversation is not over."

Cathy's back straightened. "I won't be talked to like a child, and I refuse to feel bad about what I did in there."

"I fear Sir Iris will see it very differently."

"I'd be more than happy to give him a piece of my mind too. I can defend myself, Will. You don't have to do it for me."

He sighed, looking up the wide oak stairs, torn between rage and fear. "It's not you I will have to defend," he said. "Go home, before you upset anyone else."

"You know," she said, "considering that it's women who are supposed to be weak and emotional, it's quite a revelation seeing how easily these men are upset."

She picked up her skirts and marched down the stairs. He watched her go, fearing he'd created a monster. He'd only given her a modest amount of freedom to speak and she was already doing more damage than a drunken Buttercup.

"Your Grace?" The page appeared at the top of the stairs again. "The Patroon was most insistent."

Will turned and carried his heavy legs towards the roasting he was about to get. There was no doubt about it now; he had to tell the Patroon about the Poppy magic, before Cathy destroyed herself, and him with her.

3

The beer tasted the same, and the pub's decor was just as dingy as Sam recalled, but something didn't feel right. Sam looked down into his pint, trying to ignore the feeling that this had been a terrible mistake.

"So he said that if I'd actually taken the time to get a full brief from the client, the architecture wouldn't have to be redesigned." Dave was on his third pint and hadn't noticed that Sam was only halfway through his first. "What a prick! Everyone knows that the client is the last person on Earth who knows what their real requirements are. I could have spent two days on site and been none the wiser. So I…"

The pause in the diatribe made Sam look up from his beer.

"You're not listening to me," Dave said.

"I—"

"Nah, I don't blame you. I'm a boring twat when I get onto work stuff. I just haven't had anyone I can vent at since you left."

"Since I was fired."

"Well, yeah, but who gives a fuck about that now, eh?" Dave grinned, belched loudly, and patted his beer belly. "You should've seen the boss's face when I took in the paper with you on the front page."

Sam sank a fraction lower in his seat. Only in Bath would his inheritance of Amir Ferran's empire reach the front page. It was covered in the national press several pages after the latest celebrity and political scandals. He had read two articles presenting mostly fictional accounts of his life, character, and the reasons behind his inheritance from the eccentric multi-billionaire and realised he'd never be able to read a newspaper again.

"So what's it like then?" Dave leaned in and propped his elbows on the table. He'd put on weight in the weeks since Sam had last seen him but nothing else had changed.

"What?"

"Being a rich bastard."

Dave was smiling but it made Sam uncomfortable. A gulf had opened between them, one Sam hadn't considered possible. It was as if Dave was trapped in amber and he was peering into the old life preserved with him, one he could never have again. The last time he'd drunk in this pub he was a computer programmer, coasting through life as his marriage collapsed around him. Since then his wife had been promoted, moved to London, asked for a divorce, and then dropped dead on a tube station platform. Natural causes, they said, but the former Lord Iron, Amir, confirmed that her old boss, Neugent, was somehow responsible. Then Amir passed the mantle to him and now he was sitting in his old local, head of a multi-billion global empire, the new Lord Iron. It still didn't feel real.

He'd actually had to argue with his head of security to meet up with Dave. They only agreed it was possible if he gave them twenty-four hours' notice. A car full of his staff had driven down the night before, examined the location, worked out whatever they needed to, and three of them were now seated around the pub. They were all in casual clothes, blending in as well as blokes built like tanks could, carefully watching people come through the door. Each new arrival precipitated a round of texting as they communicated with the coordinator outside, no doubt receiving information about who had just entered. The amount of stuff they could uncover in a matter of seconds freaked Sam out. No doubt they had run the same background checks on him when Amir decided to visit his humble terraced house just a few weeks before.

Sam realised he hadn't answered Dave's question. "Weird," he said. He couldn't say that while Dave had been moaning about the company Sam used to work for, he was worrying about the activities of just one of the companies he owned, and that had an annual turnover nearly five hundred times larger. He would sound like a dick. "It's…yeah, weird."

"But good weird, I bet," Dave said. "You don't have to worry any more. You know, about bills and stuff."

Something in his voice made Sam's discomfort worsen. Did he need help but couldn't ask? "Are you okay for money? I can—"

"I didn't come here hoping for a handout!" Dave caught his voice before it turned into a shout, thankfully.

"I know."

"I just wanted a drink with an old mate, for Christ's sake. I'm not a bloody charity case."

"I know." Sam became far too aware of the three plainclothes guards, all of whom were looking at him as Dave's voice rose. He knew that if there was even a hint of something turning ugly they'd intervene, and not in a way that would leave their friendship intact. "I'm sorry. I just wanted to help if I could. You'd do the same for me."

Dave leaned back in his chair and scratched at the stubble on his chin. "You could get the next round in."

Sam was glad to have a chance to back off from the conversation. He ordered two pints from the landlord who smiled at him just a bit too much and paid for them with a twenty-pound note his PA had given him. He couldn't even go to a cash point without there being some ridiculous song and dance about it.

A night that was supposed to make him feel more relaxed was giving him a headache. He watched the pints being pulled and realised he didn't really have anything to say when he got back to Dave. What did they used to talk about? Football. He hadn't had time to watch any since taking on the burden of being Lord Iron. Work. Nothing in common there anymore. His marriage.

He frowned at the bar as the lump rose in his throat. Six months ago he would have been three pints into the evening and moaning at Dave about how Leanne was never home. Dave would be drunkenly sympathetic in the way a bloke who'd never had a relationship longer than three months could be. Dave would remind him how lucky Leanne was to have him, how selfish she was to put her career first and how stupid she was to think Sam would stand for it much longer.

Now she was dead, the beer was doing nothing to fill the hollowness inside him.

"Mr Ferran?" One of his minders had come to his side. "We have to leave."

The landlord placed the second pint down and smiled again. "So nice to see you back in here, Sam."

Sam had no recollection of the landlord knowing his name before everything had changed.

"Sir," his minder leaned closer once the landlord moved away. "The pub owner has phoned the local newspaper and there's a journo and some paps on their way right now."

"Why?" Sam couldn't understand why anyone would be interested in him being there, let alone wanting to take a picture of him.

"We should take your friend home too," the minder said, ignoring his question. Sam nodded, trying not to think about how thick the man's neck looked in the polo shirt. Being surrounded by huge blokes who could crush his skull like a ripe plum didn't make him feel safe, even when they were on his payroll. "We can't guarantee what he'd say to the press in his current state."

"Shit." Sam wasn't looking forward to explaining it to Dave. He shouldn't have come.

An hour later, with Dave's complaints still echoing in Sam's thoughts, he was in the back of a limousine on the M5 back up to Cheshire. He was supposed to be staying in the hotel he now owned in Bath but once word was out that he was back, fuelling rumours that the local boy made good was planning to buy his old local and half the city, he just wanted to avoid any more reminders that it could never be his home again. That hotel was the place where they'd held Leanne's wake. Perhaps he wasn't as ready to face seeing it again as he'd thought.

He ignored a text that came through on his work phone. He didn't have the energy, but then he started to worry that it was Cathy, as she had that number as well as his old one, so he checked it.

It was from Des, his PA, a six-foot-tall polyglot with a passion for order. Sam liked his quiet efficiency and the fact that he'd never worked closely with Amir. He was sick of constantly being compared to the previous Lord Iron by the team he'd inherited and was stuck with for the next ten years. *Your mother phoned and would like you to call back as soon as possible. It's currently 6:30 a.m. local time if you want to call now.* Sam also liked the way Des prevented time zone befuddlement. A second text arrived. *I've emailed you the crib sheet for the meeting with the Elemental Court. If you have any questions, don't hesitate to ask.*

He didn't open his email. He'd look at that in the morning. There was a lot to remember, mostly names, faces, and how those people's businesses intersected with his own. From the look of the notes he'd been given already, and the small amount of coaching Mazzi—or Lady Nickel, as she was also known—had given him, the Elemental Court was nothing like he'd imagined it would be. It was a relief; he was worried he'd have to face some weird shit like Cathy mentioned about her court, with thrones and bowing and all that bollocks. It sounded more like he was going to give a speech at some sort of symposium for the wealthy elite, none of whom he'd ever heard of before. So elite, the newspapers couldn't get near them. Certainly the articles about him demonstrated ignorance of the extent of Amir's empire. His empire now. He shook his head. He just couldn't think of himself that way.

He looked back at the first text and then searched his contacts for his parents' phone number. They rarely called and Sam tried not to imagine news of a heart attack as he dialled. They would be awake, both early risers.

"Hello?"

"Mum?"

"Sam! Hello, dear, how are you?"

She sounded okay. "Fine. You called."

"Yes. I wanted to talk to you about something I saw on the telly."

Sam slid down the soft leather until his nose was level with the bottom of the windows. Had she found out about one of the atrocities carried out by CoFerrum Inc under Amir's stewardship? "What was it?"

"It was about this charity that looks after cats. In London."

He released his relief with a protracted sigh. "What about it?"

"Oh, these cats, Sam, people do terrible things to animals. I cried, I did."

"You called me to tell me that?"

"No, I called to ask you to support them. They need money to stay open. And I thought that you could give it to them. They might put your name on a plaque. Wouldn't that be nice? And you'd be saving them from—What's that noise? Where are you?"

"In the car. I'm on my way home."

"You called Australia on your mobile?" Sam had to move the phone away from his ear to protect it from the shriek. "That will cost a fortune!"

"Mum, just…just email me the details about that charity, okay?"

"Okay, dear. And we love the new house, by the way."

Sam smiled.

"And now you're not strapped for cash, you can come and visit."

The smile faded. "I'd better go, Mum. Speak to you soon."

She said goodbye three times before hanging up. He tried Cathy's mobile in case she was in Mundanus, but it went straight to voicemail. He didn't leave a message. She had her own life in the Nether with that twat of a husband. He couldn't expect her to drop everything and come and see him. He frowned as he stared out into the darkness. Cathy had all those ideas about changing things, but he knew they wouldn't have any of it. It wasn't like the struggle Leanne faced, researching the atrocities carried out by CoFerrum Inc from the inside, gathering enough evidence to expose them catastrophically when the time was right. In Cathy's world there was no press or public to put pressure on those in power. She had no leverage.

Fuck. Did he actually think that? The word *leverage* was on a "corporate wank" bingo sheet that he and Dave took to conferences. If he ever used it in conversation, along with "blue-sky thinking" and "pushing the envelope" he'd have to trash everything and go and live in a bin somewhere.

Restless, he phoned Des, killing the hours of the journey by tackling what he could from the car to free up the following morning for a lie-in. Then he filtered his emails to show the ones from Susan, the most obstructive member of his inherited team. Sure enough, every single one she'd sent him over the day contained reasons why he couldn't just change things as he saw fit. He deleted them, a petty pleasure, knowing that it didn't really matter. He hadn't just been sitting around, hoping they'd change their minds. There was another team of experts he'd put together that only Des knew about and was under strict orders to keep secret. One that would start getting Sam the information he needed about CoFerrum Inc so he could start making a real difference.

By the time he got home it was late enough for the roads leading to his estate to be pitch black and devoid of any other traffic. He still wasn't able to see the mansion without being faintly surprised that he lived there now. It wasn't as if it felt like Amir's home anymore, but it certainly didn't feel like his either. He'd let the butler go, unable to cope with how awkward he made him feel, and kept the housekeeper, Mrs Morrison. She treated him like a normal person, unlike the butler, who'd talked to him like he was some nobleman from *Pride and Prejudice* or something. And Mrs M was happy to cook and organise the cleaners, which were a necessity with so many people staying there at the moment.

At least there were lights on and more people living there than when it had first passed into his ownership. He'd taken in just over twenty people that Cathy had rescued from some kind of dodgy asylum, people who used to live in the Nether but couldn't handle it anymore. They kept to themselves mostly, uncertain of him and fearful of his being the enemy of their former patrons. Perhaps on some level they were afraid he'd kick them out one day, and planned to be able to tell the Fae truthfully that they didn't fraternise with him.

Only one of them, an elderly lady called Eleanor, actually sought him out to speak with him from time to time. Unlike the other guests, Eleanor never seemed afraid of him. Cathy told him Eleanor used to be the matriarch of the family she'd been married into. From what Sam had seen of Cathy's husband, he was unsurprised that Eleanor seemed fearless. After dealing with men like William Iris for hundreds of years, some clueless bloke with more money than he knew what to do with was probably as frightening as a kitten.

She was standing outside on the steps when the car drew up, wrapped in a shawl and leaning against the wall next to the front door. He didn't wait for his car door to be opened for him.

"Eleanor? Is something wrong?"

She shook her head. Even now, well past the bloom of youth, she was attractive in a fiery, imperious sort of way. She wore her grey hair up in the sort of bun they had in period dramas. "I stand out here sometimes, when I'm bored of talking with them all." She pointed up at the sky. "There are no stars in the Nether. I don't think I'll ever be bored of them."

"Aren't you cold?"

"No." She stared at him as the limousine was driven off to be parked. "What happened?"

"Nothing."

"Let's have a brandy."

She wasn't the kind of lady to deny a drink so he followed her in and they headed to his study. She sat down in the chair opposite his desk as he poured two glasses and placed one next to her. He already knew not to hand her a glass directly but had never been able to bring himself to ask why.

"You have the look of a man who went looking for something and has returned empty-handed."

He shrugged.

"Out with it," she said, picking up the glass to cradle it in both hands. "In my experience it's better to tell someone than to let it fester."

"There's nothing to tell." He managed less than ten seconds beneath her stare and then downed his drink. "I went back to where I used to live and met up with an old friend. But it wasn't the same."

"Someone you knew before you were Lord Iron?"

Sam nodded.

"When you were just a mundane."

"…Yeah."

"Why the hesitation? That's what you were then and most certainly are not now. No matter how much you might want that." Her smile did little to soften her words. "My dear man, one can never go back, not once you've left their world."

"But I haven't…" Sam didn't finish the sentence. He might still live in England—or Mundanus, as Eleanor called it—but he didn't live in the same world as Dave anymore. "I see what you mean."

"It can be hard to adjust. You might think you need an old friend—or any friend—at the moment, but what you actually need is a project." When he didn't say anything, she said, "It's the best thing for a lonely man. Looking for solace in others never leads to any good. A grand project, however, fills you up from the inside."

"There are dozens of projects going on."

"Are any of them truly yours? Did you think them up? Or did that team of suited monkeys tell you that they needed to be done?"

Sam smiled at her description. He wasn't fond of the committee that helped him to run Amir's—no, *his* empire. And she was right, none of the dozens of things that ate his time up were truly his. He'd only just put his secret team together, and it would take time for them to gather the information he needed. He'd been able to reverse some of the damage CoFerrum Inc had done to the environment in a few scattered locations, but trying to change the company on a fundamental level was a deeply frustrating experience.

"You need to stop thinking like one of them, too," she added. "You're no longer a mundane man with a tiny little life. Let yourself imagine doing something bigger than you ever have before."

"I want to help people," he said.

"That's a place to start." She stood up. "When you know what you want to do, don't tell me. Write it down. Keep it close. Think it through. Then when you're ready, call your monkeys and tell them what they are going to do."

He pulled open a drawer to find some paper. Maybe if he sketched out the iron gates he had in mind to make next, something else would come to him.

"And, Sam," she said, and when he looked up she was by the door. "You'll need a wife, too, one day."

"Someone to give me sons?" he said, thinking of the world she came from.

"Someone to make you smile," she said sadly, and bid him good night.

4

Will stepped through the mirror in his private chamber at the Tower and found himself in the anteroom outside Sir Iris's study. It was a modest oak-panelled room with a handful of uncomfortable chairs designed to keep anyone waiting in exactly the state Sir Iris intended. He was greeted by a smartly dressed page wearing livery emblazoned with the fleur-de-lis who told him to wait. Will eyed up the chairs and decided to remain standing, too tense to sit and relax.

Will had never been summoned to Sir Iris before and had only met him briefly on his wedding day. As Patroon of all of the branches of the Iris family, his time was in great demand, and it was rare for anyone other than the head of a family to speak to him in person. Will appreciated the reinforcement that he was no longer a mere second son, relying on his father to pass on guidance (and often orders) from the Patroon. Now, he enjoyed a higher status in Society than that of his own father. It was hardly a comfort.

There were no windows, no paintings on the walls, nothing except a stucco frieze running around the top of the wall with predictable stylised fleur-de-lis at regular intervals. He clasped his hands behind his back and started to pace, resenting the urgency of the summons only to be kept waiting. Will reined in his impatience. He might be a duke now, but Sir Iris could strip that title from him and give it to another Iris he felt was more deserving. Will reminded himself that speculation only led to worry, and that neither would help him now.

The page returned and invited Will to follow him. He was led down a short panelled hallway, lit by sprite light, with no sound save the clipping of their shoes on the polished floorboards. His guide knocked once on a large door at the end of the hallway, opened it, and then stood to one side, gesturing to Will that he should enter. When Will did so, the door was closed behind him and footsteps receded down the hallway.

Sir Iris's study was larger than the antechamber and far more comfortable. A huge stone fireplace took up most of one wall, a fire crackling in the grate, and the wooden floor was covered by a large dark blue rug. The same wood panelling covered only the lower half of the walls; the rest was covered in flocked blue fleur-de-lis paper punctuated by various portraits of men Will could only assume were ancestors or distant relatives. A window to his right overlooked a beautiful formal garden with a large fountain in its centre, all reflected into the Nether at immense cost to keep the plants alive without sunlight.

The room was dominated by a huge oak desk behind which sat the Patroon, fingers steepled in front of his mouth, staring at Will. He was rumoured to be hundreds of years old, but looked like he was in his late sixties.

Intimidated, Will clicked his heels together and executed a tight formal bow. The Patroon's stare lingered, long enough for Will to wonder whether he should say something, until it was finally broken with a wave of the hand towards the chair in front of the desk.

"Sit," the Patroon commanded, and Will obeyed. "I'm supposed to be at a recital," he said, his dark eyes still piercing beneath his bushy eyebrows. "While I am always grateful to have an excuse not to go and listen to that damned Bach for the hundredth time, I do not appreciate it being the need to speak to a man about his wife's appalling behaviour."

Will hoped his cheeks weren't burning as much as it felt they were. "Sir Iris, I—"

"Is it so hard to keep that woman's mouth shut? Are you not aware of the Charms available at the Emporium?"

"I am well aware—"

"If you have some sort of misguided distrust of them then just beat her a few times. Put her in her place." He leaned forwards, scowling at Will like he was a mouse to pounce upon. "Well? Kindly explain to me why you didn't do either of these things *before* the Court this evening? Was the debacle at the previous Court not enough of a warning?"

Will rested his hands on his knees, keeping his back straight. "Sir Iris, I gave Catherine permission to speak on both occasions. I felt—"

"I have no interest in what you felt, boy. This is what comes of pushing a child onto a throne mere weeks after returning from the Grand Tour. This isn't Mundanus. We still know how to keep women in their place and that place is not in our politics. You took the throne, against all the odds, and now you are letting your rule be undermined by your wife. What possessed you?"

"Sir Iris, I stand by my decision. Catherine has a great deal to offer, and I think Londinium could benefit from—"

"A great deal to offer? More than children? What utter nonsense is this? Your good standing does not give you the right to carry out ridiculous social experiments in public. Get your house in order, William! I know Catherine Iris is not the one you wanted—Nathaniel and the pretty younger sister would have been quite sufficient to keep our alliance with the Papavers solid—but you must do better with her."

Being spoken to this way after weeks of being Duke was like being turfed off a sun lounger into a cold pool. Will struggled to shrug off his own shock and indignation so he could try and gain a footing in the conversation. "Sir Iris, please allow me to explain why—"

"I have no interest in what childish thinking led to this mess. I can only hope that the potential you've hitherto demonstrated will prove to be more than mere good fortune. I hope you can salvage your reputation in Londinium, otherwise I will be forced to choose a more worthy Iris to take the throne until you have matured. Perhaps a political apprenticeship in the Frankish Empire would be better for you, knock you down a few pegs, get some good sense back into your head."

Will clenched his teeth. He'd visited the Parisian Court on his Grand Tour, a ruthless, brutal political pressure cooker that turned its young bloods against each other. Duels were as commonplace as hot meals and assassinations rife, but neither bothered him as much as the potential loss of power. He'd tasted a life in which he didn't have to ask permission for every critical decision, free from the constraints of being the perfect spare in case his brother got himself killed in some hot-headed sword-fight. He wanted to keep it.

But surely the Patroon wouldn't want to publicly disgrace one of the family? Not one so obviously supported by Lord Iris himself?

"I know what you're thinking," Sir Iris's smile was more a predatory baring of teeth, as if the man had forgotten how to smile with warmth or humour. "That I wouldn't dare replace such a high-profile member of the family. Perhaps you don't appreciate how many ways the Irises would benefit from placing another son on the Londinium throne. The Tulipas are very upset with you. Nathaniel may have dealt with that ridiculous widow but that hasn't stopped the Patroon's constant demands for compensation. The Rosas will rise again, eventually, and they will direct all of their efforts against you." He patted a pile of letters to his right. "I have several very promising candidates ready to take your place, and many interesting offers of wealth and favour from the various parties you have wronged. Perhaps it would simply be easier to accept them and send you off to learn some harsh lessons for a couple of hundred years."

"There is no need to threaten me, sir," Will said. What a pathetic triumph to finally be able to finish a sentence. He seethed beneath his polite smile.

"Good. I cannot bear disappointment. I would rather keep you in Londinium for now. There are other cities I want to focus on. But if you show one more error in judgement, I will personally oversee every single decision you make in office until I am satisfied you have our family's best interests at heart. If you fail to keep that wife of yours in check, I will strip you of your title and put someone more worthy on the throne instead. Do you understand?"

"Perfectly. Sir." Will stood at the flick of Sir Iris's wrist, shame and anger sitting badly in his stomach. He had never been dressed down so harshly in his life. He'd never complained and had done nothing more than try to be an impeccable son. With each step towards the door, the sense of injustice built until he couldn't bear the thought of walking out of that room being seen as a stupid child by the most powerful man in the family. He had schemed, taken risks, and even killed a man to claw his way to the life he had now, and the relative freedom it gave. He was not going to lose it all now.

"Sir Iris," he said, turning before he reached the door. "Please may I ask for your advice in a sensitive matter?"

The Patroon's hawkish eyebrows raised from a deep scowl to one of surprise. "You may."

"I believe my wife to be under the influence of powerful Poppy magic, something done to her before our marriage. I think this magic is driving her to behave in the way she is."

Sir Iris's eyes widened. "Something that survived the wedding ceremony?"

"My understanding is that it was a form of wish magic put in place before the engagement and somehow triggered after we were married."

"Could you have been influenced by this too?"

"I cannot be certain, and I don't want to blame my error in judgement on this, Sir Iris. My wife is a passionate woman, and I'm not so weak as to seek an excuse for my failings in controlling those passions. But I do believe she is driven in an unnatural way and that our marriage would be happier and easier without this magical influence."

Sir Iris stood and came around the desk. "You were right to raise this with me. I'll inform our patron." Another smile, not exactly warm, but better than the one before. "It all makes sense now. Once your wife is put right, I'm sure you will impress me again, William."

"I will do my very best, Sir Iris." Will said and then, masking his surprise, he watched Sir Iris offer his hand and shook it.

He left the study filled with relief and a warm glow from winning the Patroon's hopeful approval once more. He felt a pang of guilt at the thought of Cathy losing the Poppy magic she had preserved even when Lord Iron offered to break it. She evidently thought it benefitted her somehow. But he had to keep the throne and keep her safe. She didn't see how self-destructive that wish was making her. And once they were freed from its influence, perhaps he could get them back on track, making a family of their own and consolidating their power in Londinium. By the time he stepped back through the mirror into the reflected Tower of London, he was convinced of two things: that he was right to ask Sir Iris for help in dealing with the wish magic, and that it would be best that Cathy didn't know.

• • •

Whilst Kay and Rupert were off buying things for the office, Max read the article, looked up the address of the newspaper office, and then phoned ahead to make an informal appointment with the relevant journalist. He'd used the mobile phone Rupert had insisted he buy. Perhaps it would be useful after all.

He thought about the article as he walked across the city. It was the first in a series, apparently, claiming that Bath had a hidden history of disappearances that had taken place over the past hundred years that had never been satisfactorily explained. The first article concentrated on prominent trade unionists from Bath and its nearby towns who'd simply disappeared over the twentieth century.

Max knew his father had worked at a foundry in Walcot Street, but had no idea he was in the National Union of Foundry Workers as the article claimed. The picture in the paper was of him and his fellow foundry workers, taken after they'd declared membership of the trade union founded that year, in 1920. Max's childhood memories were a confusing patchwork of images and sensations. He could still recall the itchy wool of a jumper his grandmother had knitted him, and the short trousers he'd worn with sturdy boots handed down through three generations of boys. By the time they'd got to him there were holes in the soles so big he could put his toe through them. Then his father had got the job at the foundry and everything was better. New boots, full bellies, and his mother smiling again. He couldn't remember much more than that.

In the Chapter, after he'd been taken from Mundanus, the head of the dorm had hit them with a cane if they talked about their life before. One girl who had wept hysterically for her mother was locked in a cupboard until she stopped and thrown back in there every time she started again. She went on to become a researcher and had supported him on multiple investigations, then was killed by the Sorceress along with the rest of the Bath Chapter.

Max knew that picture of his father was taken the same year that the Arbiter dragged him into the Chapter. He was ten years old and his new boots had scuffed on the cobbles as he'd struggled against him. He knew the Arbiter had taken him from Mundanus because he saw something he shouldn't near the foundry. Nothing more. After his soul had been dislocated and he was in full training as an Arbiter, the one who took him, Collins, became his mentor. They never talked about what had happened, because it was irrelevant. Thirteen-year-old Max, with a newly fitted soul chain tight around his neck, was no longer capable of being homesick or longing for his mother's arms or his father's laughter. He was no longer curious about whether his siblings were well or if his parents missed him.

Now, over ninety years later, Max wanted to find out what happened, unlike anything he'd wanted to investigate before. Something was shifting inside him. He'd gone fishing a week before because the gargoyle had wanted to go. Somehow, once he was at the river, the desire to fish lasted longer than any physical contact with the gargoyle. Without any reason to fish other than enjoyment, Max had started to wonder if the long-term proximity to his soul was having some sort of effect on him. Not that he could say he enjoyed the fishing.

Now he was driven to find out what happened to his family in a way he never had been before. He didn't feel upset or excited or in need of any closure. It was simply an intellectual compulsion, one that had made the gargoyle so restless and unfocused that it was now pacing the empty office, waiting for his return.

Walking through the city centre, he couldn't help but keep an eye out for any of the Fae-touched or their staff that he knew by sight. He didn't see any of them in the mundane city, which was expected, but vigilance was needed now more than ever. There were the usual tourists and residents bundled in coats, hats, and scarves, heads down against the bitter northerly wind. A blonde woman playing the violin on a street corner caught his eye; being young, attractive, and talented, she would be an obvious target. After watching her and the small crowd for a few minutes he was satisfied that none of the parasites had taken an interest.

Rupert had given him a new hat and coat and new gadgets to replace those he'd had from the Bath Chapter on the grounds that, though they worked perfectly, they were apparently "antiquated shit." Rupert had given him a quick demonstration of each one. As far as Max could tell, the only difference was that they were made of Bakelite and electronics instead of brass and clockwork. Rupert seemed to be offended by the comparison, saying his were far superior to anything Ekstrand had ever made. Max thought it best to say no more on the subject, and at least his pockets clanked less than they used to.

Max wasn't sure about his new coat or the hat, which Rupert said was better than the trilby, but he was certain that people stared at him less. The coat looked like a more modern version of his old one, had more pockets, and was warmer, too. The hat was lined with fur and had flaps that could be folded down to cover his ears when it was very cold. From the way the gargoyle had laughed at him, Max decided it was better not to wear them that way.

The receptionist recognised his appointment when he arrived at the newspaper's building on the other side of the city, and directed him to the third floor. He took off the hat and his gloves in the lift and looked at the article photos before the ping told him he'd arrived.

It was a large open-plan office, similar to the space Rupert had hired in Cambridge House, filled with dozens of cubicles. Each one contained a desk, chair, computer, and telephone. It was noisy and filled with people, some rushing around, some at the desks. A couple of them glanced at him and then looked back a second time, frowning, no doubt wondering what such a strange, ugly man was doing there.

Max went to the receptionist for that floor, a man who didn't give him a warm smile in greeting. "Excuse me, could you direct me to Nita Singh's desk?"

"She's over near the back wall, third from the left," the man said, happy to point and make Max go away.

He picked his way between two rows of cubicles, listening to the conversations, glancing at screens full of words and pictures that held no interest for him. Was this what Rupert had planned for the new Chapter? The two large rooms filled with researchers in the Bath Chapter were serene in comparison. People made notes, pored over books, and wrote up reports in silence, engrossed in their work. The dining hall was different, always as noisy as this place, but that he could understand; it was where the staff relaxed and exchanged stories. How could any work get done in a place like this?

A woman was sitting at the desk that was pointed out to him, her back to him as she typed on her computer. A long black braid ran down her back and her skin was dark brown. When she turned to look at a notepad resting beside her, he saw small white balls tucked into her ears with thin white cables leading from them. It took him a moment to place them as something to do with listening to music. He'd had a briefing about it at the Chapter, not long before it was destroyed.

He went over and tapped her on the shoulder, making her yelp and tear the wires from her ears. She swivelled her chair to face him and he was met with the usual mild shock and revulsion that was rapidly replaced with a professional smile. She stood and held out her hand. "Max?"

"Yes."

"Hi." She pulled an empty chair on wheels over from a nearby cubicle and put it near to hers. "Sit down, Max. How can I help you?"

"I'd like to ask you some questions about the article you wrote about the trade unionists." When she looked at him blankly, he added, "The ones who disappeared over the last century. It's the first in a series about people going missing from Bath and surrounds."

She leaned back in the chair, frowning. "I'm sorry, I have no idea what you're talking about. Perhaps you got the wrong newspaper?"

"This is the *Herald?*"

"Yes."

"And you are Nita Singh: nsingh@bathherald.co.uk?"

"I am. But I didn't write an article about any trade unionists. I'm afraid there's been some sort of mistake."

Max pulled the newspaper from where it was tucked under his arm and showed her the page, pointing out her name and email address. Her frown deepened.

"I don't understand. This is this week's edition. It must be some sort of error….Could you just wait here a moment? I need to speak to my editor."

She took his copy with her, striding off to a corner of the room with glass walls partitioning it off from the larger space.

Max pulled the Sniffer from his pocket, palming it until he was sure that no one was watching. It didn't look anything like the old one, which resembled a small clockwork gramophone. Rupert's device was a rectangular stick of plastic, about the size of a packet of chewing gum, and seemed too light to be of any use. Keeping his hands tucked in his lap and remaining as still as possible, he touched the two small nubbins on either side of the small rectangle. It started to vibrate, but if it made any noise, it was lost in the room's hubbub. A tiny orange light flashed in the corner of one of the larger rectangular surfaces. When it turned a solid green, Rupert had told him, it was done. It worked on the same principle as Ekstrand's device did, sucking in air to detect any residue of Fae magic, but without any need for winding up. He supposed batteries were involved. As long as it did the job, he didn't care.

Nita soon returned, the frown even more pronounced and her steps hurried. She sat at her desk without saying a word and began typing on the computer. "I don't understand," she muttered.

Something new appeared on the screen. Max read it over her shoulder, committing it to memory. It was a list of photographs and what they featured—including the one of his father and the others in the article—a summary of a conversation, and the name and address of someone listed as the source.

Nita swivelled round to face him and he looked away before she noticed he'd been staring at the screen. "I'm so sorry, Mr…Max. I have no recollection of writing this piece but the notes and source details are in the database. We have to keep this in case anything is challenged or there's legal action. The entry says I entered all the details last week and my editor says she had a conversation with me about it but…but I can't remember any of it."

She handed the newspaper back to him.

"I was hoping you'd be able to tell me more about one of the photographs. Did you get it from a local historian? Someone I could speak to instead?"

She turned back to the screen and scrolled down. "According to the entry in the database they've asked to remain anonymous. I'm afraid I can't pass on any details. Perhaps the library could help?"

He noticed her hands were shaking. The Sniffer stopped vibrating but he merely dropped it back into his pocket as he stood up. "I'll try there, thank you, Ms Singh."

He left her sitting at her desk, head in her hands. Once he was in the lift he pulled the Sniffer back out, noting the solid green light on the top. He flipped the rectangle over to the small pale grey display on the other side. In dark grey typeface, a single word confirmed his suspicion.

IRIS.

5

Tom gave the butler his cape and hat, surprised by the silence of the house. Usually Lucy played the piano in the evening and as far as he knew she had no other engagements. "Is my wife at home?"

"Yes, sir," Grayson replied. "She's in the drawing room."

Usually he would go upstairs, wash, and have his valet furnish him with a smoking jacket, all to try and distance himself from his role as Marquis of Westminster. Just as it was important to put on his cape and hat when he left every morning to get into role, he needed to get out of the uniform just as much. But this time, concerned that Lucy's routine was broken, he went straight to the drawing room.

He opened the door and found the room cooler than she normally preferred. A fire was burning low in the grate and he could see the back of her head where she was seated on the sofa, her blonde hair arranged neatly enough but with a few more strands hanging loose at the sides than he was used to seeing.

"Lucy?" he asked, closing the door behind him. "Are you well?"

She started, as if she'd been concentrating on something, but by the time he had rounded the sofa she was standing and didn't seem to have any embroidery or score sheets that could have absorbed her so.

"Thomas, oh, hi—hello. Dear." She bobbed up onto her tiptoes to kiss him on the cheek. She could only reach it if he bent down. Not for the first time, he wished she were taller. "I had no idea it had got so late." She tucked the wayward strands behind her ears and smoothed down her dress, clearly unprepared for his arrival.

"You seemed distracted."

"Oh…just thinking." Her smile was forced. When he frowned, she looked away. "I confess I was feeling a little homesick."

"Rather homesick," Tom corrected. "'Homesick' is a state of mind, not a small animal."

"Yes." She tried to smile again. "Of course. How was your day?"

"Tedious." He sighed. "Thanks to my sister's latest antics, I spent all afternoon pandering to Bertrand Viola's petty requests instead of the things I should have been dealing with, just to make sure he doesn't have any other reasons to complain." Cat had no inkling of how much trouble she caused. Whether it was in Londinium or Mundanus, she always found a way to make life as difficult as possible.

"Shall I get you a brandy?" Lucy asked.

He nodded, feeling tired. "Every time I go to Black's, someone corners me and complains about something she's said or done. Cat always maintains she hasn't done anything, but she doesn't appreciate how all of this nonsense about the need for change is making the men of the Court thoroughly bad-tempered. That can hardly be good for their wives, but Cat is incapable of understanding that."

Lucy was suspiciously quiet as she poured his drink. She was petite and not unpleasant to look at. She wore her dresses well and was an accomplished pianist. But as he let his eyes roam over her waist and the bustle of her dress, he felt nothing more than a sense of duty to care for her, as he'd promised in front of the Oak. They'd been married almost a year and the feelings he'd hoped would blossom still hadn't even formed buds. Would it never happen for them? She seemed to be fond of him. Why? She barely knew him. Her affection only made him feel more distant from her.

He sat heavily on the sofa, his starched shirt collar making him feel choked. He winkled a finger into the knot of his cravat and loosened it so he could undo the top button. He should have changed first. The brandy tasted good enough to take his mind off it, and he took a moment to savour the warmth it spread through his chest. Lucy perched on the armchair nearest the fire and he noted that she looked pale. Then he realised that she probably prepared herself before his return home each evening, but for whatever reason had not done so this time. Had she worn makeup all those times before? He only noticed now that there was an absence of it.

Tom leaned back and a crinkling noise came from the cushion he rested against. Lucy shot out of her chair and, faster than he could twist round and investigate, she had stuffed her hand behind it and pulled something out, something now hidden behind her back.

"What was that?"

"Nothing. Just a score. I'll take it to the music room."

She was lying. Tom put his glass down, mindful of his temper rising. He took a deep breath, keeping it in check, always careful to not succumb to the same rages his father had. He stood and put himself between her and the door. Just his height alone made him imposing enough to make her shrink back. "Please show it to me, Lucy."

Her cheeks reddened. "I don't think that would be a good idea."

"Why not?" Was it a letter from a lover? No, he didn't believe that; Lucy was a devoted wife, always doing all she could to make his life easier.

"Because…because it hasn't been written for men to read."

Now he was just confused. "Lucy," he said again, stern enough for her to bite her lip and hold it out towards him.

It was a printed booklet, not unlike many he'd collected in Mundanus during the years he had spent hunting for Catherine, written by local historians about some obscure slice of history that no publisher would be interested in. It was printed on A4 paper with a grey cover, folded in half and stapled. *Recipes for Happiness and Fulfilment* was written on the front in a no-nonsense copperplate. A recipe book? He wouldn't have given it a second glance had Lucy not behaved so nervously around it.

He flipped it open at a random page. *Know Thyself* was written at the top. Had he not seen the diagram beneath, he might have been forgiven for thinking it was a rather twee effort to explore some sort of feminine philosophy.

Lucy squeezed her eyes shut as his widened and his mouth

fell open. It was a picture of female anatomy in cross-section with unspeakable things such as *ovaries* and *fallopian tubes* labelled neatly. Beneath it was a brief explanation of the functions of each part. Incensed and embarrassed in equal measure, he flipped the page to find questions in bold with answers written below them. The first he saw, *What is an orgasm?*, made him slap the pages shut before he could accidentally scan the text below it.

"Like I said, it wasn't written for you," Lucy said, taking a step back. "Oh, Tom, there's no need to look like that."

"Like what?"

"Like you've just swallowed a bee."

"Where did you get this?"

Lucy folded her arms. "None of your business. It was written for women."

"Written by whom?" He held up a hand. "Oh for the love of… it's Cat, isn't it?"

"I've no idea," Lucy said, but he didn't believe her. "Besides, even if it was, it's nothing to do with you."

Tom waved the booklet in the air. "This is filth!"

"It's education."

"It's exactly the sort of thing that corrupts women."

"Oh, sweet Jesus, Tom! Will you just be quiet and sit down?"

Stunned into silence, Tom found himself sitting and staring at the tiny woman sitting herself down. She'd never raised her voice before, let alone barked an order like that.

Lucy composed herself faster than he did. She smiled at him, just as if they were seated across from each other at dinner. "Thomas…I would like it very much if you could listen to what I have to say."

"Is this how wives speak to their husbands in the colonies?"

Lucy rolled her eyes. "Since I moved here and married you I have done everything that has been expected of me, have I not?"

Tom nodded.

"I even speak like you do now, and believe me, that isn't easy.

So, seeing as I have done everything a good wife possibly could, please will you listen to me and not speak until I'm ready?"

Tom took another breath to protest. Something about the way she was talking to him seemed disrespectful in the extreme, but when he thought about it, she hadn't asked for anything too unreasonable. With another nod, he acquiesced.

"Every woman in Albion should know this stuff, and they should learn it from their parents and governesses."

When Tom opened his mouth to protest she held up a hand and gave him a stern look. Who was this woman? Had that booklet done this?

"Now, it might be a shock for you to learn that I already know everything in this booklet. I was taught all I needed to know about my body, about sex, and about how it all works before I left California."

All Tom could do was blink at her. Not even he knew all of the intricacies of female anatomy and he considered himself well educated.

"And that's the way it should be," Lucy continued. "Now, I've been in Albion for nearly a year, long enough to see that something here is really screwed up, and I figure that you're just as oblivious as the rest of them."

"Now look here—"

"I haven't finished," Lucy said, raising her voice enough to shock him into silence again. Was he cursed with having to care for difficult women? "Something is rotten in Albion. You guys send young men into Mundanus for the Grand Tour and yet even though they spend four years living in the modern world, nothing changes here. In America both the young women and the men travel in Mundanus, and both bring back knowledge of progress. My mother has just as much influence over the way our family is run as my father, and I'm talking about financial decisions, not just who wears what and how their damn houses look! Why do only the men have any real power in Albion?"

"Because it's the natural—"

"Goddamn it, Tom, I haven't finished! Albion is stuck, and it needs people like your sister to change it. I suggest you stop being angry about something as stupid as women here being given the education they should have and start being angry about the way they're having to find it out from a secret pamphlet."

Tom pulled off his cravat and tossed it onto the arm of the sofa, loosening his collar further. After what had been said, it didn't seem so important to be perfectly attired. A painful throb was building behind his eyes and he just wanted everything to be simple again. Even hunting Cat in Mundanus had been easier to bear than this life of politics and the ground shifting beneath his feet every five minutes.

Lucy moved from her chair to sit next to him. "I'm sorry that was hard to hear. But it isn't just me that feels this way, and not just your sister either."

"It's my fault she's the way she is," Tom said, letting himself sink back into the cushions. He didn't have the energy to hold himself rigidly straight anymore. "Father used to beat her. Terribly. I should have…" A tightness in his throat threatened the steadiness of his voice, so he took a breath and waited until it passed. "I should have intervened, when I was old enough. But I never did. If she'd felt safe at home, she never would have run away and been corrupted by Mundanus."

"Oh, Tom," Lucy took his hand and kissed it. "Cathy wanted to find her own way, more than she wanted to get away from home, I'm sure of it. Don't blame yourself. Your father can be pretty scary—sorry—quite scary." She stared at him so intently that he was drawn to look back at her. He saw nothing but compassion in her pale brown eyes. "It must have been so hard for you, trying to be a good son and a good brother when your father was like that. And then having to find her and bring her back….I know you wanted to see so much on your Grand Tour. You've never talked to me about it. It might—"

Tom stood and grabbed his cravat. "It's all in the past," he said. "No point dredging it all back up again." He looked at the booklet in his other hand, uncertain of how to proceed. He considered confiscating it, but he couldn't risk it being found in the house and he couldn't be seen to condone such material. He went to the fireplace and threw it into the embers. By the time Lucy had dashed over to his side the paper had caught alight, rejuvenating the dying fire.

"Tom!"

"I'll forget I saw that, for your sake. But if I find another, or if one of the residents brings it to my attention, I will investigate and haul whoever is responsible in front of their Patroon. I'm going to change for dinner, and we'll never speak of this again."

"You can be better than this," Lucy said as he headed towards the door. "Just let me talk it over with you. It's not what you think."

"It's not what you think, either," he said. "This isn't some romantic intellectual movement. It's an attempt to disturb the order of things and cause chaos. Otherwise known as sedition!"

"That's—"

"And you can be better than this too," he added. "You can set an example and make it clear you disapprove. You're the wife of the Marquis of Westminster; don't forget it."

He left the room and shut the door behind him, his stomach cramping and headache worsening. As he climbed the stairs he told himself he was doing the right thing. If that was the case, why did he feel so wretched about it?

•   •   •

By the time Cathy got home after the Court, she felt terrible. Even though Will was clearly so afraid of what Sir Iris was going to say to him, she'd just scored points off him, without any consideration of how he was feeling. With her blood up, she'd felt invulnerable, filled with satisfaction with how shocked the men of the court had looked when she put that stupid Peonia in his place. Not even Bertrand Viola had been able to cow her.

That triumphant feeling and her irritation that Will was clearly not on her side had pushed away any compassion about the summons. Cathy didn't regret any of what she'd said in the Court, but did regret not giving a second thought to how worried Will was about Sir Iris, and wanted to apologise. She waited up for a couple of hours, and then received word from the Tower that Will was sleeping there that night.

Now that she was dressed and ready to tackle the day despite a sleepless night, Cathy found herself both hoping for and dreading his return. Navigating a path between her near-constant frustration at Society and her love for Will was harder than she'd imagined it would be. Now she understood why the few romantic films she'd seen in Mundanus ended at the part where the couple got together. Even Doc Brown and Clara's story had the tricky middle bit skipped out. There was the getting together, then the kids, not the time where they learned how to be a couple. Cathy shuddered. She didn't want to get to the kids part.

Cathy went to her study, trying to draw comfort from the fact that even though Will wasn't as keen for change as she was, he wasn't a monster like his brother or Bertrand Viola. *It could be worse*, she thought. *We'll figure this out.* On the way, she checked in with Carter about her movements for the day and reassured the bodyguard that she still didn't need him to stand outside of her study whilst she was dealing with correspondence.

She sat at her desk and whispered the Key Charm with her hand over it to unlock all of the drawers. She pulled out a pen and her notepad.

> *To-Do List*
> 1. *Burn down the patriarchy*
> 2. *Apologise to Will and work out a way forward*
> 3. *Write to Eleanor*
> 4. *Check on how the escapees are doing in Mundanus*
> 5. *Get Coll to buy me Plants vs. Zombies 2 for the iPad*
> 6. *Research batteries for TV and DVD player*

At the knock on the door she invited in the butler, Morgan. They'd settled into a routine and, as expected, he entered with a stack of envelopes on a silver tray.

"Did all of that arrive today?"

"Yes, ma'am," he replied. "Is there anything else I can do for you?"

"No, thanks."

The letter on top of the pile was from Margritte, and the wax seal on the back had been stamped with the single feather motif that the four of them used to indicate the need for the reader to be alone when reading the enclosed letter. It also meant that after she'd read it the ink would turn into dust, so she moved the waste-paper basket closer, ready for afterwards.

> *Dear Cathy,*
>
> *I regret the way our meeting ended yesterday. It was clear you are not happy with the idea of a Ladies' Court. I should have told you that William and I discussed it but it simply slipped my mind. As you know, he visits regularly with the Charms required to keep me hidden, and inevitably we talk about what occupies our thoughts. He does want to help but both he and I feel you wish to achieve far more than Society could accommodate as quickly as you wish. It is so frustrating being unable to help you publicly, and I fear you may have felt William and I colluded behind your back. I can only assure you that this is not so. We all have the same end goal, and a desire to see each of us safe and happy as we achieve it. There is a long and difficult road ahead of us and I hope our friendship will endure.*
>
> *With love,*
>
> *M*

Cathy watched the words turn to dust, folded the paper inwards to collect it all, and tossed it on the fire. Secrecy Charms were all well and good—and critical for her secret cabal—but she missed being able to read the words over a few times to digest them. She had been angry that they'd discussed the idea of a Ladies' Court behind her back, but half of that anger was the needy, ugly fear that Will preferred the company of the stately and refined Margritte over her own. She had to make sure that fear didn't make her into an arsehole about his friendship with Margritte. Of course Will doted on Margritte; he was responsible for the awful situation she was in now. Cathy sighed. What a bloody mess. She added *Write nice letter to M* to the list.

Flipping through the rest of the envelopes, Cathy saw that there were none from her fellow conspirators and, happily, nothing from Dame Iris either. Cathy hadn't seen her since the last time she visited. She couldn't help but smile at the memory of her fainting when Eleanor had appeared at the doorway. The moment when Dame Iris realised she no longer had any power over her was one Cathy would never forget.

One envelope towards the bottom of the pile caught her eye, as the handwriting was unlike that of Society ladies. It was all in uppercase, the letters spaced too far apart to look right.

There was no wax seal on the back. Cathy opened it, finding a single sheet of paper inside with the words all written in uppercase letters again.

SPEAK LESS AND SMILE MORE. STUPID WHORES LIKE YOU SHOULD STAY OUT OF

A knock on the door made her jump and stuff the paper back into the envelope before she finished reading it. "Yes?" Her heart thumped uncomfortably as Morgan entered with his silver tray again.

"I'm sorry, ma'am, you have visitors."

Cathy looked at the clock. At this time? She picked up the calling card offered to her on the tray, noting the folded top left corner informing her that the individual was there in person.

Mrs Charles Rhoeas-Papaver
Aquae Sulis

"Oh shit." What was her mother doing in Londinium? She picked up the second card with its own folded corner.

Miss Elizabeth Rhoeas-Papaver
Aquae Sulis

Cathy noted how Elizabeth's had a beautifully painted poppy

flower in the lower right corner. Did their father know about that embellishment? "Bollocks. Not her too. This is all I need."

Morgan, no longer disturbed by her language, simply pulled the tray back to rest in place in front of his chest. The sound of her sister cooing at the entrance hall floated down the hallway. "Shall I inform them that you are not receiving visitors?"

"If you'd met my mother, Morgan, you'd know that would make no difference whatsoever. Show them in."

When Morgan left Cathy realised she was still holding the horrible letter. She stuffed it into the top drawer and locked the desk with the Key Charm as the sound of her sister's excited gabble grew steadily louder. She had time to stand and check her hair in the mirror—and get annoyed at herself because inevitably she'd still be a disappointment—before Morgan knocked again.

As he announced them Cathy smoothed her dress and tried her best to fix a smile on her face. Perhaps if she hid how much she didn't want to see them, things would go more smoothly and they'd go away sooner.

Her mother swept into the room as if she owned it, dressed in a dark red dress with a dramatic black hat and gloves, and kissed her on the cheek. "Don't pretend to look pleased to see us, that fake smile is too tedious for words. Apologies for the hour and unexpected visit. I would have written and arranged it, had I known we were coming."

"Mother and Auntie Lavandula had the most appalling row last night," Elizabeth said as she entered. She was wearing an emerald-green dress and looked as perfect and beautiful as ever. Cathy immediately felt the familiar sense of being ugly, plump, and ungainly next to her. "Catherine, you are positively wicked for not telling us how divine this house is. Why did you not invite us as soon as you moved here? I would have wanted to show it off to everybody."

"I…had other things on my mind," Cathy said, and endured another kiss on the cheek, this time from her sister.

A row? They'd always been thick as thieves. Cathy didn't appreciate being reminded of her aunt, the Censor of Aquae Sulis, a ruthless, cruel-hearted woman. She'd never told her mother how the Censor had picked her up to take her out for tea, only to throw her out of the carriage into Mundanus to be picked up by an Arbiter. At least her uncle was better disposed towards her.

"The house is splendid, Catherine," Mother said as she sat down. "Did you choose the decor?"

"Yes," Cathy said after a slight pause, not wanting to admit that the only room she'd really chosen anything for was her library. The rest was mostly suggested by Will and the interior designer sent by the Agency, back when she still had dealings with them.

"Mmm." Her mother didn't need words to convey her disapproval.

"So…" Cathy moved towards one of the chairs around the fireplace, gesturing for them to join her there. "What brings you to Londinium?"

"Auntie Lavandula has been beastly," Elizabeth said, cheeks flushed with excitement. "It's all your fault, Catherine."

"Oh, well there's a surprise," Cathy said. "It's always my fault, isn't it? Even when I live in another city."

"It's you who—"

Her mother cut off Elizabeth's words with a glare. "I have brought Elizabeth here for the season."

"It doesn't start for another month!"

"I know it's early. I want your dressmaker to make her new gowns in the latest Londinium fashion."

Cathy felt like her mother was on a fast-moving carousel and was trying to pull her onto it too. She didn't want any part of this fun-fair. "Can we go back a minute? Why are you bringing her to me?"

"Because I want you to secure a good match for her."

Cathy half laughed, half choked. "Me? Isn't Father supposed to sell her off to the highest bidder?"

"Catherine!" Elizabeth was genuinely affronted. "Oh, Mother, don't leave me with her. She's so horrid to me."

Her mother looked tired and Cathy noticed how pale she was.

"Elizabeth, go and take a turn about the gardens; I've heard they are beautiful."

"But I don't want to see the—"

"I want to speak to your sister in private."

Bottom lip protruding, Elizabeth flounced out of the room in the most dramatic way she could get away with, narrowly avoiding a collision with Morgan, who was about to bring in tea and cake.

When the refreshments had been left and the door closed, her mother took off her hat, tossed it onto Elizabeth's chair, and leaned back. "I barely slept last night. Elizabeth knows enough to feel like there's some drama that makes her special, but not all of it."

"She thinks she knows enough to blame me. Was that just her usual rubbish?"

"Partly. Catherine, you know that news of your exploits here has not been well received in Aquae Sulis."

Surely one of the few benefits of being Duchess was not having to endure this rubbish from her mother anymore? "Exploits? You make it sound like I've been robbing banks."

"Don't be difficult. You know what I'm talking about. Cutting husbands out of communication between a family and the Duke? Just the mere act of your speaking in the Court has upset a lot of people. I've heard rumours of a 'Ladies' Court.' How you persuaded William to allow all of this I have no idea."

Cathy picked up the tea strainer, decided against using it to bat her mother on the forehead and instead poured the tea. "What has any of this got to do with Elizabeth?"

"Your aunt is very upset about the way you're behaving."

"It's none of her bloody business! She's the Censor of Aquae Sulis, not Londinium!"

"She holds you responsible for the antics at the last ball of the season."

"Why me? I wasn't even there!" Cathy had been delighted by the lack of invitation to the annual masked ball.

"There were women there dressed as men, the most horrendous

pamphlet making the rounds, talk of women's rights—who else would be at the centre of that besides you?"

"There's no proof of that. And as for what I do in the Londinium Court, that's up to me. And Will, I suppose. Not her."

"For goodness' sake, Catherine, you may be woefully lacking in many respects, but you're no fool. How you rule in your city has an impact on all the others. Whatever changes you force through here will put pressure on the Censor and Master of Ceremonies to dig in deeper or change themselves. You're unsettling everything."

"Good. That's what I'm trying to do. Aunt Claudia has been queen bee for far too long and hates the thought of any other woman having an opinion of her own, let alone any sort of power. I'm glad she didn't invite us to that ball. It would have been awful. But you have to ask why she was so scared of me being there."

"She isn't scared of you, Catherine! She's embarrassed to be related to you. Besides, I didn't come here to discuss politics. Is that lemon drizzle cake?"

Cathy nodded and cut her mother a slice. "I'm not a matchmaker. You know I hate all of this…" she wanted to say *bullshit*, but she was sure that wouldn't help. "It goes against my principles. You know how much I hate the fact that women are treated as property. Why the hell would I agree to sell off my own sister?"

Her mother abandoned the cake. "Oh, hang your principles! I just want her married off, and there's no way we're going to make a satisfactory match with Claudia being obstructive. She's excluding Elizabeth from the best salons and dinner parties at which she should be meeting eligible gentlemen. You must help us."

Cathy clenched her teeth and counted to five. Margritte had told her the technique had saved her on some occasions. "You're not listening to me. I'm not going to undermine what tiny amount of progress I've made here by participating in—"

"Catherine, I know very well how you feel about it, and that's just something you'll have to deal with. I need her to be married and every time we've been on the brink of settling a contract, something has gone wrong. First it was Nathaniel; Poppy insisted you be married to William and that went out of the window." Her mother picked up the fork again, chasing the cake around the plate with it as she spoke. "Then we tried to match her with a Viola but the family wouldn't commit and there were at least three different Rosas in the running but none of them would marry until you were married and you were off having your little rebellion, so that was impossible. Then their family collapsed and the number of eligible young men has become woefully low."

"Does Father know you're here?"

"He will by this evening. Catherine, you owe us. Your actions have resulted in Tom being married off to a colonial and your sister rapidly becoming the laughing stock of Aquae Sulis. Claudia thinks that snubbing you will bring you into line, but that's only because she has no idea how stubborn you are." She abandoned the cake again. "I am asking you, nicely, to give your sister a fantastic season and every opportunity to milk your status. She won't embarrass you. She'll positively thrive!"

"I can't believe this."

"She's had such a difficult start. We couldn't give her a proper debut because of your antics, and it was only because the Censor and Master of Ceremonies are my siblings that we could get away with taking her to balls to meet eligible young men without one."

"My heart bleeds for her."

Her mother slapped the arm of her chair, eyes filling with tears. "Catherine, why must you make everything so bloody hard? I just need you to do this one thing for me."

Cathy stared at the unshed tears. She had never seen her mother cry. She'd never seen anything other than disapproval, anger, and disappointment. She'd seen her smile on many occasions—brittle, empty masks of smiles and the occasional real one for Tom or Elizabeth when she wasn't being petulant. There was something else behind this.

"Why now? Why the urgency?"

A single tear broke free and then her mother swiped it away, the mask restored. She busied herself with her cake fork.

"Is she pregnant?"

Her mother's shock was genuine. "Catherine Rho—how could you even think such a thing? Her maidenhood is still very much intact."

"Is it Father? Has something—"

"Listen to me." Her mother edged forwards in her seat. "I know I've not been the mother you wanted. I know I haven't been the kindest or most understanding person and that you're angry with me."

"Of course I bloody am! The last time I saw you, you drugged me and dressed me for a wedding I didn't want to have!"

"I know, I know." She closed her eyes. "I know you will never forgive me, but I promise: this is the only time in your entire life that I will ever ask anything of you. Do you want me to beg? To bargain with you? Offer something in return?"

Cathy shrank back from her mother's desperation, repulsed. "No," she said, realising that despite everything, she didn't have it in her to turn her mother and sister away. "If it's that important, she can stay." Her mother's relief made her worry she'd made a terrible mistake. "But I'm not going to negotiate a contract or any of that crap." Her mother's back straightened at the use of the word but she stayed silent. "I'll...I dunno, put on a ball or something. Introduce her to people—"

"The *right* people, Catherine. Wealthy, preferably, and well respected."

"Yeah, yeah, all that bobbins," Cathy said. "Don't worry, Will's really good at that sort of thing. He'll know who's a good candidate. But I'll only tell you and Father who the match is if Elizabeth likes him. That's non-negotiable."

Her mother stood. "If he's wealthy and powerful, she'll like him. Do try and be kind to her. I don't want her to lose any weight or look sullen, so you need to keep her spirits high. She always looks her best when she thinks you approve of her."

"That might apply to you, not me," Cathy said, following her mother to the door.

"I think you underestimate the power of your approval, Catherine," she said. She paused, kissed Cathy on the cheek, and put her hat back on. "Thank you. This means a great deal to me."

Cathy managed a smile and then slid down in her chair with relief once her mother had left. She rested a hand over her stomach, feeling like everything had been churned up inside her by her mother's visit.

Then Cathy remembered the letter. She retrieved it from the drawer, steeled herself for the contents, and pulled the piece of paper out of the envelope. Unfolding it, she found only black dust. Cathy stared at the blank page, trying to recall the wording before throwing it into the fire. There was nothing to be done when nameless enemies used the same Secrecy Charms as her friends. Then the door burst open and Elizabeth flew into the room.

"Oh! How wonderful! How many new dresses may I have? I don't want any like that one you're wearing now, it's simply hideous. Now, sit down and listen carefully. I have a list of characteristics my future husband must have and they are all very important."

6

Sam applauded, stifling a yawn. He'd lost track of how many speeches he'd sat through since he'd arrived, and none of them had contained anything of use.

They were in the swankiest hotel in Manchester, all thirty-two of the Elemental Court, and the atmosphere was charged with excitement when he entered the conference room. Mazzi came straight over to him, shaking him warmly by the hand and guiding him to meet a few people before the first item on the agenda started. He was introduced to Lord Copper first, a short man with black hair and dark brown skin who spoke with an unidentifiable accent that sometimes sounded Spanish. He met Lady Silver, whose long auburn hair featured a prominent white streak that seemed to glow. She was from Russia and smiled often, but didn't spend much time with him.

Then the speeches started. He'd sat there, eager for answers to so many questions. He wanted to learn about their history, the relationship each of them had with the Sorcerers, whether any of them had had dealings with the Fae. But none of them talked about anything like that. Most gave a potted summary of business growth, tonnes extracted, projects in the pipeline—all the sorts of things found in the *Financial Times* that had never interested him.

Lord Gold was a jeweller, and Sam had almost laughed out loud at hearing about a necklace he was working on as part of his presentation. But then Sam realised he was as much a cliché: Lord Iron, the blacksmith. Mazzi had told him that sometimes they were chosen thanks to an affinity when working the metal. Sam listened intently when Lord Copper spoke, hoping for just a passing reference to the way copper rendered the Fae weak and their magic inert. Nothing. He spoke passionately about how his personal intervention had increased the number of tonnes of copper being shipped out of Zambia and Sam's shoulders began to knot with tension. He was certain there had been something in the information Leanne had left to him about the acid runoff from a Zambian mine creating horrific ecological problems.

As Sam was the new kid on the block, he was supposed to speak last. Mazzi had said that not all of the court would speak, which was something, but the longer the day went on, the more uncomfortable Sam felt. Most of the people there were the sort of hard business execs he was allergic to; they spoke of "achievements" that were environmentally devastating. It was all about driving up profits and production with nothing about how short-sighted the activity was. Everything they talked about sounded like mundane super-rich crap.

There was no hint of anything esoteric when they talked about the element in their title, nor any sense that they embodied its qualities, as he had been told he embodied iron in the eyes of the Fae. Sam knew he was more than just a super-CEO; he'd walked a path between the worlds, broken the beauty of Exilium, and scared the shit out of Lord Poppy. But he had the feeling that if he talked about any of that, they'd laugh him out of the room.

In the breaks for coffee and pastries, he found himself drawing inwards as one by one they all came to meet him. Several of them seemed like nice people, warm and friendly. One in particular, a woman "representing Chromium," as she introduced herself, seemed like the kind of person he'd happily have a chat with in the pub. Lady Aluminium, on the other hand, set his teeth on edge. Something about her voice, perhaps, or her manner. She was obviously someone who'd been born into wealth. In any case, when she asked to have a quiet word with him he was tempted to say no.

Instead, he decided to be polite: "Of course."

"I'm looking forward to your presentation," she said, drawing him into a little nook around the corner from the rest of the...of the what? Delegates? Reps? It didn't feel like a court.

"Yeah," he replied. He had no idea what he was going to say, even though he had no fewer than two fully written presentations with him and a third half-baked.

"Call me Alicia. I was good friends with Amir. I was sorry to hear of his passing."

Sam forced a smile, trying not to think too much about the way the previous Lord Iron had committed suicide right in front of him to pass the mantle. "It was a bit of a shock for everyone."

"Indeed. Presumably for him, too, because we were on the brink of signing a deal."

"That's the thing you want to talk about?"

Alicia was as tall as he was in her high heels, reed-thin with the sort of cheekbones he'd only seen in computer games. "Yes. Perhaps you've come across some paperwork regarding the South African Vanadium proposal?"

"Not yet, sorry."

Alicia twisted away from him and clicked her fingers. An aide he hadn't noticed hurried over with a small attaché case. "I have a copy of the proposal here, along with the contract Amir agreed to over the telephone. He was due to sign it as soon as it arrived but…" she shrugged. "He passed before he could, I suppose. Very sad." She offered him the folder she pulled from the case. "I'm sure you'll agree it's most beneficial." She leaned in close. "Better to not mention it to Titanium; he'll only want to make things difficult." Then she straightened and held out her hand, which Sam shook reluctantly. "Looks like it's time to go back inside. Oh, I think it's your turn to speak."

"Better get my notes together," Sam said, and walked a few paces away until she left.

He pulled out his phone and almost called for a taxi, but reconsidered. He couldn't run away from this. He opened his texts and fired a new one to Cathy.

Any chance we could go to the pub soon? I can come to London no trouble. Could do with a friend who thinks most of the stuff they're supposed to do is bullshit :)

Sam swiped to his presentation notes and the words just swam before him. "Fuck it," he whispered, and went back to the meeting room.

Mazzi gave him a warm smile when he entered, doing all she could to make him feel at ease. It wasn't helping, but he could have hugged her for trying. Sam went up to the front, put the paperwork on the lectern, and looked at the assembled. Men and women from all over the world looked back at him expectantly. He thought of the funeral, of Leanne's mother sobbing in the front row. Had any of the people in front of him accidentally killed any of their employees? Maybe. Probably. He knew several of them ran business empires responsible for the misery of many people, and deaths too. He cleared his throat.

"Hi, everyone. My name is Sam, and I'm the one Amir chose to…I'm the one he chose. I've prepared a presentation—well, two, actually, but after watching the others today I know neither is right." A few smiled, most didn't. "My team, the one I inherited, wrote one of them. It's got all the figures in it. All the business stuff, you know. But I'm not really into showing off about that sort of stuff, so I'll skip that one."

He scanned the faces of his audience and saw the polite attempts to mask their confusion. Many looked like they were trying to decide if he was taking the piss out of them.

"The second presentation I wrote is mostly me trying to give this potted summary of who I am and…and it basically boils down to me not being a hardcore business kind of bloke." He watched the glances exchanged, the shuffling in the chairs. "I guess that's a bit of shocker, seeing as Amir was like, Mr Business Mogul, but I'm…" he shrugged. "I'm just a blacksmith." He picked up the folder, ready to walk out of the room and leave them to it, but he thought of Leanne, of the way gathering the dirt on the activities of these people led to their separation. To her death. He put the folder back down again.

"I'm making changes, though. I'm rolling out a programme of improvements, making sure that all of the mines, plants, forges, foundries, and whatever the hell else I own now will meet the highest environmental protection standards, regardless of what the local compliance requires. I'd like to see you doing the same."

Backs straightened, eyebrows raised, both Copper and Alicia looked far from pleased. Mazzi closed her eyes.

"The environment and how we can protect it is something I really am interested in." He let the silence hang for a moment, feeling the hostility towards him building. He wanted to just leave the room, not press it any further, give in to the social pressure to shut up.

He thought of all of those files in storage that Leanne left to him. Her legacy. How those boxes, dozens and dozens of them, catalogued suffering and destruction caused by the very people staring at him. He wanted to yell at them, but they were all there together, facing him standing in front of them, alone. All in their expensive suits and dripping with power. "I...I...um...I just worry that this endless striving for growth and profits just isn't sustainable. For you or the environment! We need to think about a bigger picture here."

"Iron, we *are* the bigger picture," Copper called out, making many of them smirk. "The people in this room make the world go round. Did Amir not tell you? Without us—without your predecessor's predecessor we wouldn't have had the industrial revolution. We make the world a better place."

"Do we? Really? But what about the pollution and—"

"We cannot micro-manage every single cog in the machine," Copper said. "The benefits far outweigh the costs."

"That's easy for you to say," Sam said through gritted teeth.

"Lord Iron is very new to our world," Mazzi said, twisting to face the rest from her front-row seat. "Amir did very little to prepare him. Can we all just give him a little time to—"

"But Mazzi," Sam cut in. "Amir deliberately didn't prepare me because he knew another person like him would be toxic. He chose me *because* I'm not like him." *And not like all of you.* "I'm looking at this from the outside and I'm wondering what the hell this is all for. Making money? You all look like you have enough. More than enough."

"Amir chose a fucking communist," someone muttered.

"I'm not a communist. I'm not a hippie, either, before you go there. I just don't think we're doing the best we could. Leaving aside the environmental responsibilities we have, there are others that none of you have mentioned once. What about protecting people?"

"From what?" Alicia asked.

"The Fae."

He scanned the faces, ranging from confused to a mocking amusement and a lot of disbelief. He looked at Copper. "You must know about this. Copper's used as much as iron is."

"Fae? I don't know this word."

"*Es 'hada' en español*," said Lord Titanium, and Copper frowned.

"Is this a joke?" Alicia asked.

Sam looked at Mazzi, waiting for her to back him up. She'd spoken to him about the Sorcerers and the Fae. She folded her arms and shook her head. "Not now," she mouthed.

"I'm done here," Sam said. "Actually, no, I'm not. I think we need to do better. We need to improve pollution control, working conditions, and dealing with environmental damage."

Lord Copper yawned and checked his watch. Scanning the rest of the faces, Sam could see the room was closed to what he was saying. He wanted to grab Copper by his very expensive lapels and shake some responsibility into him, but instead Sam picked up the folder. "Someone has got to think about more than bloody profits," he said, and left the silent room.

7

When Will heard Sophia's light babble coming through the schoolroom door down the hall he headed towards it, each happy syllable driving away the weight of the meeting with Sir Iris from his shoulders. Coming straight to the mundane nursery wing the moment he returned home had proven to be a good decision.

The sight of a carriage already parked outside of his house when his own drew up that morning had made him frown. It was hired from the stables in the west of Londinium, used primarily by visitors from Aquae Sulis who reached the stables via a Way to cover the majority of the journey with a carriage to reach their final Londinium destination in style. Will had feared that his mother had come to take Sophia home.

Relieved to hear from Morgan that it was in fact Cathy's family visiting, he'd avoided the library where the reunion was taking place and headed straight for the green baize door leading into the nursery wing. The sound of his little sister's happy chatter as soon as he'd stepped through into Mundanus was just what he needed to feel better.

"Sophia!" he called, and was answered by the sound of running feet and the schoolroom door being opened. She peered into the hallway and beamed at him.

"Will-yum!" The hug, tight and all-consuming, followed swiftly. "I'm building a bridge! Triangles are best. Come and see!" Her golden ringlets bounced as she did. The scars left by the thorn attack had yet to fade and her neck, arms, and hands were covered in tiny red lines. They never seemed to bother her, though. "Is Uncle Vincent here?"

"Yes, he's helping me, come and see."

Will allowed himself to be pulled into the schoolroom. Cathy and Vincent had decorated the plain white walls with dozens of posters showing animals, places around the world, planets, and an alphabet made of cartoon people. It was the antithesis of the room he'd been taught in, which had had whitewashed walls and nothing but a fleur-de-lis frieze that ran around the room. The governess he'd had as a child, a sour-faced woman who seemed to despise children, would have swept through this schoolroom like a hateful tornado, ripping all the distractions off the walls.

His uncle was sitting at the large table in the centre of the room, making small balls of Plasticine. Dozens of drinking straws had been cut into quarter lengths and were piled next to him. At the other edge of the table was a rudimentary bridge made of the straws and Plasticine, along with the remains of some failed attempts.

They'd never made the formal decision to have Uncle Vincent tutor her instead of a governess; it had just happened organically. Vincent didn't seem to care that spending so much time with her in Mundanus was ageing him. Between him and Cathy, Sophia was surely getting a bizarre education, but she seemed to be thriving and that was what mattered.

"This is engining," Sophia said proudly, barely pausing when Vincent corrected her gently. "I'm very good at it."

"Engineering?" Will asked. "Why engineering?"

Sophia answered before Vincent had a chance to draw a breath.

"When I'm a princess, I'm going to be an engineer too. I need to learn how to build bridges for all my people, so they can cross rivers without getting wet. Look! This is how you make a pyramid."

She let go of his hand and started sticking straws together with the balls of Plasticine.

"One of Cathy's ideas?" he asked his uncle, who nodded.

"Sophia asked her how she could learn how to build bridges and Cathy hit upon all this. Haven't a clue how she came up with idea, but—"

"Look, Will-yum!" Sophia held up a pyramid shape she'd made.

"The square goes on the bottom, and then you make more and join them up. I'm going to build a bridge between this table and the window and then my dolls can drive across it."

"They have a carriage now?"

Sophia's bottom lip pouted at Will. "No, Will-yum. A car! A big one that goes very fast. Like Cathy used to drive."

"I beg your pardon?"

"Cathy used to drive a car. She drove from Manchester to Londinium in twenty-five seconds and didn't knock anyone over!"

Will looked at Vincent, who shrugged good-naturedly. "Cathy likes to make up stories as much as Sophia."

"But it's true!" Sophia protested. "I'll go get it."

She ran out of the room towards her bedroom. Will looked at his uncle, still dutifully pulling chunks off the hard sticks of Plasticine and working them into balls. "Do you mind all this?"

"The engineering or the stories?"

"I mean the unorthodox education."

Vincent shrugged. "It's probably more useful than Latin. Cathy doesn't limit her, that's all. And Sophia's sleeping better again."

"You don't have to stay." Will immediately regretted saying it when he saw the flash of worry in his uncle's eyes. "I don't mean that you should go. Not for a moment. But you must have your own business to attend to, your own commitments? Sophia is—"

"I'd like to stay." Vincent put the stick of Plasticine down and looked right at him. "I want to stay in Mundanus with her. Her nursemaid is nice enough, and Cathy comes when she can, but she's got so many responsibilities. That little girl deserves some proper attention." He gave a smile. "Besides, I find the company of a small child to be far superior to that of most of Society."

Will sat at the table. "But if you stay here, how will you meet anyone else? Don't you want to start a family?" Will knew his uncle's wife and sons had died in some sort of accident over a hundred years before. No one had ever told Will the details. It was one of those topics that one never brought up. Perhaps that's why Uncle Vincent spent more time in Mundanus than most—what was the point of living on in the Nether, protected from the ravages of ageing, when the people one loved the most were long dead? But surely he'd grieved enough?

"I had one, Will," he said with such sadness. "Couldn't risk going through that pain again."

"Look! It's an Audi TeePee!" Sophia cheered from the door, thrusting a large model car towards Will. "My dolly princesses ride in it and go very fast." She paused, looking at Uncle Vincent. Silently, she put the car on the table, moved to his side, and wrapped her arms around him. "Don't have a sad, Uncle Vincent. You can play with my dolly car too."

Will watched his uncle scoop Sophia up and envelop her in a bear hug, squeezing his eyes shut and kissing her hair. Vincent loved her so deeply, more than her own father did. The thought made him uncomfortable.

The sound of the baize door opening made Will stand. Morgan appeared at the door. "The Duchess is now free, your Grace."

"Thank you, Morgan. I need to go now, Sophia."

"Awww." Her bottom lip stuck out again.

"I'll come back soon, I promise."

He smiled at his uncle as he hugged Sophia goodbye and then left them to bridge-building. Morgan was waiting for him on the Nether side of the baize door. "Something else, Morgan?"

"It seems that the Duchess's younger sister may be a guest for an extended stay. I thought you should know. The Duchess seems rather upset about it."

Will frowned. "Thank you, Morgan. Is she still in the library?"

"Yes, your Grace, and Miss Rhoeas-Papaver has been shown to her room. Mrs Rhoeas-Papaver has returned to Aquae Sulis."

Will thanked Morgan and headed for the library, hoping he'd planned the right approach. He had to make this marriage work and bring her onside, wish magic or not. There was no way to know what solution Sir Iris was planning to combat the effect of Poppy's magic, nor how long it would take, and he couldn't risk another misstep.

He knocked on the door to Cathy's library, heard the sound of a drawer being shut, and then Cathy called him in.

"Oh! Will, you're back!" she said, standing up so fast that she almost knocked her chair over. A fountain pen rested on her desk, uncapped, and she seemed on edge.

Will shut the door behind him. "I didn't want to disturb your mother's visit."

Cathy sagged. She looked so tired. "She wants me to get Elizabeth matched and—oh, I don't want to talk about it. It's such bollocks and I just…" She shrugged. "I'm sorry I was horrible to you last night."

He took a step towards her. This was a good sign. "Thank you."

"I'm not sorry about what I said in the Court," she added, and he sighed.

"We need to talk."

"I'm not going to apologise for what I said to that pillock."

"Cathy." He went to her and took her hands, uncurling them from fists until she held his. He had to keep calm and cool her passion enough to make her see sense. "I want to have a conversation with you, not a fight. What happened last night in the Court can't be undone. I want to talk about how we move forwards."

Cathy's eyes narrowed. "You're managing me."

Will laughed. "Of course I am. It feels like every time we talk we end up arguing."

She looked away, a slight blush on her cheeks. "I know."

"I need to talk to you about what happened with Sir Iris."

She bit her lip and looked back at him, fearful. "Was it awful?"

"Thoroughly."

"Was it because of what I said in the Court?"

"Yes."

She closed her eyes. "Shit."

"Come and sit down."

They sat in the two chairs he'd originally bought for her library (the sofa was her own addition). He recalled her radiant smile when he first showed it to her, weak from the knife attack. He needed a way to keep both her and his Patroon happy. Was that even possible?

"I would like to say some things, Cathy, and I would like you to listen. Right to the end."

She nodded, pale. "It's bad, isn't it?"

"Sir Iris was furious. Somehow he heard about what happened at the Court."

"Hang on," Cathy said. "He heard what really happened, or some misogynistic interpretation of it?"

Will silently counted to three. "I haven't finished yet. He thinks I'm a weak husband and a poor duke for letting you speak in the Court. No matter what I said, no matter how clear I was that I supported you, he was adamant that what…we've done is unacceptable."

Cathy took in a breath but mercifully stopped herself from launching into a predictable tirade against the Patroon.

"He made it clear that if I allow you to continue to speak in a political capacity, he'll strip me of the Dukedom and send us to the Frankish Empire. We do not want this to happen, trust me. The Parisian Court would be the end of us and most certainly the end of your—our—dreams of change in Society."

Cathy's fists were balled up again, but she stayed quiet.

"I need you to understand the position I'm in, Cathy. I need you to understand that the man who is furious with you—and with me—can take all of this away in a moment and put another Iris in my place. He already thinks I'm too young to be Duke. He treated me like a naughty child. It was humiliating, and I never want to feel that way again. I don't want to silence you, but I cannot—I will not—let that man take everything away from us. And if we don't think carefully about what we do next, that's what he's going to do."

Will watched Cathy's face carefully, seeing the anger, the frustration, and the fear play across her features. He reached across the gap between them, took her hand, and kissed it, pressing his lips against her skin twice, three times. "I love you. I want to keep you safe, you and Sophia. I want to make you happy, and I fear I cannot do any of those things as long as my Dukedom is under threat." He looked into her eyes. "Help me, Cathy. I need you to think this through with me, without rage, without attacking this 'patriarchy.' I need you to work with me."

She drew in a breath, and he heard it catch in her throat. She was shivering. He cupped his hands around hers, holding it tight, hoping that she could rein in her emotions enough, despite that damned magic working against them. "Is there anything more?" she asked, and he shook his head.

"I'm making your life difficult, aren't I?" She said it with sadness. "I always knew I would. Didn't I say, back before we were married, that we'd be a poor match?"

He gripped her hand tighter. "No, Cathy. That's not the way to see this."

"What other way is there? You want me to be someone I'm not. You want me to play the game, don't you? That's what you mean when you say you want me to work with you. You want me to stop being such a pain in the arse. But what you're really saying is that you want me to stop being who I am."

"No." He shifted to the edge of his chair until their knees were mere inches apart. "No, Cathy. I don't want you to stop being clever and passionate. I want you to use that cleverness to direct your passion in a way that won't harm us."

"But that's impossible!" She pulled her hand away from his. "Don't you see, Will? The Patroon wants to put a stop to what we're doing because it's a threat! We want to change things, and the fucking Patroons want everything to stay the same. Forever!"

She was spiralling away from him and back into her rage. "Darling," he said, keeping his voice calm and low, "Cathy, I agree with you! That's what they want and that's what they'll get if you continue to speak out in the Court. Do you understand? We need to change tack."

"Change tack?" Her eyes welled with tears. "You're backing out of this, aren't you? You want power more than you want change."

"No, Cathy, I want power so we can make these changes! Can't you see? What we have here is so fragile. I'm too young. I don't have allies I can truly trust, I don't have friendships spanning centuries or people indebted to me or favours to call in when things are difficult. I'm too easy for him to replace! This has nothing to do with whether I support you or not; it has everything to do with how we stay safe now and how we build a place in Society so we are protected."

"What do you want me to do? Put all my plans on hold for a few hundred years until you feel safe again?"

"I want—"

"You want me to smile and curtsy and be nice to those... those monsters who make their wives into dolls and rape them every night?"

"Good God, why in the worlds would you say such a thing? Most husbands are true gentlemen. I just want you to understand that Society is not going to change under your sledgehammer, Cathy. The Patroon will cut us down and—"

"But what about Lord Iris? He wanted you to be Duke! The Patroon is just trying to frighten you!"

"Lord Iris wanted an Iris on the throne. I was simply the best placed. And he can get a child from us whether I am Duke or not." He saw that flicker of fear again. "I would rather be Duke whilst dealing with whatever Iris wants from us. I would rather have some control over our lives than none at all. The only way to make any changes and the only way for us to achieve any sort of freedom is to get to the top of the ladder and stay there."

"You want to be Patroon?"

Will shook his head. "Even I know I'm too young for that. But one day, perhaps. Right now, I'm just trying to stay on the highest rung I can. I know you want everything to change, but it can't happen as fast as you want. I'm sorry, I know you don't want to hear that, but even in Mundanus life for women didn't change overnight, did it?"

Shaking her head, eyes down now, Cathy was looking inwards.

"I'm not saying you have to stop everything," he said. "There are women you want to help and you should help them. All I'm asking is that you don't do it in the Court. I think this needs guerrilla warfare rather than a battering ram."

"But there's a huge gulf between helping women secretly and making our Society fair. I want us to reach the point where women aren't in need of any help. How can that happen if nothing changes publicly?"

"Just give me time," Will said, catching hold of her hand again. "Please. Give me time to work out how to secure our position. I'm trying hard to be what you want me to be, Cathy. Can you try hard for me too?"

She chewed her lip, a single tear running down her cheek that she swiped away angrily. "Did he say we couldn't have a Ladies' Court?"

"Not explicitly, no, but—"

"If I can have the Ladies' Court, I'll stay quiet in the main one. Even though it's exactly what they want."

It wasn't ideal—what havoc would she wreak with a room full of wives who'd be interrogated by their husbands as soon as they got home?—but he could see how much it was taking from her to concede the main court. He'd delay the first Ladies' Court as long as he could, at the very least until Sir Iris provided a solution to the Poppy magic. Will kissed her hand again. "Thank you."

Will went to the fireplace and pulled the bell cord to ring for tea. Cathy was silent and introspective; the skin between her brows pinched tight, her hands balled up once more. What forces worked through her by Poppy's design? How much did that wish control her actions? She was rebellious even before it was made. Was he deluding himself into thinking Sir Iris could present a solution that didn't change who she fundamentally was? He went back to Cathy, leaning down to cup her face in her hands and kiss her deeply.

"I love you," he whispered, the skin of her face hot beneath his hands.

"I love you too," she whispered back. "But it's hard, Will. It feels like I'm being pulled in different directions. I have to change Society and I hate giving in to Sir Iris's threat but I hate making you upset too. And I know you're trying. And I know you could just 'fix' me with some bloody Charm, and I'm so glad you'd never do that. I know you're trying to make the best of a bad situation, but I'm scared I won't make any difference. I'm scared I won't be able to change anything because I love you."

Will kissed her again, as if he could somehow kiss away the guilt he felt for using the Lust Charm on Cathy. No. It was the right decision. If they hadn't consummated the marriage, it would be even worse for them now.

The sound of Morgan outside pulled him away from her lips, leaving her face tilted up, flushed, eyes closed and lips still poised for his. At the knock on the door she blinked and jumped and they both smiled at each other. In that moment he felt hope again.

He returned to his chair as Cathy called Morgan in. The butler arranged the tea and buttered crumpets that Cathy liked for elevenses and left them after a small bow.

Will put two crumpets on one of the plates and handed it to Cathy. "When is the next visit from Dame Iris likely to be?"

The crumpet that was halfway to Cathy's mouth was put back on the plate, untouched. "I have no idea. I'm hoping…never. She hasn't been back since I stood up to her."

Will raised an eyebrow. "What exactly did you say to her the last time she was here?" He remembered the day of the Dame's last visit clearly. He'd been up most of the night, as had Cathy—she'd been handling the fallout from her radical actions at the asylum and he'd been saving Margritte from his brother.

Cathy stared down at the crumpets, watching the melted butter soak into them. "I made it clear that I wasn't going to take any of her abuse anymore."

Will waited. "And…?"

"And I smashed a bottle she brought with her. Some potion or other. Something evil."

Will suddenly lost his appetite. "And…?"

Cathy looked at him. "And I told her that if she ever tried to coerce, Charm, or curse me ever again, I'd tell Sir Iris what she did to his first wife. Eleanor." She took in the shock on his face and swallowed. "One of the ladies I rescued from the asylum."

Will slammed his teacup down. "The former Dame Iris is alive and you didn't tell me?!"

Cathy winced. "Eleanor asked me not to. Really, Will, she asked me to keep her a secret until she works out what she wants to do now she's free. The current Dame Iris cursed her and tricked Sir Iris into thinking she was mad, and it's all a big fucking mess and—"

Will held up a hand. "All right, all right. I understand." He sat back, taking it all in. "Where is Eleanor Iris now?"

"I can't tell you that."

"You don't trust me?"

"I promised her. I wasn't supposed to tell you about her at all. We've managed to keep a lid on the asylum stuff so far. I thought it was for the best. The staff were paid off and are being protected, like all the people at risk from the asylum. We're still working out what to do with them all in the long term."

"Could you contact her? Please, Cathy, I need to speak to her. She could help us."

Cathy nodded. "Okay. I'll ask her."

Will watched her pour the tea, realising how much he'd underestimated his wife. She was blackmailing Dame Iris? He smiled. She was inspirational.

• • •

As he left the newspaper offices, Max wrote the name and address of the source in his notebook and headed back towards Cambridge House, stopping to sit on benches every couple of streets to rest his leg. He chose a route that took in some of the main centres of Fae-touched activity, passing the Holburne Museum to go back into town via Great Pulteney Street. He bought a latte at Jacob's Coffee House on Stall Street and sat by a window on the second floor to watch over the crowds walking between the coffee house and the Pump Rooms, heading towards the Abbey. Most were tourists, all behaving as they always had. He didn't see anything unusual and yet couldn't stop himself scanning the street for any sign of one of the parasites.

The city had never been so at risk. After the Chapter was destroyed, at least Ekstrand had had the monitoring room, which enabled him to see where the parasites came in and out of the Nether. Now they were blind, and it was just a matter of time before the parasites noticed.

A song burst out of one of the pockets of his coat, draped over the chair next to him. He waited until it stopped, noting the irritation of the innocents at the other tables of the coffee house. None of the old tools of his job would have made a noise like that, but Rupert had replaced all of them with his more modern designs. It might be some sort of alarm. But he couldn't work out which one was making the noise without pulling out the Opener, Sniffer, and more in front of innocents.

The song started again and a man at a nearby table said, "I think that's your phone going, mate."

"Oh, the mobile phone," Max replied. "Thank you. Will it stop eventually?"

"Don't you want to answer it?"

Max nodded and began to rummage through the coat. He thought it would ring, like a telephone, not play a song that sounded like a wireless. Halfway through the third burst of song, accompanied by tuts and stern glares from the other patrons, he finally found it.

He stared at the screen. There was a green phone in a circle and a red phone, with dotted lines in between. The telephone number of the caller was displayed above it.

"Press on the green one and swipe across," the man said, miming the action. "It's one of those smartphones. My daughter bought me one for Christmas. Takes some getting used to."

Max followed his instruction and the song stopped. "Thank you," he said to the man, and pressed the phone against his ear as he'd seen the Londinium Arbiters do in Trafalgar Square.

"Max? It's Kay. From the office."

"Yes. I remember you."

"There's something dodgy going on in Victoria Park. You need to go and check it out."

Max frowned. "I thought you were buying supplies."

"We did. We made tea, Rupert told me about my job and about the Fae-touched, and then the alarm went off from one of the Sniffers in the park."

Rupert hadn't wasted any time, and she sounded rather calm for someone who'd just been introduced to an alternate reality. Max could tell the gargoyle was still in the bathroom, so the briefing hadn't got that far. And Sniffers in the park? Rupert hadn't told him anything about that. "Where in the park?"

"Near the children's play area. It's showing up as Peonia—is that right, Rupert?" There was a muffled "yeah" in the background. "It's just gone off, so if you go now…"

Max was already shrugging his coat on. "Proceeding to the scene now."

"Cool. Keep us—holy shit!"

A flash of the office interior burst into Max's mind, Rupert and Kay sitting cross-legged on the floor with half-eaten burgers on paper and cardboard cartons of chips beside them, both looking up from a laptop screen. Kay was staring, slack-jawed, right at him—or rather the gargoyle.

"Sorry I scared you," it said in its gravelly voice. "I gotta go and help."

"Yeah…" Rupert said to Kay with a mouth full of half-chewed burger. "That was the next thing I was going to tell you about."

Max blinked away the image, returning his attention to the coffee shop. A glance at the mobile helpfully showed a red phone symbol labelled *end call*.

He limped down the stairs as the gargoyle opened one of the windows, climbed out, and scaled the wall to the roof. Max knew it was heading to the main Peonia residence in the town, hoping to spot something if the Fae-touched stayed in Mundanus and went home into the Nether through the house gates. It was going to take longer, having to keep high and out of sight of the mundanes, but Max knew the gargoyle would take the best route.

The sky had brightened further and the clouds had broken enough to give stretches of blue sky. It was still cold, but innocents would be walking in the park, and there would be children, too. Max walked as quickly as the ache and the walking stick allowed, heading for the park he knew well. The bracers Ekstrand had made kept the gargoyle silent as it made its way towards the top of Lansdown Road by the inconvenient and circuitous route that kept it out of sight.

Victoria Park was huge and sprawled over more than fifty acres of land, but Max knew the paths well enough to get to the children's play area without consulting one of the maps posted on boards around the perimeter. He passed families bundled up against the cold wind and tourists walking with maps in their hands. He kept his collar turned up and folded down the flaps that ran around the edge of the new hat, not caring if it looked amusing or not.

He listened to snippets of conversation as he passed couples and people speaking into mobile phones, but nothing was relevant. Then he heard the singing. It drifted on the breeze, light and female. A nursery rhyme, repeated twice, then again. He stopped, not wanting the sound of his cane to interfere, then headed towards it as quick as he could. It was coming from the northern side of the play area. He cut through a cluster of trees, emerging near a row of benches overlooking the adventure playground.

"Half a pound of tuppenny rice, half a pound of treacle…"

A woman sat on one of the benches, staring straight ahead, singing quietly. A large pram was parked next to the end of the bench.

"That's the way the money goes…"

The woman was young, wearing a black woolly coat and a bobble hat. Max moved closer.

"Pop goes the weasel."

Her back was straight and her right hand rested on the handle of the pram, pushing it up and down just enough to rock it gently. As he rounded the bench enough to see her face he expected her to turn at the sound of his approach. But she stared out, looking away from the pram, oblivious to him.

"Half a pound of tuppenny rice…"

Max hooked his cane over his forearm and reached into his pocket to rummage for the Sniffer.

"Half a pound of treacle…"

He pulled it out and pressed the button to start it off.

"That's the way the money goes…"

As the Sniffer sucked in the air barely feet away from the woman, he closed in and stood in front of her. Her eyes focused too slowly on the buttons of his coat. She looked up, not flinching at the sight of his expressionless, ugly face.

"Pop goes the weasel."

"Is that your child?" Max pointed at the pram.

"Half a pound of tuppenny rice…"

He was too late. He moved around and peered beneath the lace-edged canopy. Shaded from the sunshine and tucked neatly beneath a yellow blanket was a lump of mud, crudely formed into the shape of the stolen baby.

The Sniffer detected Peonia magic, as Kay had said.

The mobile phone sang in his pocket again. Moving away from the woman, who was still singing, he looked at the screen. The same number as before was calling him. It took two attempts for him to swipe the button, and it finally stopped singing. He lifted it to his ear, turning his back on the victim.

"Where are you? Have you found anything?" It was Kay again.

"At the park. I've found a victim. She needs to be taken in and…" He stopped. There was no Chapter to take her to. "I need to speak to Rupert."

"'Sup?"

"Sir, there's a woman who's been Charmed and her baby has been stolen. She's singing a nursery rhyme repeatedly and is detached and unemotional. She seems oblivious to the fact her baby has gone."

"There's a chance it'll be broken if the baby is brought back to her. If not, we'll make the Peonia lift it before we take them to the Patroon. I'll send Kay to keep an eye on her whilst you get the baby back. How many Peonias are there in this city?"

"Only one family, sir. But you can't send Kay. Her soul's intact; she'd be at risk."

"Whoever took the baby isn't going back there in a hurry."

"But where will we take the woman afterwards? She can't just—"

"Max, get the baby back, for fuck's sake, let me worry about the rest."

The call ended. Max wasn't certain if the Sorcerer appreciated all the clean-up involved in a breach of this kind; his former Chapter Master would have handled it all. Getting the baby back was first priority, though. If it was taken into Exilium before he could retrieve it, they might never get it back. But whoever stole it would have to take it into the Nether first, as there were no places in Bath that led straight to the Fae prison. Ekstrand had made certain of that a long time ago.

He set off towards the ·Peonia's residence when a flash of Lansdown Road appeared in his mind. The gargoyle was up high, watching a young man hurry up the hill carrying a large leather bag. It was rigid, flat-bottomed, and big enough to hold a baby temporarily. Max could see that it wasn't tightly closed at the top and could only assume the baby was still alive. After a last glance at the singing woman he set off in pursuit. He had to get to that parasite, and make it clear to all of them that there was still someone watching over this city. Otherwise that stolen child would be only the first of many.

8

Sam raided the hotel minibar as some arsehole from the government talked on the news about how there wasn't enough money to keep paying for all the beds in a hospital straight after a report about how they'd spent millions bombing people in some distant nation. He found the remote, flicked over to another channel with a programme about some superstar he'd never heard of looking for a wedding dress, and turned the TV off. Everything was fucked, and now he knew why. The most powerful people in the world didn't give a shit about anything except money. And why was there no fucking lager in the fridge? He laughed at himself mirthlessly. As first-world problems went, that was pretty shitty.

There was a knock on the door. Assuming that Des had finished dinner and wanted to go through the diary with him, he went to the peephole and saw Mazzi on the other side of the door. He opened it and went back to the fridge without greeting her.

Mazzi entered, closed the door behind her, and put down her briefcase. "What the fuck was that?"

"I could ask you the same thing!"

"What's that supposed to mean?"

"You let me stand there and look like some fucking nutjob."

"You did that all by yourself, Sam."

"Why didn't you back me up? You know about the Fae. You talked to me about them! Why didn't you support me?"

Mazzi shrugged off her black jacket, revealing a deep red silk blouse that rippled as she moved to the window. "Because I don't know what I believe. Amir told me all sorts of stories, towards the end, and I...I don't know what to think about it."

"But Copper must have!" He watched her shake her head. "And you talked about the Sorcerers like you knew them!"

"I know some people commissioned some very particular pieces from Amir, that he called 'sorcerers.' He told me about iron and copper protecting people from the Fae, but I thought it was a metaphor!"

"Bullshit! You said it like it was true."

She looked down into the street below. "You didn't need any doubts, then. Amir had just killed himself and bled all over you! And then you started saying the same sort of things he mentioned to me and I...I don't know. Maybe there is something more to it—"

"There is!" Sam yanked a bottle of wine from the minibar and looked for the bottle opener. "I've seen the Fae, I've crossed over to their world." Her stare made him want to smash the bottle against the wall. "Christ! Don't look at me like I'm some fucking lunatic. Why would I make shit like that up?"

"Fair point."

Sam pulled the cork from the bottle. "Drink?"

Mazzi shook her head. "No. I have to go and meet a friend. Look, what you did down there was stupid. I'm not talking about the Fae part, I'm talking about the environmental stuff."

Sam poured a large glass for himself. "I could have said a lot more. It's important to me."

"That's the stupid part. They could see that." She came over to him, stood close enough for him to smell her musky perfume. "These are the wrong people to make into enemies."

He stepped away and took a large swig of the wine. "I'm pretty certain they're the wrong sort of people to make into friends. Present company excluded."

"Fine. I get it. You're not one of us. Not yet." Mazzi headed for the door after collecting her jacket and case, looking thoughtful. "What are you doing next Wednesday?"

"The diary knows, not me."

"Clear the day. I'm going to help you."

"To do what?"

"To understand what it is to be one of us. Amir thought he was doing the right thing by keeping you ignorant, but I don't think it was. I'll pick you up, okay? 10 a.m."

Sam nodded and watched her go. Even after the glass was empty he didn't feel any better. Was she telling the truth about Amir and what she knew about the Fae and the Sorcerers? Whatever game Mazzi was playing, it was clear that no one else in that room had known what he was talking about.

And she was right about him being stupid. Not because of what he'd said; because of what he *hadn't* said. He'd had the opportunity to really drive home what those bastards were doing to the Earth and he'd let himself be intimidated out of it by some stern faces and privilege.

Sam's phone rang and the number displayed made him smile. "Cathy! God, it's good to hear from you."

• • •

Max's leg was throbbing with pain by the time he reached the street the gargoyle was waiting on. It was hiding in a bush across the road from the large Victorian villa it had tracked the Peonia to, taking care to keep out of sight.

The house was detached and set back from the road, surrounded by a high wall. It wasn't an anchor property that Max recognised, so he walked round to the side, checked that no one was watching, and got out the Peeper to check the house was reflected into the Nether. The new version of the tool looked quite similar to Ekstrand's: a small telescope in two sections that could be twisted. Rupert's was made of some sort of Bakelite, rather than brass, and felt much lighter. Max pressed one end against the brick of the garden wall and twisted the casing until a tiny green light flashed on the side. The Sorcerer seemed to have a fondness for little green lights.

Max peered through the lenses, seeing the Nether beyond the wall. Satisfied, he pulled an Opener from his pocket and stuck the pin of the door handle into the brickwork. After one last check to make sure no innocents were nearby, along with a check from the gargoyle's position too, Max turned it.

The outline of a doorway burned its way into a rectangle until a new door appeared and Max stepped through. The Nether's silver sky was now above him and he glanced back into the green and blue of Mundanus before pulling the Opener out and letting the door close and disappear behind him.

He took a couple of steps towards the house, knowing from the gargoyle that the Peonia had gone in through the back door and was unlikely to be looking out of the windows. There was no sound of cars or birdsong any more, but the silence was broken before he reached the house.

A horse-drawn carriage was coming down the Nether street and pulled up outside the gates. Max carried on. If the visitor was unaware of the crime in progress they would be a distraction that could give the Peonia the chance to get the baby into Exilium. If the visitor was the one taking delivery, Max would be ready.

Max heard the gate open as he reached the front door. A footman was holding the gate open as the passenger got out of the carriage. Disinterested, Max tried the handle of the front door. Like most reflected properties in the Nether, it was unlocked, so Max carried on inside and let the door close behind him. He didn't want to knock and alert the Peonia to his arrival.

A baby was crying in a room off to the right from the entrance hall. A maid rushed out of it, pale-faced, only to run into Max and scream.

"Is there a mirror in that room?" he asked as sounds of servants hurrying from other parts of the house battled with the baby's crying.

The girl shook her head and then squealed as the door-knocker was employed behind them.

"Whatever is the—" A butler froze at the far end of the hall. "Get out of his way!" he hissed at the maid who shrank back against a wall to let Max pass.

He'd made it to the room that contained the baby before the door was opened. "It's the Master of Ceremonies!" he heard the maid squeak before he went in. Surely Lavandula wasn't involved in something like this?

The room contained a large dining table and chairs. The leather bag was open on top of the table and, judging by the sound, the baby was still inside. Oliver Peonia was standing next to it, looking inside with an assortment of expressions ranging from horror to despair.

"Marie, it smells dreadful," he said without looking up. "Have you found something…"

He stopped when he saw that it wasn't the maid.

"Oh…dear…" he muttered, stepping away from the bag as if that could somehow distance himself from the crime, too.

Voices in the hallway pulled his eyes from Max to the door. "I insist," a male voice, rather effete, rose above the butler's protestations. Max recognised the Master of Ceremonies before he saw him, having spied on his conversation with Ekstrand weeks before the Sorcerer died.

"Oh dear, dear me." Oliver took out a handkerchief and tried to wipe away the sweat on his face before Lavandula entered in a burst of perfume, powder, and pale blue silk.

"Oliver, my dear boy, I do hope I'm not interrupting something? Ah! Maximilian, of the Bath Chapter, a delight to see you again my dear chap, it's been *an age*."

Oliver bowed deeply, his eyes flitting between the most powerful man in Aquae Sulis and the large leather bag. "I…perhaps this isn't…I don't wish to be rude, but…"

"I just happened to be passing when my driver spotted Maximilian heading towards the house. I say, shouldn't someone be doing something with that child, wherever it is? It is rather noisy."

"The maid is getting something for it," Oliver stammered. "Perhaps we could retire to the drawing room to…" He trailed off as Max headed towards the bag and looked inside.

The smell was pungent and the baby was red in the face but otherwise unharmed. Max turned to Oliver.

"You're in possession of an illegally acquired child, an innocent you kidnapped from Royal Victoria Park less than one hour ago. Oliver Mascula-Peonia, in accordance with the Split Worlds Treaty and with the sanction of the Sorcerer Guardian of the Kingdom of Wessex, I'm taking you into custody." He thought it best to keep his arrest speech the same as it always had been. If he said anything different, they'd know something had happened to Ekstrand.

Oliver's flushed face suddenly took on a greenish tinge and he slapped his hand over his mouth.

"Maximilian," Lavandula began in a voice normally reserved for those with emotions to sway. "I'm sure there's been some sort of misunderstanding. Oliver is a good boy and there must be a perfectly reasonable explanation for this. Isn't that so, Oliver?"

Oliver nodded and belched into his hand, now very pale.

"I have ample evidence to present to his Patroon and will press for his expulsion from Nether Society," Max said.

"Oliver is a close friend of the Duke of Londinium."

"That makes no difference to his guilt."

"And the Duchess of Londinium is my favourite niece," Lavandula continued. "It would be rather uncomfortable for me to have to explain that I didn't intervene."

"You don't have the right to intervene, or to interfere," Max said. "The Peonia has violated the terms of the Treaty and will be punished accordingly."

The Peonia darted over to a large vase in the corner and vomited into it. Lavandula slipped a lace handkerchief from an inside pocket of his jacket and held it over his nose. "Perhaps it would be better to discuss this somewhere quieter that doesn't contain anything… recently expelled."

"There's nothing to discuss." Max took two steps towards Oliver before the young man vomited again.

"Look at the boy. Does this suggest a cold, calculating individual, capable of kidnapping? Or does his reaction speak of someone who has been terribly manipulated?"

"Irrelevant."

Lavandula touched his arm though Max had no idea why—the Master of Ceremonies would know that he was immune to Charms, thanks to his dislocated soul. "You said you're here with the sanction of the Sorcerer Guardian of Wessex. Ekkie and I have been friends for a long time and I need to speak with you about him."

The maid entered after a brief knock on the door, carrying a bowl of water and some towels. "I've come to change the baby's nappy," she said with a timid glance that flickered across the three of them. She settled upon looking to Lavandula for permission to continue, who nodded to her.

"Now, you'll surely want to take a clean, quiet baby away with you, so why not step outside with me whilst it's seen to?" Lavandula continued. "Oliver gives his word that he and the baby won't go anywhere, don't you, dear boy?"

"Yes," Oliver croaked. "I give my word."

The mention of Ekstrand was a potential problem, so Max acquiesced. He also wanted to determine whether Lavandula was the one who put Oliver up to stealing the child. If the Peonia was desperate enough to attempt escape the gargoyle would warn him.

The staff cleared the hallway as the door was opened and Max knew they'd all been listening in. Lavandula suspected the same and steered him towards a drawing room.

"You may not know this," he said once they were in private once more. "I have no idea what he chooses to share with you— but Ekkie and I have had a special understanding for quite some time now. We usually take tea together twice a month, always on a Monday, and should we need to inform each other of anything out of the ordinary we write to each other." Lavandula took a step closer and lowered his voice even further. "Ekkie didn't keep our last appointment and the Way he created so that I may visit him discreetly has been closed for over a fortnight. I've sent three letters enquiring about his health and have received no reply. We have taken tea together for over two hundred years and he has never missed an appointment in all that time."

Max considered potential responses. Telling Lavandula that

the Sorcerer of Wessex was murdered would solve the problem of his curiosity, but would lead to too many new questions. He'd want to know who the replacement was and Rupert had made it very clear that he wanted to keep a low profile; otherwise, the Sorceress would probably come after him again. If Lavandula had any hint that things were in flux, without a reliable Bath Chapter, the innocents of Bath would be at terrible risk. Kidnappings would be just the start. If word got out that there was no one to hold them accountable to the Treaty, the parasites might even tell their patrons it was worth the risk to enter Mundanus via the Nether. Max, not the most imaginative of men, could only assume it would be chaos.

"Naturally I'm rather concerned about my sorcerous friend," Lavandula continued. "If he is unwell I should dearly like to send a note, perhaps a gift—not that he would accept it, but the thought would be there. If he is going to be away for a prolonged period of time then we need to make alternative arrangements. I'm disappointed he didn't feel the need to write to me before, if truth be told."

Max didn't want to be the one to make the policy decision on the fly. "I will pass on your message," he said. It wasn't a lie; he would just be passing the message on to another Sorcerer.

"I look forward to hearing from him soon. Now, regarding the Peonia boy. His family have fallen on hard times recently. Their standing in Aquae Sulis has suffered since the Rosa debacle, despite my nephew-in-law's best efforts to protect them that night. Even though my sister publicly absolved them of guilt, they've been overlooked on many an invitation." He leaned in close, conspiratorially holding the lace handkerchief to one side, as if they were standing together at the edge of a ballroom. "I understand the father has taken to drinking too much and the elder brother has washed his hands of them all. Doubtless Oliver acted out of desperation, perhaps hoping to elicit help directly from his patron if he brought her a gift."

"The motive is irrelevant," Max said. "He contravened the Treaty."

"But minor contraventions happen all over Albion, and I'm sure that there are a few that are overlooked in favour of maintaining good relationships in the long term. If Ekkie were here he would agree with me. The baby can be returned and no further harm need be done. I will personally ensure that Oliver doesn't do anything in Mundanus that would contravene anything other than the laws of fashion and you can escape the bother of taking him to the Patroon—who is a terribly boring man—and be home in time for dinner. I'm sure you can appreciate that as the Master of Ceremonies I have a great capacity for discretion. Not a soul would know."

"I don't share your interpretation of the Treaty, Mr Angustifolia-Lavandula. Harm has already been done, and your discretion doesn't change the fact that the Peonia has committed a crime."

"But it makes no sense! If you won't show mercy to the boy, then please, as a gesture of goodwill and in acknowledgement of the good relations between myself and Ekkie, won't you allow me just a few minutes—in your presence—with the boy to uncover who pressured him into this act?" When Max didn't immediately reply, Lavandula took a step closer. "Surely it is in your interests that I be informed about the villains in our midst? You won't be able to convict them with only the Peonia boy's word against them. Allow me to learn their identity so that I may be able to keep a close eye on their behaviour henceforth. I'm sure Ekkie would be so relieved to hear you and I are helping each other to keep the mundanes safe."

Max suspected Lavandula had another agenda—probably more than one—but he was right; if someone else was using the Peonia, it would be hard to get enough evidence to present to the relevant Patroon without help. With Cathy living in Londinium, he no longer had an Aquae Sulis resident to help him.

"We'll speak to him first," Max agreed. "Together."

Lavandula left with a smile on his face, used to being the man everyone else in the room followed, and went back to the one in which they'd left Oliver Peonia. The maid was holding the baby now, rocking it to sleep in a clean makeshift towel nappy. The original and the vase with its malodorous contents had both been removed from the room. The Peonia was sitting at the dining room table, head in his hands, a glass of water next to him. When he looked up to see Max and Lavandula coming back in, he stood, still deathly pale.

"Now sit down, dear boy, and have some more water." Lavandula looked at the maid. "Perhaps we could have tea?" She bobbed a curtsy and left with the baby. "The Arbiter and I have had a conversation, and we just have a few questions to ask you."

Oliver sat down again, trembling. "Am I going to be thrown out of Society?"

"It depends upon what you tell us now," Lavandula said.

Max pulled out a chair and sat down on Oliver's left, Lavandula taking the seat to Oliver's right. "It actually depends on my judgement, and as things stand you will be expelled from Society before the day is out."

"I wasn't going to keep him."

"I didn't think you were," Max said. "You were planning to take the baby to your patron?"

"No. I was going to take him back to his mother. She won't even notice he's gone. She's still at the park and thinks everything is fine."

"So you admit you cast a Charm on an innocent in Mundanus."

Oliver bit his lip and then nodded, too ashamed to look at either of them.

"But whatever possessed you, dear boy?" Lavandula asked. "Your family behaves impeccably, when they're not being manipulated by those filthy Roses."

"I…" His voice trailed off, his cheeks blazing red.

"Why take a child only to return it to the mother?" Max asked. "Did you plan to do something to it?"

"No!" Oliver seemed genuinely horrified. "I only had to prove I'd done it, and then I could take him back!"

"Who would require that proof?" Max asked.

Oliver looked down at his hands and then jumped when the tea was brought in.

"If you say nothing you cannot improve your situation,"

Lavandula said once the servant had left. "It cannot get any worse. Better to tell us, dear boy. If you're truthful, I may feel moved to defend you when you face your patroon."

Oliver looked at him with shining eyes. "Would you really? Gosh, that would be so terribly decent of you."

"Well, I have been known to be terribly decent from time to time." Lavandula smiled. "I'll be mother, shall I?" he said, waving a hand at the tea. He poured milk into three cups as Max stared at Oliver. As Lavandula tended to the teapot, Oliver seemed to come to some sort of decision.

"It's part of an initiation," he said finally. "I'm so dreadfully ashamed. Things have been rather difficult of late, what with the Rosas and mother being made ill with the shame of it, and father hasn't been himself either. I set up some rather interesting investments in India whilst I was on the Grand Tour, and I got a letter last week informing me that the Prince of Rajkot has revoked all of my trade rights, effective immediately. My elder brother is in Jorvic and refuses to help, and I confess I was desperate for a change in fortune." He accepted the tea offered to him and the cup rattled in its saucer. "Then two days ago I received a letter. It said that as a second son, I was invited to join a secret society, one established to help those of us often overlooked."

Lavandula's eyebrows shot so high the powder on his forehead creased. "A secret society for second sons? I've never heard of this."

"Well…it's a secret," Oliver said.

"But I make it my business to know all the important secrets," Lavandula replied. "This one has thus far eluded me. It must be newly established."

"I beg your pardon, your Grace, but the letter said they've been established for over four hundred years. Of course," Oliver added at Lavandula's pursed lips, "it may be a lie."

"This secret society told you to steal a baby?" Max asked.

"Not straight away. It said that if I was interested in knowing more, I had to leave a peony petal in my top hat when I went to the assembly rooms for cards. I did, thinking I had nothing to lose and everything to gain. I thought, seeing as the reason for the invitation was simply the matter of my birth, I couldn't possibly get it wrong."

"Do you have the original letter?" Max asked.

"I'm terribly sorry, Mr Arbiter, but the ink slipped off the page as soon as I read it. Dashed Secrecy Charm or some such." Oliver frowned into his teacup.

"I take it you left the petal in your hat," Lavandula prompted.

"I did, your Grace, and I played the most appalling cards all evening, I was so nervous. When I retrieved my hat at the end of the evening there was a note tucked inside the inner band. It said that only the most…" he looked up as he struggled to remember the wording, "…committed, trustworthy, courageous, and discreet of individuals are permitted to join the Second Sons. I must confess, I was rather disappointed. I'm trustworthy and I try my best to be discreet, but I wouldn't dare call myself courageous. I'm not the likes of Will—I mean, his Grace the Duke of Londinium—and I couldn't say that I'm committed, as I've never had cause to discover such a quality within myself." He set the teacup and saucer down on the table, clasping his hands together over his knees. "The letter detailed three ways in which I could demonstrate some of the qualities required to gain an invitation to an initiation. I don't recall the third, but the first was the…procurement of an item of lady's underwear." His cheeks flushed and his eyes darted to the Master of Ceremonies. "A specific lady's item of underwear."

"Not my sister!" Lavandula gasped, the handkerchief flying up to his lips once more.

"Yes, your Grace. I couldn't dream of doing something so despicable, so I settled on the second. It said I had to steal a mundane child without the parent noticing, take it to my house, walk around the grounds with it three times, and then return it to Mundanus."

"You found kidnapping an innocent less morally reprehensible than stealing underclothes?" Max asked.

"The mother doesn't know! And they weren't just any underclothes, Mr Arbiter. I felt this was the best way to gain membership without any damage done in the long term. If I had stolen something from the Lady Censor, it could have been used to embarrass her and I simply couldn't bear the thought of it."

Max noted how Lavandula smiled. "I take it that none of the correspondence was signed with a name?"

"Not even a scribble," Oliver said. "I can only assume someone is watching my house to see if I have taken the child, and they'll have seen both of you come inside. I've failed so utterly! I cannot describe the utter shame and embar—"

"Hush now," Lavandula said. "The milk is spilt and beating your breast about it helps no one."

Max went to the window and looked outside. There was an expanse of flagstones reaching up to the garden wall with no one in sight beyond in the mists. "I doubt anyone is watching, Peonia. They would have to linger in the mists and your kind aren't fond of that. And they'd be seen watching over the wall. More likely they'll take your word for it or bribe one of the staff to corroborate your story."

"I didn't think of that," Oliver mumbled. "I'm such a buffoon."

"And even if they did see myself and the Arbiter enter, it can only make your story more thrilling," Lavandula said, patting Oliver's hand.

"I doubt the Patroon will be thrilled by it," Max said. "Time to go."

"Oh, now, Mr Arbiter, do sit down and finish your tea," Lavandula said, putting a hand on Oliver's shoulder to stop him standing up. "Surely you can have a Bath bun whilst we consider the facts before us."

"I have considered the facts. Regardless of the reason why he did it, the crime was still committed. While I waste time here a woman is sitting in Victoria Park, Charmed, rocking a pram containing a lump of mud. That is not acceptable."

"I can take the child back right after I've walked round the house!" Oliver said. "It won't take more than a minute or two at the very most. It's a modest house, Mr Arbiter, and then I can return the child and lift the Charm."

"You will take that child back immediately and lift the Charm under my supervision, and then you will accompany me to your Patroon."

"Maximilian, dear chap, do please sit down and consider the wider picture here. There is a secret society encouraging young men to commit crimes in Mundanus. Surely that's worthy of investigation? If you push for Oliver's expulsion from Society, how will we discover the scoundrels behind it?"

Max frowned. The thought of not dragging the Peonia to his Patroon seemed...unbearable. Interesting. He'd never considered allowing such a severe breach to go unprosecuted and now even just the suggestion of it was eliciting a reaction within him that could only be described as emotional. Surely that was impossible?

Lavandula interpreted his silence as temptation. "After all, what else could they be coercing young men to do? Surely it's more important to identify the ringleaders than punish one silly boy for a brief error in judgement? I'm certain Ekkie would agree with me. If you have Oliver exiled from Society, there will be no way to trace them. Why not give him a stern warning now and put him to better use flushing out these people? We'll all be better off if they are expelled rather than this dear child. Look at him. He's as harmless as syllabub."

Max looked at the Peonia, his round cheeks flushed, lips pale, face covered in a sheen of sweat. Perhaps the Lavandula was right. Having someone in the Nether rooting out these people would be more useful, and more than that, having a parasite that was terrified his stay of execution would be revoked at any time could be useful. While the new Chapter was getting established, he'd need all the help he could get, even from the most unlikely places. And if Lavandula didn't get his way with this, it would only increase the likelihood of him pressing more forcefully to see Ekstrand.

"All right," he said. "Take the baby round the house so it will be reported if they bribe the staff. Then take the child back and restore the mother. I will be watching you every step of the way. If any harm comes to the child or the mother, I will drag you to your Patroon without a second thought."

Oliver let out a breath. "Oh, thank you, Mr Arbiter, your Grace, thank you so much!"

"When the Second Sons get in touch, you must inform me right away," Lavandula said. "I want to see any letters from them, so don't read them until I'm with you."

"I will visit you in two days," Max said, "and I will want a full report."

Oliver nodded. "Shall I fetch the baby from the maid?"

Max and Lavandula nodded and he bolted from the room. Lavandula stood after dabbing his lips with his handkerchief and then beamed at Max. "I knew you were a reasonable man. How thrilling! Secret societies and our very own mole—I think that's the new word for it that all the youngsters are using—and my sister has no idea whatsoever. I simply cannot wait to find the ringleaders and see if they've stolen anything from her. I'll be able to tease her for at least a century! I could kiss you!"

"That won't be necessary."

"No. I think not."

9

Just being back in Mundanus made Cathy smile, even though the wind was bitterly cold and the clouds looked ominous. After three days of her sister living at Lancaster House, being a world away was the best thing for her spirits.

Elizabeth seemed to amplify everything. The house was ten times more gorgeous and the bed was the most heavenly thing anyone in the worlds had ever slept on. The need for new ballgowns—for events not even arranged yet—rivalled the need for oxygen. Will was the most handsome and dashing Duke, and of course, Cathy was simply the worst Duchess ever, whose backside shouldn't come within a mile of any thrones anywhere, ever. Cathy had taken to shutting herself away in different parts of the house and not telling anyone where she was except for Morgan, who had also developed an astute sense of where not to be when Elizabeth was on the prowl.

Hiding was the only way Cathy could keep up with everything. Between her secret meetings, conspiring with Natasha to produce and distribute the pamphlets, and managing the properties in which she was hiding the people from the asylum, there was little spare time. With none of her own staff working for the Agency anymore she felt blind, expecting retaliation for emptying the Agency's secret asylum. At least she'd been able to bring the asylum staff onside, but it was just a matter of time before someone was tracked down and it all came out. Some of the people she'd rescued were keen to find relatives and berate them for abandoning them to die in Mundanus and some had darker plans, but Eleanor was keeping them in line at Sam's estate.

Life had become an exercise in spinning plates whilst waiting for the floor to open up beneath her. By the end of each day she flopped into bed, utterly exhausted yet unconvinced she'd really achieved anything. She was worried about Charlotte, who was losing weight, and worried that Will would exercise his marital rights again now that things were settling down between them. It didn't help that she wanted to rip his clothes off him, even though she was terrified of becoming pregnant. Mundane contraception was becoming a more attractive risk as each day went by.

Walking down Shaftesbury Avenue with her nose tingling in the cold and no one asking her for anything was such a simple joy. Just wearing jeans and trainers again had made her practically skip along the street. The lure of a mundane life was as strong as ever. She tried not to wonder where her ex was, and which film star he was probably shagging. Not for the first time, Cathy wondered whether to ask Sam to break the wish magic acting upon Josh. She couldn't make her mind up about it, getting tangled in guilt and envy and the basic fear of opening herself to the prospect of ruining Josh's life for a second time. Surely he would be devastated to lose the lifestyle he had now. Wasn't it kinder to just leave him alone?

It felt like her life with Josh at university had happened decades ago, to another version of herself. The old fear that somehow she'd lost who she really was crept back into her chest like a weasel returning to its favourite cubby. No. She hadn't lost sight of her own desires—they'd just changed.

Meeting Sam felt indulgent, even though she was there partly to get a message to Eleanor. He didn't seem to mind where they met, so she picked the American-style diner opposite Forbidden Planet on Shaftesbury Avenue and persuaded Carter that a quick look around would do no harm at all. She'd left the shop with a bag full of new books for her library, including a hardback with crossed flintlocks on the cover that a random woman in the shop had gushed about.

Even though she didn't feel she needed a bodyguard, it was the easiest way to stop Will fussing about where she was and what she was doing. He was more relaxed than he'd been after the attack on her and Sophia, especially now that Thorn was back in custody, but he was still overprotective. Was that the Iris in him, or simply love mixed with paranoia? Either way, now that Carter was in her employ she felt better about it. Carter had got used to chatting with her, making it less awkward between them now, though it was sobering when she remembered that he could snap a person's neck like a twig.

Carter had insisted on going into the diner first, checking the staff and even the table she pointed out that she wanted to sit at to make sure it all appeared normal. There were no other customers, which surprised her. He was subtle about it—to anyone else it just looked like he was scanning the room for a friend and somewhere to sit, but she knew he was working.

They sat at a table at the far back of the room. Carter straightened up when three huge men came in and scanned the room.

"They're security men, your Grace," he said to her. "Your friend is probably on his way."

Cathy looked at the three men and their thick necks, trying to imagine Sam being escorted by them. It seemed ridiculous. But he wasn't a hapless computer programmer anymore. He was Lord Iron. She still hadn't got used to it.

The security men had taken an interest in Carter, and they gave each other long looks. One whispered into a hidden mic. Cathy was tempted to tell them to just go out back and have a pissing contest, but a limousine pulled up outside the diner and another huge man got out of it, followed by Sam. She waved when he came through the door and he smiled, heading over.

He looked different. He was wearing a black cashmere overcoat and was clean-shaven, his hair neater than usual. As Sam approached the table she realised that he seemed broader, perhaps even taller. Maybe that was confidence.

"Hi, Sam," she said. "This is Carter; he's here to make sure I don't get mangled or crushed or something."

"We met, briefly, at your house," Sam said to him, then turned to her. "Can we talk in private?"

"I'll be at the table over there, your Grace," Carter said.

Sam sat opposite her and Cathy shuffled along her seat so there was no risk of their knees touching. Up close, she could see how much healthier he looked. When he shrugged off his coat she could see muscles beneath the long-sleeved white shirt he was wearing, and she couldn't help the little ripple that went through her stomach.

"I wish I could hug you," Sam said. "I'm guessing that's still totally not allowed?"

Cathy nodded, wishing it wasn't true and then blushing a little. "You look great. So much better. I mean healthier. Healthy. You look…"

"I've spent a lot of time in the forge," he said, picking up the menu.

"So the Lord Iron thing isn't just an empty title? You really work iron like a blacksmith?"

"Yup. I still don't quite believe it myself. Feels good, though. Like I've been doing it forever."

It was hard not to stare at him, especially his shoulders and arms. "The milkshakes are great here," she said, scanning the menu to keep her eyes busy. "And the burgers too. It's usually packed."

"Oh, I hired it out," he said. "Makes security less twitchy."

"So this Lord Iron thing is working out for you then."

He looked up from the menu and half smiled with a shrug. "In some ways. Christ, it's good to see you, Cathy. I need to talk to someone who understands all this shit."

She started to reach across the table but caught herself in time. Even though she was gloved, she didn't want him to break the wish magic, nor that of the wedding band. She'd watched him break the curse on Natasha just by holding her hand. Somehow, all the power he had now only made him more magnetic. She was far from impressed with herself. "Let's get the food order in first, I'm starving. I've usually had elevenses and about a gallon of tea by now."

The waitress flirted with a totally oblivious Sam as they made their orders. Carter and Sam's security men sat at opposite sides of the diner, watching the doors and keeping an eye on them. It seemed silly and made Cathy want to go over and introduce them to each other. Perhaps they could become friends and exchange tips. Did security men do that?

"How are you, really?" Sam asked, his hands flat on the table, leaning forwards slightly.

"I'm fine."

"Really?"

She laughed. "Yes. Well, you know, I'm worried about stuff and I mostly just want to run away and watch *Adventure Time* and eat pizzas and forget the Nether ever existed, but shakes and a burger with my friend will have to do."

"Is he treating you well?"

"My husband?" Sam gave a nod that conveyed all the ways he couldn't stand Will. "He's not like the others. I know you haven't got off to a good start with him, but he's not as bad as you think."

"He's a posh thug. He held a sword to my throat!"

"He's an Iris. They tip over into being arseholes at the drop of a hat. He was scared you were going to take me away from him."

"He doesn't know you at all, does he?"

She smiled at that. "He knows me better now. And he knows I'm here with you and he was fine about it." She didn't mention the fact she'd had to persuade him for over an hour to reach that point, and he probably only acquiesced because it was the only way for her to get his letter to Eleanor. "That's enough about Will. How are you?"

"Listen, Cathy, if you ever want to leave that bastard and all that fucked up Fae shit behind, you can. Come to me. I'll make sure they can't touch you."

She sighed and leaned back. "What is it? What's going on?"

"Nothing. I just know how much you hate it. I know you're scared of them. I just want to make sure you know you have an alternative. I couldn't help you before, but I can now. I have flats in London that are built to keep Fae magic out. I have houses and hotels all over England. If you're in Bath, there's a hotel you can go to, any time of day or night, and they'll take care of you until I can get there. If you want to leave him, just call me and I'm there."

She blinked at him, surprised by his earnestness. There was definitely a new confidence to him, a strength that hadn't been there before. "God, if you'd said that to me a few weeks ago I would've taken you up on it like a shot."

"You still can."

"No. I have work to do." She saw the sadness in his eyes, the frustration. She knew he was thinking of his wife, the one he couldn't save. "I can't just swan off into the sunset, knowing what I do."

"You don't have to be brave for everyone else."

"Bollocks. If I'm not, who will be? I looked for someone else to change Society, believe me, and they don't exist. It has to be me."

"Yeah? How's that working out for you?"

Something in Sam's tone made her scowl. "You don't think I can change anything."

"What? No, I didn't mean that. It's just that I'm trying to make changes too, and I'm mostly getting nowhere. No, worse than that, I'm making enemies."

The milkshakes arrived and Cathy listened as he described what his wife had been uncovering before she died, how hard it was for him to change things and how disappointed he was with the Elemental Court. As he spoke, she heard the loneliness beneath his words, saw the weight of his wife's legacy on his shoulders, as well as what the previous Lord Iron had dumped on him. She wanted to put an arm around him, or even just rest her hand on top of his, knowing what it was like to feel like the only swimmer trying to go to the opposite shore from everyone else.

The burgers arrived and he paused. "Wow. Sorry to just dump all that on you."

Cathy smiled. "It's okay. You needed to vent. I know the feeling." Again, she resisted the urge to take his hand. "I know it's hard, but you have to remember what an amazing opportunity you have. I mean, shit, all that money, that power. You could really make a difference."

His frown lifted. "You think so?"

"I think you'd have to be a special kind of fuckwit not to."

Sam threw his head back and laughed. "No one talks to me like this anymore. They're all employees or rivals or…I dunno, maybe friends but still dangerous, or ex-Fae-touched and kind of terrified of me. Cathy, I was wondering if you could do something for me." He reached into his pocket and then put four USB memory sticks on the table. "Can you keep these for me? Hide them somewhere safe in the Nether?"

"Is all the stuff Leanne found out on them?"

"Yeah. I'm worried that they'll try to destroy it once I make my first move, before I have a chance to work out how to fix it all. They won't know about you."

She put them in her pocket when Carter was looking at the entrance. "No problem. I'll keep them safe."

"Take this too." He passed over a folded piece of letter paper. "These are the places I own in London and Bath, and my estate in Cheshire. You can go to them at any time. I'm serious about what I said, Cathy. I know you want to stay and fight, but if you ever change your mind, you'll always have somewhere safe to go."

Cathy stared at the paper. She was afraid that if she took it she'd lose her nerve and take the easy way out.

"Just taking it won't do any harm," Sam said. "And I'll feel a hell of a lot better."

With a shrug, Cathy slipped it into her pocket. "I don't need rescuing, okay?" She took out the letter that she'd brought with her from Will to the former Dame Iris. "Whilst we're exchanging things, could you pass this letter on to Eleanor for me?"

"Sure." Sam tucked it into the inner pocket of his overcoat, not worrying about whether his security guards saw. "She's a character. I like her."

"Is she happy?"

Sam shrugged. "I think she's still working out what to do. She's content for now, but I wouldn't exactly say happy. She was a big deal in the Nether, right?"

"Yeah."

"I think she misses that. So, what's been going on with you?"

Cathy didn't know where to start. She settled upon the Court nonsense first. He listened intently, tucking into his burger and nodding and laughing when she told him about taking the piss out of the men who'd got upset.

"They have no idea what it's like in the real world, then," Sam said. "Christ, Leanne would have got on so well with you."

There was an awkward pause. "She must have been amazing, doing what she did."

"Amazing and annoying. It fucked our marriage up. You know, I've read stuff about activists and campaigners, and they couldn't have been happy. If they were married it must have been to saints."

Cathy nursed the dregs of the milkshake, feeling that was too close to the bone. It wasn't a happy path she was on. And Will was hardly a saint.

"So you're going to drag those men into the twenty-first century, kicking and screaming?"

"That's the plan. And I need to sort out the Agency, too." She told him about the slavery, the asylum and what the gargoyle had told her about the people trapped in the basement of the Agency headquarters, forced to magically anchor a building in the Nether without a real property in Mundanus. "It's totally fucked up. That's why I can't leave, Sam. I have to do something. I'm going to tell all of the women in Londinium about how evil they are, but before I do that, I have to make sure Ekstrand helps me to keep the Agency off my back. One of them already tried to blackmail me, and now I've screwed up their very lucrative asylum they're bound to try something else."

"Ekstrand doesn't give a shit about anyone else," Sam said bitterly.

"But Max and the gargoyle said he took over the Agency or something like that, so I have to try. I want to see if I can persuade him to free those people at least. I just don't know how to find him or Max. I could go through my uncle, he knows Ekstrand, but my aunt hates me and I daren't risk going to him when she might have poisoned him against me. She's really angry with me at the moment."

"I know where Ekstrand lives," Sam said. "I'll take you there if you like."

Cathy reached across the table and then snatched her hand back. "Thanks, Sam," she said, blushing.

He grinned. "No problem." He looked at her hand. "You're worried about me breaking the wish magic?" When she nodded, he smiled sadly. "I wish we'd met before all this shit happened."

Cathy didn't know what to make of that. "Yeah," she said, and thought back to when they first met, how different everything was. "Do you remember when Ekstrand made me take you into Exilium, and that faerie recognised you and I walloped it? You were so shocked."

"Shit, yes! I never thought I'd look back on that and laugh. You took care of me there. You didn't play any games with me."

"We were both pieces on the same board."

"What are we now, then, now I'm Lord Iron and you're a duchess?"

Fucked, was Cathy's first thought. "Survivors." She gave him her best smile. "And fighters. We have to be. Keep going, Sam. We'll get there in the end."

• • •

Will tried to coax the smoke-coloured cat over for a scratch behind the ear, but it wouldn't budge from its spot by the window. It didn't like him, and after several visits to Tate's house in Pimlico, Will was starting to feel the same way about the cat. It always hissed when she opened the door to invite him in, as if it thought he was there to hurt them. Far from it—he and Tate had settled into a mutually beneficial business arrangement. He had access to all of the artefacts, potions, and Charms sold at the Emporium of Things in Between and Besides at a fraction of the price and compensated her well for them. There were no difficult questions or any transaction records for the extraordinary number of Shadow Charms and others he'd had to use to keep Margritte hidden. The mark-up that Shopkeeper imposed was exorbitant and Will was glad he no longer had to pay for anything with tears of regret or sighs of unrequited love or whatever took the Shopkeeper's fancy at the time. Both he and Tate preferred the Queen's pounds to form the basis of their transactions.

Tate stood at the window, making the most of the brief spell of sunshine, staring through a jeweller's loupe at the sapphire he'd just given to her. She wore thick gloves with intricate stitching that he assumed offered some sort of protection. He let his eyes run down her back, the slender curve of her hips and the shapeliness of her legs. The cat hissed at him. He looked away.

"It's a beautiful gem, Mr Iris. First-generation magic, very powerful."

So Lord Iris himself had given it to the Patroon, as he'd hoped. "And does it do what I described?"

"Yes." She tilted the gem to capture the light in different facets. "Whoever wears it against their skin will have any magic other than that of the Iris broken. And if it's worn continually, it would protect against anything else being cast. This is rare, Mr Iris. Your patron obviously wants to protect someone very well."

Will smiled to himself. In one thing, at least, he and his patron's feelings were aligned. "Any side effects or other things woven in?"

"Well, the wearer might feel the other magic being broken, depending on what it is. Nothing else that I can see, but the more subtle effects are very difficult to see in first-generation jewels." She raised her eyebrow to let the loupe fall into the palm of her other hand. "Do you want me to set it into a piece of jewellery?"

"Yes. What would you suggest?"

She considered it against the white of her glove. "Too large for a ring of any taste. It would be wasted on a bracelet and tiaras always look best with lots of small jewels. I'd say a necklace. It would make it easier to maintain contact with the skin." She looked at him, a wicked glint in her eye. "There is something possessive about this jewel. Perhaps it would suit something tight about the throat. Yes. A choker. Elegant and functional, wouldn't you agree?"

He didn't like what she implied, and how, deep down, he agreed with her. "How soon could you have it finished?"

"I could prioritise it and have it for you in three days. That would be reflected in the cost."

"That's no concern. Set it with diamonds. Something eye-catching. Not too ostentatious."

She nodded and dropped it back into the small velvet pouch it had arrived in. "I'll send word when it's done. I think you should pick it up in person. It's too valuable to send via courier."

"Agreed." Will stood and retrieved his cane from the umbrella stand by the door. "And the other special order, to remove scarring, how is that progressing?"

"Another month at least, I'm afraid. I cannot make it any faster. But the choker won't delay it. It's the…curation of certain base ingredients that takes the time."

Will said his goodbyes, gave the cat one last glance only to see it looking steadfastly in the opposite direction, and left the house. He got into the taxi waiting outside and asked to be taken to the stables on Bathurst Mews.

Even now, when the gem was on its way to being made into a gift, he still had his doubts. Cathy had moved away from that mundane-made-Lord when he was at the house before, fearful his newfound power would break Poppy's magic. She wanted that wish's power, even though she said that all of her actions were her decision. She clearly feared she would be less decisive without it, so he'd have to keep the gem's true purpose from her.

He pressed his fist against his mouth as he wrestled the guilt into submission. He was trying so hard to be a good husband, to care for her and be all she wanted him to be, but it was simply impossible. There was no way he could accept the gem—a solution he himself had brought about!—and then not use it. The Patroon would check. And fundamentally, he still wanted the outcome. He needed her to slow down, consider her actions and words more carefully, and breaking the wish magic was the only thing he could bear to do to her to make that happen. Trying to reason with her, counsel her, had achieved nothing.

He sank lower in his seat as he admitted the other reason for hiding the gem's purpose to himself: if she knew the wish magic had been broken, would protecting her wedding band be incentive enough to stay away from Lord Iron? He believed her when she'd said that they weren't lovers, but surely the temptation to run away to her old life in Mundanus was still within her. Was the love she professed for him enough to keep her in the Nether? Was the desire to help people enough? Without the wish magic to assist her that desire might lose its lustre. He had to make sure he gave her everything else he could, without losing his Dukedom in the process, to keep her at his side.

He tried to push his worries about Cathy away. He had other decisions to make and concerns that made his head ache. The Agency was one of them, thanks to Cathy's recent actions. He'd learned a great deal about the organisation from Mr Bennet, enough to make him want to gain control over it—and also to understand that he couldn't. Even though he controlled Tate, who supplied the Agency with everything magical that they required to function, it was ostensibly owned by the Sorcerer of Wessex, Ekstrand. He didn't even know how to find the man and doubted that he would be interested in a negotiation even if he could locate him. He still had to decide what to do with the wretched Mr Bennet to punish him for blackmailing Cathy. He was convinced there was some way to use him, he just hadn't settled upon it yet.

Then there was Margritte. They needed a long-term solution and neither of them had one to suggest. She was dependent on him and the Charms he supplied to keep herself hidden; Nathaniel would have her assets and property watched closely for any sign of her. She had no allies she could trust to withstand the temptation of selling her out to the Irises and her son had been stripped of all power and influence, exiled from the very city that he might have been able to mobilise to help her. Will felt his responsibility weigh heavily upon him, knowing that he couldn't keep it up forever due to the cost and risk of discovery, but failing to see a viable alternative.

And then there were the disgruntled men of the Londinium Court. Bertie Viola needed to be kept happy; otherwise he would nurture dreams of seizing the Dukedom for himself. Will wasn't prepared to offer him much more than he already had. And there was Elizabeth Papaver to match, as he knew that Cathy wouldn't have a clue about who was both eligible and desirable. He needed to take some time to give that proper consideration and make some arrangements. He wanted peace restored in the household.

And there was the child he and Cathy had to conceive.

"That'll be twenny quid," the driver called from the front, and Will paid him. He hadn't realised that they'd arrived at the stables.

In minutes he was back in the comfort of his own carriage and travelling home on a Nether road. The silence after the roar of mundane London was welcome. He wondered what crisis Elizabeth had engineered in his absence and whether he'd be able to sneak through the house to play with Sophia for half an hour before anything else demanded his attention. When the carriage pulled up outside Lancaster House he was delighted to see that no carriage was parked up outside.

Greetings exchanged with Morgan, mundane coat and gloves deposited, Will listened for Elizabeth and smiled at the silence of the house.

"Miss Rhoeas-Papaver is with the dressmaker, your Grace," Morgan said, "and the Duchess has not yet returned. Would you like me to bring tea to your study?"

"Please."

In the peace of his study, with the fire lit and tea at hand, being the Duke of Londinium was quite enjoyable. A rattling in the door and the appearance of a golden letterbox in the wood made him stand and stretch. What now?

The wax seal displayed the fleur-de-lis, and he recognised his brother's handwriting as soon as he turned the envelope over.

My dear brother William,

 I am en route to Londinium and desire a private audience with you at your home. There is highly sensitive matter we need to discuss. Clear your diary for the afternoon; I'll be with you shortly after this letter arrives.

 Nathaniel Reticulata-Iris
 Chancellor of Oxenford

"Dear brother", eh? And how rude to demand he clear his diary. He might be Duke of Londinium, but to Nathaniel he would always be the baby brother. Will tossed the letter onto his desk and pulled the bell cord next to the fireplace. "Morgan, my brother is soon to arrive. He may wish to stay for lunch."

"Very good, sir. I'll bring tea and refreshments upon his arrival."

Morgan cleared the small tray bearing Will's teacup and the cold teapot, leaving Will to pace his study. It had to be about Margritte. He shouldn't have rescued her from Oxford Castle, truth be told, but he'd been so appalled by the way Nathaniel had taken the city and how brutally he'd treated Margritte that he couldn't leave her at his brother's mercy.

Sweat prickled under his collar and he realised he was still dressed down for Mundanus. By the time he'd been correctly attired by his valet Nathaniel's carriage was pulling up the drive. It had been glamoured to bear the Chancellor of Oxenford's crest. Of course, Nathaniel couldn't bear to be seen to arrive in a hired Londinium carriage.

Will moved away from the window of his study and did his best to prepare himself. He had to pretend he knew nothing of Margritte, and to be appalled by the news of her disappearance. Above all else he had to resist the urge to score points off his brother.

"Come in," he called when the door was knocked. He gave his calmest, most polite smile when Morgan announced Nathaniel and showed him in.

Even though Nathaniel looked tired, having power after

decades of waiting obviously suited him. He strode into the room with his arrogant swagger and made straight for Will.

"Brother," he said, looking into his eyes as he shook Will's hand with both of his. "I am glad to see you so well."

Morgan withdrew silently as Will surreptitiously attempted to work the blood back into his crushed hand. "It's good to see you in better circumstances, Nathaniel. I trust you're enjoying life in Oxenford?"

"I find it fits me well," Nathaniel said, casting his eye over the room. "And you?"

Will, all of his guards firmly in place, nodded. "Londinium is a challenge, but one that I relish."

This was nothing more than an exchange of pleasantries to fill the air before the tea arrived. Nathaniel was holding something back, like a man pressed against a door with a monster on the other side of it. There was a pent-up energy within him, suggesting ongoing stress that couldn't be resolved by shouting at someone or duelling, Nathaniel's preferred means of making things go his way.

Tea, finger sandwiches, and a Victoria sponge were brought in and left by Morgan. As soon as the study's door was shut Nathaniel went to the fire, running a hand through his hair. He was wearing it longer than Will, giving him a Byronic air.

"Will, I need your help."

He hadn't expected his brother to be so direct. Will permitted himself one tiny moment of satisfaction that after all the years of tormenting him, his brother had been reduced to coming to him with such desperation. "You have it, of course. Is there a problem in Oxenford?"

"It's gone beyond that," Nathaniel replied, staring into the flames, unable to bring himself to look at Will. "That streak of piss Alexander Tulipa didn't have the decency to crawl into a hole and accept defeat."

Will remembered Alexander—more specifically, the chilling resemblance between him and his late father. "He was vice-chancellor, am I right?"

"Yes. I threw him out that night we got you back. He went to the family seat at Hampton Court, as was his right. But he didn't stay there. He went to Jorvic."

Will's heart raced at the mention of the city in which he'd been hiding Margritte. "Ah, that's why I haven't seen him in the Court. Why Jorvic?"

"The Tulipa Patroon has been visiting there, apparently. A few of them have. Sir Tulipa, Sir Ranunculus, Sir Digitalis, and a handful more. There to discuss the 'Iris Issue,' by all accounts. They don't like the way we've taken two cities in as many months. I managed to squeeze it out of one of the people at the masked ball in Aquae Sulis. Shame you weren't there, Will. I would have appreciated your company."

Will felt a chill descend. Even though he'd managed to placate his own Patroon, he still wasn't safe from the interference of the other families. Once Patroons got involved there was more chance that the Fae would be drawn in, and someone who coveted his position could be supported in trying to take it for themselves. He himself was proof of how well that could work. "All talk, no trousers, I should imagine," he said, forcing himself to be light to hide his fear.

"Well, quite. The deuce of it all is that Alexander managed to gain an audience with his Patroon. He made a formal complaint about what happened at the Hebdomadal Council and said his mother was abused or some rot. All whining nonsense, designed to make me sound like an utter cad."

"How tiresome," Will said. "Surely not of any concern, though. He's whining at losing his status; surely the Patroon would see that and take whatever he says with a pinch of salt."

Nathaniel twisted to look at him. "That bitch was married to the Patroon's favourite nephew. The one who tried to murder your wife. He wasn't best pleased at the justice you dealt, but knew Lord Iris was backing you up and that you had every right. Alexander Tulipa has made out that his damn mother is some sort of saint and that I have no right to keep her at my pleasure. He probably skimmed over the fact that she kidnapped you, had you beaten, and was probably planning to kill you! Sir Tulipa has believed every damn word of it and is kicking up a stink."

Will poured the tea as he listened, then thought better of it. "Brandy?"

Nathaniel nodded. "He's demanded an audience with myself, Margritte Tulipa, and Sir Iris. 'To uncover the root of the problem,' he said. She *is* the root of the problem!"

Will unlocked the tantalus. "And Sir Iris has agreed?"

"He's fed up of that fool writing to him all the damn time. He asked for my side of it, I told him the truth and he can see I'm in the right. What she did to you was despicable!"

What I did to her was worse, Will thought. *I killed her husband, and she forgave me.* He poured a generous brandy for each of them, keeping silent.

"Sir Iris agreed with what I did but says that for the sake of good relations—a quiet life for him, that is—he feels we should allow this meeting. He said Tulipa won't be satisfied until he sees the damn woman and hears her side too. Hears her side? What kind of man is he? This is all about the nephew, and he's taking out his impotence on me. It's a bloody farce."

Will gave Nathaniel his glass and watched him down half of it in one gulp. "It sounds like a trial."

"I said as much to Sir Iris, and he assured me that I was beyond reproach. I exercised my right and behaved impeccably. He thinks that when Sir Tulipa sees her and hears from her own lips what she did to you, he'll back down."

Will hoped the thrumming of his heart wasn't as loud as it seemed in his own ears. "Perhaps the only thing to do is grin and bear it. I understand your anger at having your judgement challenged this way, but if—"

"Will, I don't have her."

Will stared at him, hoping that Nathaniel believed his shocked expression. "I beg your pardon?"

"I don't have her! I locked her in the tower at the castle myself.

By the next morning she was gone. I've been looking for her ever since but someone must be hiding her. I wouldn't put it past that Patroon, forcing this 'non-trial' when what he really wants is to force me to admit I lost the first prisoner I ever took! My first act as Chancellor, no less!" He downed the rest of the brandy. "I can't admit that I've lost her. Tulipa is pressing for the meeting to happen as soon as possible, and Sir Iris has told me it has to be tomorrow! He said it will be just a formality, and she'll be returned to my custody or punished by her Patroon—he isn't sure which way it will go but either way, he'll see that justice is served. What am I to do? Fall into Tulipa's trap? Confess I'm unable to keep one damn whore under lock and key? He'll strip me of the Chancellor's chain, Will. We'll be a laughing stock."

Will was tempted to let his brother keep believing it was a Tulipa plot, but with Sir Iris involved and the honour of his family at risk, he couldn't do it. He saw his own fear reflected in his brother's eyes. While he had little love for Nathaniel, the man had been ready to duel the Rosa in Aquae Sulis for him when everything had come to a head. When he'd been taken by the Sorcerer of Mercia, Nathaniel had torn through Londinium and Oxenford to find him, throwing everything else aside to see him safe. This was the strength of family. "I doubt it's Tulipa, Nathaniel. Yes, he might be able to make you look a fool, but when that moment passed, Tulipa knows Sir Iris would destroy him for such a slight."

Nathaniel nodded, breathing out as he thought it through. "Yes, you're right. Of course. I've lost my mind with worry. Thinking such ridiculous things…" He rested a hand on Will's shoulder. "I knew you'd talk some sense into me. I can't go to anyone else with this. Father would be appalled, and there's no one in Oxenford that I trust, and…" His head drooped a little. "It's so hard. Being untouchable. Maintaining perfection. If this hadn't happened I'd be so much further ahead than I am now. But I've lost so much time and energy searching for her. The blasted Shopkeeper is starting to ramp up the prices for the Seeker Charms, and I can't keep my demand for them hidden for much longer if I have to—"

"I'll help you," Will said.

Nathaniel looked at him, all the arrogance and posturing falling away. Will saw another young man, terrified of being humiliated and punished for his imperfection. For the first time in his life, he realised how similar he and his brother were.

"You will?"

"Yes, I'll help you find her. I have better contacts in Londinium than you have in Oxenford. The people who knew her well are keen to keep my approval. I'm sure I'll be able to find something out."

"I would be indebted to you, more than I can express."

Will patted his shoulder and pulled away. His brother's gratitude, a rare and valuable commodity, wasn't the only incentive. If he stood by and watched Nathaniel being stripped of everything and sent to the Frankish Empire—or worse—he'd never be able to forgive himself.

But then he saw Bartholomew so clear in his memory, dying on the floor, blood dripping from his own sword. An innocent man that he'd killed, a woman's life that he'd destroyed, all because of these political games. Was he willing to betray Margritte and destroy her life a second time, just for the sake of his family's honour? Was that not perpetuating the motion of the very machine that had done so much damage already?

His family's honour was more than a mere romantic notion, though. In such dangerous times, caught up in that machine from which there was no escape, the best allies he had were his own family. They might not have been the most loving, but they would never betray him. It was them against the worlds. His brother keeping the throne of Oxenford, his father remaining at the head of such a successful branch of the family, his Patroon remaining pleased with him and his brother—all of these things would help to keep his position secure and him, Cathy, and Sophia safe.

"You're my brother," he said. "Family comes first."

10

"You let him go?"

"Yes, sir." Max tried to read Rupert's expression. The Sorcerer of Albion seemed more incredulous than angry. "I questioned him first."

"And then you decided it was better to give him a slap on the wrist and make him into a spy than hauling him in front of the Patroon, like regulations dictate?"

"I did."

Rupert grinned and clapped Max on the shoulder. "That's great!" He looked at the gargoyle, whose stone eyebrows were higher than usual. "And you weren't with him, obviously."

"Obviously," the gargoyle confirmed.

"I don't understand why you're so pleased." Max watched Rupert toss his report into a tray on his desk. One of his golems— Benson or Hedges, it was impossible to tell—rolled over and cycled through the attachments on its right arm like a robot from the back of a 1950s comic book. It picked up the report with the pincers it had chosen for the task, swivelled around, and wheeled to a filing cabinet on the other side of the room, narrowly avoiding the gargoyle, who scowled at it with suspicious stone eyes.

"You made the right call, and that was to fuck regulations in the ear. You used initiative. That's awesome!"

"All Arbiters use initiative in the field."

"Ah, but not while breaking the rules, Max." He rested his hand over his heart. "I'm proud of you, you rebel. Now all we need to do is teach you how to use a computer to write your reports and we'll be golden."

"I also need the use of a holding room, in the Nether," Max said. "Somewhere secure to put a puppet into for interrogation when I make an arrest."

"I'll sort that out." Rupert sat down on one of the new office chairs.

Now the office had three desks, two of which had computers resting on them. There were chairs, a handful of filing cabinets, waste-paper bins, and even a large potted plant. The space was still mostly empty, though. In the far corner of the room was the camp bed that he'd slept on. He had no idea where Rupert was living now, and it was clear Rupert wanted to keep it that way.

"Where's Kay?" Max asked.

"She'll be here any minute. She wanted to walk from her hotel to the office via the streets reflected into the Nether, to get her head around the city."

"But she'll be vulnerable!" the gargoyle said, appalled.

"Oh credit me with some sense," Rupert snapped. "I gave her something to protect her, not that I think she'll need it. Lavandula saw you bust the Peonia and get your Arbiter on. He knows the city is still being policed."

"You need to decide what to do about him wanting to see Ekstrand," Max said as the lift pinged. "Perhaps you should introduce yourself as his replacement, otherwise—"

"No," Rupert said. "If I do that it'll be all over Albion before you could say 'more tea, vicar, no thank you, it makes me fart.' And if that happens, *she'll* know. The best thing for me is for everyone to think I'm dead."

Max and the gargoyle had speculated about the woman behind the destruction of the Chapters and the murder of the other Sorcerers. The only thing they knew about her was that she seemed to be the sister of the late Sorcerer of Essex, Dante. Where she was now, what she planned to do next, and why she'd committed all those murders was beyond anyone's knowledge. "I know why you want to stay hidden, but it's not the best thing for the innocents," Max said.

"Lavandula needs to be convinced that…" He stopped as Rupert stood up and patted his pockets. "What are you looking for, sir?"

"All the fucks I give about Lavandula and what he thinks…oh, that's right, there aren't any."

"But—"

Rupert picked up one of the pencils in a pot on his desk and flipped and caught it again. "Look, I know you're worried about what the parasites will do, but honestly, it's several orders of magnitude less important than what that woman will do next. You don't slaughter all the Sorcerers in the world and hundreds of people just for shits and giggles. She's got more planned and what's really getting on my tits is that I have no fucking idea what that is. *That* is the thing to be worried about. I don't like having a mortal enemy who's developed her own blend of magic, and I like her running around doing fuck knows what without my knowledge even less."

"So what are you going to do about it?" Kay asked as she walked over.

"I'm working on something. It's not ready yet. So in the meantime, you need to get up to speed."

"I have about ten thousand questions," Kay said, dumping a small rucksack on the second desk. "Morning." She smiled at Max and then gave a second, nervous smile to the gargoyle. It grinned back, baring so many stone teeth that she shuddered and busied herself with her bag and computer.

"I can answer them," Rupert said. "And Max here can do Arbiter stuff"—this was accompanied by a vague wave of the hand—"But only after you help me get some books, Max."

"I can get books," Kay said.

"Not the ones I'm talking about," Rupert replied. He looked at Max. "They're in Ekstrand's library. I gave that librarian of his—"

"Petra," the gargoyle said, making Kay jump.

"Yeah, her, I gave her a list of the ones I wanted but she still hasn't brought them over. I've phoned three times but there's always an excuse. I want you to go over there with me to pick them up."

"You're worried about magical protections?"

"No! That Petra woman obviously doesn't trust me. And she sounds all weird on the phone. She knows you. She might be more cooperative if you're with me."

"Is this the lady who might come and work with us?" Kay asked.

Rupert shrugged. "I thought so, but she hasn't left the house since her old employer died, so it's all a bit up in the air at the moment. Ask the gargoyle those questions whilst we're out. He'll know most of the answers about the Fae-touched and how they're policed, right, Max?"

Max nodded and the gargoyle padded silently over to Kay, who shrank back from it, her wheeled office chair moving away with her. "Ask me anything you like," the gargoyle said, grinning again.

"Do you bite?"

"Not people I like," it replied as Rupert grabbed his coat.

"Brill, okay then, see you later. Don't eat her," he said to the gargoyle. "Don't look so scared!" he said to Kay. "It's only a lump of stone with a soul trapped inside it, animated by arcane means."

She scowled at him. "We need to discuss my pay," she added as they left. That was met with another wave of Rupert's hand.

Rupert's hire car was parked in an allocated space at the back of the building. Max got in the passenger side, resting his walking stick next to the door once it was shut. As the engine started the car was filled by a noise that Max could only assume was some sort of modern music. Rupert switched it off and pulled out into the city centre traffic.

"Are there any topics that shouldn't be discussed with Kay?" Max asked, aware that she'd found the courage to start asking the gargoyle questions.

"Not that I can think of. We need to bring her up to speed as soon as we can. She's got a brain like one of those super-absorbent kitchen towels, Max, like on the adverts, you know."

"No, sir."

"So retentive. And she has a capacity for logic and problem-solving that's just a fucking joy to see in action."

"She seems to be handling it all very well."

"Yeah. I thought she would. She always seemed disappointed with the world. I think I just made it complicated enough to hold her interest. I might make her my apprentice." He started to laugh.

Max tried to fathom the joke and failed. "I thought there were rules against women being taught the arcane arts."

"There are. But who's left to get on my case about them now? Fuck the rules. Listen, have you heard anything about Margritte Semper-Augustus Tulipa on your excursions into the Nether?"

"No. The Tulipas are primarily resident in Londinium and Oxenford, as far as I know. Is she causing problems?"

"Maggie? No. I'm just worried about her. I have no fucking clue what's happening in Oxenford and…" He shrugged. "It's complicated. I want to clear the air with her. We sort of fell out over…something. You got any contacts in Londinium?"

"Yes. Would you like me to ask about her whereabouts and well-being?"

"Yeah, that'd be awesome. Shitting crikey, I need to get control of the traffic system here. I can't be doing with all these pissing red lights."

They travelled the rest of the way across the city in silence punctuated by Rupert yelling obscenities at other drivers. Occasional snippets of the gargoyle's conversation with Kay floated into Max's consciousness. She seemed very excited by the concept of his soul being trapped inside the gargoyle by the chain that hung round its neck, forgetting her fear of it with each question.

"How did you meet Kay?"

"I heard about her from one of the Dons at the university. She helped me with a riddle. One sent by Ekstrand, funnily enough. I couldn't crack it. She got it in, like, ten seconds. We became friends after that. Can't be arsed with stupid people, Max. They bore me." He pointed down the road they were driving along. "Down there on the right?"

"Yes. Do you know fifty more people as clever and adaptable as Kay?"

"Not that I'd be willing to work with. Don't worry. We'll find that woman who tried to kill me, deal with her, and then tech can make up the staffing shortfall. I know you're used to a Chapter with dozens of staff but, let's face it, your old boss wasn't exactly moving with the times, was he?"

"I'm not worried," Max said as the car pulled into the drive. "I also disagree with your appraisal of what it takes to run a Chapter and police Wessex effectively, let alone the entirety of Albion."

Rupert either didn't hear him or was choosing to ignore him. He got out of the car, shrugged his coat on, and strode up to the house as Max struggled to get out. By the time he'd limped over, Rupert had pulled up the hood of his hoodie and buttoned his coat. "I'm freezing my nuts off here. No reply—she must be in the Nether." He chewed his lower lip. "I want to stay in Mundanus for now. Just in case."

Max pulled the knuckle-duster from his pocket, put it on, and knocked three times. He had time to slip it off and drop it back into his pocket before the door opened.

Petra was dressed in black and her normally perfectly styled blonde hair was tied back in a lopsided ponytail with strands hanging around her face. Her eyes were red and puffy and her makeup was streaked. "Oh, Max. It's you."

"And me," Rupert said, stepping into sight.

"Oh." She looked disappointed. "I knew you'd come for them in the end."

"Look, it's bloody freezing out here."

"Come in," she said reluctantly, and shut the door after them. The house wasn't much warmer. "Sorry I didn't hear the door. I was in the Nether library."

"Have you got the books I want ready?"

Petra wrapped her arms about herself. Max noticed that she was wearing the same suit as the last time he saw her, over a week ago. There were ladders in her hosiery and food stains on her blouse. "I've put them to one side but you can't take them out of the library."

Rupert pulled his hood down. "Oh, for fuck's sake, we went

through this on the phone. I'm not coming here every time I want to look something up. They're not safe here. She knows where this place is."

"You're not safe here either," Max said. "Why not close the house down and come and work with us?"

Petra looked utterly horrified. "I can't leave the house! Who will take care of it now Axon's gone?"

Max looked at the dust collecting on the hallway table, smelt the mustiness in the air. "I'm not sure you can take care of the anchor property and the Nether property too, not by yourself."

"I've been focused on the library," she said, looking away. "That evil woman took some of his books." She looked at Rupert. "You are going to get those back, aren't you? And she stole some other things too."

"Eventually. If you give me those books, I'll be able to find her more quickly."

Petra rubbed her left eye, frowning at him. "Come to the library, then."

"No, it's in the Nether."

She started to chew a thumbnail. "I shouldn't let you," she muttered. "He wouldn't like it."

"Ekstrand's dead!" Rupert said. "He is literally incapable of giving a shit about who goes in his library, or anywhere else in this house!"

"I'm the only one left who cares and I know he wouldn't like it!" she shouted back at him. "You don't deserve those books! Get out!"

"I need them," Rupert said, stepping towards her. "They used to be mine! Ekstrand stole them from me! That's the only reason I know about them!"

Petra grabbed an umbrella from the nearby stand and held it in front of her like a sword. "I told you to get out!"

"Petra," Max said, hobbling round to stand between her and Rupert. "We need the books and we need you. You're wasted here. Mr Ekstrand tasked me with protecting this city from the parasites and it's hard. If you helped us, it would be easier to protect the innocents and easier for Rupert to find the one who killed Mr Ekstrand before she kills again. Do you understand?"

The umbrella wavered, as if she barely had the strength to keep it held up. "I need to make sure the library—"

"Oh, for the sake of fuck!" Rupert made her jump. "Look, if you won't let me take the books, I'll have to go through this place top to bottom and pull out every damn diary, notebook, scrap of paper and see if—"

"No!" Petra's horror made the umbrella waver even more.

Rupert peered through the doorway to the living room. "All sorts of interesting shit in there. Yeah, scrap the books, I'll just take the whole fucking house and throw you out. That solves the problem just as well."

Petra let the umbrella fall to the floor. "I'll get them, if it means you'll go."

"I won't stay a minute longer than I have to, trust me."

"Make sure he doesn't touch anything," she said to Max, and then left, glancing over her shoulder a couple of times to make sure Rupert was staying put. When he took a step towards the living room she hurried off, making him chuckle.

Max looked at Rupert, standing with his hands in his pockets, rocking back and forth on his heels. "Was what you said about the books true? Were they yours?"

"Sort of," he replied, but said no more.

Petra returned with a cardboard box full of books. "They're all here. But you must promise to take care of them, and if you don't need them anymore, please do bring them back."

"Why? No one else is going to use that library. No point you staying here, like Max said." She didn't have anything to say about that so Rupert went over and took hold of the box. She was still holding it after several beats, then sagged once he'd prized it from her grip. "Good. They're all here. Come on, Max. Weird-ass hybrid Sorcerer-killer to hunt, parasites to police and all that."

Max went over to Petra as Rupert struggled to open the front door whilst holding the box. "You don't have to stay here," he said once Rupert was outside. "This is my mobile number. We have a new Chapter starting up at Cambridge House on Henry Street, top floor. Come and help us. We need people with experience." He scribbled the number on the notepad next to the telephone that Axon used to use.

She took the piece of paper. "Maybe," she said. "I just…I don't feel like I can just abandon everything he made, and…"

Max saw the tears well in her eyes and knew he was the last person who could offer any solace. Even the gargoyle would be better equipped than he. Rupert was calling him. "I have to go."

Petra closed the door behind him, a loud slam that echoed off the perimeter wall. The fountain at the centre of the drive was dry, and some litter had blown in from the street to gather at the edge of its plinth. He'd never appreciated all the work Axon did until he was gone.

Rupert beeped the car horn and Max made his way over as fast as his leg would allow. Rupert pulled out of the drive the moment Max's door was shut and sped off down the street. Halfway back, he looked at Max. "She wasn't always like that, I take it."

"Petra is one of the most skilled and well-read people I have worked with," Max said.

"Does she have family to go to?"

"I have no idea. I don't know anything about her life before working for Mr Ekstrand."

"Bit weird, him having a woman working so closely with him."

Max didn't reply and Rupert didn't press him. They remained silent all the way back and in the lift up to the office. Kay was spinning in her office chair, knees tucked up under her chin as the gargoyle gave it another flick with a claw to make it spin again.

"Okay, so if you contain Max's soul, and that's the seat of emotion, how come the other half of you, the Arbiter bit, still gets up every morning and goes to work? Doesn't that need some sort of desire or motivation? Are they separate from the soul? And if they're separate—"

"You weren't lying about the ten thousand questions," Rupert said with a grin. "And I can probably answer that better than anyone else here."

Kay stopped her chair spinning by grabbing the desk, her eyes rolling for a couple of seconds afterwards. "Okay, I'm listening."

Rupert set the box down on his desk. "Part of the training all Arbiters go through is conditioning—you know, positive and negative reinforcement stuff. Max was conditioned to the point where he needs to investigate anything related to Fae activity when he's in the field, so he can pursue leads without the need for any messy emotional desire. He has to keep policing, has to prosecute, has to protect the innocents. He physically can't help himself now."

Kay's eyes widened and she exchanged a look with the gargoyle. "You mean...he was...I dunno...programmed?"

Rupert looked up at the ceiling tiles, considering the question. "Yeah, I guess so. Who wants pizza for lunch?"

"Isn't that unethical?"

"Pizza is never unethical."

"I mean what was done to Max! Did you do that to the Arbiters who worked for your Chapter in Oxford?"

"Me?" Rupert pointed at his own chest. "No! *I* didn't. Pepperoni or Meat Feast? Or both?"

"Pepperoni," Kay replied quietly. "I'll go and collect. I need a walk."

• • •

Sam dozed in the back of the limo as it sped towards Bath. He and Cathy had agreed that him walking through a Way between the cities at Bathurst Stables wasn't the best plan when neither of them were sure how the magic worked, and whether he would break it. He decided to drive and meet her near Odd Down Park-and-Ride. She'd said it was only a short walk away from the stables in Aquae Sulis that she'd reach using the Way from Londinium.

He'd caught up with a couple of phone calls and was now trying to catch up on some much-needed sleep. He'd been working late every night since the terrible meeting with the Elemental Court, scanning the last of the information Leanne had gathered in the early days of her research that only existed on paper. Thankfully, as time had gone on, she'd backed up onto disks, which were easier to move onto flash drives.

Now that Cathy had a copy, he was less worried about someone tracking down the storage. He'd already moved it all to a different unit, under a different name, but his enemies were resourceful and very motivated to find it.

Enemies? Had he overreacted? He'd been working at full tilt since then, covering his arse, all based on a few reactions from the people in that room. Was this just paranoia?

Even under examination, that gut instinct to protect himself and prepare for battle remained intact, as did his horror that none of them seemed to have any idea about anything other than the normal, "mundane" world.

What had he been expecting? A room full of people in robes, incanting all sorts of weird shit and declaring him Lord Iron? As relieved as he was that it wasn't an intimidating court with rituals and bizarre rules, he'd been hoping for more. Titles like "Lord Iron" and "Lady Nickel" and "Lord Copper" weren't the sort of thing that dry businesspeople in suits came up with for themselves. And he was convinced Mazzi knew more than she was letting on. Why had she suddenly clammed up on him, after being so open the first time they'd met? Was it because he was turning out to be a disappointment? A danger?

He wanted to speak to someone who understood the roots of the Court, but with dismay he realised the only viable candidate was Ekstrand. Would that crazy, selfish bastard talk to him and Cathy? He wished he knew another Sorcerer, someone he could question without the baggage he had with Ekstrand.

Mazzi had said that the Sorcerers commissioned special pieces made of pure iron from Amir. That meant there had to be some sort of means of contact between whoever was the current Lord Iron and the current Sorcerer of wherever. It was clear from the way things had been handled after Amir's suicide that there were rules in place—not being allowed to radically change his business interests for ten years being one of them. Even though he was beginning to question who exactly would enforce those rules, surely there were similar mechanisms in place for dealing with the Sorcerers that he could exploit.

Just because Amir hadn't trained him in any esoteric skills, nor even mentioned them, didn't mean the previous Lord Irons were ignorant. As soon as he'd taken Cathy to see Ekstrand, he was going to start some digging into who they were and whether they'd left any diaries or notes behind that could explain what exactly the roots of the Elemental Court were, and what he was capable of as Lord Iron. Once the decision had been made, sleep wasn't far behind it.

"We're five minutes away from Odd Down Park-and-Ride, sir," the driver said, waking him.

Sam sat up and tried to work the crick out of his neck. "Thanks."

He looked out of the window, seeing the darkening sky. It wasn't even five in the evening. He hoped Cathy was okay waiting for him.

He'd been relieved to see her looking so well when they met in the diner earlier, the best he'd seen her in a long time. Perhaps she was right to stay in that life. Perhaps the fight put that spark in her, the feeling that she had something to tackle head-on. It didn't stop him wanting to take her home with him to Cheshire, wrap her in a blanket, put a whisky in her hand, and tell her she didn't have to see any of those fucks ever again. He'd seen one of them stab her and could still hear that child screaming and the sickening thud of the blade going into Cathy's chest. She said that husband of hers was different, but he remembered her talking about the marriage and how it was the last thing she wanted. She'd argued so passionately for help with Ekstrand, and that soulless fuck had ignored her. Surely she was just deluding herself. Maybe it was the only way to cope.

They reached a roundabout and the driver took an exit off it straight into the park-and-ride. A rather cold-looking Cathy waved at his car, her bodyguard beside her. Of course Carter was with her. Sam had forgotten about him.

"You weren't waiting there for two hours, were you?" he asked when they climbed into the car.

"No, only a few minutes," Cathy said through chattering teeth. "Ooooh, but it's so lovely to be properly cold! That wind is absolutely bitter!"

Sam smiled at her and the way the tip of her nose was red. "It loses its novelty pretty quick."

He directed the driver to Ekstrand's house, and they reached it in the deepening twilight. A solitary light was on above the front door, but no others. "Shit," Sam said. "Don't tell me we came all this way and they're not bloody in." Then he noticed the dry fountain and the litter and leaves that had gathered around the front of the house. Something was wrong. He didn't want to worry Cathy, who didn't know that the house was usually impeccable. Maybe Axon just had the flu or something.

"There's a Nether version anchored there, though, right?" Cathy asked, and Sam nodded. "I can knock and be heard in the Nether house, it's fine. Oh, hang on! Won't you…break the Nether house? Being Lord Iron and all?"

"I didn't break yours when I visited," he replied. "I guess the magic that anchors the buildings is hidden away in something. I have to touch it to break it, remember?"

She smiled. "Oh yeah. I forgot."

They got out of the car and Cathy asked her bodyguard to stay inside it, worried that the Sorcerer would be intimidated by him. Carter insisted on getting out of the car, but compromised by staying back from the doorway when they knocked.

Cathy marched up to the door and after whispering a few words that Sam couldn't make out, rapped on the door with the knocker three times. It seemed to reverberate through the entire house, with an echo that sounded wrong, somehow.

They shivered on the doorstep as the sky grew black. Cathy

knocked a second time and then just as she was about to try a third time, the door opened.

Sam hardly recognised Petra. It seemed she was having the same difficulty recognising him.

"Sam?"

"Petra?"

"What happened?" they asked each other in unison.

"Can we come in?" he asked. "It's freezing." When Petra gave Cathy a wary look, Sam said, "This is Cathy. She's been here a few times before, but you never met."

"You're the puppet that Max knows?"

Cathy frowned. "I'd prefer not to be called that. But yes, I'm the one."

There was a moment of hesitation. "I'm not supposed to talk to you."

"Petra, please," Sam said. "Everything's changed. I'm Lord Iron now. And I vouch for Cathy, okay?"

Petra stared at Sam. "Lord Iron? That's what it is. How...never mind. Come in." She almost shut the door in Carter's face.

"That's my bodyguard," Cathy said. "Can he come in too?"

After another hesitation, Petra stepped aside for Carter and then shut the front door.

Something was definitely wrong. The place felt abandoned. Then Sam remembered that he'd always been in the Nether house. Perhaps they didn't use the anchor very much. "I need to speak to Ekstrand and so does Cathy. Is he in the Nether?"

Petra looked away. "I—I'm afraid he's not available."

In the light cast by the hallway chandelier, Sam took in the extent of Petra's dishevelment. Why hadn't Axon opened the door?

"Petra..." he began, but she rallied herself.

"Perhaps it's something I can help you with?" she said, smoothing her skirt and trying to tuck some of the strands of hair away from her eyes.

"I want to talk to him about the Agency," Cathy said. "Do you know anything about it?"

"Probably not enough for your purposes, I'm afraid." Petra's smile was horribly brittle.

"Then maybe you could tell me if there's a way I can get in touch with the Arbiter, Max. He visits sometimes, but—"

"Oh, that I can help with!" Petra fished a piece of paper from her pocket and went to a notepad by the telephone. "He gave me his new mobile phone number earlier. I'll just write it down for you."

Sam looked around as she wrote. A couple of strands of cobweb hung from the chandelier and there were dried shoe prints on the black and white floor tiles. Axon never would have stood for that, mundane house or not. He saw the ladders in Petra's stockings and how greasy her hair looked. When she turned around to give the number to Cathy, he saw a woman desperate to make it seem that everything was fine when it most definitely wasn't.

She directed that fragile smile at him. "And how can I help you, Sam?"

"I wanted to talk to Ekstrand about the Elemental Court and being Lord Iron," he began. "My predecessor didn't leave me any information about the more…unusual aspects of my new job."

"Well, I know a little. Did you have a question about the protocol for commissioning a piece of pure iron? I know about that."

"Anything would be great."

"Well, when you became Lord Iron, a letter will have been sent to all of the…" her voice faltered but she took a moment and then cleared her throat. "All the Sorcerers of Albion, detailing who you are and how you can be contacted."

Sam had no idea if the letter had been sent out. No one had mentioned it to him— perhaps the knowledge had been lost over Amir's stewardship. Then again, he couldn't imagine Ekstrand allowing anyone else to read his correspondence, so maybe she just hadn't seen it.

"Then whenever a piece is needed," Petra continued, "the Sorcerer sends a representative with a seal, made of iron, to prove they are who they say they are so the negotiation for the work can be carried out."

"How do I recognise a seal?"

"Oh I think you just do, because the first Lord Iron made them and they're pure and…" She shrugged. "I was told he or she will just know when they see one."

"Can I look at Ekstrand's seal?"

Petra bit her lip. "I…"

"Or talk to him about the rest of what the job involves? It's really critical, Petra, I'm sure you understand."

"I don't know where he…" She looked up the stairs.

At first Sam thought she was searching for something; then he realised she was trying to stop tears from falling. "Has he passed away?"

Petra looked like she was going to deny it, but then broke down, twisting away from him and Cathy as her body shook with heaving sobs. Carter looked away, distinctly uncomfortable, and Cathy stepped back too. Sam went over to Petra, knowing how that grief felt and hating the thought of her alone in the huge house, suffering.

"I'm so sorry," he said, and she turned to face him, mumbling some sort of apology. He put his arms around her, feeling her bones and the way the suit hung from her shoulders. "It's going to be okay. What happened? Did Axon die too? Are you alone here?"

She stopped crying, as if a switch had been flicked, and pulled away from him. She fished a handkerchief from up her sleeve and wiped her face, the strangest expression forming upon it.

"Petra?" Sam asked, worried she'd catastrophically lost it and was about to start laughing hysterically.

"I'm so tired," she said. "I don't think I've slept or eaten properly since he died." There was no emotion in her voice, as if it had been stolen away.

"Sam," Cathy said nervously. "What did you do to her?"

"Nothing!"

"You broke some sort of magic," Cathy said. "Um, Petra, how are you feeling?"

"Very calm," she said. She rested a hand on her stomach, focusing inwards, as if she needed to consider the question carefully and consult her own body. "I need to eat and to sleep. Urgh, and to have a bath. I must look terrible."

"Do you feel anything else?" Cathy asked, staring at Petra's hand in a way that made Sam feel that she was seeing something he wasn't.

Petra considered the question. She did seem different, even though she looked exactly the same, and it wasn't just the sudden end to her grief. She seemed…distant in a way Sam would never associate with her. All the times he'd visited before she'd been warm and engaged, bright and eager to help. It was like he was looking at a shell of her.

"I feel like I'm missing something." She looked around the hallway as if seeing it for the first time. "I'm not supposed to be here."

"Where are you supposed to be?" Sam asked, disturbed.

"I have no idea," she replied. "I just know it isn't here. How curious. I feel like I've been…dreaming for so long, I've forgotten what it's like to be awake."

"You've been under a spell," Cathy said with authority.

"She was a Sorcerer's librarian!" Sam said. "It's impossible. He hated the Fae; there's no way he'd let someone work with him so closely if they had any of their magic on them!"

Cathy shrugged. "That's what it looks like to me. I don't know you, Petra, but I've seen curses being broken before. Either Ekstrand didn't know or he didn't care. Either way, I reckon someone got to you."

"I think you're right," Petra said. "I'm sorry. This is a lot to take in. I need to clean myself up and get some food." She looked at Sam. "I don't know where he kept the seal, I'm sorry. There might be something in one of the books in the library. Once I'm feeling stronger, I'll do some research. I'd let you do it yourself but there are powerful protections on them and I'm not sure whether you'd be immune to sorcerous magic. Could you leave a contact number for me?"

"Sure," Sam said, wondering how she could be so calm. Perhaps it was shock. "Are you going to be okay here? Have you got some family? Somewhere else you can go?"

Petra shook her head. "I don't think I have any family. I can't quite remember where I came from, before I came to work here."

"Could Ekstrand have stolen your memory?" Cathy asked.

Petra smiled faintly. "Sorcerous magic doesn't work that way. Whatever has happened to me, I doubt it was Mr Ekstrand's doing, though I suspect he was happy to benefit from it."

"Shit, aren't you at least angry about it? He must have exploited you! I'm angry and I barely know you!"

Petra shook her head. "No. I don't feel much of anything. It's such a relief. I was overwhelmed by emotion. It feels like I've just been plucked out of a hurricane and left on a desert island somewhere. It's blissful."

Sam gave her his card, having written on the back. "That hotel is a short taxi ride away. Go check yourself in, charge the taxi to the hotel, I'll arrange it all."

"You don't need to do that."

"Sam collects waifs and strays," Cathy said with a smile.

"And I own the place, so it's no big deal. Stay there as long as you need to. Okay? Just don't stay here by yourself."

Petra nodded. "I just need to pack a few things first."

"Was it the war?" Cathy asked. "That killed Ekstrand? The gargoyle mentioned it a while back."

"Yes," Petra replied, "But not the war he thought he was fighting. It all seems so…far away now. So long ago. It was less than a fortnight. I think. But then, I can't remember how long I've been here, so don't take my word for it. It feels like I was working for Ekstrand forever." She blinked a couple of times. "And now I'm free. But I don't really feel that way. It's so very confusing." She looked down at the card. "I'll take you up on that offer, Lord Iron, thank you."

"Sam, please, I'm just Sam," he said.

"No, you're not," Petra replied with a moment of her former intensity. "You're master of the blood and star metal, brother to the binding metal, and protector of the innocent. You're woven into the fabric of the world on a level deeper than most can even conceive of and you haven't even come into your strength yet." She rested her hand over his heart. "And you freed me. I won't forget it."

Sam looked down into her eyes, struck by the feeling that one day, that would be important. It was all getting too weird. He stepped back from her. "Time to go," he said, shaken.

11

Will struggled to manage his guilt as he arrived at Sir Iris's house. He'd received a letter asking him to come and speak to Sir Iris regarding Margritte Tulipa. She had been brought to Sir Iris's house earlier that evening, delivered personally by Nathaniel at the request of the Tulipa and Iris Patroons. Having engineered it all without Margritte's knowledge, the only thing left for Will to check was whether her trust in him remained intact and what she was planning to say. Whether he could bear to look into her eyes was another question yet to be answered.

Last time, the mirror at the Tower had brought him straight into the waiting room so that he could sweat the correct amount before being dressed down. This time the mirror brought him out of a matching glass hanging in the hallway of Sir Iris's household. When he asked the page who'd been waiting for his arrival if he could speak with Margritte, he expected to have to justify why. It seemed no orders had been given to keep her isolated, and William was escorted straight to a room guarded by two burly men in Iris livery.

The door wasn't locked and he was shown inside. There was a chair and a desk within, along with a lit fire. There were no paintings and, obviously, no mirrors. The window was covered by locked shutters. He wasn't sure what the room was usually used for. It wasn't comfortable enough to be a study and was too plain to be a receiving room. Perhaps there were dozens of rooms simply set aside to hold nervous people as they waited to see the Patroon.

Margritte was standing in the corner farthest from the door, ashen-faced, with her arms wrapped about herself. When she saw that it was Will and not another Iris she let out a sigh of relief and went over to meet him in the centre of the room. He kissed her hand and noted how it trembled, even though she was otherwise composed.

"I'm so sorry, Margritte, I just got the news. I failed you."

"Oh, you did more than I could have asked for. You always said there was a risk your brother would escalate. You were right."

Will noticed a tiny bit of blood under her nose. "Did he hit you? I'll beat the—"

"No, no." She blushed and dabbed at her face with a handkerchief stained with fresh blood. "The Seeker Charm he employed was so powerful it made my nose bleed. Nathaniel wasn't exactly gentle, but he didn't hit me this time. I thought he was going to take me back to Oxenford, but I don't think he has. Where are we?"

"Londinium, in my Patroon's household. I made enquiries, and I'm told Sir Tulipa is on his way. There's to be a discussion about what happens now. Nathaniel insists you should be held at his pleasure, but your Patroon disagrees. Sir Iris has agreed to discuss it with him."

"I've been thinking," Margritte said, starting to pace. "Nathaniel didn't have any idea who hid me from him, and I didn't say a word when he asked me. I doubt he will bring up the fact that I've been free of him all this time, so the Patroons will assume I've been in his custody. I won't tell them otherwise, Will. They don't need to know what you've done for me. I can't imagine it would be received well by your Patroon."

Will hid his relief. He'd been hoping she would see it this way. He'd counted on her nobility and she hadn't failed him. He pushed down another surge of guilt and smiled at her. "Even now, you seek to protect me?"

"Are you not trying to do the same? Why are you here, if not to help?"

He nodded, neglecting to mention that he had been summoned by his Patroon. "I've asked to speak to the Patroons. Nathaniel is no doubt going to emphasise the fact that I was returned to him after you took me. I'm going to make it clear that we resolved our conflict, and that he jumped to conclusions he shouldn't have in the heat of the moment."

"There's no way to hide the fact that I wronged you, Will."

"No, but if they know I have no desire to see you punished, it may soften their judgement and make it more likely that Sir Iris will release you into the care of Sir Tulipa. That is the best outcome we can hope for, I fear."

"He's my uncle," Margritte said. "I would rather face his wrath than that of your family. I was ready to do that before your brother intervened in the Sheldonian, and I still am. I behaved terribly and I take responsibility for it."

"I plan to keep any mention of the Sorcerer from my testimony," Will said. "I take it you intend to do the same?"

She nodded. "Unless they force me, I plan to say it was all me. And I have no intention of telling them anything about what you confessed to me in Rupert's prison. That is in the past, and we have been victims enough of these sickening games they play with us."

"Thank you," he said, all the while knowing that he'd cast the Seeker Charm that had made her bleed. His men, disguised with a glamour, had stormed the room in which she was hiding and thrown her through a Way into a house in which she was kept under guard until Nathaniel arrived, having received a tip-off from him. He was moving her around the board to protect his own pieces and although he felt wretched about it, he would still execute his plan. "I will do everything in my power to press for leniency. Sir Iris knows how hot-headed Nathaniel is, and he'll want to keep relations civil between himself and the Tulipa Patroon. This will all blow over."

"Will, if I don't have the opportunity to do so myself, please will you convey my warmest affection to Cathy for me? Tell her… tell her I'm sorry I won't be able to continue to help her."

"Now, don't speak like that!" Will said, hearing the tremor in her voice. "I'm sure you'll see her yourself, very soon." He heard a clock striking down the hall. Nine o'clock in the evening. Sir Iris would be sending for him soon. "I need to go now, before Sir Tulipa arrives. Have courage, Margritte. You're not alone."

How he hated himself as he smiled so sweetly at her and held her hand for one last, brief moment. But he had to stop thinking this way. He was doing the right thing for his brother, for his own blood, and that counted for more. Besides, the Tulipa Patroon would probably do no more than tell her off and send her to some country house for a couple of years until it faded from Nathaniel's memory. It wouldn't stop her secretly meeting with Cathy, and surely it was better to just get it all cleared up, rather than her living in hiding indefinitely.

As he walked back to the sitting room, Will tried to get his fears in check. Margritte was right that it was better for everyone involved that the Patroons know nothing of her escape from the castle, and therefore it was very unlikely to come up. What worried him more was how much detail the Patroons would want about what happened to him and why, after being driven to such extreme behaviour, she'd suddenly changed her mind and released him. He had mentally prepared for as many varied questions as possible, and short of having a Truth Charm slapped on him or on Margritte— highly unlikely given that both families were being represented in the room and neither would want to risk secrets being revealed—he simply had to trust his ability to talk Margritte out of trouble.

• • •

It was almost midnight when Sam returned to Cheshire. Petra was at the hotel in Bath, hopefully feeling better by now, and Cathy was back in Londinium, satisfied with Max's telephone number and being a step closer to negotiating some protection from the Agency. Cathy promised she wouldn't tell anyone about Ekstrand's death, even though it hadn't occurred to him how sensitive that information was until she explained that the Fae-touched in Aquae Sulis would have a field day if they knew.

He couldn't stop thinking about the way Petra had changed. None of it made sense. Even if he accepted that Ekstrand had overlooked a Fae spell or curse or whatever had been done to her, why did she still seem so strange after he broke it? What did the spell actually do, apart from making her grief so severe? Had it made her love Ekstrand? It would explain why his passing caused unbearable grief. But why would anyone associated with the Fae make a woman devoted to a Sorcerer?

All the times he'd seen Petra before, she'd seemed happy and fully autonomous. She'd stood up for him against Ekstrand; she wasn't just a devoted servant.

And then there was the way she spoke to him at the end of the visit. Like the Prince had spoken to him in Exilium. There seemed to be a longer title for him—or rather, a formal job description, known by those involved in magic. Master of the star and blood metal? It sounded stupid, and yet…something in those words spoke to a deeper part of himself.

Nah. He was just getting carried away.

Halfway home he'd texted Des, asking who the Lord Iron was before Amir and where that man lived. He didn't recognise the name mentioned in the reply—though Des told him he was a famous man in his day, even buried in an iron coffin—but he did recognise the address. Amir had simply moved into his estate and extended the house. Sam called Des then, eager to know more, but Des said he had no knowledge of any notes or artefacts left to Amir by the previous Lord Irons. When Sam asked if he could find out if the previous Lord Iron's PA might still be alive, or maybe some member of staff he could ask, Des had laughed. "He died in the 1890s, sir."

"But I asked for the one before Amir."

"He was, sir. Amir took on the mantle of Lord Iron in 1891."

That had to be a mistake. Amir hadn't looked much over forty, if that. Not over a hundred years old.

But…what if they lived longer? Surely Mazzi would have mentioned that? Why did it feel like there was a massive gulf between the way the Fae and Petra saw him, and the way the rest of the Elemental Court did? Was the truth somewhere between the two, like most things? Or was he in the horrible position of the Fae and Sorcerers knowing far more about what he was and actually being the most knowledgeable source?

Most of the household was asleep when the car pulled up, but as usual, Eleanor was standing outside the front door, despite the bitter cold.

"You look tired," she said to him as he got out of the car. "Did you have a good day?"

"I saw Cathy," he replied, going over to her. "She asked me to pass this letter on to you."

Eleanor peered at it. "Perhaps you could be good enough to put it on the table in the hall for me. Is she well?"

"Yeah, very."

"You like her."

"She's a good friend."

Eleanor stared at him with pursed lips. "Hmm. Well, time for bed."

She followed him inside, collected the letter he left for her, and headed for the stairs.

Sam pulled off his gloves and looked at the hallway. Which parts of the house were original? Could he learn something from what was built here before, left behind by the previous Lord Irons?

"Eleanor," he called, making her stop halfway up the stairs. "Do you know anything about architecture?"

"I can tell my Doric from my Corinthian." At his blank face she said, "A little. Why?"

"Can you tell me which part of this house is older than the rest?"

She turned and came down a few stairs until their faces were level. "My dear man, 'older' is a relative term. Do you mean older than this part, or older than the east wing, or the oldest part of the whole house?"

He frowned. "It's not just one old house extended around the late eighteen hundreds?"

She smiled. "Oh, this is going to be an education for you. Get a torch. I'm going to take you on a tour."

• • •

Sir Iris actually smiled when Will entered his study. At least, Will chose to believe it was a smile, rather than indigestion. It was hard to tell.

"Sit down, William," he said, gesturing to the same chair in which Will had squirmed a couple of days before. "I trust the gem meets with your satisfaction?"

"Yes, thank you, Sir Iris. It's perfect. It's being set into a piece of jewellery and will be given to Cathy before our next public appearance."

Sir Iris gave a nod. "I have something else to give you before you leave, but before that, tell me what I need to know about this business with Margritte Tulipa."

"Margritte and I had some difficulties, but we resolved them."

Sir Iris raised an eyebrow, fixing that hawk-like glare on Will. "Perhaps I should be more clear. Nathaniel has told me what happened at the Hebdomadal Council when he took the city. Sir Tulipa has told me what he thinks happened there. Both of them mention you being present and you being the reason why Margritte was taken into custody, but neither of them have explained what happened to you *before* that to my satisfaction."

"Before I do, I feel you should know that Margritte was overcome with grief, following the death of her husband."

"The lawful challenge and execution of her criminal husband," Sir Iris interjected, "carried out with the blessing of Lord Iris and in accordance with the laws of Londinium."

"Yes," Will said, increasingly uncomfortable. "She made some poor choices that resulted in…" He looked at his Patroon, at the set of the ancient man's jaw, the way he was scrutinising him. Skimming over the details to protect Margritte simply wasn't going to work. "Sir Iris, I fear that if I begin this story, I will have damned Margritte Tulipa by the end of it."

"If you speak the truth, it sounds like she's already damned herself."

"I feel she lost her reason, in her grief and rage, without her husband to guide her. She recovered and we made amends. Nathaniel judged swiftly and in the heat of the moment, which he is entitled to do, as Chancellor. However, I feel it should be known that Margritte went to the Hebdomadal Council to turn herself in and put everything right." Even as he spoke, he realised he'd have to reveal more than he wanted. How would he be able to explain anything about the huge holes in his story without condemning her?

"Why are you trying to protect her?"

"I…feel somewhat responsible, considering what I did to her husband."

"What you did to her husband? Why make it sound as if you are guilty of something unsavoury? He sent an assassin to kill your wife!"

"But Margritte did not, sir. She had shown nothing but kindness to myself and my wife during our first days in Londinium." He paused. How could he explain his sense of duty to Margritte without revealing how the Rosas had successfully duped him into thinking Bartholomew had sent the assassin? It would make him seem like a fool in the eyes of a man as cold and uncaring as the Patroon. "However, I understand that you need to know what happened before you speak to her Patroon."

"Nathaniel said you were beaten."

Will felt his cheeks flush with shame. "I had a split lip and a bruised eye when I saw Nathaniel. I think he feared I'd been hurt more than I had."

"He saw enough to know you'd been mistreated."

"Yes, Sir Iris, I cannot say otherwise."

"I grow tired of feeling I need to winkle this story from you like a piece of lobster meat from a claw. Do you want me to assume you were foolish enough to fall into the hands of a woman, mad with grief, who struck you hard enough to split your lip?"

"No, sir, I do not!" And then it all unfolded in his mind. He had to tell him everything, despite what he'd just agreed with Margritte, otherwise he would look like an incompetent child. In light of the threat Sir Iris had made the last time he was in that study, he simply couldn't risk it. Sir Iris sent Nathaniel to find him—he even gave him his sword to get him back and take Oxenford if he could—because he knew something had happened to him. Without a sufficiently terrible crime committed against Will, Nathaniel's seizure of the throne would look more like the brutish act it actually was, rather than one of political retribution. Will rubbed the replacement wedding band he'd acquired to disguise the fact that Rupert's trap had destroyed the real one. Of course, Sir Iris knew something more than a grieving widow was involved. He was just waiting to hear how he explained it.

"Margritte Tulipa used my wife's better nature to arrange a meeting between myself and her. She'd been trying to coax Londinium residents to live in Oxenford and destabilise my Dukedom, so I thought that clearing the air would be preferable to any further escalation of her grievance with me.

"Before the meeting, I procured every Charm I possibly could to protect myself. I can produce a list, should you wish to review it. I took armed footmen, one of whom had taken a Clear Sight Charm, and agreed to meet with her at a mundane inn between Oxford and London on neutral territory as a gesture of goodwill. I took all of the precautions one can before meeting with a potentially hostile individual. Alas, none of them are effective when that individual is a Sorcerer."

Sir Iris's shock was mildly gratifying. "I beg your pardon?"

"Margritte Tulipa persuaded the Sorcerer of Mercia to help her try to force me to make a public announcement absolving her husband of guilt. He broke all of the Charms and magical artefacts on my person and literally opened the floor beneath my feet to drop me into a prison cell."

"So that's what destroyed your wedding band," Sir Iris said.

"And my sword, sir, to my shame."

"There is little to be done when a Sorcerer intends one harm, William."

"It was his men who inflicted the injuries. Whilst I was tied to a chair and unable to defend myself."

"Even after this, you forgave her?"

"She realised she'd gone too far. When she saw that I was hurt, she came to her senses. As I said, Sir Iris, it was the madness of grief. She released me, despite the Sorcerer's protestations, and insisted on going to the Hebdomadal Council to answer for her crime and assure everyone that I was safe. She is a brave and noble woman. She just lost herself for a while."

Sir Iris leaned back in his chair, still regarding Will closely. "And why did you not come to me after this?"

"To what end, sir? To complain like a child? I forgave her—and besides, Nathaniel had taken her into his custody, insisting it was an Oxenford matter. I had no intention of doing anything but supporting my brother's judgement. As for the Sorcerer of Mercia, not even Lord Iris could make a complaint against his behaviour. I felt it best to let Nathaniel make his judgement in his own time and to focus on consolidating my own rulership. As you know, sir, I have had a lot on my mind of late. Better to move forwards than to dwell on one woman's mistake."

"I'm sure Sir Tulipa would have agreed with you, were collusion with a Sorcerer not involved. Thank you for making me aware of this. Terrible shame about the sword. It was a fine blade. Irreplaceable. Have you commissioned another?"

Will hadn't even thought about it. His blade was hundreds of years old, with its own history before it was passed to him. He had no idea who to commission a new one from, as his had been a magical weapon Charmed to look and feel like steel. "I haven't yet had the opportunity."

"I'll see to it. And I will bear that sword in mind when discussing compensation."

Will almost said that he didn't feel compensation was necessary, but that was guilt rather than reason. As far as his Patroon was concerned, he was an innocent man, one who'd avenged his wife and maintained his family's honour and proven himself in a righteous duel. Margritte had colluded with a Sorcerer to take the Duke of Londinium prisoner, having him beaten before reevaluating her actions and belatedly trying to make amends. When he thought of it like that, he feared for Margritte.

"Is there anything else you feel I should know, William?"

Will shook his head, knowing that it was all out of his hands now. It was as if he'd taken a handful of seeds he'd hoped to nurture himself and tossed them into the grinding of wheels of power at a level above him. It was foolish to have even tried to help Margritte. "No, Sir Iris. I can only repeat that Margritte and I have made amends, and that she sought to put things right."

"Yes, yes," Sir Iris said, disinterested. "Now"—he opened the top drawer of his desk and took out a blue velvet pouch—"I have been instructed to give this to you."

Instructed? There was only one who could instruct his Patroon to do anything, and Will was uncertain whether it would be a gift that he'd want to receive. He accepted it from Sir Iris, pulled open the drawstring, and tipped the contents onto his palm. A golden wedding band sparkled in the sprite light.

"Lord Iris commanded me to tell you that he is pleased that you are seeking to protect your wife from unsuitable influences and trusts that you will give him what he has asked for very soon."

Will removed the mundane replacement and put the new wedding band on his finger, feeling it adjust to a perfect fit. "I am his obedient servant, sir."

"I look forward to seeing you make your mark on Londinium, William. You may leave."

He stood, bowed, and then went to the door.

"A word of advice, William," Sir Iris said as he reached for the door handle. "An excess of sympathy will not serve you well as Duke. Especially for the weaker sex."

"I will bear that in mind, Sir Iris. Thank you." He left and closed the door behind him in relief.

As he walked away, he reviewed the conversation in his mind, checking every detail he could recall and convincing himself he hadn't put a foot wrong. Nathaniel's reputation was intact, he'd told the truth, and he had explained losing his wedding band and sword in the only way that could have satisfied his Patroon that he wasn't incompetent. The only risk to him now was that Margritte, having realised he'd gone against his word, would reveal that he'd been hiding her. What if she told the Patroon about the confession she'd got from him inside the Sorcerer's prison, that he knew Bartholomew was innocent and that the Rosas had successfully duped the mighty Irises?

The fear melted away when he realised how the words of a woman known to associate with a Sorcerer would be regarded. After his testimony, nothing she said would be trusted. He was safe and his family was as strong as ever. It didn't make the ache in his breast go away.

• • •

Sam had been lifting floorboards, clambering in the loft space, and examining scratched marks on the stone lintels above several doors in the east wing of the house for over an hour. Eleanor directed him, slipping back into a role of authority that evidently came naturally to her. She was educating him on the long history of the house, which she believed was first constructed in Norman times. One of the original windows was still there in one of the back bedrooms in the central section of the house, one she was convinced was Norman in design.

"The Irises are very proud of their heritage," she told Sam after she'd pointed it out to him. "I've seen a lot of Norman construction as a result."

"They were the bad guys, right? The ones who tried to kill Robin Hood."

"It was far more complex than that, my dear man. The so-called Robin Hood wasn't the paragon of social justice that the mundanes have crafted. Though, in fairness, a fair few of the Normans were just as bad as people like to think. I know, I've dined with some of them. The current Duke of Londinium is descended from William the Conqueror. Did you know that?"

Sam shook his head, still processing what she'd just said about dining with the Normans. "I know he's an arsehole."

Eleanor laughed. "I can see why you get along with Cathy. Not that she'd agree with you. She's quite taken with him, I think. You don't have a chance."

"What? I didn't—"

"Now follow me," she said, disinterested in any defence. "You said you wanted the oldest part of the house. I think it's downstairs, but it's been covered over."

"So is this how you've been keeping busy?" Sam asked as he followed her down the back staircase, its stairs warped and uneven with age. "Playing architectural detective?"

"Amongst other things," she replied with an enigmatic smile. "Reading this house to learn its history didn't require a great deal of work. In the Nether, property is hugely important to us. We learn how to read a building like one reads a book. They all have their own narratives and stories to tell. This house is too modern for our tastes—there have been too many additions over the centuries. It's refreshing to spend time in it and trace what each of your predecessors added and took away. I always wanted to change the house I moved into when I became Dame of the family, but of course, I never expressed that desire. It would be unthinkable."

"Why? Surely things wear out and need to be changed to stay fit for purpose?"

"Oh, you misunderstand me. I meant it would be unthinkable for a lady to alter a house structurally. Each Patroon adds a little bit, makes his mark, there's no way to stop that. My husband built a new wing of the house several hundred years ago to keep the business of running the family separate from our home." She paused at the bottom of the stairs, as if she needed all of her attention to hold the memory. "He did it for me. I complained about the young bloods littering the hallway and pacing so much they wore the flagstones down. So he built the new wing to have lots of receiving rooms without the pressure of fitting our family life into them too. Most of the young ones now have no idea what our—his—family house is like. Only the most important people see the real home."

Sam waited, happy to listen. She so rarely talked about her former life. "You sound like you miss him."

"I do. I loved him. I still love him."

"Even after he threw you into that asylum to die?"

She turned to look at him. "That was an act of love. He could have done far worse. It was that weevil who replaced me who deserves my anger and hatred. Not him."

Sam didn't know what to say to that. Besides, what did he know about good marriages?

Eleanor carried on down the narrow hallway, one that Sam hadn't been down before, and came to a stop at the end, where a door led to the rest of the house ahead of them and a second door on the right opened onto stairs down into the basement. She patted the wall on her left. It was uneven and looked old. "This is the oldest part of the house. That bedroom with the window is above it. I think something has been walled off here, though." She beckoned to him and he followed her through the door to the rest of the house. She took him to the adjoining games room, opening the door to switch on the light but stopping him in the doorway. She patted the left-hand wall. "On the other side of this is the hallway we just walked along. But take a step back and you can see how far apart the wall of the old hallway is from this wall. It's too thick. There are no doors to any cupboard or small room that I think should be here."

Sam did as she instructed, and saw what she meant. "But how thick are the walls?" he asked as they went back into the narrow hallway. Sam pressed his hands against the wall, feeling the undulations. It felt solid enough. He knocked on it. No echo, nothing to suggest any space was behind it.

"I think it's the original cob, plastered with lime and whitewashed," Eleanor said. "My educated guess is that it's about a yard thick. If that's so, there's a space at least three or four yards across between this wall and the games room next door that's been sealed off." She twisted to Sam, grinning ghoulishly. "It's probably where the first Lord Iron walled up his enemies to die in the dark."

"Jesus, Eleanor!" Sam said, and she laughed.

"You modern men. So soft. Well, I'm for my bed. Good night."

"Good night. And thanks!"

Long after she'd gone, Sam found himself still standing there, hands on the wall. He wanted to see what was in the space behind it. No, more than that; he felt a pull towards it.

He closed his eyes and told himself he was just tired. That he'd wanted to find something so badly that his mind was playing tricks on him. He wasn't even sure what he was looking for. After finding out several Lord Irons had lived here over hundreds of years and made additions to the building, he wondered if something was being protected here, in this house. As far as he knew, all of his predecessors had lived there, even Amir, who had properties all over the world.

Eleanor was right about there being too big a space between the hallway and games room for it to be just a wall dividing the two. What was hidden in there?

"Sod it," he said, resolving to get a sledgehammer from the toolshed near the forge and demolish it in the morning. The worst that could happen was damaging a wall that could be easily repaired. That and finding skeletons, but he tried not to think about that.

12

Cathy looked out of her carriage window as it drew to a stop, chewing her lip. "Looks like we're here," she said to Carter. "Have you stopped sulking yet?"

Carter reddened. "I wasn't sulking, your Grace. It's just harder to protect you when you change your itinerary at the last moment."

"This may be nothing," she said, gathering up her reticule as the footman lowered the step. "I just have to check, that's all."

It wasn't as though she'd planned to visit the Lutea-Digitalis household. She was meeting Natasha in less than two hours and had a mountain of correspondence to plough through. But something in the letter she'd read that morning from Mrs Lutea-Digitalis, former Marchioness of Westminster, had made her worry. At first she'd thought it nothing more than a courtesy letter to remind the Duchess of her existence, but it went on to express her great interest in the Ladies' Court and her hope that the fortunes of the women of Londinium were soon to change. The handwriting was hurried and distinctly emotional. Why would this lady, well respected in the city, be so keen for fortunes to change?

The footman helped her down and she walked up to the front door, Carter shadowing her as usual. She pulled the chain for the bell, and a rather shocked butler answered the door.

"Your Grace!" He bowed.

"I know you aren't expecting me," Cathy said. "Is Mrs Lutea-Digitalis receiving guests this morning?"

"The lady of the house is at home, your Grace. Please do come inside. May I take your cloak?"

Cathy could hear the hurried footsteps of several servants

down the hall to the left. It was a rather austere house, with only a dramatically arranged vase of foxgloves to brighten the entrance hall.

"If you would like to follow me?"

"Is Mr Lutea-Digitalis at home?"

"No, your Grace. I understand he's attending to business elsewhere."

She was shown into a claustrophobic drawing room, filled with ornaments and heavy drapery as loved by the Victorians. She couldn't see a spare inch of wood on the mantelpiece, covered as it was by a fringed cloth. A portrait of Mr Digitalis in his finery dominated the chimney breast. Carter scanned the room and then assured her that he'd wait outside.

Mrs Digitalis stood nervously next to the fire, wearing an early Victorian gown with sloping shoulders that, combined with her fearful eyes, made her look horribly diminutive. She had a heart-shaped face with large brown eyes and sallow skin. She curtsied deeply. "Your Grace, what a delightful surprise."

Cathy suspected that saying "bollocks" to that blatant lie probably wasn't the most Duchess-like response. "Sorry I didn't send a note ahead, Mrs Digitalis. I probably should have." She didn't explain that she hated the stilted and carefully arranged visits that happened after she sent word ahead. Having a shocked butler and a host caught off their guard wasn't exactly pleasant either, but at least she was likely to see more of what was really happening in the household. "Oh, please don't look so nervous, I'm not going to eat you!"

A high, slightly strangled giggle escaped from her throat. "Please, call me Wilhelmina. Would you like to sit down?"

As if on cue, tea was brought, along with shortbread. Cathy imagined there'd been a debate about what to serve, it being on the early side of sociable hours. "I received your letter." She watched the flush rise up Wilhelmina's neck. "I'm delighted you approve of the new court."

"I...I confess, I am very interested to see what is discussed there."

"Well, that's one of the reasons I came," Cathy said, accepting the cup of tea that had been poured for her. "As the former Marchioness of Westminster, I thought you'd have a wealth of knowledge about the issues women face here."

Wilhelmina was paying a great deal of attention to the teapot as she poured her own cup. "You flatter me, your Grace."

Cathy reined in the impulse to roll her eyes. She was so tired of these false conversations with people half-terrified of her, resembling awkward dances where every move was mirrored by a complementary step as each evaluated the other. "Hardly. You'd have to be mostly dead not to have picked up a few things over the past couple of hundred years."

Wilhelmina stared at her over the teacup, uncertain whether to laugh or be offended, it seemed. She erred on the side of caution and smiled.

"You were there at the last Court," Cathy continued. "Surely by now you know I want every woman to feel able to speak her mind?"

"Indeed. Though sometimes it's not the wisest course of action."

"Do you think I did the wrong thing in speaking up?"

Wilhelmina almost dropped her cup. "Oh, no, not at all, your Grace! I didn't express myself adequately. I simply meant that sometimes, speaking one's mind can have...undesirable consequences."

This was it. Cathy could see she was desperate to tell her something. "In your letter, you mentioned a hope that fortunes will change for the women of Londinium. Did you include your own amongst them?"

The nod of Wilhelmina's chin was almost imperceptible.

"But your family is respected and you have a beautiful home, and..." Cathy paused, wondering how much more conversational rope she needed to pass out to this poor woman. "And something's wrong. Isn't it? I know we're supposed to say bland pleasantries to each other for at least half an hour before you might even consider telling me what it is, but I'm not very good at them and you can trust me. As Duchess, I serve you. I came here to listen to you."

"I watched you stand up in that room and speak so clearly,"

Wilhelmina said after a long pause. "And I watched your husband too, your Grace. He looked so proud when you made the announcement. How I envied you, even as that awful man was so rude to you. I watched you stand there and challenge him. I saw that you were unafraid. I couldn't stop thinking about what would life be like, if I could feel that too."

Cathy put her cup down. "Are you afraid?"

"Yes."

"If you tell me why, I will do everything in my power to help you. I promise."

Wilhelmina looked into the fire, at the hearthrug, at a crystal vase, the mantelpiece—anywhere except at Cathy. "My husband is a very unhappy man. I would like to be able to blame it on his loss of status, but he was hardly happy when he was Marquis, truth be told. Lots of things upset him. I never know what he will be like when he comes home. Sometimes he's angry. Sometimes he's miserable. Sometimes he goes from one to the other in a heartbeat. It's always my fault.

"I try to make him happy, but I never know the right thing to say. And then when I decide to say nothing at all, he accuses me of being cold and uncaring. When I try to make conversation he thinks I'm mocking him. It always ends the same way."

Cathy feared she knew what that was. She stayed quiet, trying to be present without imposing herself. Wilhelmina was clearly struggling to talk about it, as if each sentence had to be physically pushed out of her. It wasn't like when Cathy suspected something was wrong at Charlotte's house; there was no sign of any Charm controlling the way she spoke. Cathy suspected it was simply hard for Wilhelmina to confess that she was suffering.

"It's so hard to talk about it. I never have. I think…I think I should show you. I'm using a Charm, your Grace. Will you permit me to remove it in your presence?"

Confused, Cathy nodded and watched as Wilhelmina removed a pin from her hair and whispered some words. The breath caught in Cathy's throat as the purpose of the Charm revealed itself.

Wilhelmina's right eye was bloodshot and the skin around it yellowed with faded bruising. One cheek was swollen to twice the size of the other and her jawline varying shades of purple and green. She undid the collar of her dress and several buttons below, showing more bruises on her collarbones.

Cathy saw a flash of her father's stick, of his fist, of the grimace he wore when he hit her and told her it was all her fault for not trying hard enough. She started to shake as she watched Wilhelmina roll back the sleeves of her dress to reveal more bruising and a swollen wrist.

"I…" She looked at Wilhelmina, who was shaking just as much, and realised how hard it had been for her to reveal the abuse. "He does this to you?" Cathy watched her nod. "No matter what he has said to you, this is wrong." She felt a rush in her chest, a sharpening of awareness into the sure knowledge that she had to do something about it. Not only for Wilhelmina but for all the women in Society hiding the abuse she was sure was happening far more than anyone spoke of. "Will you let me protect you?"

"How? He's my husband. He owns me. He can do what he likes to me."

The words chilled Cathy. That was how everyone else saw her in relation to Will, but not how *she* saw herself. Snippets of the conversation with Will about Sir Iris, about the need to slow down, go carefully, protect *his* power in Londinium flickered through her mind, mixing with the sight of Wilhelmina's bruises. The rage roiled within her, inexpressible, useless and exhausting. It was like she was constantly stretched taut between explosive ranting or total emotional implosion.

Now, seated across from another woman who was being abused as she had been, Cathy knew she had to do more than just hold herself together. Wilhelmina had reached out, making Cathy responsible for her future safety. She had to step up.

"No, your husband *can't* do what he likes to you," Cathy said. "I won't let him. I want you to pack a bag and leave with me. Right now."

"But he'll be angry! He'll—"

"I don't care how he feels," Cathy said, standing up and holding out her hand. "I care about you. I know you don't want to make a fuss or make it worse, but I'm not going to let him hurt you ever again. And until I change the law in this city, you'll have to stay as my guest where you will be safe and cared for. And I don't care if he comes banging on our door or who he shouts and screams at. He won't hurt you again."

Wilhelmina looked hopeful, but then she crumpled. "I couldn't possibly stay at your house! It's just not the done thing."

"Neither is speaking in the Court, and you know what I think of that." Frustrated, Cathy took a moment to put herself in Wilhelmina's place. She'd never tasted an independent life, had never had the opportunity to imagine herself as anything but at the mercy of the men in her life. As the previous Marchioness she would have friends, rivals, all manner of people who would devour any gossip about her. No wonder she was afraid. "I want you to come and be my guest," Cathy said. "I won't tell a soul about the reason why, if that's what you want. I might have to tell Will if he starts making a fuss, but only if I must. Okay? I won't humiliate your husband publicly. I'll just keep you safe until I can change things. I promise."

Wilhelmina took her hand and stood. "I'll be as quick as I can."

"Don't tell any of your staff that you intend to stay longer than a few hours and only bring the essentials. I can give you whatever else you need. Tell them you're packing for…"

"Lawn tennis," Wilhelmina said. "It's all the rage, apparently."

The pin was replaced and the Charm restored, hiding her injuries but not the fear and hope that waxed and waned with every moment. Cathy followed her out of the room. "Mrs Lutea-Digitalis will be returning to Lancaster House for lunch, Carter."

"Very good, your Grace."

Cathy was all too aware of the butler standing nearby, listening in. "And afterwards, she's promised to show me how to play lawn tennis." The butler wasn't to know that she had as much interest in lawn tennis as Bertrand Viola had in the rights of women.

Carter's eyebrows twitched with surprise but he said nothing. Wilhelmina returned to them shortly afterwards, holding a small carpetbag. Even though she looked nervous, it was nothing that couldn't be explained by the fact the Duchess had taken an interest in her.

"Ah, ready to go?" Cathy asked her.

"I think so." Wilhelmina looked at the butler. "I'll send word when I'm on my way home. Tell my husband to eat without me if I'm not back."

"Don't look so worried!" Cathy said as they left, deliberately light for the butler's benefit. "I'm sure you'll win."

• • •

When Max finally had a chance to actually look for the address listed as the source of his father's photo on the journalist's computer, he started to suspect it was false. He couldn't visualise it, which was unusual, considering his knowledge of the city. New buildings were being constructed at the edges of the city all the time and he might have missed it. When Kay found him wrestling a large ordnance survey map in the office that morning, she offered to help.

"We can Google it," she said, and then laughed at his lack of response. "Come over here, I'll show you."

He and the gargoyle watched over her shoulders as she tapped the keyboard and then moved the thing he'd been told was a mouse, even though it didn't look much like one at all. She'd made a map of the city appear and with each movement of the mouse, made it zoom into the supposed location of the house in the address.

"Doesn't look like Google knows about anything being there, map-wise."

"Who is this Google?" the gargoyle asked. "How does he know all these maps?"

"Okay, tomorrow, I'm going to give you a tour of the twenty-first century, starting with Google. It's more than just maps. Let me change the view."

She clicked on something and the drawn lines of the map changed into something that looked like an aerial photo of a field right at the edge of the city. He could see a small building tucked near the hedge.

"Looks like a farm, maybe? Not really big enough for a house. Maybe there's a farmhouse further up the hill or something. Google can still be a bit rubbish when it comes to rural locations. This photo may be out of date, too. There's something at the address, at least. Are you following up on the Peonia thing?"

"No. This is something I discovered before that. A journalist has been Charmed to forget something, and I'm investigating why."

"Awesome. That the only address you've got for them?" When Max nodded, she said, "Want me to see if I can find out about the farm? It'll only take a few minutes. It'll give you time to make me a cup of coffee." She grinned at him.

By the time Max hobbled back from the kitchen with the coffee, she was collecting a couple of sheets of paper from the printer. "It used to be a farm, ages ago, but not anymore. The plot of land and the original house is listed in the Doomsday Book—how cool is that? There used to be a forge there too, but it's not in commercial use. That might be what that outhouse was—it's listed as being at the bottom of the hill."

"You learned all this from Mr Google?"

"Max, you are adorable. Sort of. It was in the press a couple of years ago. Housing developers tried to buy the land but the owner refused, apparently. That owner is a Mr Ferran. Is that the name of the person you're hoping to find there?"

Ferran? Max was certain that was one of the names for Lord Iron but it had been a long time since his Chapter briefing on the topic. "No. I'm looking for a Robert Amesbury."

Her fingers flew over the keyboard. "The only reference I can find to a Robert Amesbury in Bath is a police officer in the 1990s who won the George Medal for gallantry. Stopped a kidnapping, according to this. I can't find anything else, and nothing tying him to that address."

Now Max appreciated why Rupert had recruited her. "Thank you. That's very helpful."

"Have you seen Rupert?"

"No."

"He hasn't been in yet? I'll get on with what he told me to do yesterday, then. Wanna take a look?" She did something unfathomable and the screen changed to show another map of Bath, this time the centre and its more familiar streets. "I'm making a map of the Fae-touched properties with a backend database that stores everything we know about who lives there, tied in with the sensors Rupert has already put around the city. When I've finished it, it'll give us real-time information about whether they're in Mundanus and doing anything dodgy."

The gargoyle peered at it. "I thought you did English Lit."

"I did. Everyone knows how to use computers now, though. This isn't uni-level stuff. I did a project similar to this at school and whatever I don't know about, I just Google or look on YouTube. When this is done and tested, we'll roll it out over the whole country and then when something happens, we can direct you to the exact location. Much better than patrolling."

The gargoyle was staring at her. "You're like some sort of wunderkind."

She snorted. "Nah. You're just really out of touch. I'll print out that map for you if you need to go and check that place out."

Less than an hour later, Max stood at a gate at the edge of the field in the printed photograph. Behind him there was a row of new houses, and the field to the left was being churned up by diggers. By the look of things, once the development was finished, the field in front of him would be the only one left in that square mile.

The building shown in the photo was a ramshackle stone outhouse that seemed to grow out of the hillside. He could barely see it through the brambles that had grown between it and the edge of the field. There was smoke curling up from a corner of the roof, however, so he assumed someone was there. He opened the solid metal agricultural gate and trudged through the mud towards the building.

He could hear someone singing as he approached. He didn't recognise the song, but the man's voice was strong and tuneful. As he got closer, the building looked sturdier. The walls were made of stone and although some small stones had tumbled from a few places, the walls were so thick that it didn't make much difference to the structure. Thick bands of iron had been attached as if to keep the rest of the stones in place, and it had a corrugated metal roof that looked like it had been nailed over old slate tiles. The smoke was coming from the top of a pipe protruding from the corner of the roof. There was only one window, tiny and covered in cobwebs, through which a warm yellow light shone into the dank January gloom.

Max went round to the other side of the building and found a door with peeling green paint and a horseshoe nailed to it. Even though the paint had seen better days, the huge iron hinges that also held the wood together were well oiled and rust-free. Max rapped on the door and the singing stopped. When the silence lingered, Max knocked again.

"Go away! Don't want anythin' you're sellin'!" The voice was deep, with a broad, west country accent.

"I'm not selling anything."

"Be off with yer!"

"I need to talk to you about the photos you gave to the journalist at the Bath *Herald*."

"Piss and sawdust! Don't know what you're talkin' about! Bugger orff!"

"Are you an amateur historian? Is that how you pieced it all together?"

"If you don't get orff my land, I'll call the police on yer!"

"But it's not your land, Mr Amesbury."

There was a pause. Max looked at the article Kay had printed out for him. The Robert Amesbury in the photo was dressed in a police uniform with gleaming buttons, smiling with pride as he accepted his medal. The voice coming from inside the outhouse sounded more like an irate farmer. "I'm assuming you're Mr Robert Amesbury. The one who won the George Medal."

There was the sound of a bar scraping across the door from the inside, and then it opened, just a crack. A man in his sixties with a shock of wild white hair and a beard squinted through it. "Who are you?" The accent wasn't so thick this time.

"My name is Max. You gave some photos to a Bath *Herald* journalist and a feature was written about it." He pulled the newspaper page from his coat pocket and showed it to the man.

The man's eyes widened when he saw it. "I didn't think she believed me." He frowned at Max. "I told her to keep me anonymous. Fat lot of good that did. So what do you want?"

"I went to see her about one of the people in the photos. She couldn't remember writing the piece."

He was expecting confusion, but instead the man closed his eyes. "Not again. Wait there." The door closed and was then opened again after a minute or so. "You'd better come in, then."

Max entered to find the interior surprisingly warm. A fire blazed in a large hearth at the far side of the room, a huge set of bellows mounted next to it that had seen better days. There was a stone sink in the corner, a makeshift bed, and a few piles of clothes. The floor was nothing more than uneven flagstones with an old tea crate overturned and set in the middle of the room to form a table. The space was lit by several lanterns hung from hooks in the wooden rafters. On the far wall an old blanket had been hung up. Max suspected it had just been used to cover something up.

Amesbury dropped a wooden beam back into iron brackets on either side of the door to brace it shut and looked at Max, hands in his pockets. He wore several layers of clothes, all with holes and frayed edges, along with an old pair of boots.

"You won the George Medal for preventing a kidnapping. Did that case lead you to uncover the other people who've disappeared over the years, detailed in that article?"

"Now, just wait a moment," Amesbury said. "I've no idea who

you are. 'Max' isn't much to go on. Who sent you? Are you with another paper?"

The broad accent was gone and Max could see it was just an act, maybe to keep the developers away. "I'm an investigator, Mr Amesbury. I've been working on disappearances from the city of Bath and surrounds for many years now. I was hoping we could work together on one of the groups detailed in the article, the trade unionists from the foundry on Walcot Street."

"Long time ago, that one. Would've thought you'd be more interested in something recent."

"I'm very interested in why the journalist forgot about an article she wrote days before. And why that didn't seem surprising to you."

"What sort of things do you investigate? Only disappearances?"

Max shook his head. "Anything unusual."

"One of those Forteans, are you?"

"No. Am I right in thinking that you're Robert Amesbury?"

He nodded. "I suppose you're wondering why I'm living here, seeing as I used to be one of the golden boys on the force."

"I am."

"I'd tell you, but you'd laugh in my face."

"I definitely won't, Mr Amesbury. Were you hoping someone would come forward with more information, or an offer of help?"

"Something like that," Amesbury muttered.

"The article had a result, and that's me. I suspect I can help you, but unless you tell me more, that won't be possible." He waited as Amesbury considered his words. "For what it's worth," Max added, "it isn't the first time I've come across somebody who has forgotten something that just happened to them. And not just a misplaced memory. It's like it never happened at all."

"You can sit on that crate over there, if you need to," Amesbury said, pointing to one partially buried by a pile of clothes. He went to stand near the fire, watching Max closely. "I haven't told anyone this before. Not sure why I'm telling you, truth be told, but you don't seem like the kind of man prone to flights of fancy."

Max pushed off some of the clothes and perched on the tea crate.

"Years back, there was a girl at the university who played the piano. She was tipped to be the next big thing. She'd noticed someone following her around and reported it. No one did much about it. Then she just disappeared one day. She was due to play at a concert. Her parents travelled down from London to see her—they spoke to her that morning and she was excited—and then when the concert was about to start, the manager of the venue had to go out on the stage and tell everyone she hadn't turned up. A couple of hours later I was called in.

"'Course it came out that she'd filed a complaint about someone stalking her, and it was suddenly number-one priority to find her. It was one of those disappearances that was bound to end up on the telly. Kids go missing every day, but the press like the pretty blondes. The fact that she had a musical career ahead of her was exactly the sort of thing those vultures like. So I gets to work and then my boss calls me in to the station. 'Drop it,' he says. 'We know where she is, and she's fine.' I offered to call the parents, he said he'd do it himself. I thought nothing much of it.

"Less than a year later, another music student goes missing. I look into it. This lad was due to play a concert at the same place as the girl. Bit of a flimsy connection, seeing as there aren't that many places to play in the city, but I took it to my boss as an avenue I was going to pursue. 'Drop it,' he tells me. 'We know where he is, and he's fine.'

"I went home that night, and I drank half a bottle of Jack Daniels.

"I told myself it was just a coincidence. I told myself all sorts of crap to make myself feel better. I had a wife then. She wanted me to get promoted. Then a complaint comes in from another student about someone following her back to campus from town. I could see it happening all over again. She was a cellist. I went and interviewed her without telling my boss. I found out the next time she was due to go into town, and I told her I would follow her and see if I could see this stalker.

"I more than saw him. I stopped him taking her."

Amesbury stopped, staring at the floor for a while before jerking towards the pile of logs next to him and heaving another one onto the fire.

"Want me to carry on?"

"Yes."

"You're a good listener. I don't know what that man said to her, but he was like a hypnotist or something. He just went over to her, said something, and she was in this trance. I hit him over the head with my truncheon. Not the way it's supposed to be done, I know, but I didn't want to take any chances."

As Max listened, he recalled the case Amesbury was talking about. It was one of the biggest failures of his Chapter ever documented; they suspected a parasite was involved but never identified who it was.

"I took the bloke into custody. I delivered him to the station myself, where he was checked over by a doctor and put in a cell. I wrote up the paperwork, filed it, and went home."

"That's what you got the medal for?"

"No. That was for something else. No, the bloke I hit over the head disappeared from the cells overnight. No one knew anything about him when I went in the next day. My report was gone. The student decided to change university the very next day. All total bullshit. I wrote it all up and I went to my boss, just stormed in when he was having this meeting, and told him I was filing a complaint against him. Then this man…" Amesbury covered his face with a grimy hand. "Then this man said, 'Is this the one you were telling me about?' and then…then…everything went to shit."

"You somehow forgot it all happened?"

"More than that. I forgot everything. Who I was. Where I lived. When people told me I thought they were lying. I was sectioned. They thought I'd had some sort of psychotic break caused by stress. Stress! I know what stress does to people. It isn't that."

"How long ago was that?"

"Going on for twenty-odd years now. Lost my wife. Lost my

job. Lost my place at the home they put me in when they did all those cutbacks. 'Care in the community,' they called it. I was on the street for a while. Then about three winters back I found this place. It was snowing and I needed somewhere warm. I came inside, put that beam down to keep the door shut, and then…" He shrugged. "Then I got better. Instantly. Like I was my old self again. But I stank and I was older and I had nothing. Nothing except my mind back."

Max nodded. He'd been Charmed and something about this place broke it. The iron on the building, perhaps? It was a working theory, especially given his suspicion about the landowner, one that would need further investigation. "And then what did you do?"

"I won't lie. I cried. A lot. My wife had divorced me over ten years ago, and I didn't even realise. I 'lacked mental capacity.' She lives in Spain now. With some bloke she met on holiday. I tried to persuade her to see me again but she won't. She gave me some money but I don't feel safe anywhere but here. I thought you might be Mr Ferran coming to kick me off his land."

"No. Do you have any theories about what was done to you?"

"Hundreds, but they're all ridiculous." He glanced at the blanket behind him. "I decided to do my own investigation. My old boss is still in the force. Much higher up now. And the disappearances are still happening. I started to make connections and…I thought I might be going too far. I was scared the madness was coming back. I needed to talk it through with someone, someone not in the force. I couldn't find anyone who'd listen. I went to the paper, presented it all like a case. That lady loved it. Said it was compelling and that she'd run it. Now you say she can't remember. She won't be writing the rest of it up, then. I'm the only one who knows what really goes on in this city. And it all goes back over a hundred years. Someone here, some organisation or hidden group or something, doesn't like troublemakers. Those trade unionists were some of the first. Five men disappeared one night and no one ever found out why. Oh, people think they were killed, but no one investigated. Or maybe they tried and were done in like me." Amesbury frowned at him. "You're not giving me anything here. You're a strange one, if you don't mind me saying. I've no idea whether you think I'm mad or not."

"You're not mad. I believe you," Max said. "I need to look into a couple of things that might give you some answers. Can I come back to see you in a couple of days?"

"Yes! You really believe me?" He suddenly looked ten years younger. "But don't tell anyone I'm here. Please."

"I won't. Thank you for your time, Mr Amesbury. I appreciate it."

They shook hands. The joy of being treated with any respect seemed to cancel out any of the usual discomfort caused by Max's lack of expression. He left Amesbury's squat, listened to the beam being dropped back into place behind the door, and then hobbled off. He needed to speak to Rupert about the possibility of recruiting Amesbury, to Petra about whether Mr Ekstrand had ever told her about a Mr Ferran, and to the gargoyle about the way he was wasting time resting his chin on Kay's desk, gazing at her as she worked.

13

The next morning, once everyone in the house was awake and warned about the impending demolitions, Sam took a sledgehammer to the cob wall that Eleanor had shown him the night before. He'd expected her to wait nearby and see what was revealed, but instead she asked if she could use the car and driver for a day trip. Wherever she planned to go, she certainly dressed well for it.

For old mud and straw, the wall was surprisingly tough, but the hours he'd put in at the forge paid off and he was able to gouge a good chunk out of the wall without breaking a sweat. Eleanor's estimate was fairly accurate; it was about a metre thick and there was a space behind it into which he could poke his fingers. After a couple more wallops with the sledgehammer to open the tiny hole up, he struck something metallic.

The strike sent reverberations through him and the house. It felt like he was still vibrating long after the din had stopped. The housekeeper came and asked if everything was all right, and he sent her away with brisk reassurances, his heart pounding with the thrill of discovery. The vague pull he'd felt the night before had strengthened into something stronger, reinvigorating his excavation until he'd made a hole big enough to fit his head and shoulders through.

He grabbed the torch and switched it on before pushing it through the hole ahead of him. Then he climbed in, the wall thick enough to support his torso as he pushed himself through to see what was on the other side.

There was a gap of only a few centimetres between the inner side of the cob and what looked like a slab of iron. When Sam brushed it with his fingertips he knew, on a level deeper than he could ever hope to express, that the first Lord Iron had placed it there, that it was pure iron with only an infinitesimal amount of carbon and something else...manganese, yes, that's what it was. The smith who'd trained him to use the forge told him that iron that pure was made in modern arc furnaces. Sam knew the slab had been there for hundreds and hundreds of years.

He paused. How did he know that? No answer presented itself. He wished Cathy were there to talk it over with him, to spark ideas. Yet again, the pull to go and get her out of that house, away from that life, flared up within him. He pushed it aside as he examined the slab as best he could. It felt mostly smooth but with some imperfections. The torch did little to help; it seemed they were too small to be picked up by the light.

He shuffled back out and realised he was covered in filth. The wall would have to come down. He had to get some help to do it properly. Jim was at the forge today. Hopefully he wouldn't mind helping out. He called Des and cancelled his meetings for the day. Nothing could be more important than this.

· · ·

The tea rooms were pleasant enough, though they were past their best. Will had one of his men check the interior beforehand and had been assured that there were no Charms or anyone from the Great Families present, nor anything to suggest that the place was anything other than it appeared to be. Even though Eleanor was no longer Dame, he wanted to be careful. Unwilling to share the space with mundanes and their screaming children, he'd paid the owner a generous sum to rope off the conservatory section of the establishment, so they could take tea in peace.

He'd dropped Nathaniel off on the outskirts of Oxford, having elected to return him home via mundane means so they could talk about future plans. His brother was all smiles, now the Tulipa problem was resolved. Neither of them had been called back by Sir Iris, and neither had been informed of the outcome of the Patroon meeting. It irritated Will that he hadn't been told—after all, he was the wronged party in their view of events—but Nathaniel seemed to revel in not having to attend to it any more. Of course, he had no affection for Margritte, nor a wife to upset with bad news about her friend and co-conspirator.

The lack of a wife was evidently on Nathaniel's mind. They debated whether he could choose his own now that he was Chancellor and, unsurprisingly, Nathaniel thought he could. After Will waved him off at Oxford Castle, he read some of the letters that had arrived whilst he'd been tangled up in the Tulipa business. The only letter of any real interest was one from Bertrand Viola, telling him that a cousin who'd been abroad for many years had decided to return to Londinium and that he would like to sponsor the cousin into the city, with Will's permission, with a view to him taking his late brother's property. Will noted that the cousin, Harold Persificola-Viola, was unmarried. By the time he'd reached the outskirts of Worcester, he had a plan that could help secure both his and Nathaniel's positions admirably. All he had to do was speak to Eleanor, get what he could from her, and then get back to Londinium via the Nether to make arrangements swiftly.

"William." The voice made him jump. He'd been so caught up in his plans that he'd missed Eleanor's arrival.

"Lady Eleanor," he said, standing to kiss her gloved hand. At least he'd already met her and was expecting her elderly face. It helped that she had left Society before he was born, so he wasn't shocked by her appearance. He had no earlier memories of her to form a comparison. He pulled back her chair for her and saw to her comfort before resuming his own place.

"A lot on your mind, I see," she said, smoothing down her dress. "Only to be expected. Well, these tea rooms have seen better days, but they'll do. Safer than my travelling back to Londinium, I felt."

Will nodded and signalled to a waitress to bring the tea and cake selection he'd already ordered. "Not that we've seen much of the current Dame Iris since your last visit."

Eleanor's wrinkles deepened as she grinned wickedly. "I shall never forget the look on her face. Ah, Cathy dealt a master stroke that day. How is she?"

"Well, thank you. And I trust you are well also?"

"As well as can be expected. You have a fine wife there, William, but one that will cause you no end of problems."

Will frowned. "Is it possible for her to be both?"

"Why, yes, of course! She's loyal, passionate, strong, and sharp as a pin. You just have to find the right way to direct her energies. Like those fine stallions one sees at the races. The ones fast enough to win are the hardest to care for."

"I'm not sure she would appreciate being compared to a horse."

Eleanor laughed again. "I agree. I wish you could have seen her when she came to the asylum, William. She was quite remarkable. Nothing much to look at, but she spoke straight into the hearts of the people there. Not many in our world can do that. As impressive as it was, I imagine you were quite vexed by her actions."

"Not all consequences of her actions that day have been vexing, Lady Eleanor—your freedom being the best example of that."

She beamed at him. "Oh, yes, I see why she's so taken with you. Aren't you simply the most handsome boy? What does Sir Iris make of you?"

Will was still uncertain about how to react to her open compliment. It seemed the Truth Charm was still very much in place, despite her residency with Lord Iron. "He thinks I'm too lenient with my wife, but he's pleased with what I've achieved."

"Yes, all very impressive, so soon after your Grand Tour. This tea is very disappointing. Is that supposed to be a macaroon? Heavens, what in the worlds has happened to Mundanus?" She cast her disapproval over the selection and chose a scone. "Are you too lenient with your wife?"

Will paused, choosing to spread butter on his toasted tea cake as he considered his response. He felt he was being evaluated, but he wasn't sure which standards he was being measured against. "I find myself walking a difficult line between accommodating Cathy's desire for change and keeping my Patroon satisfied. I fear it is impossible to satisfy both of them."

Eleanor tested the scone she'd spread with jam and clotted cream, seemed to find it agreeable enough, and then fixed a keen eye on him. "Who do you feel is more important to keep happy? And tell the truth, now. I can't abide falseness over elevenses. It wreaks havoc with my digestion."

"Sir Iris," Will said. "Without his support, it doesn't matter how happy I've made Cathy. We'd be exiled or worse."

"Been threatening you, has he?" She nodded in response to his acknowledgement. "He does that with all the young bloods, my dear. He has to lick you into shape, just like the Dame does with all the new chicks in the henhouse. I remember when he dressed down your father for something far too inconsequential for me to recall. I could hear him two rooms away." She sighed wistfully.

Will tried to imagine his father in front of that desk and found himself smirking. "Are you satisfied with the arrangements that have been made for you, Lady Eleanor? Cathy seems to think you are safe with Lord Iron, but it's hardly ideal."

"'Satisfied' implies contentment, and I am not content. But these are strange times and one must do one's best. Now, William." She dabbed at the corners of her mouth with her napkin and poured the tea again after seeing a deeper colour emerge from the spout. "Tell me why you asked me to tea."

"To ensure your well-being, Lady Eleanor. I feel as responsible for you as Cathy does."

"And?" Her intense stare reminded him of Sir Iris. "Come now. It's clear you want something else, and I'd wager it's a little titbit of information about my husband, something to help you through these difficult early days when you've come to his attention. It's always a shock, having to go there and answer to him directly instead of having your father take the brunt of the storm and pass on a little rain to you."

Will didn't want to admit to his hope, even though she'd laid it bare before them. "Your well-being is my first priority, Lady Eleanor."

"Of course it is, dear boy. I'm your wild card. You have no idea what to do with me, but you're certain I'll come in useful at some point, much like those lovely boxes that gifts arrive in. Oh, don't look so embarrassed. It may soothe you to know that I knew all this the moment I read your letter. I simply came to meet you to see what you're like. I only saw you so briefly before. I wanted to see if you're as handsome as I recalled. How lucky Cathy is, to have someone as delightful as you to look at for the foreseeable future."

Will suppressed the irritation that he'd wasted an entire morning. Was there nothing he could winkle from her?

"And now you're wondering how to salvage a wasted morning." She reached across the table and patted his hand. "Don't worry, you're not that transparent to everyone. I simply see a lot of myself in you. Now, it may come as a revelation to you, but I still love my husband and I'm unwilling to give you the upper hand over him. I could be a great help to you, William, but I am not in the habit of inconveniencing myself for no return."

"I understand."

"So, in light of that, should you still wish to gain my assistance, you should turn your attention to how you might be able to offer me something I cannot refuse."

"If only all conversations could be so straightforward," Will said, aiming his most disarming smile at her.

"I find it quite refreshing. Now, you're an intelligent boy, and I've told you everything you need to know to deduce the rest. If the tea were better, I'd enjoy another cup with you, as you're far more pleasing to the eye than Lord Iron. But as it's not, I'll bid you good day."

Will stood as she did, allowing himself to puff his chest a little after her last comment. He watched her leave, mentally placing her at the edge of the board. A queen to bring into play, if he could find a way to do so. Until he did, he'd have to content himself with the moves he'd planned on the drive up. It was time to solve some problems, and he knew which pieces to move to do so.

• • •

By the end of the day, most of the cob wall had been wheelbarrowed out of the house and dumped in a huge pile outside the back. The waifs and strays, as Cathy called them, came and chatted at points, entertained by the industry unfolding in front of them, but Sam shooed them away as soon as he saw that there was something on the iron slab that wasn't just a roughened surface. From that point, only he and Jim were allowed in the small hallway, and he got the estate manager to put locks on the doors that gave access to it. He was happy to keep the victims of the Fae and their minions safe, but there was always the possibility that some of them might go back to that world, and the less they saw of anything important, the better.

He had a couple of portable floodlights brought in and elected to finish the demolition once Jim's working day was over. Even though he'd only paused for lunch and comfort breaks, he seemed to have a boundless amount of energy that was constantly replenished every time a few more inches were exposed.

It was about two metres high above floor level, one and a half metres wide, and a metre thick. It was an absurdity in the centre of a house, serving no discernible purpose; it wasn't holding up any of the floor above it nor supporting any other structure. He went down into the cellar and found that it probably went down as far as the foundations of the entire house, as the wall of the cellar ended about a metre from the slab he'd uncovered on the floor above. It felt as if it had always been there, with the house built around it. For all he knew about the first Lord Iron, that might well have been true.

Once he'd brushed it all off, clearing ancient cobwebs and newly created dust from the surface, he sat on one of the stools that had been brought in and stared at the iron.

At first the bumps and grooves didn't make much sense at all. There was no writing or any symbols per se, just seven large bumps and a series of lines that weren't joined to each other, seeming random in the way they curved and wobbled across the iron.

Then he noticed a curve that looked like the Thames, recalled from a time when Leanne had gone through a phase of watching *Eastenders* that he'd endured for the sake of getting half an hour of cuddling on the sofa. Of course, he'd got quite hooked on the stories too, but he'd never admitted it. In the credits, it panned across a map of London and the particular bow in the river around the Isle of Dogs.

He fetched an atlas from Amir's library and soon discovered that most of the lines related to rivers. There were discrepancies, but he knew that the slab was so old, some of the rivers were bound to have been altered by people at some point or other.

One of the seven lumps was near a line he suspected was the river Dee in just the right position to suggest that it was his house. It was only a couple of miles away from a recognisable bend in the river before it curved away to head east into Wales. The other six dots were located all over England, one clearly in North London, and one in a place near enough to the river Avon for him to suspect it was near Bath. Were these Lord Iron's houses? Places of some other significance? Whatever the lumps referred to, he knew this was precious knowledge, something he felt he should know, or perhaps already did but couldn't quite recall. It was like trying to remember all the kids in his class in the first year of primary school, something he once knew but had been lost long ago.

He heard the house phone ring and ignored it, staring at the slab and trying to work out the possible locations of the other lumps. There was a knock on the door between his corridor and the rest of the house.

"Mr Ferran," Des called through the wood, "there's a 'Petra' on the phone for you. She says you told her to call any time."

Sam put the atlas on the floor and hurried through the door to take the phone.

"Petra! Hi! How are you feeling? Is the hotel okay? Do you have everything you need?"

"I'm very comfortable, thank you, and feeling better. I have a question for you, something relating to your being Lord Iron. If you don't mind?"

Sam went back into the corridor to stare at the slab as he talked. "Go ahead."

"You also go by the name of Mr Ferran—the hotel room you arranged for me, for example—and I was wondering if that has something to do with your new role."

"Why do you ask?"

"Max is investigating something relating to the Fae-touched kidnapping people from Bath, and he's come across a man living in a shack on some land that belongs to a Mr Ferran. I thought the coincidence was so strong, I'd ask if you know anything about the property."

Sam didn't like the thought of Max knowing where Petra was, but she must have told him—how else could he have known? He supposed they were friends, though having seen how utterly heartless Max was when it came to helping victims of the Fae, Sam felt that friendship was misplaced. He couldn't deny that Max had uncovered a potential lead for more information regarding his inheritance, though, so he swallowed down his initial urge to hang up and replied instead.

"Mr Ferran is a name I inherited, along with Lord Iron." Sam's eyes drifted towards the line he'd pegged as the river Avon. "So if the land belongs to Mr Ferran, it belongs to me now. Tell me, do you know if this property's north or south of the river?"

He listened as Petra asked the same question of another person who was with her, presumably Max. "It's south. Right on the edge of the city. Max thinks it might be an old forge. It has a waist-high hearth and a set of bellows next to it."

Sam's heart quickened in his chest. The seven lumps on the map represented forges. "Give me the address," he said. "I'll look into it."

14

The ache that had settled into Max's leg was growing painful by the time he reached the shack on Mr Ferran's land late that evening. He'd spent too much time on his feet and needed to rest, but with the prospect of new information on its way from the unlikely Lord Iron, he couldn't yet.

As he hobbled towards the gate by the light of his torch, Max considered how different Petra had seemed at the hotel. She had called him on his mobile phone, asking him to go over and talk to her. Thinking it was about the way Rupert had treated her, or the possibility of her joining the Chapter, he'd agreed. He hadn't expected the story about what had happened with Lord Iron freeing her from a curse.

Max couldn't understand how Ekstrand could have either not known about the Fae magic or had ignored it. Neither seemed possible. Max wondered if he should have noticed something, whether he'd lost his edge since the injury, but he couldn't recall any reason to suspect that Petra was a victim of Fae trickery. Granted, a female professional working so closely with a Sorcerer was unusual, seeing as all of their apprentices were only ever allowed to be male, but she was such a superlative and knowledgeable librarian he thought it was simply a matter of Ekstrand overlooking her sex to benefit from her work.

Petra had said she felt lost. That she didn't belong and that until she understood what had happened to her and where she came from, she couldn't work for Rupert. Max suspected her traumatic experience had also made her distrustful of Sorcerers in general. It was a loss to their budding Chapter, but no one could force her.

She promised to keep in touch after she facilitated the fact-finding exercise in relation to Lord Iron, and he'd left her at the hotel.

Max opened the gate, felt the cold mud seep into his shoes as he misjudged where the worst of the puddle was, and closed the gate behind him. He saw a light in the sky before he heard the drone of the engine and paused, wondering if that was Lord Iron on his way.

As he waited, Max saw an image of his old Chapter House through the gargoyle's eyes as it approached the building hesitantly. He'd decided to send the gargoyle on a fact-finding mission whilst he headed for Mr Amesbury's shack, for efficiency's sake. Max didn't want the sculpture housing his soul to linger too long, no matter how unlikely it was that the Sorceress was still watching that building. It wasn't just the risk, it was also the fact that the sooner Max got the information he was hoping the gargoyle would find there, the sooner he could move toward a prosecution and potentially find the people abducted. Perhaps even his father.

Max knew that the Chapter would have a record of his statement when he was first brought in. He couldn't remember giving it, nor what exactly had happened the night the Arbiter took him, but he knew the procedure and had to assume the same was done for his case. Hoping it would contain some details about what happened to his father, he decided to take the risk of sending the gargoyle into the Chapter whilst he progressed with the investigation in Mundanus. It was more efficient than leaving it to pine for Kay in the empty office.

The engine he'd heard was getting louder, so he decided to stay near the gate as the helicopter crested the hill. It circled a couple of times, shining a large light on the ramshackle building, before heading off. It was too steep for it to land; Max decided to carry on and let Lord Iron catch up.

Lord Iron had been true to his word; he'd looked into the land and the building on it, confirming that it was an old forge owned by his predecessors and passed on to him. Max had taken the opportunity to ask about the foundry on Walcot Street where his father used to work. Lord Iron had come across it in the search for information on the old forge and when Max explained that it was all connected to innocents disappearing from Mundanus, Lord Iron had offered to come down to Bath to pass the information on. Max suspected he also wanted to see the old forge.

Robert Amesbury was opening the door as he arrived, looking up at the sky nervously. "Oh, you again," he said to Max. "Was that a helicopter?"

Max nodded. "Can I come in?"

There was only a brief pause before Robert nodded. "It's too cold to talk on the doorstep."

Max went straight to the hearth when he entered, warming his hands as Robert dropped the beam to hold the door shut.

"Didn't expect to see you so soon," he said. "Got the answers faster than you thought?"

Max nodded. "I'm here to offer you a job," he said. "One that I think you'll find very rewarding."

Robert shook his head. "I can't leave this place for too long. I wouldn't be any use."

"Someone is on the way who can help you with that."

Robert frowned. "I think you might be overstepping the mark."

Max glanced at the blanket, still draped on the back wall. "I can understand why it would appear that way," he said. "But you're an excellent investigator, and you're already involved."

"Involved in what, exactly?"

Max paused, distracted briefly by an image of a door in the Chapter building being opened by the gargoyle, revealing rows and rows of file storage boxes.

"In uncovering the kidnapping of people from the city of Bath. As I said before, I've been conducting my own investigation, and we cover a lot of common ground. I think you would be a very valuable member of the team, but first there's someone you need to meet. Someone who will be able to help you."

Robert had folded his arms, scowling. "Not some bloody psychiatrist? They were useless."

"That's because they didn't know what had been done to you."

"Who, then?"

"Mr Ferran."

Robert paled. "The man who owns this land? He'll evict me! Why did you—"

There was a loud knock on the door, and Robert jolted away from it. "You bloody idiot!" he hissed at Max.

Max went to the door. "There's nothing to worry about, Mr Amesbury." He lifted the beam and opened it, finding a huge man in a suit there, instead of Sam. "Are you Max?" he said in an incredibly deep voice. He looked past him, into the room, taking in Robert and the fire and the general state of the place.

When Max nodded, he pressed his ear, whispered something, and in moments stood aside as Sam came into view.

"Hello, Max," Sam said.

"Mr Ferran," Max said, and tilted his head respectfully. "Thank you for coming."

Max made room for him to come in, leaving the guard to stand outside. Robert's eyes were wide with fear and he shuffled from foot to foot, uncertain of whether to bolt or to brazen it out. With the huge man blocking the doorway, there was nowhere to go. Max closed the door and dropped the beam back into place.

"I'll move out," Amesbury said to Sam. "I just had nowhere else to go. If you could just give me a couple of—"

Sam held up his hand. "I'm not here to throw you out." He looked around the room, taking in the fire and the bellows. He pointed at the crate coffee table. "Is there an anvil under there?"

Robert nodded. "Too heavy to move. I think it's been there since the place was built."

"It's a very old forge," Sam said, brushing the wall with his fingertips. "I had a conversation with Max about this place. And about you. He said you weren't well until you came here. Has he explained why?"

Robert's eyes darted to Max. "Hadn't quite got that far."

"We haven't discussed anything other than the mundane," Max added. "I wasn't sure where to start."

Sam nodded. "Yeah. Understandable. Okay." He looked at Robert. "My name's Sam. And we have something in common."

Robert's eyes tracked up and down Sam's cashmere coat, the smart shoes covered in filth. "That so?"

"We both stumbled across something we shouldn't have. Saw something or heard something that certain people work very hard to keep hidden. It made you into a problem, and they solved it in the only way they can, short of killing you. For me, they took my memory and every time I tried to talk about what happened that night, I started spouting bits of nursery rhymes. Like I was insane or something."

Robert's shoulders dropped and his mouth fell open.

"Sound familiar?" Sam asked, and the older man nodded.

"Since then, life has changed a lot and I know things now that back then, I would never have believed. It was all just this month-long head-fuck, mostly." He took a step closer to Robert. "There are things in this world that we're told aren't real. But they are. And you won't believe us when we start to tell you about it. But it's all true. I know this man"—Sam jerked a thumb at Max. "He's not the easiest bloke to get along with, and his old boss was a total douchebag, but he works hard to keep people safe and that's why I'm here. He wants to help you. I do too."

Robert stared at the floor, unable to sustain the eye contact. "I lost everything."

"That's what they do," Sam said softly. "They destroy lives and they don't give a shit about anyone. Max told me you feel safe here, but that when you go out for anything longer than a short period of time, you don't. That right?"

Robert nodded. "It feels like that fog comes back when I go too far. I get the local shop to deliver food, and I try not to go out unless I really have to."

"You feel safe here because…" Sam paused, looked at Max. "You gonna tell him or should I?"

"It's aliens, isn't it?" Robert said.

Sam laughed. "It's not aliens."

"You were put under a curse," Max said.

"A curse? What, like a witch?"

"Sort of," Sam said. "Look, there's no way to make this sound anything but stupid. Since I was one of their victims, my circumstances have changed. I break that magic now. This place was built by…one of my predecessors, and I think it's strong enough to keep the curse at bay. But when you leave it, it comes back. I reckon you still don't feel all that great, even when you're here."

Robert was frowning at the crate. "I had every bloody diagnosis under the sun. None of them were right, so I'll give you the benefit of the doubt."

"Better than that," Sam said, taking another step forwards. "I can break their curse on you." He held out his hand. "Just shake my hand."

Robert snorted. "This is…"

"Stupid? Crazy?" Sam asked. "Yeah. I didn't believe any of it either. Till it fucked my life up. Just shake my hand. If you don't feel any different, you can call me the crazy one and I'll leave."

Robert looked at Sam's hand, up at his face, then back at his hand. Then he shook it, vigorously, as if once he'd made the decision, he was going to put everything into it.

He gasped like he'd just been underwater and was overdue coming up for air. Shocked, he grasped Sam's hand with his other one, pumping it up and down before lurching forwards and wrapping his arms around him in a bear hug. "It's gone!" he said before his voice gave way to a shuddering sob.

Sam clapped him on the back, practically holding him up, and grinned at Max over the man's shoulder. Max looked away, focusing instead on an image of a file that had been plucked out by the gargoyle. "Maximilian—né Matthew Shaw" was written at the top.

Max had forgotten his first name, the one given to him by his parents. Maximilian was the name given to him by the Chapter Master when he passed the trials to qualify as Arbiter, the same day the chain was put around his neck. He wanted the gargoyle to flip through the pages to the witness report and case summary, but for some reason it wanted to read every sentence. Max looked back at Amesbury and Sam.

Amesbury was sitting on the crate, looking shocked as Sam crouched in front of him, hand on his shoulder, talking to him softly. Eventually Amesbury blinked a few times and twisted round to look at Max. "Tell me about this job."

"I think the person who did this to you is involved in the disappearances, and it's my job to find out who that is so they can be prosecuted."

"No judge is going to believe any of this. Where's the evidence, the—"

"It won't be tried in a mundane court," Max said. "The people I police aren't bound by mundane laws. You need to be fully debriefed, and there's a lot to explain, but it boils down to this: My job is making sure that what happened to you never happens to anyone else. We failed you, and the people taken, but the one responsible can still be stopped. Do you want to help me find him?"

"Yes."

"And when it's done, do you want to help me to stop anything like it happening to other innocents?"

"Christ, yes!"

Max nodded. "That's good enough for me."

"Do you have anywhere to go?" Sam asked, and when Amesbury shook his head, he said, "I'll sort that out. Max, I have a file for you on the foundry you asked me about."

"The one in Walcot Street?" Amesbury asked, assuming correctly that the photo and information he'd supplied for the newspaper article had something to do with it. Max nodded.

"It used to belong to my predecessor," Sam said. "There's some notes inside it about trouble they had with people going missing after they declared their intention to join a union. Amir got involved when people started accusing the foreman of bumping off troublemakers. He worked out it wasn't that at all. It all came to a head one night and he intervened personally. Very personally."

Max had a flash of the witness statement through the gargoyle's eyes. "He injured a man who was leading more men away from the foundry."

Sam nodded. "Amir slashed his right arm with a sword. I reckon it was one of…" He glanced at Amesbury. "One of the people like Cathy's family. He seemed powerful but he was definitely a man."

Max stayed silent. The haziest of memories was returning, of a cold night hunkered down in an alleyway, hoping to see his father, who hadn't come home the previous night. He could remember a finely dressed gentleman drawing a sword and another man in the shadows. Shouting. Nothing more. But he couldn't be certain if it was a memory or a construct formed by the gargoyle reading his statement, given when he was ten years old.

"After that night," Sam said, "Amir put up some pure iron gates around the foundry and spent a few nights in a place nearby. The dodgy bloke never came back, and it all settled down again. They never did find the missing staff but I reckon they weren't killed. I reckon they were taken to…" Another glance at Amesbury. "You know."

Max nodded, briefly distracted by a note in the case summary. *Iris activity detected outside of foundry.* Then another toward the end. *No blood present. No evidence that Iron injured a third party. Unreliable witness. Request from Lord Iron to leave foundry alone. Insufficient evidence to pursue further.*

Max saw the file being swiped off the table by a stone paw. The gargoyle was angry. And rightly so. It was poor work. Probably one of the old Arbiters reaching the end of their usefulness. When would that happen to him?

"Max?"

Sam was looking at him expectantly.

"I'm sorry, could you repeat that?"

"I suggested we get Mr Amesbury cleaned up, and I can get that file for you, okay?"

Max nodded. "Yes. Thank you for your assistance, Mr Ferran."

• • •

The worst thing about Catherine being Duchess was that Elizabeth knew she would do a much better job and she'd never get the chance. Her elder sister was literally the worst person in the world for the role and yet it had just fallen into her lap, with no effort at all. Typical. It was so unfair.

What really galled Elizabeth was that Catherine never had to try for anything. All those stupid French verbs just seemed to stick in her head, like the Latin and all the silly history dates. No matter how hard Elizabeth had tried (and she liked to think she worked very hard in the schoolroom), that sort of thing just befuddled her. Catherine would always look at her like she was some sort of donkey as she struggled through the lessons.

Then when it came to things Elizabeth found easy, like singing and dancing and making the grownups smile, Catherine didn't care at all. More than that—Catherine ridiculed her for enjoying them. It made Elizabeth want to scream, then and now!

Being Duchess didn't suit Catherine at all. She always looked worried and distracted and if it weren't for the staff shooing her through the day, she'd be late for everything. Elizabeth knew that if *she* were Duchess, Londinium would be a much more exciting place. She'd have parties at least five nights a week and a lawn tennis tournament and a minimum of three balls a month, each with its own theme. Londinium had such grand buildings, and she could fill them with sprites and beautiful things and people and her stinky aunt would simply die of jealousy. She could just imagine the Censor in a swoon, bemoaning the fact that Londinium was the most fashionable place to be since *Elizabeth* became Duchess and if only she hadn't been so cruel to her. Yes, the Censor would have to say that—with an audience around her—before dying. Hopefully with horrible blotches all over her face so that everyone remembered her like that.

Of course, in her fantasy, Elizabeth the Duchess was married to Nathaniel, as she should have been. He was so tall and dashing. They would have been a perfect match. She would have settled for William—she'd been forced to admit to herself that he was far more handsome than she remembered, especially since becoming Duke of Londinium—but no. Catherine had ruined all of that too.

Thanks to her sister, Elizabeth was left adrift, waiting and waiting and waiting when suitors should have been beating down the door to take her to tea. She should have amassed a collection of at least a dozen full dance cards since she'd arrived, and there hadn't been one ball. Not one! What was her sister doing? What could be more important than making sure her darling baby sister was married to the best eligible bachelor in the city?

What made everything harder was the fact that she had no insider knowledge. In Aquae Sulis she knew exactly whom to pursue—without looking like she cared about them at all, of course—and whom to avoid. In Londinium she had only her general knowledge of the Great Families to guide her. She knew to avoid the Buttercups and Wisterias without exception and that the Violas were the wealthiest. But whether there were any eligible Violas was a mystery to her. Catherine should have told her all of this the day she arrived! But no, she was always busy, either locked up in her boring library or her boring study, writing boring letters. She'd just watched her bring home the most boring-looking woman ever and they'd gone to the guest wing and had all sorts of private conversations and Catherine hadn't thought of her once. Not once. No introduction, no swift briefing on whether that boring woman happened to have a dashing son or handsome brother. She could scream.

Elizabeth finished her latest letter of complaint to her mother—not that it seemed to do anything—and sent it off with a Letterboxer Charm, rather than handing it to one of the staff to send. They all seemed to like her sister far too much to be reliable. It was utterly baffling why they looked at her with such fondness. Perhaps it was Lord Poppy's doing.

She called the lady's maid and told her to arrange her hair in a different style because she was so bored of the current one she could cry. The maid did a passable job with a few touches that impressed Elizabeth. Not that she gave any of that away; it was best to keep the staff on their toes by expressing mild dissatisfaction so they tried harder the next time.

Another half an hour was idled away by penning a letter to Cecilia Peonia, whom she missed dreadfully, ending with a promise to ask the Duke of Londinium if Cecilia could come to stay with her. Elizabeth beamed at herself in the dressing table mirror. A stroke of genius. If no one else was willing to spend time with her, they couldn't refuse her a visit from her best friend.

Elizabeth practised her smiles in the mirror and her coquettish glances over her fan. She couldn't let her skills diminish during this social famine. Satisfied that she could easily out-charm practically every single woman in Albion, she decided to hunt her sister down. Perhaps if she tormented her enough, Catherine would relent and hold a ball, just for some peace and quiet. It always worked with Daddy.

When Elizabeth emerged from her bedroom, she could hear the clomping of her sister's feet coming up the stairs. She sounded like an elephant. How William could bear her, Elizabeth had no idea. No wonder he was never at home.

Planning to pounce on her as she headed down the hallway, Elizabeth waited tucked around the corner. Surprise was always preferable. Catherine couldn't think very quickly when she was caught off guard and might agree to something if she was flustered.

But then the footsteps went the other way. Elizabeth peered round the corner to see Catherine heading towards the other wing, the one containing her bedroom. Perhaps she had a headache and was going to lie down. Elizabeth grinned. Even better.

Elizabeth followed, her dainty feet—the smallest and prettiest in Aquae Sulis—making no sound at all. Catherine went past her bedroom and headed towards the green baize door at the end of the corridor, the one leading to the nursery wing. Whatever for?

Once Catherine had gone through, Elizabeth picked up her skirts and scurried over to it as fast as she could. She opened the door, heard nothing in the Nether wing, and then closed it again. Catherine must have gone into Mundanus.

Elizabeth bit her lip, wondering whether a few minutes of ageing would be worth finding out whatever Catherine was up to. She tried to imagine her sister sitting in a newly decorated nursery, stroking the crib, wishing for a baby. Elizabeth was sure that was what took up at least half of the time for most new brides. But it just didn't fit with Catherine. She covered her mouth as a new possibility occurred to her. Perhaps Catherine was planning to run away again! Elizabeth rested her hand over her heart as she imagined the thrill of catching her sister doing something despicable. She could tell William, and he'd be so grateful he'd find her the most wonderful husband. He would punish Catherine, too. Nothing but good could come of it. Elizabeth whispered the usual Charm and stepped through.

It was colder and fresher on the other side, and Elizabeth immediately regretted going through. If she didn't find Catherine packing a bag within thirty seconds she'd go back to the Nether.

Elizabeth could hear those clomping feet pacing a room to the left. It was labelled "The school room," and the door was still open. She tiptoed closer, managing to catch a glimpse of brightly coloured letters pinned to the wall. They'd already had the room decorated? Was Catherine pregnant or just planning a long way ahead? Neither seemed plausible.

"Ah, Max, great," Catherine said, and Elizabeth shrank against the wall, holding her breath. She didn't realise someone else was there.

Her heart began to pound. Max? Catherine was having an affair! She clamped her palm over her mouth to stop the delighted squeal erupting from it.

"How are you? Yeah. Petra gave it to me. I hope you don't mind me calling."

Calling? Was she on a telephone? Elizabeth had seen the butler using one in the mundane wing at home whilst she was growing up. Using a telephone was strictly forbidden. At least, it had been in their home when they were children. Her excitement ebbed. It wasn't nearly as exciting as her sister sneaking off for a lovers' tryst, but she still listened in, just to be sure it was a lover on the other end of the line.

"Listen, I wanted to ask you about the Agency. I'm not their favourite person in the world, and I'm going to make it worse soon. I thought Ekstrand was in charge of it—I think that's what you said when we went to Green Dale—but Petra said he was dead and…"

A pause. Who was Ekstrand? Why was she talking about the Agency and not declaring her forbidden love? Urgh, Catherine couldn't do anything right.

"No, don't worry, I'm not going to tell a soul. Why would I do that?"

Elizabeth perked up. A secret, then.

"I know he's my uncle, but I'm not a complete arsehole, Max. I know what they'd do if they knew. It'd be bloody chaos. Will there be a replacement? I don't know how the whole Sorcerer inheritance thing works."

A Sorcerer had died? That was Ekstrand? And why would their uncle be mentioned? He was Master of Ceremonies, he had nothing to do with—oh! She remembered the ball the night the Rosas fell. How her uncle had been returned by the terrifying Sorcerer. Was that Ekstrand? No wonder her uncle would want to know if he had died.

"That's good. No, I won't say anything to a soul. And has this new one taken over the Agency? He doesn't? Oh, right. Okay. I only ask because I want to know if you have any sway with the Agency, now Ekstrand isn't in charge of it. Shit. I'll have to think of something else, then. How's the gargoyle?"

Gargoyle? Was Catherine referring to a particularly ugly mutual friend, or a project of some sort?

"Cool. Well, take care of yourself, okay? And good luck in Bath. I hope your new boss isn't as much of a dick as Ekstrand was. I will. Bye."

There was a strange beep, and then it sounded like Catherine was heading out of the schoolroom. Elizabeth made it to the green baize door in three balletic leaps and dashed through it, not pausing once until she was back in her bedroom.

Elizabeth flapped her hands with excitement. A Sorcerer had died and this meant that no one was looking after the Agency. What was the Agency? Were those the people who managed the staff? Elizabeth knew she had stumbled upon an important secret, even if she didn't fully understand all the implications.

She had to make the first important choice that all good secrets gave: whether to use it to do the most harm as possible, or to achieve the most gain.

Sometimes, on the rarest of occasions, a terrible secret could do both. That had only happened for her the once, a few years ago, when she discovered that their governess, Miss Rainer, had been secretly giving Catherine books she shouldn't read. Elizabeth had held onto that secret for weeks, trying to work out the best way to use it. Should she blackmail the governess? Her sister? Should she steal the books and give them to someone else who would want them and give her better things in return?

In the end, the most perfect use of the secret had revealed itself. Miss Rainer had been particularly mean to her that week— Catherine was always her favourite—and said that if she didn't learn how to conjugate all the verbs in her French book, she wouldn't be able to sing at a recital for all of the Aquae Sulis children. Elizabeth knew there was no way she'd remember all the silly endings to those words and had blazed with the injustice of it. She knew that her beautiful voice would impress everyone and make her the darling of the show and to have that stuffy, boring woman who taught them about the stuffiest, most boring things deny her the opportunity was simply unthinkable. So Elizabeth had waited for the perfect moment over dinner, just when her father was particularly sour-tempered and irritated with Catherine, and let the secret fall from her lips.

Elizabeth smiled at the memory of her father's face. Catherine had kicked her repeatedly under the table, but she didn't stop. After talking about the books in the most innocent way she could, Elizabeth described the lessons they'd had, mentioning things that had excited Catherine the most, like "Peterloo," as she was certain those were the lessons that would make her father angry since he and Catherine were the exact opposites of each other. She'd watched with glee as her father went to Catherine's room and used a Charm to reveal all the hidden books. She did feel the slightest pang of guilt when Catherine sobbed to see them being burnt on the fire, and when Father started to beat her until she screamed the nursery wing down. But she brought it on herself—and besides, when Elizabeth heard that the awful governess was going to be replaced right away and that her recital appearance was no longer under threat, there was no room for anything but joy.

This secret about the dead Sorcerer was trickier to exploit, being slightly confusing, so she decided to work out who would like to know about it the most and how useful that could be to her. The only people she could think of were her uncle, who was most definitely not her favourite person in the world, and William. Surely he would want to know that his wife was talking to a gentleman on a telephone without his knowledge? And William had been tangled up in the Rosa downfall, so he would probably be very interested to hear anything about that scary Sorcerer. But what he was probably most interested in was the fact that Catherine was planning to do something that would upset the Agency. He would be so grateful for the warning. Grateful enough to find her a wonderful, rich husband.

Yes, Elizabeth thought, going to the window to look down on the gardens. Her mean sister would get into the most appalling trouble whilst she gained favour with the Duke of Londinium. That would do nicely.

15

Stopping off at the Tower instead of going straight home had been a mistake, Will thought. So many people wanted to talk to him, most of them men who were concerned about the Ladies' Court. Most of the conversations boiled down to clumsy fact-finding attempts, of varying subtlety, to discover how they'd be looked upon if they kept their wives at home that night.

Will had done his best to allay their fears, knowing that if Cathy had heard only a fraction of what they'd said she'd be threatening to burn down the entire city. While he wasn't as old-fashioned as many of them, he could understand their fears. They were probably terrified that their wives would attend one Ladies' Court and come back home speaking like Cathy, challenging their authority. By the time Mr Lutea-Digitalis came through his door, he was hungry, tired, and just wanted to get it over with as quickly as possible.

"I need to talk to you about a matter of some delicacy," Digitalis had begun, and Will had sighed inwardly.

"You have my ear, Mr Digitalis."

"I don't quite know how to say this, your Grace, but…but it seems that your wife has decided to steal mine."

Will half laughed, he was so surprised. "I beg your pardon?"

"I went home this afternoon after visiting a friend and was told that the Duchess took my wife back to Lancaster House after a visit. I was delighted. There was talk of lawn tennis or something or other. The hours passed, I ate dinner alone, somewhat disappointed that my wife had failed to send a message of apology, and then it grew late."

Will glanced at the grandfather clock in the corner. It was half past ten. "And your wife has still not returned home?" Thoughts of highwaymen made his stomach clench. If a woman travelling alone had been attacked, it would be—

"She's still at Lancaster House, your Grace. I received a message from the Duchess stating that my wife was going to stay the night. When I enquired whether she was unwell—I could think of no other explanation—I received this message." He handed a piece of letter paper to Will, recognisably from the Duchess's desk.

Mrs Lutea-Digitalis will be staying with me at Lancaster House for the foreseeable future, sir. I suggest you consider why I might believe that to be a necessity.
Catherine Reticulata-Iris
Duchess of Londinium

"Forgive me, your Grace, but I have no idea why the Duchess would say this. I didn't know what to do, other than seek your counsel."

Will folded the piece of paper and kept hold of it. "I have not been at home today," he said, struggling to manage his anger and embarrassment. "I shall make enquiries upon my return and send word to you in the morning. I'm sure it's a simple misunderstanding that will be easily resolved."

Digitalis made a rather pathetic attempt at a smile after realising his Duke had no intention of returning the evidence of the Duchess's interference. "Thank you, your Grace. I shall not mention this to anyone else, of course."

"And you can trust my discretion," Will said, coming round his desk to shake the poor man's hand. "Don't worry, all will be well."

Will kept up the reassuring smile until he was alone again. He was just about to tell the page outside his door that he was returning home for the night when there was another knock.

He sighed. What more chaos had Cathy wrought? "Come in."

Tom entered, looking grave, even for him. "Your Grace, apologies for the lateness of the hour, but I feel you should know about an investigation I've started, one involving seditious material being distributed throughout Albion."

"Does it directly challenge my authority?"

"Not directly, your Grace, but it's most—"

"I trust you to handle it, Tom." As Marquis of Westminster, it was one of his primary tasks, after all.

"I've been unable to trace the source using magical means," Tom said. "I need to extend the investigation into Mundanus. Would you be able to provide—"

"Whatever you need is at your disposal," Will said. "If you need men, arrange it with the Head Yeoman. Just give me a report when it's all done."

Tom looked like he wanted to say more about it, but could sense Will's desire to leave. He bowed. "Thank you, your Grace. Good night."

After Tom left, Will informed the page of his departure, pulled the cloth off the cheval mirror that was positioned behind a screen in the corner, and whispered the appropriate Charm.

Stepping out into his study at home, he fought to keep his temper in check, Cathy's letter to Digitalis crushed in his fist. He pulled the cord next to the fire, and Morgan arrived very quickly.

"I'm sorry the fire isn't lit, your Grace, I didn't—"

"Is Mrs Lutea-Digitalis currently a guest here?"

"Yes, your Grace."

"Would you be kind enough to find my wife and tell her to come to see me?"

"Yes, your Grace. Would you like me to light the fire?"

"That won't be necessary." Seconds after Morgan left there was a rather timid knock on the door. Had Cathy been waiting down the hallway for a sign of his return? "Come in."

Elizabeth entered, all smiles. "Good evening, William."

"Oh. This isn't a good time, Elizabeth."

Her pout was carefully constructed to convey disappointment without too much peevishness. "But there's something very important I need to talk to you about."

"It will have to wait until the morning. I have serious matters to attend to."

"But this is a serious matter too."

Will gave her a glare he'd learned from his father. "Tomorrow, Elizabeth. I bid you good night."

Defeated, she gave a small curtsy and left.

He had enough time to unlock the tantalus and pour himself a brandy before there was a second knock. "Come in."

Cathy entered and he could tell from the wary look on her face that she expected trouble. "You're back."

He held up the crumpled letter and her cheeks reddened. "I've just had a very confused and upset man in my study at the Tower come to ask me why my wife won't let his return home."

"Don't get angry, Will, you don't—"

"It's a bit bloody late for that! Why do you keep doing this to me? I think everything is fine, and then I go out for the day and come back to discover you've stormed in somewhere and removed people from their homes and I'm left to deal with the consequences."

"Oh, don't be so stroppy! You're making it sound like I've done that loads of times and it's only been twice. I haven't 'stormed in' anywhere and I haven't removed people from their homes. I freed them from a dodgy asylum and gave sanctuary to a woman in need. Don't make it sound like I'm some sort of firebrand that you have to—"

"You have written a letter to a man telling him his own wife cannot come home and implying—in a rather brutal manner—that he may be responsible for that! What possessed you?"

"He is responsible!"

Will tossed the letter onto his desk. "He has no idea why you'd say such a thing."

"Bollocks!"

Will closed his eyes, pinching the skin above his nose to try and fend off the headache. "Do you have any appreciation of how far you have overstepped the mark?"

"What mark is that? The one arbitrarily drawn by the men of Society to stop us doing anything other than pleasing you?"

Will groaned. "Oh, God, Cathy. Don't bring your opinions on the patriarchy into this."

"Why the fuck not? This is exactly what the patriarchy does! You haven't once asked me why I thought it necessary—you're more worried about a letter upsetting some man-child than the woman I'm trying to protect. I didn't go to their house for fun, Will! She asked for help and she showed me what he does to her."

Will folded his arms, struggling to think of a reason why he shouldn't just go and find the Digitalis wife and take her home, rather than fighting with Cathy. Then her final words seeped through the anger. "What does he do?"

"He beats her black and blue. She's terrified of him. Can you imagine how hard it was for her to show me? She wears a Charmed hairpin to hide it all. It's…" Her voice cracked. "It's awful."

He saw the tears in her eyes and it all made sense. He recalled the soirée at the Peonias' in Aquae Sulis and the moment he saw the bruising on her arms and shoulders. "So you rescued her."

"I couldn't leave her there! What would you want me to do— see that bruising and her black eye and just say, 'Oh dear, well, that's such bad luck. I can't possibly do anything to help as it would upset your husband. See you at the Ladies' Court'?!"

The sarcasm set Will's teeth on edge. There was passionate and there was disrespectful. "You could have come to me. Made me aware of the problem, rather than being the bull in the proverbial china shop."

Cathy's hands were on her hips now, strands of hair fallen away from the neat arrangement pinned at the back of her head. "And what would you have done? Had a quiet word with him over billiards? 'Gosh, I don't want to overstep the mark, dear boy, but could you possibly stop beating the shit out of your wife? There's a good fellow.' Yeah, like that would have done anything."

"There's never any middle ground with you, is there, Cathy? No quiet way, no alternative solution that keeps everyone calm and—"

"And the men in control. No. I've lived most of my life in that middle ground, being beaten behind closed doors. No one said anything. No one stopped it happening. How can I be one of them? How can I have this supposed power as Duchess and do fuck all with it? What is the fucking point of us, Will?"

"Please don't talk like that."

"She's been used as his punchbag for over a hundred years. His first wife died from a 'fall down the stairs.' Oh, come on, Will! Fuck what Society thinks should happen here! As far as the old boys' club is concerned everything is fine as long as no one makes a fuss. But it's only fine for them. There's no one else to help her, no one to stop it from happening, no marriage to take her away. I did the only thing I could. I don't give a fuck if Mr Digitalis is upset because his wife hasn't come home. On what fucking planet is that more important than her being able to sleep tonight without being afraid?"

Cathy sagged, the rant over, and went to rest against the back of the sofa. Sobered, Will looked at her, at how tired she looked, how the rage seemed to crash through her like a tornado he saw tear through a cornfield in America, leaving her disheveled in its wake. "You know I can't bear a lady to be hurt," he said quietly, approaching her. "When I saw what your father had done to you, I wanted to take you away then and there, put you somewhere safe."

She watched him get closer, arms wrapped around herself. "But you didn't. You put Society first. You cared more about what my father would say to your father."

He stopped. "I moved the date of the marriage. I didn't just forget about it!"

"My point is," she said quietly, "you stayed within the rules. The rules that suit men. My father could have beaten me to death between that night and our marriage date, for all you knew."

"This is all academic now," he said, irritated.

"Well, it isn't for Wilhelmina. This is her life. And her safety. And her right to live without fear. All I did was put her first. That's why he can't stand it, and why it frightens you. It's breaking the rule you all defend the most: that men are more valuable than women."

Will closed the distance between them, drawn by the nobility in her eyes. No one else could make him want to shout with rage and hold them close in the same moment. She enraged him, and yet he couldn't help but admire her. She was bold and fearless in a way he could never be. He wrapped his arms around her. "You drive me insane," he whispered in her ear. "You are so infuriating and so…" He gave up trying to find the words and kissed her instead. He wanted to claim her, possess her and take her fire into himself. That passion of hers just needed to be redirected, as Eleanor had said.

She didn't respond at first, then slowly her head tilted and she reciprocated the kiss, sliding her arms out from between them so he could press his hips against her. He felt her arms circle him, her hands slide across his back as she closed the embrace.

"No, wait a minute," she whispered after reclaiming her lips. "We need to sort this out."

"I'll work it out, leave it to me," he whispered between tiny kisses on her cheek, then down her neck.

"No, Will, we need to change the law."

"Tomorrow," he said, weaving his fingers into her hair to hold her closer as he nuzzled her neck. "We'll talk about it tomorrow, I promise. It's late." There was no way the law could be changed without the Patroons destroying him. It was too ridiculous to contemplate. He'd have a few words with Digitalis, frighten him into committing to treating his wife better. He'd obey, knowing the Duke was watching over his wife, and she would be safe and Cathy would calm down again.

"But—"

He kissed the words away. "I want you," he said, letting her see the lust in his eyes. "I don't want to talk about anything, I just want to be with you."

Twisted in his grip, the elegant braiding of her hair finally gave way and it tumbled around her face. He could see her battling to stay rooted in their argument but also how she wanted him, so he redoubled his efforts, pressing her against the sofa as—

A piercing scream filled the house, making both of them jump and break apart. His first thought was of Sophia, but she would be asleep in the mundane nursery wing.

"Elizabeth!" Cathy said, and headed for the door.

Will grabbed a sword from its mount on the wall and dashed after Cathy, who was already opening the door. "No, Cathy!" he shouted, and pulled her back, moving her behind him as he drew his sword. He could see Carter running ahead as the scream died away and melted into crying.

It was coming from the main entrance hall. All over the house there was the sound of staff rushing to help. He could hear Morgan shouting at them to stay back.

"Miss Papaver?" he heard Carter say and then gasp. By the time Will emerged into the hall himself, Elizabeth was clinging to Carter, sobbing.

Will followed Carter's horrified eyes to a large glass case standing in the middle of the tiled floor. Its edges were contained in an elaborately decorated gilded frame, and there was a pool of blue silk around it that looked like it had slipped off the case. But it was what was inside that made him stop and hold a hand back to keep Cathy in the hallway.

"No, stay there," he said quietly. "Carter, take Miss Papaver to her room. Morgan, take her some sweet tea and a hot water bottle."

Carter picked up Elizabeth, who was hysterical, and carried her up the stairs as Morgan hurried off, ashen.

"What is it?" Cathy said, but he had no words, so he just held up his palm again, wanting her to stay back.

Will approached the case, letting the sword drop to the floor, forcing himself to look at the woman inside the case. She was standing, rigid as a mannequin and posed as if someone had just leapt out from around a corner in front of her and yelled *Boo!*, her hands both held level with her shoulders, mouth agape. The dress was a dark blue and in a style that was familiar but he couldn't place it. Her face was hidden by the glare of sprite light against the glass.

As he got closer and the reflected light shifted, he could make out her face and he stopped, a chill running through him. It was

Dame Iris, but not as he remembered her when she'd last visited. Instead of her beautiful, youthful face, she had that of an ancient corpse, desiccated and grey-skinned, with hollow cheeks and straw-like hair. But her eyes still looked moist in their sockets, and as he stared, they moved to look at him.

He yelled and jumped back, every hair on his body standing on end. Cathy rushed in, saw the case, and stopped as if Dolled by a Charm.

"Cathy," he said, rushing over to her, hoping to turn her away before she saw the Dame's face, but it was too late. All of the colour drained from Cathy's lips as the Dame fixed her dreadful stare on her.

Then the Dame's eyes dimmed somehow, glazing and losing their power, and her body crumbled to dust, as if time ran differently inside of the case. Only then did Will notice the fleur-de-lis motif running through the gilded decorations.

Cathy started shaking violently. He wrapped an arm around her and turned her away from the case, as she seemed incapable of doing it herself. "Oh my God," she whispered, again and again. "Oh my God."

"Come on," he said, steering her back down the hallway, desperate to get her away from it as much as himself. He was shivering too, he realised, and remembered the brandy in his study. "It's over, you're all right, come on."

"It's not over," she stammered. "Don't you see? It was a warning. She disappointed him, so Lord Iris did that to her. It couldn't have been anyone else."

He nodded, squeezing her tighter against him. "He won't do that to you."

She said nothing, but he could tell he was doing little to comfort her. What could he say to soften the impact of such a horrific demonstration of power?

He sat her on the sofa in his study, lit the fire himself, and poured her a brandy. She took the glass when he offered it to her but just held it, as if the notion of actually drinking the brandy was beyond her. She was in shock. He covered her with a blanket that had been left draped over another chair and downed his drink, pouring another with a shaking hand. Did Sir Iris know that his wife was dead? Yes, he must, just as he had known when Cathy was being attacked.

And Cathy was right; it was a warning. The last time Dame Iris had been in their house she'd come with a potion that Cathy had smashed, and she had been outmanoeuvred. This was the final warning, after several reminders of what Iris had wanted from them since their wedding. Whether Cathy wanted it or not, they had to conceive a child soon, otherwise the same would be done to her, and he simply couldn't bear the thought of it. He would secure the appropriate Charms from Tate when he picked up the choker. With the Poppy magic broken and their patron satisfied, he could keep her safe.

Would Sir Iris be distressed by the death of his wife, or the fact that he'd been unable to protect her, despite being Patroon? Will found it hard to imagine the old hawk being moved to tears, even now.

Then Will realised that a queen had been removed from the board. He had another one, waiting. What had been a grotesque warning for Cathy could actually be an opportunity for him.

"Don't worry, my love," he said softly, bending down to kiss her hair. "I'll do everything in my power to keep you safe."

16

As excited as he was to have discovered another of the first Lord Iron's forges on the edge of Bath, and to confirm the theory that the seven lumps on the slab of iron mapped out the locations of six others, Sam couldn't put everything else off forever.

Eleanor had told him he needed a project, something grand to fulfil him. One idea was starting to form, still too nebulous to put into action, but one he had been brewing at the back of his mind following the night he had met Max and Robert Amesbury at the old forge.

Sam wanted to protect people from the Fae. When he lifted the curse from that man and saw the overwhelming relief and gratitude in his eyes, Sam felt happier than he had in a long time. It was the same when he'd broken the curse on Cathy's old teacher, and it felt right on a deep level, like it was what he was made to do. He had all sorts of fanciful notions about expanding the number of buildings protected from their magic, perhaps even setting up protective barriers around public spaces. What he really wanted to do was find a way to give a place the same quality that he had: the ability to break their magic. The buildings he owned that worked as a block didn't go far enough; they could only stop the Fae entering or magic finding someone inside, and besides, people still had to go out.

He'd tasked Des with hunting through Amir's files, looking for anything that might have been passed on to him from the other Lord Irons, but nothing had turned up yet. So he'd gone back to his other legacy, the one left by his wife.

Every moment he hadn't been occupied since, his mind had replayed the speech he'd made to the Elemental Court. Though the details were fading, the sense of shame was not. He'd stood in front of those people with the mindset of a man with no career prospects who lived in a terraced house and fretted over whether he should buy a brand-new computer game or wait for it to be cheaper secondhand. His life had changed and he had just as much right to stand up in that room and make his case to those people, and he'd wasted it.

Leanne would have been appalled.

Sam had decided that if anything was going to change, it wasn't enough for him to sort out Amir's legacy; he had to push the rest of the Elemental Court to start taking responsibility for their actions too. He'd prepared everything using a laptop he'd disconnected from the internet and kept with him at all times. Sam knew he was taking a risk, but if he made an example of one of them, surely the rest would fall into line.

He moved onto his main computer and opened his email client to look at the draft letter he'd saved the night before.

> *Copper,*
>
> *The last time I saw you, in Manchester, it was pretty clear you and I have different ideas about how a cost-benefit analysis works. You said "the benefits far outweigh the costs" when expanding upon your thoughts about how you and the rest of the Elemental Court make the world a better place.*
>
> *Look, we're both busy people, so I'm not going to dress this up. You were talking utter shit. Your activities do not make the world a better place for the thousands of people directly affected by your mining activities.*
>
> *You have dozens of companies and hundreds of mines, so let's get specific. Attached to this email is evidence that the people who work in your largest Zambian copper mine are paid less than they need to survive, and are given poor-quality safety equipment or in some cases, none at all. Accidents are common. There have been several deaths as a result.*
>
> *You'll also see several reports that your PR monkeys have managed*

to keep hidden from the press, detailing how gross negligence has led to no fewer than seven major environmental incidents over the past three years. Your mine, that you own and are ultimately responsible for, has polluted rivers and groundwater supplies and resulted in the poisoning of several thousand people with copper sulphate and manganese. Your company has failed to compensate the victims who are continuing to suffer the effects of this. The reports also feature grim reading about the sulphur dioxide air pollution in the area surrounding the nearby refinery and smelter, owned by your company.

If you don't replace the current management of the mine, lift its pollution control and health and safety practices to those of the highest world standards and then compensate the people whose lives your activities have damaged or destroyed, then I will release this information and the original evidence to the press. And I will make sure your name is tied to this. No hiding behind subsidiary companies and parent companies and all that crap. You will be held responsible in the eyes of the world press.

You have twenty-four hours to demonstrate a commitment to improving the conditions for the people who work in and live near your mine before I go public with this.

Lord Iron

Sam read it through, decided that he'd made himself clear and didn't just sound like an arsehole, and clicked 'send.'

Leaning back, Sam wondered what Copper would make of his demand. "Bring it on," he thought. He imagined Leanne smiling at him. A ping indicated new email. That was quick.

How I run my operation is no business of yours. I suggest you focus on your own affairs. If you threaten me again, I'll take it to the rest of the court.

Copper

He was about to reply when there was the sound of a helicopter coming in to land. Shit! Mazzi! He'd forgotten about her offer to help him understand what it meant to be one of the Court.

Des knocked and entered. "Sir, Lady Nickel is arriving. There wasn't anything in the diary."

"That's my fault. I'll be going out with her and I'm not sure when I'll be back. I'll call you when I know what I'm doing."

"I'll carry on with the file search then. Have a good trip, sir."

Once Des had left, Sam switched off the laptop and locked it in the safe, then went out to greet Mazzi. Instead of her usual sharp suit, she was wearing jeans and a thick padded jacket with stout walking boots.

"Where are we going?" Sam asked.

"Forest of Dean," she replied. "Get changed into something warm and easy to climb in. You need to wear boots. I'll wait for you. Okay?"

Within the hour they were flying over England, Mazzi more introspective than usual. He was happy to look down at the dull green fields and the naked trees, thinking through his plans. He still wasn't sure if he trusted her, even though he couldn't deny that he found her company strangely reassuring. Perhaps it was simply the fact that she was so comfortable in her own skin and at ease with her power. Would he ever be like that?

They landed in the grounds of a private house a mile or so from the edge of the forest, where a car was waiting for them. Once they were ensconced in the back of the Mercedes and the glass dividing them from the driver was closed, Mazzi turned to him.

"I've thought a lot about the last time I saw you," she said. "I wasn't truthful with you. I'm going to put that right."

Sam folded his arms. "Okay. Which bit?"

She shifted, as if uncomfortable. "The Fae, Sam. Listen, Amir never said anything about Sorcerers or Fae for most of the time I knew him, and we were very close. A couple of years ago he told me about them. He said he'd had dealings with the Fae in the past— unpleasant ones—and that he'd made a few pieces for Sorcerers."

"And you didn't believe him."

"Well, no, not at first! Come on! Of course I didn't. I thought he was going senile. The Court was already worried about him. He was supposed to name a successor—we do that as far in advance as possible—so everyone can get to know him or her. He kept being evasive. He told me, in private, that he thought the Fae-touched were trying to infiltrate his business. He was paranoid, I suppose, because things kept going wrong with the hopefuls. Then he realised it was him. Not the Fae or Sorcerers or anything like that. Him. He was somehow poisoning them."

Sam nodded. "I met one of them and I heard about a few others. It's why he chose me—at least, that's what he said. Because I hadn't been poisoned or contaminated or something."

She nodded. "Amir was very well respected in the Court and a very powerful man outside of it. But then he started asking the others weird questions. Especially Copper. Asking if they'd noticed the same thing. If they'd had dealings with the Fae or the Sorcerers."

"Copper must have!"

Mazzi shook her head. "He hadn't. Not directly. No one else had. People started to turn against him. A group of them came to me. Copper, Silver, Lead, a couple of others. They said they thought Iron was losing it and made it clear that if I believed him, I'd be frozen out of some critical deals. I went to Amir and laid it out for him and he agreed that regardless of what he really knew, it was clear the Court couldn't handle anything out of the ordinary. So he stopped talking about it. And then he picked you."

"And then I stood up there in front of everyone and started spouting the same shit that he did."

She smiled. "More or less. If I'd supported you in front of the others, it wouldn't have gone well for me. And I didn't want to tell you that they thought Amir was crazy, not after you started saying the same things."

"So do you think Amir was crazy?"

She shook her head. "No. He wouldn't make anything like that up. And it fit with a few things I'd been wondering about. That's why we're here. I want to share something with you that makes me think there's more to us than the others think. I hope it will make you realise you're closer to being one of us than not."

One of us. He'd never liked that phrase. It always meant there was a "them," and he was usually in the latter. "If the others don't think the same way, what 'us' are you talking about?"

"The Elemental Court," she replied as the car slowed. "Just keep an open mind—you'll understand what I mean soon."

"Have you brought any of the others here?"

She shook her head. "This is your place. Not theirs."

He saw a sign for Clearwell Caves. "Why are you so keen for me to become part of the Court?"

"Because we all need each other," she replied. "And because I'm worried that if you don't, you'll make more enemies than you can handle. You're planning to fight them, aren't you?"

"Not all at once."

"Don't." The car stopped. "We're here. Remember, keep an open mind."

• • •

The only advantage of being born a Poppy was that the Charm to put oneself into a deep, peaceful sleep was one of the first ones Cathy was taught. That night, she was tempted to use it for the first time.

It had taken over an hour to stop shaking and even now, after a poor night's sleep, she could still see the Dame's face every time she closed her eyes. When she was able to think with any clarity at all, she made Will promise that he wouldn't send Wilhelmina home until they'd discussed a long-term solution. Will seemed to recover much faster and had agreed.

The last thing Dame Iris had tried to do was give her a pregnancy Charm. That Lord Iris would murder her over such a failure both terrified and enraged her. Yet more proof that women were disposable things. Would he have done the same to Sir Iris for a similar misdemeanour? She doubted it.

Regardless, she felt responsible, even though she'd had to defend herself to maintain sovereignty over her own body. Dame

Iris was determined to rule her life, and she couldn't endure her harassment. She clung to the idea that Lord Iris didn't have to kill Dame Iris to make his point. It wasn't her fault he was such a cold, inhuman bastard.

But there was no getting away from the fact that he was capable of such things, and that she had avoided pregnancy longer than he wanted. Will simply refused to discuss the topic, as if their having a child was inevitable. He was more concerned that they conceive the child enjoyably, rather than having something foisted upon them with Fae magic. He just didn't understand.

It felt like every conversation they had now was just a breath away from another argument. She could see him just switching off whenever she tried to explain her actions, as if he'd already decided she'd done the wrong thing and the reasoning behind it was irrelevant. If anything, she felt she was making things worse. The longer he was Duke, the more motivated he was to keep all the men happy. What did she expect? They perpetuated their own dominance.

She'd pretended to be asleep when he woke, his slow stirring into consciousness enough to make her wide awake in moments. He'd been wrapped around her and his arm had felt heavy. She'd wanted to push him off and run out of the house, out of the Nether, just keep running from this toxic life where women could be turned into death statues just to form an exclamation mark at the end of an order. But she stayed still, waited until he had stretched and held her breath when he kissed her experimentally in the hope she'd wake. She felt wretched, needing comfort but frightened that if she reached out to him, he'd be lustful again. She was certain the death of Dame Iris had made him all the keener to give his patron the child he desired.

Will left and in the silent bedroom she could feel the pull of despair. She'd considered her freedom from Dame Iris one of the few victories she'd had, and now it was a source of guilt and fear. She'd managed to save Natasha, free Charlotte from her curse, and inspire Wilhelmina to ask for help, but what else? The fabled Ladies' Court still didn't have a date for its first session, and she had never even wanted a separate court. She was planning to use it as an opportunity to tell more women about how the Agency treated its staff, and to urge more of them to do what she had. Max's news about Ekstrand made it riskier, though. Not that Ekstrand would have defended her against any retribution, but at least Max would have been able to warn her, maybe.

Margritte had stopped answering her letters, and she doubted Will was going to even consider a change to the law regarding the status of wives as property. Once word of what she'd done got out, she knew the number of hate-filled letters would increase. Not that the idiotic ones sent by frightened men really bothered her; it was the more considered ones from women that really stung. The ones begging her to consider the example she was setting for the younger women of the city, the ones trying to persuade her that being a woman in Society was all about subtlety and the persuasive arts. One even offered to teach her how to manipulate her husband into doing what she wished. It made her want to scream.

It felt as if she were a very angry ant waving its antennae at an elephant to make it change its course. The elephantine mass of Society just lumbered on, oblivious, uncaring.

What if staying to fight had been the wrong decision?

A Letterboxer rattled the door and three letters shot through before the gilded letterbox disappeared. From the bed she could see that one was from Charlotte. She would save that one until last.

She pulled on her dressing gown and padded over to collect them, yawning. She didn't recognise the handwriting on the other two and she was tempted to just throw them onto the fire. Most of the worst letters were sent to her privately, with only a handful a week coming through the household post. She decided to open one of them. Nothing inside a letter could be worse that what had been delivered last night.

> *You will send Mr Digitalis's wife home immediately. You have no right to interfere in a marriage. If she is not at home within the hour, there will be consequences.*

"Oh, piss off," she muttered to the letters as they slid from the page. She caught the dust in the envelope—at least she'd learned the best way to deal with anonymous threats—and threw it onto the fire to catch on the last embers.

She opened the second.

This is your final warning. We told you to stop. Return Mr Digitalis's wife to him immediately, or the next time you leave your house, you will be taken from your carriage and I'll show you what a real man—

She crushed the letter in her fist, taking a deep breath before she threw that onto the fire too. "Well, Mr Digitalis, what noble friends you have," she said to the flames.

She pulled the cord, needing caffeine, before opening Charlotte's letter.

Cathy, I need you. Come at once, please. Don't tell any of my staff you are coming, and pretend you haven't been invited. It's about Emmeline.

Yours,

C

Charlotte's daughter? Cathy remembered her from the secret meeting at Mr B's bookshop and how gentle she was. She couldn't bear the thought of something happening to her. Cathy opened the door to find her lady's maid on the other side of it, about to knock. "Help me get dressed, quick, I have to go out." She spotted one of the parlourmaids lurking a few steps away, probably wondering if a new fire should be set in her bedroom. "Tell Carter to ready the carriage, I'm leaving as soon as I'm dressed."

As soon as she was ready she flew downstairs. Just as she was reaching the bottom, the front door was opened by Morgan. She'd thought he was doing it to let her out and realised too late that it was actually to admit Bertrand Viola.

Bertrand was far more attractive than his late brother Freddy, but the cold glare he always reserved for her made him unappealing in the extreme. "Good morning, your Grace."

Cathy endured the usual scan of his eyes up and down her body. "I suppose you're here to see the Duke."

"Indeed. There are some matters regarding Londinium that need to be discussed in private."

"Oh, in private? You mean, between men."

His smile was as sharp and cold as a knife. "Yes."

"And there was me thinking that business relating to Londinium was supposed to be raised at the Court. I have the feeling you prefer to discuss politics without women present, though."

"The complexities of running a city can only be truly understood by the male mind, madam. It's better suited to problem solving."

She looked pointedly at his groin. "If you have a problem that can only be understood by a man, perhaps a doctor would be a better person to confide in."

A small patch of red flared across his pale cheeks. "How dare you imply—"

"I do hope that whatever ails you improves soon, and that the Duke and I will see you at the next Court."

Bertrand stepped towards her, the half cape of the coat making him seem even taller and broader. "The Duke of Londinium is a fine man, and I am constantly impressed by his ability to rule in such difficult circumstances." She could smell aniseed on his breath. "Though I do think he could benefit from some advice regarding wives and boundaries."

"I hardly think you'd be the most qualified to give it," she replied, having to crane her neck to look up at him even though she was standing as tall and straight as she could. "After all, the Duke isn't the kind of man who would gag his wife with a Charm because he can't cope with her having an opinion." Cathy watched his nostrils flare and knew she'd gone too far. "Yes, I guessed. There's no other explanation for the gulf between the man she speaks of and the man I've actually met. Why don't you prove me wrong by lifting it from the poor woman?"

"You are simply the most dis—"

"Your carriage is ready, your Grace," Morgan said, and Bertrand stepped aside, unwilling to cause a scene in front of the staff.

"The sooner you realise how unnatural your behaviour is, the better," Bertrand said as she passed him to go out. "For all of us."

Cathy tried to think of a retort, but the moment passed before she could. Once he'd stalked off towards Will's study she realised how much she was shaking. She looked at Morgan's concerned expression. "Don't worry, Morgan. One more enemy isn't going to make a whole lot of difference, is it?"

"I fear it isn't the quantity you're acquiring, your Grace, rather the quality."

She headed for the carriage, hoping she'd managed to cover her mistake. She wasn't sure who'd come out of that encounter as the victor, but at least she knew that Bertrand wouldn't be at home when she arrived at his house.

• • •

Sam had followed Mazzi and the guide that greeted them at the visitors' centre down into the caves under the Forest of Dean. He'd skidded down slopes, knocked his hard hat against uneven rock, and gazed across a cavern with an underground pool. He felt fantastic.

At first he'd thought it was just the change of scenery after being stuck in his study, drafting that email to Copper. But as they went deeper into the old mine, he suspected there was something more. Every now and again, Mazzi would twist round to check on him, reciprocating his excited grins with broad smiles as the guide chattered to them about the long history of the place and the ochre that was still being mined there.

"This is as far as we can go on the tour," the man said eventually.

"Could you give us a few minutes before we go back?" Mazzi asked, and the man nodded.

"I need to check on some safety rail repairs, seems as good a time as any," he said, and left.

Mazzi came to Sam's side, leaning against the same outcrop of rock. "Well?"

Sam tried to put it into words. "I feel...brilliant. Like I could run a marathon or climb a mountain. Not just a physical thing...like I could do that and write the most amazing code at the same time. I can't remember the last time I felt like this."

She nodded.

"You knew I'd feel this way," he said. "Did Amir like it here too?"

"He did. It's how I felt when I visited Ravensthorpe in Australia."

"A nickel mine?"

She nodded. "I don't feel it here. If I'd just told you this is how you'd feel here, you'd never have believed me, right?"

"Right."

"This is what makes you one of us," she said with certainty. "We all feel this, for our own elements. None of the others really talk about it. Copper thinks this feeling is all about the numbers, the tonnes being extracted per day and the sheer thrill of the money being made. But he's wrong. It's deeper than that. Amir understood. I think you do too."

And in that moment, he did. He could feel the iron in the rock around them, not in any amount worth mining out as ore, but still there. Below them, some metres below, he knew there was a richer deposit, just like he knew that his feet were at the ends of his legs. When he focused on the feeling, his pulse increased and he wanted to get that iron out, with a pickaxe and brute strength if needed. He just knew it had to come out of the ground.

Then it frightened him. What was making him feel this way? It wasn't natural. Was this what Amir had done to him? Infected him somehow with his blood? This was all part of being Lord Iron. Breaking Fae magic was just another facet. When he beat the iron in the forge and felt solid and real and fully himself, that was just another facet too. Was there any of his old self left?

When Sam pushed aside the high from being in this place, the sense of the iron ore deposits just begging to be mined, the hankering to be back in the forge, all he could find were two things he believed about himself. He wanted to protect people from the Fae. That started way before Amir got his hooks into him, he was just better equipped now. The second was that he wanted to protect the environment. Now Sam was starting to realise that the roots of humanity's drive to rip the ground open and take everything that was there, regardless of the consequences, were in the very court Mazzi wanted him to feel part of. She was hoping that if he felt this way, his talk of environmental responsibility would be forgotten.

Now Sam knew there was no reasoning with them. Satisfying this craving was all they cared about. And money.

"This is why," Mazzi said, "I want you to get along with everyone else. I know it's not your scene, but we're all just doing what we're made to do. Maybe you could remember that when you next deal with them?"

Sam looked at her. "I won't forget it," he said, forcing a smile. "Thanks for bringing me down here. Everything is so much clearer now. Let's go back up; I need to make a phone call."

17

"Come in." Will was expecting to see Cathy, thankful that she hadn't bumped into the foul-tempered Bertrand whilst he was in his study earlier. "Ah, Elizabeth."

"Is this a better time?"

He stood and went round his desk to her. "Yes. Did you manage to sleep?"

"A little."

"Do you want to sit down? There was something you wanted to discuss with me."

He gestured to the sofa and she sat, taking a moment to arrange herself in a way Cathy never did. Despite the shock of the night before and the poor sleep that resulted, Elizabeth's face was still just as fresh and pretty as it always was. Will sat down on the other sofa, the coffee table between them.

"Who was that lady in the…"

"That's nothing for you to worry about. It was an Iris matter."

She looked frightened, and understandably so. "What happened to her?"

"She died and the case was removed from the house."

"Why—"

"Forgive me, Elizabeth, but it's all over now and I have no desire to speak of it. Now, what did you want to tell me last night?"

The worry in her eyes was rapidly replaced by a flash of mischievous excitement. "Oh, yes, that." She edged forwards. "I discovered a secret yesterday, one that I thought might interest you."

There was a wicked glint in her eye. Will doubted that any secret she might value would interest him, but he played along for the sake of keeping her happy. "Oh?"

"Do you recall the Sorcerer who appeared at the ball in Aquae Sulis before you married my sister?"

"It would be impossible to forget him."

"Well," Elizabeth paused, ostensibly to take a breath, but he knew she was trying to build anticipation. "He's dead."

"Dead? Are you sure?"

"Yes. I am absolutely positive. He had something to do with the Agency, but now he's dead, there's no one who really cares about it, which is why I'm telling you."

Will stayed quiet. There was no way she could know his desire to take over the Agency, surely.

"Because of Catherine," Elizabeth continued. "She's planning to do something that will upset the Agency, but the Sorcerer who used to look after it is dead now, so she won't have any protection. As her husband, I felt you should know." She smiled, clearly delighted with herself.

Will smiled back, pleased that the way was clear to seize control of the Agency. "How did you discover this?"

"I overheard a conversation—purely by accident—between Catherine and a man called Max." She bit her lip, revelling in the attention. "I wonder if they might be having—"

"Max is an Arbiter of Aquae Sulis," Will said, noting Elizabeth's disappointment. "They met?"

"She phoned him! On a telephone! In Mundanus, the schoolroom."

His breath caught in his throat. Did this vile girl know about Sophia? Then he remembered that Vincent had taken her out on a day trip the day before. The secret was still safe, but he decided to have the door locked as long as Elizabeth was snooping around the house.

"The mundane schoolroom in the nursery wing? That you just happened to be in at the same time?"

Elizabeth didn't blush like Cathy would have; she simply smiled sweetly and fluttered her eyelashes a little. "Pure luck!"

"You are a resourceful young woman. Now, I have been considering a match for you, but I wasn't sure whether you were mature and clever enough for the one I had in mind."

Her face brightened at the mention of a match. How could she and Cathy have come from the same mother? "Oh, but I am, William! I was clever enough to come to you with this information, was I not?"

Will nodded, wishing her sister was so easy to manipulate. "Yes, I can see that you're just the sort of brilliant, beautiful young woman a bachelor of this calibre would want to take as a wife."

Elizabeth's eyes widened. "Oh, I am. Perhaps you could tell me a little about him?"

"He's a very well-travelled gentleman, seasoned, one might say, by just the right amount. He's just returned to Londinium after being abroad for a few years and is settling into a very fine house as I speak." Will couldn't help but tease her, it was so easy. He knew all she cared about was the wealth and the status. "He plays a fine game of billiards, so I'm told, and is very fond of music."

"Oh! I can play the piano, the harp, and the harpsichord. The Censor of Aquae Sulis put on a concert just so that I could sing. She said I have the voice of an angel."

"Even better." Will paused, drawing it out, amused by how she was steadily leaning forwards, straining to hear the family name. "He's extraordinarily wealthy," Will said, and she beamed with delight. "But of course, he is a Viola, so that's to be expected."

"A Viola!" she clapped her hands in delight. "Oh, he sounds perfect. Do you think he will like me?"

Will smiled, knowing that as they spoke, Bertrand was on his way to tell his cousin about the match. Harold had only been back in the city for a couple of days and was already proving to be useful. Bertrand was satisfied that Will had put his family first in matching a desirable young woman with close family ties to the Duke and Duchess to his cousin. Of course, Bertrand had the added incentive of knowing that if he failed to persuade Harold to agree, the proposed marriage between his daughter and Nathaniel Iris would be withdrawn. Will was simply happy to get Elizabeth out of his hair. "I'm sure he will find you irresistible, Elizabeth. You are the jewel of Aquae Sulis, after all."

"Oh, I must tell Mother!"

"It's already in hand," he said. "I've asked her to come to Londinium this afternoon to chaperone you on a visit."

"This afternoon!"

"Yes. You have a few hours yet; Harold isn't free until four o'clock. Should she find the match agreeable, and with your father's blessing, the contract will be signed this evening. The Violas are not fond of long engagements, so the speedy wedding your mother asked for can be accommodated."

Elizabeth jumped to her feet. "Oh, what shall I wear? I could positively burst." She darted over like a hummingbird to kiss him on the cheek before running to the door. "Thank you so much, darling William. I knew you wouldn't let me down!"

The room seemed so still after Elizabeth left. Will savoured it for a moment and then pulled the bell cord.

"Ah, Morgan, has my wife surfaced yet?"

"She just left, your Grace. I can only assume she forgot about a commitment, as she left in a great hurry. I didn't have any time to remind her about the visit this afternoon." At Will's blank expression, he added, "Princess Rani of the Princely State of Rajkot has requested an audience at short notice."

"I'm sure Cathy can handle that. She won't forget a royal visit. I'm going to be out for the rest of the day. Have my carriage readied; I'll be leaving in half an hour."

Morgan bowed and left. There was still the matter of Digitalis and his wife to settle, and Will intended to keep his promise to Cathy. However, now that he could see an alternative solution to the problem presenting itself, he was hoping that by the time they saw each other again, it would all be resolved without any need for such ridiculous ideas as changing the law.

The Peonia boy was less pale than the last time Max saw him, but he was still just as nervous and sweaty. Max had arranged to meet him at the coffee-house near the Abbey as it was an easy location for the boy to get to without having to be gone from the Nether for too long.

He was sitting in the corner of a room on the first floor, back to the wall. When Max hobbled in, he stood to attention, in the most conspicuous way imaginable.

"Sit," Max said, and the Peonia did so.

"Gosh," he whispered. "All this derring-do isn't anything like how they describe it in the adventure books, is it? I couldn't manage my breakfast this morning."

"Make your report and then you can leave," Max said as the Peonia pulled out a handkerchief and dabbed his forehead.

"Well, I got in," he said, with a grin. "I couldn't believe it. 'Oli,' they said, 'not only did you steal a baby and return it without the mundane noticing, you managed to gain the favour of the Master of Ceremonies whilst you did it.' I didn't know what they meant, but they spotted me talking with Mr Lavandula the day afterwards and he never really spoke to me before and, well, they assumed I'd impressed him. I didn't let on that they'd got the wrong end of the stick, of course. You were right about them not watching the house, thank goodness. They gave the boot boy ten of the Queen's pounds to report me taking the baby round the house three times. All worked out jolly well, considering the circumstances."

"Who are the members?"

"Ah, well, I haven't met them yet. But I can tell you that the usual haunt is Lunn's, in the upstairs room, and I'm supposed to meet everyone there tomorrow night. I was supposed to be lunching with them there today, but there's something going on in Londinium. They wouldn't tell me what it is, but it sounds jolly exciting to go on a jaunt like that. Something about seeing the Duchess and making sure she has what's coming to her. Delivering a gift, I suppose. So they're not all bad, Mr Arbiter."

"You can go now," Max said, and watched the Peonia scurry out like a child who'd escaped a beating. He pulled his mobile from his pocket and called Catherine. It went to answerphone. "Don't leave your house," he said. "There's a group associated with illegal activity in Aquae Sulis who are travelling to Londinium and may intend you harm. Oh. This is Max. Call me when you—" It beeped loudly, but he was fairly certain it had recorded.

• • •

Cathy stifled a gasp when she saw Charlotte. She'd lost even more weight, her face was quite gaunt, and she was dreadfully pale. Once the butler left the room Cathy embraced her, disturbed by how thin she felt, and kissed her cheek.

"What is it?" she whispered. "What's wrong?"

Charlotte held up a finger, telling her to wait until the tea had been brought in. Once they were alone again, she went to her embroidery box and pulled a seashell from beneath the silk skeins. She whispered a Charm into it and set it down next to the teapot.

"We can't be overheard now," she said. "Thank you for coming."

"Have you been eating? You look so thin!"

"I can't. It's so hard, pretending to still be cursed. I don't know how much longer I can bear it. Smiling when he says such awful things, looking pleased when he…" Her face crumpled. "When he touches me. I could not hate a man more."

Cathy moved to sit next to her, putting an arm around her. "Oh, Charlotte. This isn't going to work. We need to think of a better solution."

"I didn't ask you to come to talk about me," Charlotte said, wiping away stray tears. "It's Emmeline. She's being married off."

"Do you know who the—"

"Nathaniel Iris."

"Oh no! Shit!"

Charlotte nodded. "I am beside myself. I cannot possibly allow that to happen, but if I express my unhappiness he'll know the curse has been broken and he'll cast it again and I can't bear that. I know I shouldn't be so selfish, but even if I do speak out against the match, he won't take any notice. I have no voice here! Whether I choose to speak or not."

She broke down and Cathy held her tight as the worst of it passed. "We have a little time before he comes back. I saw him as I was leaving. He's with Will."

Charlotte nodded. "Afterwards he's going to see Harold, to press him into marrying your sister. Oh, that sounds terrible. I mean—"

"Elizabeth? Hang on, who's Harold?"

"Bertrand's cousin. He's been away for over fifty years, I've no idea where. He's another of Lady Violet's favourites. He's quite harmless—a bit of an idiot if you ask me, but there isn't a cruel bone in his body. Bertrand got all of those. I'm sure your sister will be safe."

Cathy felt as if she'd missed half of the conversation. "I've never heard of him, or this match. When did it happen?"

"Yesterday. Bertrand spoke with the Duke at the Tower." Charlotte looked at Cathy over her handkerchief. "Nothing was mentioned to you?"

Cathy shook her head. "He didn't say a bloody word."

"They've made a deal. If Harry marries your sister, Nathaniel will marry Emmeline. Of course, Bertrand is over the moon! His daughter in a high-status position, something the Violas have been sorely lacking over the past hundred years thanks to Freddy, may he rest in peace. And both marriages tie us to the Duke's close and extended family."

Cathy shook her head. Will had been busy. And he hadn't shared any of it with her. "I don't believe this."

"So you see, there's nothing I can do," Charlotte said. "But the thought of that brute with my darling girl…" She broke down again. "After what he did to Margritte I can't bear the thought of it."

"Have you heard from her?" Cathy asked. "She hasn't replied to the last three letters I sent her. I'm worried she's angry with me."

Charlotte dabbed at her nose and shook her head. "I haven't. But surely William would know if something had happened to her. She may just be busy, trying to find allies. Have you asked Natasha?"

"No, I haven't seen her. She's been setting up new distributors for the pamphlets."

"Cathy, I don't know what to do. Benedict has just gone on his Grand Tour, so he has no idea what's going on. Emmeline doesn't know yet and I don't have the heart to tell her. I hoped that you might…" her voice trailed off.

"Will won't listen to me."

"But I thought he—"

Cathy shook her head. "He isn't one of us, Charlotte. I hoped he was, but he isn't." Her throat clogged and she felt a sudden overwhelming sadness at hearing herself say that. But it was the truth. "Do you have any allies?"

Charlotte pointed at her, with the saddest smile. "I was cursed for decades, Cathy. Everyone thinks I'm some vacuous doll."

Cathy looked down at her gloves, feeling the pressure. What could she do? She took a deep breath. "Okay. There are two problems here. The first is that we can't let Emmeline be married off to that misogynistic fuck." She smiled at the way Charlotte gasped. "The second is that you staying here, pretending to be cursed, is killing you."

"The first is more urgent," Charlotte said, pouring the tea. "Bertrand was talking about contracts being signed within days, and the Violas don't like long engagements. Probably because the wife is usually unwilling," she added bitterly.

"We can't approach any of the Violas, or your patron, I assume?"

Charlotte shook her head. "No. Not looking like this. She'll know something is wrong, and it could create more problems than solve them. I'm one of her favourites."

Cathy nodded. "That's what usually happens when those lot get involved. Look, we could just get you and Emmeline out."

"Out?"

"Into Mundanus."

There was a flash of excitement in Charlotte's eyes, and then she looked away, shaking her head. "No. I couldn't do that. Everything is so different there now. How would we survive? And the Violas would come after us."

"I have a very powerful friend who would protect you. They wouldn't find you."

"No. I couldn't possibly. I used to be brave, a long time ago. Not now. There has to be another solution!"

Cathy understood her reluctance. Being so dependent on a stranger wasn't exactly a great solution either. "Okay. How much do you care about being successful in Society?"

"Not a jot," Charlotte said. "I would be happy to retire to the country and so would Emmeline. She's too intellectual for this world and I find it hollow."

"Maybe we could kill two birds with one stone," Cathy said. "What if I told an Arbiter that Bertrand stole you from Mundanus? He'd be booted out of Society and Nathaniel would break the contract if the father of his bride were dishonoured."

"I've heard that in those circumstances," Charlotte said, "the entire family is expelled. Or taken by the Arbiters and put to work. I couldn't bear it. If only he'd committed some other crime, something unrelated to me, then Lady Violet would probably pension me off. I've borne children and she's too fond of me to just abandon me. But Bertrand's spotless and he has the Duke's favour, too."

Cathy sighed. "You're right. We can't risk you being kicked out, you can't say anything to your family elders, and you have no leverage. So the only option is to approach this from the Iris side."

"But Dame Iris hates you."

"She's dead," Cathy said, and Charlotte blanched. "Lord Iris killed her because she…didn't meet his expectations."

Charlotte shuddered. "This is hell. A very beautiful hell."

"Sure you want to stay? Mundanus can be quite wonderful."

"Better the hell I know," Charlotte replied.

Cathy stood, draining her cup in a couple of loud gulps, fearing that if she dwelt upon Dame Iris and this gilded hell too much, she'd break down. "I'll think of something. I promise. Hang in there. And eat something. You're going to need your strength, okay?"

They embraced. "Sisterhood," Charlotte whispered in her ear. "Sisterhood is our strength."

Cathy said goodbye and left the house. She climbed into the carriage, Carter getting in behind her, and waved to the ghost-like woman watching from the window. As soon as they were away, Cathy slumped, exhausted. The brave band was disintegrating; Margritte unresponsive, Charlotte fading away, and Natasha elsewhere, admittedly working for the cause, but still absent. Where was that feeling of strength and invincibility she had felt that night when the four of them were united? Where was the sense of hope, of potential for change?

Was she doing enough? Will would say she was doing far too much, but they were still getting nowhere. She thought back to her lessons as a girl, how the suffragists had argued peacefully and calmly for the vote for fifty years or so to no avail. She could understand why they had shifted their tactics. Faced with the wall of silence and oppression, what else was there to do but escalate?

Deeds not words. Was it time for her to take more radical action? But what could she do in her world, where women could be Dolled, cursed, and Charmed into obedience?

"Some days," she said to Carter, "do you just want to burn everything down to the ground and start again?"

He blinked at her. "I can't say I've ever felt that, your Grace."

"You're lucky," she sighed. "But what if—"

There was a flash of light outside the carriage, casting the darkest shadows she'd ever seen in the Nether, and the horses whinnied in alarm. The carriage lurched to a stop so fast that Cathy was thrown into the opposite wall, only stopped from banging her head by Carter's quick reflexes, catching her with one of his huge arms.

She sat back and was about to call out to the driver to ask what had happened when she noticed the most awful silence.

Carter sprang into action, locking the carriage doors.

"What's happening?"

"Please stay calm and still, your Grace," he said, starting to lift the seat cushion he'd been sitting on. "I believe we're about to be attacked."

18

Bennet looked very different from how Will remembered him. His suit had been cleaned and mended, as had he, but Will was certain he used to be taller. Perhaps it was something to do with the slump of his shoulders or the way that he looked like he was trying to take up as little space as possible.

"Mr Bennet," Will said, nodding to the guard to leave him in his study. "I trust your spell in the Tower has given you time to reflect upon your actions."

"Yes, your Grace. I could not be more filled with regret."

"Blackmailing the Duchess of Londinium is such a severe crime, you're lucky to be alive."

"Yes, your Grace, lucky and so very grateful that you're a merciful Duke."

The snivelling suited the wretch's face, with its weak chin. He disgusted Will, but at least he hadn't given into his desire to have him executed for putting Cathy through such a distressing experience. Was a couple of weeks in a stone cell after an occasionally painful interrogation enough of a punishment? He wasn't sure, but he had to move quickly and Bennet was more useful to him alive.

"I will pardon your crime, in light of the fact that you've been most cooperative, on one condition."

"Anything, your Grace!"

"I intend to take control of the Agency. I have reached an accord with the Sorcerer, as he has lost interest in it. I already supply all of the potions and Charmed artefacts it uses to run its operation, so it is in our mutual interest that I take over responsibility for it."

Bennet's mouth fell open. "He lost interest?"

Will smiled and gave a slight shrug. "Sorcerers. They have other concerns, wouldn't you agree? And after I worked so closely with him to remove the criminal Rosa family from our midst, he considered me trustworthy enough to ensure I would see everything done properly with regards to the Agency."

"And...and how may I help, your Grace?"

"You will convey this letter to Mr Derne and advise him of the change in circumstances. You can assure him that the supply of goods will not be interrupted as long as I have his full and unconditional support. If I do not, I will sever the supply and replace him with a more cooperative individual. Then you will obtain the file on Mr Lutea-Digitalis, former Marquis of Westminster, and the one held on my wife. You will bring both of them to me. And then you will wait for your next instructions."

"Am I to understand that I am now in your employ, your Grace?"

"That would imply that you would be entitled to a wage, when you are simply working off a debt. This may change if you prove to be capable of more than blackmailing a defenceless woman convalescing from a near-fatal knife attack."

Bennet had the grace to look ashamed at the mention of the crime. "I will do everything I possibly can to prove my worth to you, your Grace."

"Good. Take this, then, and come back as soon as possible. If I'm not here upon your return, you will wait in the antechamber. Do not let those files out of your sight."

Bennet approached his desk and held out a quivering hand. Will gave him the letter. "Derne will need to give you something in response to that," Will said as he placed it in Bennet's hand. "If he refuses to comply, then return and tell me so. If you fail to return, I will come to the Agency myself and replace the entirety of the managerial staff. If you fail to return because you choose to flee rather than see this through, I will hunt you down and kill you. Do you understand?"

Bennet nodded with the earnestness of a terrified man. "I shall return as fast as I can, your Grace. And thank you."

Will watched him leave, satisfied, and then glanced at the clock. It was almost noon. He checked his cravat using the hand mirror he kept in the desk drawer, tidied away a few loose strands of hair, and then called in a page to brush down his frock coat and give his shoes a brief polish.

As the clock struck the hour, he went to the mirror behind the screen, pulled away the silk cloth, and said "Lady Eleanor is welcome in my study."

A few moments later she stepped through. She looked immaculate, dressed in an Edwardian-style dark blue gown with her silver hair swept back and arranged artfully. "William," she said, and held out her hand.

"Lady Eleanor," he said, bowing to kiss the back of her glove. "A pleasure to see you again."

He covered the mirror again as she walked further into the study, taking in the details. "A move to the Tower was exactly the right thing to do, William," she said, nodding with approval. "Far more history and gravitas than that imperial administration building. I never liked Somerset House. This place makes a statement. What do you feel it says?"

"That just as the Irises took this mundane land and made it theirs, we have taken our rightful place once more."

"Which is?"

He smiled. "Looking down on everyone else, evidently."

She laughed. "Oh, you look very handsome when you're pleased with yourself. Tell me what's put that sparkle in your eye."

"If you would care to sit, Lady Eleanor, I have some news."

Eleanor sat down with the grace of a queen and regarded him expectantly.

"The woman who tricked your husband and usurped you is dead."

There was the briefest widening of Eleanor's eyes, nothing else. She calmly folded her hands on her lap. "Well, that is an interesting turn of events. Did she meet with an accident?"

"No, Lady Eleanor. She was found wanting. Lord Iris expressed his displeasure most viscerally."

"A specific failing or was a proverbial straw involved?"

Will paused, considering his options and remembering her plain speaking.

"Why do I have the suspicion that it has something to do with your wife?"

"Because that's correct. Did Cathy explain the reason why she wanted you to help her intimidate that woman?"

"I assumed it's because she had the poor girl under her thumb and was making her life a misery. It's what she was best at, after all."

"That's true, but there was another reason." He leaned forwards, making her naturally reflect the movement. "The former Dame Iris was tasked with ensuring that Cathy conceives my child within the next month. Just before she revealed you, Cathy destroyed a potion that the Dame had ordered her to drink, most probably one to guarantee conception."

Eleanor's eyebrows arched. "I do hope the problem does not lie in your ability, William."

He flushed. "It does not, madam. We have consummated the marriage but Cathy doesn't want a child. And with all of the pressures upon us, and the attack on her person and the fact that I seem to be constantly fighting fires she's lit unwittingly, we haven't yet achieved our goal."

"She doesn't want a child? I don't understand."

"She fears that Lord Iris has plans for our baby, and without knowing what they are, she's reluctant to give him what he wants. If I may be so bold, could I ask if he insisted upon the same when you were newlyweds?"

She shook her head. "With marriages and fertility spanning hundreds of years, it was all very relaxed. Of course, I fell pregnant only two months after marriage. One doesn't like to make people gossip, after all." She paused as she considered something. "Well, this is a kindness, William, explaining the trap ahead before you lead me into the woods."

He smiled. "I thought a great deal about our conversation in the tea rooms. You said you still love your husband and that you are not content. It seems to me that there is only one path to your contentment, and it has opened ahead of you."

She looked down at her gloved hands. "I am not what I once was."

"And that is why we are going to see Lord Iris. Lady Eleanor, would you permit me to facilitate your return to Society and the rightful place that was stolen from you? Though you would be eminently capable of engineering it yourself, I believe that I could tell a tale that would be truthful and cast you in a most favourable light."

"And yourself in the process."

Will smiled. "Of course, Lady Eleanor. And in light of what I've just told you, I'm sure you can appreciate why I'm so keen to gain favour with our patron."

"You may facilitate, dear boy. But I have one question first. Pray tell me: why, when you have such privilege, do you not simply cast a Charm upon your wife to bend her to your desires?"

He flicked a speck of dust from his desk. He couldn't tell her about the Lust Charm. What if that truthful tongue of hers repeated it to Cathy? "Because, I confess, I have been a victim of Charms that rule the heart and I could not bring myself to do that to my love."

"You said 'could not' instead of cannot. I take it that has changed."

Will sighed. "I must satisfy our patron, Lady Eleanor. What other choice do I have?"

• • •

Cathy went to look out of the window, but Carter pulled her back, dropping the seat cushion back into place to do so. "Forgive me, your Grace, but you should stay away from the windows. Please, tuck yourself into that corner as best you can." She obeyed. "They will have frozen the horses and Dolled the driver and footmen. That means there's more than—"

The glass of the window farthest from her and closest to Carter smashed inwards and she saw a masked face, that looked like Pantalone from the commedia dell'arte with a shock of fake red hair, peering in. The wearer focused on Carter, said something, and blew sparkling powder towards him.

Carter just shook his head at the masked attacker and punched him through the gap in the broken window, square in the face. "If there's anyone else out there planning to do more than Doll me, don't bother; I'm an elite with the highest security clearance and have immunities to—"

A movement at the other window made Cathy shrink back. "Carter!" she yelled, and then there was the terrible sound of a gunshot. It pierced the glass, shattering it, and Carter slammed forwards, his head cracking against the far wall of the carriage before he collapsed.

Cathy screamed at the sight of him crumpled in the space between the seats, her ears still ringing from the shot. Then the carriage door started rattling. It would only be moments before the lock was shot out and she was right next to it.

She dived away from it, crouching down to keep away from the window, squeezing herself next to Carter.

"Oh God, Carter," she whispered, blinking away tears. She shook his shoulder but he didn't respond.

She could hear voices outside, a little distance away, an argument of some kind. Perhaps murdering a man wasn't in the plan. There were more than the two she knew of, and even if she made it out of the carriage and into the mists without them seeing her, there was no guarantee she'd be able to find her way back to the road again.

As low down as she was, Cathy noticed that the seat cushion wasn't firmly back in place. Carter had been about to open it up, presumably to find something to help. His arm was draped across it, so she gently moved it off, weeping at the way it dropped so heavily against his body when she let go.

The cushion was the top half of a lid, and beneath it were two shotguns. She'd never even held a gun before, but she'd seen them in enough films to know which end was the dangerous one. Cathy pulled one out of the clips that held it in place as a hand reached through the broken window of the door to her right to unlock it from the inside.

Please be loaded, please be loaded. She shifted away from the door, having to half sit on Carter's back to give her room to point the gun at the arm. The argument had stopped and now she could hear laughter outside, reminding her of a bunch of drunken men watching a friend trying to do a handstand at the student union. "Come on, old chap, open the bloody door!" one of them cheered.

"Get away from that door or I will fucking shoot you!" Cathy yelled. She was aiming for Ripley levels of badassitude and was horribly disappointed by how high and squeaky her voice sounded.

The hand stopped fumbling for the lock and withdrew. She whipped her head round to look through the other window and saw the top of another Pantalone mask, this one with bright blue hair, approaching the door.

"I mean it!" she yelled.

The hair got closer and she moved the barrel of the gun towards that door instead. She aimed high and pulled the trigger, blasting a hole through the top of the door and its frame. The knockback slammed against her shoulder, making her cry out, and if it hadn't been for the seat behind her it would have knocked her over, she was so unprepared for it.

At the sound of running footsteps, Cathy risked a peep over the lower sill of the window. There was no one there, nor on the other side of the carriage. It sounded like they were receding into the distance, but she didn't trust the noise, thinking they might be trying to lure her out.

"Carter," she said. "Carter?"

She rested the shotgun on the seat and felt his back, trying to find where his wound was. If she could staunch the bleeding, he might survive. She couldn't find anything.

Fumbling her fingers around his head, Cathy tried to feel if he was still breathing without standing and exposing herself through the windows. As she brushed his forehead she could feel something wet and she pulled her fingers back to see blood.

Cathy couldn't stop the tears then. She just sat, crumpled up next to him, staring at the blood on her fingertips, until there was a snort from one of the horses and a string of expletives from the driver. She felt the carriage rock as the footmen got off the back.

"Your Grace!" they yelled, and she finally let go of the shotgun, knowing the gang must have fled. A pale face appeared at one of the doors, and she unlocked it with shaking hands.

"He's dead," she wept. "They killed Carter!"

One of the footmen reached in to feel Carter's neck. "No, your Grace, he's alive."

In her shock, she'd forgotten to check his pulse. Cathy laughed at her idiocy and it rapidly degenerated into something hysterical. "Pull him out," she told them. "Let's get him in the recovery position."

"But your Grace, we need to leave—it isn't safe!"

"They won't come back," she said, patting the shotgun. "Pull him out. He's all squashed and he needs air."

They did as she ordered and then helped her out too, glass tinkling on the cobbles as it fell from her hair and clothing. Glancing back to see where the shotgun was, she spotted a flattened bullet on the floor of the carriage.

"Was he Charmed against bullets?" she asked the footmen, who both shrugged.

"I reckon he'd be a poor bodyguard if he weren't," said the driver, coming round to see what was going on after calming the horses. "I'm so sorry, your Grace. They made something flash like a firework to startle the horses and then Dolled us all. Weren't a thing I could do about it."

Cathy knelt beside Carter and examined the gash on his forehead. There was a nasty lump with it, but it didn't look too bad. The force that knocked him forwards had made him bang his head against the inside of the carriage and simply knocked him out. She fetched a clean handkerchief from her reticule and pressed it against the wound. She thought of her father, how he'd been Charmed to be protected against shrapnel and bullets before going to fight in the First World War.

Then she imagined what Will was going to say. Cathy groaned, feeling the bruise from the shotgun blossoming on her shoulder. "Okay, you all need to listen. When the Duke asks what happened, you tell him the truth, but I didn't fire the shotgun, Carter did. Right?"

They all frowned at her.

"He wasn't knocked out," she added. "He just banged his head, that's all. If the Duke thinks I did that, and that Carter was out of action, he'll sack him and never let me out of the house again. Understand?" They all nodded. It helped that she paid their wages, but they were still uncomfortable. "I know you don't want to lie to him, but this way, Carter will be fine. Agreed?"

They did. The driver climbed up to his seat and fetched a flask of tea that was shared round and before long they were laughing about what she'd yelled at the gang. Cathy grimaced. "Don't mention that bit, either."

• • •

Will knelt in front of Lord Iris, feeling the intensity of the gaze on the top of his head. There was no sense of anger or disapproval, just his patron's usual iciness.

"You received my gift."

Gift? Will realised he meant the case and…her. "Yes, my Lord. A most eloquent demonstration of your expectations."

Lord Iris reached down and with one of his long fingers lifted Will's chin until their eyes met. "And what did your wife think of it?"

Even though Will had already seen his blue eyes and knew there was no pupil or white or anything human about them at all, his heart still faltered at the sight of them boring into him. "She was rather shocked and distressed, my Lord. But she understood the meaning well enough."

"Have you come to make excuses for her?"

"No, my Lord. I came to discuss another lady of our family."

Iris glanced towards the edge of the clearing. "You brought another into Exilium but not into my domain."

"I needed to explain what has happened to her first. Our family is incomplete, Lord Iris. We are without a Dame, and the women of the family are without guidance. I wish to offer a solution in the form of the lady I've brought with me. She was the former Dame Iris, before the one who displeased you."

Lord Iris tilted his head. "Eleanor did not meet the expectations of her husband. She was replaced and died."

"For all intents and purposes, my Lord. The one who displeased you wove a web of deceit and despicable lies, convincing Society that Lady Eleanor had gone mad so that she could be usurped. In order to preserve the perfection of the family, Sir Iris was forced to send Lady Eleanor to an asylum in Mundanus to live out her days—"

Lord Iris stood as leaves and iris flowers in the clearing were pressed back by a sudden blast of cold radiating from him. "He said nothing of madness! Why did he not bring her to me?" He stared at the edge again, whispering something as Will frantically tried to think of a response.

Will had no idea why Sir Iris had decided to hide Eleanor away rather than bring her to his patron. Now he was thinking it through, it did seem rather poor form to not bring his wife here first. Then he feared it was because Sir Iris hadn't wanted to save Eleanor and simply wanted a new wife. "Because—"

"Because the usurper executed a brilliant plan, my Lord," Eleanor said from the edge of the clearing. Will turned to see her give a deep curtsy and then straighten again with some effort. "My husband knew that even if you could help me, the damage I had done in Society by offending the idiots of the Court with no more than the truth would make it untenable for me to remain in my position. Better to lead you to believe that he had lost interest in me, so you would simply let me go and he could take another wife quickly, to preserve order within the family."

She took a tentative step forwards and, seeing that Lord Iris was expecting her to continue, spoke again. "It was a very delicate time for the Frankish Empire. With war ravaging Mundanus, the mundane underpinnings of our power were under threat. He acted swiftly and decisively to limit the damage I had done, but he was also proud and he loved me. The reasons behind the action he took may not have been perfect, my Lord, but to everyone else outside of the family, perfection was swiftly restored once I was gone. He had a wife who was beautiful and devoted, willing to destroy anyone who threatened him or the family's honour. Not the one he loved, but the family came first."

Lord Iris stepped down from his living throne of wood and flowers and walked past Will towards Eleanor. Will stood, unable to read what the Fae intended. Iris stopped halfway across the clearing and beckoned her further in. "And why did you not come to me for help?"

"Because you do not exist to resolve my difficulties, Lord Iris. I exist to serve and please you, and if I am found wanting, I accept the consequences. My enemy exploited the complacency of our marriage and my sense of security. I never dreamt that a daughter of an inconsequential family would even contemplate destroying my life. That was a dreadful mistake, and I was willing to pay for that deviation from perfection."

"And as Mundanus stole the youth from your body, did you not regret this? Did you not nurse hatred towards your husband for abandoning you?"

"No, my Lord. I nursed a hatred towards the one who took my place, but not him. My husband was thinking of the family and of how we represented you. The perfection of our family required that I be absent, and I accepted that. I still love him, dearly."

"Your devotion pleases me," Lord Iris said, closing the distance between them. "You will return to your husband and resume your position as Dame with my blessing." He wrapped his arms around her, his long white hair draping down like silk, obscuring her from

Will's sight. Then the Fae released her and to Will's surprise, she still looked the same.

Lord Iris took a step back and cupped Eleanor's face with his hand in a remarkably tender way. It was jarring, seeing him be anything but cold and detached. Eleanor gazed up at him, her eyes shining, beatific in her devotion, as Lord Iris ran his thumb across her cheek.

Something flaked away from her face in its wake, making Will tense, but then he saw youthful skin revealed, as if it had been there all along. With gentle strokes, Lord Iris brushed away the age from the rest of her face, as if excavating her youthful self from the wrinkled woman standing before him. As he worked, fresh irises grew around them, the stems stretching up and the blooms bursting as if a month had passed in but moments. Lord Iris plucked one, cupped his hand around it, and whispered whilst looking at the others around them, moving further away from Eleanor. When he dropped his hand away the petals twisted into the shape of a butterfly, as did all of the fresh blooms, rising up in chaotic flight to obscure Eleanor from sight. Will heard her laughter, as light and bright as an excited debutante, as the rippling blue mass of wings covered her.

Lord Iris returned to his throne and Will stood back, wishing that he could be dismissed rather than stand there without any certain purpose. But when he saw the way Lord Iris watched and the first hint of a smile he'd ever seen on his patron's face, Will realised that he was witnessing something remarkable. He could see a flicker of excitement, too, something he'd never associated with Lord Iris, something he'd never even believed possible. Then he remembered that mere hours ago, Lord Iris would have sat on the same throne while Eleanor's rival probably begged for her life. He would have stolen the youth from her body and created the case around her. Will shuddered. They were nothing more than pets to the Fae, things to do their bidding and relieve the boredom of eternity.

How could he ever feel safe? How could he ever protect Cathy and Sophia from creatures such as this?

Lord Iris snapped his fingers and a faerie flew in from the trees surrounding the clearing and hovered in front of its master. It seemed to take an order without the need for words and flew off, leaving a shower of sparkling blue. When it left, Lord Iris leaned back, watching as the butterflies started to fly off, their work done.

Dame Iris stood with the poise and confidence of a queen, her hair raven black, her lips full and deep red, her skin flawless. Her dark blue eyes were bright with joy and no little triumph. Her gown had been replaced by one made of silk and iris petals, revealing an hourglass figure and a creamy décolletage that Will made himself look away from immediately. She was dressed as if about to step into a ball, her dark blue opera gloves adorned with diamond bracelets that sparkled in the dappled sunshine reaching through the trees.

"You are restored," Lord Iris said. He looked at Will. "I am capable of benevolence towards those that please me."

Will inclined his head. Had he not pleased his patron? Then he realised he was talking about Cathy. Not that this was the sort of display of affection she would appreciate.

A figure moving through the trees towards the clearing caught Will's eye, and he saw Sir Iris approaching. He too looked younger, but only by a few years. Perhaps Lord Iris was rewarding Eleanor further with a less aged husband for her reunion.

Sir Iris stopped at the edge of the clearing, taking in the back of the woman before him, Will, and his patron without showing any sort of reaction. He bowed deeply and awaited his patron's invitation, which was given with a beckoning finger.

"My Lord," he said, keeping his eyes fixed on the Fae as he drew level with Eleanor. Will admired his self-control. Surely he knew that was Eleanor? How could he resist looking at her?

"Your first wife has told me what you did," Lord Iris said, and for the first time, Will saw a flicker of fear in his Patroon's eyes. "She has satisfied me that you put the family and my desire for perfection first." Lord Iris spread his hands. "This is all I ask of you. Of any of you."

Will felt that was aimed at him and Cathy, but he stayed silent.

"Your second wife has already paid her debt, as has your first. You, however, are indebted to me now and when the time comes, you will give me what I ask for without hesitation."

"Gladly, my Lord," Sir Iris said.

"In a moment," Lord Iris whispered, "you will turn and look at each other and know that despite the evil of others, you are reunited once more. And your love will endure as your enemies are forgotten. The love I will see in your eyes will be pure and unbreakable. No one will come between you ever again."

As he spoke, Will watched his patron lean forwards, a hunger beneath his words. There was something about the way he described it, as if it were more a fantasy of his own than anything to do with the people in front of him.

"Now," Lord Iris said, and stared with longing as the man and woman before him turned to look at each other.

Will kept his focus on him, watching his patron's eyes widen and the smile appear, just briefly, before the coldness crept back. Will smiled to himself too, not because of the joyful reunion unfolding nearby, but because he would be leaving this place with more than he'd hoped for. Not just an association with something that clearly made Lord Iris happy, but also the suspicion that his patron was longing for a reunion of his own. The question was, with whom?

19

Sam flicked through ten news channels in his Manchester office, his smile broadening at the sight of the same things appearing in the scrolling headlines at the bottom of the screen. Lord Copper had ignored his polite request, and his warning, so Sam had executed the next part of the plan.

Leanne's friend Martin Barclay had done sterling work with the information Sam had sent him. He'd listened to Sam's ideas, too, agreed to the plan to increase the pressure on Copper with a huge breakout story about the horrific conditions of several copper mines that supplied metal to prominent UK companies. Just like Lord Copper's mines, those companies had been hiding the information about their suppliers.

As expected, a CEO from the mining company had resigned and the usual bollocks about internal enquiries and rigorous reform were trotted out. Both Sam and Martin agreed that nothing significant would actually happen, so they'd held back more information on further abuses of workers and the environment so that they could pile on more pressure when the time was right. Martin had picked a slow news day, called in some favours with his press contacts, and mobilised hundreds of members of his environmental pressure group to blog, tweet, and generally push the stories on social media too. He'd just received a text from Martin on a burner phone he'd acquired for that very purpose, telling him that the *Daily Mail* was going to run a two-page spread. "It's the first time those bastards have ever taken an interest in one of my press releases!" Martin had crowed.

There was a single knock on his door and then Susan, one of Amir's board whom he'd been purposefully avoiding, stormed in.

"What the fuck are you doing?" she yelled. "I've just sacked the head of Pin PR for—"

"Sit down," Sam said.

"*You* leaked that stuff to the eco-twats! Is this your idea of being a hero?" she shouted, ignoring him. "Do you think that this is going to do anything? It's probably going to make things worse for those poor bastards in the mines. If you keep pushing this the mines will be shut down and they'll lose their jobs. It's the only employer in the region! What the fuck is the point of protecting the environment when it means people are going to starve and—"

"They won't shut them down," Sam said. "They're the most productive in Copper's portfolio. The deposit is too big for him to just give up on. He'll be forced to improve conditions."

"He doesn't control that sort of stuff!"

"Well, he fucking should!" Sam stood up. "I told you lot that things were going to change, and if I waited for you, nothing would happen!"

"You can't just fuck over the other people in the Court like this!" Susan said. "They're going to come after CoFerrum Inc and we're not exactly saintly either, you know."

"What the fuck do you think I've been working on over the past two weeks?" Sam pushed his chair back, moving round his desk to face her. "I already knew just how bad things are. I've got a team of people overhauling every mine, foundry, and factory Amir left to me and within a year all of them are going to be the cleanest operations, the most environmentally responsible, and the best employers in the world."

Susan paled. "You've broken the ten-year rule; you're not supposed to make any major changes to Amir's company until—"

"But he planned to do this," Sam said, not caring if she believed the lie or not. "I found some old files of his, planning it all. He just didn't get the chance to see it through."

"That is such bullshit!"

"Prove it's not," Sam said, having already decided that the worst they could do was set the Elemental Court on him.

"I don't need to. If those files were real we'd already know about them and you wouldn't have had to hire a team in secret. You went behind our backs."

"I had to! This is supposed to be mine, you know. *I'm* Lord Iron. Not you!"

She looked away, so furious she couldn't speak, as if he'd said something worse.

"Oh!" He shook his head. "I'm such an idiot—I should have guessed. You were one of the potentials! You thought he would pick you!"

"I have no idea why he chose a cretin like you, but I thought he saw something I couldn't," she replied. "I was wrong. You were just a mistake. He was starting to lose it and now I see how bad he got. Fuck Amir! And fuck you. I quit."

Sam's desk phone started to ring. He shrugged at Susan. "If that's the way you feel, you'd better tell HR. Just don't forget the NDA you signed. If you go to anyone else in the Court, if you take any data with you on anything to do with my shit, I'll roast you."

"Oh, piss off, you fucking hippie!" she said, opening the door.

"Give your phone to Des on the way out," Sam said, loud enough for Des to hear. "He'll send your personal belongings to your home address."

She slammed the door behind her. The phone was still ringing. He took a moment, glad she was gone and hoping she'd take some of the others with her, then picked up.

"I know you did this," Copper said.

"I told you I was going to do something," Sam replied, sitting back down. "Question is, what are you going to do about it? It's going to get worse if you don't sort your shit out."

"I'm cutting you out of the Bolivian deal."

Sam struggled to remember what that even was. There was something mentioned about it at the Court, but he'd mostly tuned out by that point of Copper's talk, unable to concentrate whilst he was reeling from how disappointing they all were. "Whatever."

"And I'll tell you this. It's going to get worse for *you* if you don't sort *your* shit out."

"You're mistaking me for someone who gives a fuck. Now, if you'll excuse me, I've got more important things to do."

He put the phone down and tilted his chair back, ignoring the phone when it started to ring again. Was this what his life was now? Angry phone calls and people coming into his office to shout at him? It was like *Dallas* or some other shitty soap opera he used to watch as a kid so he could stay up late. Rich people stamping their feet at each other when they didn't get their own way. Sod them.

There was another knock on the door, one he recognised as Des. "Come in."

"Sorry to disturb you, sir."

"You're not going to jack your job in too, are you, Des?"

The man smiled. "Not planning to, sir. There's a lady on the line, says she needs to speak to you about something private. She called your unlisted number, sir, the one no one's supposed to have."

Sam sat up. It couldn't be Cathy; she'd call his mobile. "Put her through."

Des went out and moments later the phone rang again. Sam picked up.

"Hello?"

"Is this Lord Iron?"

"Speaking."

"Good morning. My name is Beatrice. I'm a representative from the Sorcerer of Essex. I was wondering if I could come to see you regarding a commission."

Sam straightened. "The Sorcerer of Essex?"

"Yes. Dante would like to commission a piece, but is unable to travel and wants me to come to discuss it with you. It's quite complex and he doesn't trust other means of communication."

"Umm, yeah, come to my place in Cheshire. Do you know where that is?"

"I do, Lord Iron; it was in the latest communication sent out by your staff. I shall be with you by this evening, if that's convenient?"

"Great, see you then," Sam said, and put the phone down. So the wheels surrounding his becoming Lord Iron had been turning. And maybe Petra wasn't as much of a rarity as he thought. Maybe all the Sorcerers had women working for them as well as men.

He rubbed his hands together. Maybe she could tell him more about the Sorcerers and what they expected of him. Maybe she'd know where that forge near the Thames that he'd seen on the iron slab was. Either way, his first commission was a milestone he was more excited about than his first threat from a member of the Elemental Court.

• • •

Elizabeth descended the stairs in her new gown, feeling quite pleased with herself for needing only two hours to get ready for meeting her future husband. Of course, no contract had been signed and Mother hadn't even met him yet, but she was confident all would go smoothly. She was beautiful and accomplished and everything a man would want from a wife. He was rich and came from a good family. It couldn't be more perfect.

She wondered whether he would want to stay in Londinium or establish his new family elsewhere. As long as he didn't want to live in Jorvic or Aquae Sulis, she'd be happy with anywhere else in Albion, as long as the house was at least as nice as this one. Elizabeth was just about to start making decisions about whether she wanted to have her wedding gown in the empire line or something with a fuller skirt when she became aware of a cluster of servants near the front door.

"What's happened?" she asked the butler.

"The Duchess hasn't returned. Neither has the Duke."

"Oh, he's not going to be back until this evening. Is something wrong?"

The butler moved so that he could keep glancing out of the

window as he spoke. "The Maharaj Kumari of Rajkot is due any minute, and the Duchess isn't here to receive her."

Elizabeth rolled her eyes. "My sister is the worst Duchess in the history of Albion."

"They're here!" one of the maids called. "Look at all the carriages!"

They all went to the windows and Elizabeth felt a spike of envy at the sight of the Princess's entourage rolling up to the house in over a dozen carriages. Why couldn't William have found a prince for her to marry?

"Are we expected to give lunch to all of them?" asked one of the maids.

"It was unclear in the message," the butler replied, his forehead shining with sweat.

"Is she the princess who went to the ball in Aquae Sulis?" Elizabeth asked, but no one seemed to know. She couldn't think of any other princesses visiting Albion. It was so unfair. Cathy didn't care a jot about how lucky she was to have royalty visit. How typical that she'd forgotten. She thought of no one but herself.

One of the footmen jumped down from the back of the most ornately decorated carriage while a man emerged from another. He was dressed in brightly coloured silk that made Elizabeth feel very drab in her white Regency gown. She marvelled at the colour of his skin, at his hair worn long and braided at the back and at the curved sword hanging from beneath the saffron-coloured sash wrapped around his waist.

He marched up the steps and the butler shooed the staff into a receiving line, pausing when he came across Elizabeth, who ignored him and continued to watch from the window. The Princess was being helped from the carriage by a very attractive footman.

When she stepped out, the Princess paused to have the silks of her sari arranged as a set of four bodyguards with their own curved swords got out of the second carriage and arranged themselves behind her.

Elizabeth had never seen so many jewels worn by a single

person. From the tiny gems stitched into the embroidered cloth to the larger ones set into her tiara, the Princess glittered with the most astounding wealth. Elizabeth pouted. The Princess was beautiful, too, and that really was too much. Her skin was so smooth and its dark brown against the reds and golds of her regal clothes looked so attractive compared to her own milky skin. Her black hair was so long it brushed the hem of her sari even though it was partly braided and arranged beneath the tiara. Elizabeth's eyes narrowed. Surely it was only so smooth and perfect because of a Charm?

There was a loud knock at the door. After a moment with his eyes closed, as if in prayer, Morgan opened the door.

The man on the doorstep gave the slightest bow, one acknowledging an equal, and said, "Her Royal Highness, Maharaj Kumari Rani Nucifera-Nelumbo."

He stood aside as the Princess climbed the steps. Elizabeth could see a drop of sweat roll down the side of Morgan's head. This was ridiculous. Trust Cathy to insult someone on an international scale without even realising it.

"Your Royal Highness," Morgan said, and then bowed, moving aside to admit her.

Elizabeth saw the edge of the Princess's silk slipper cross the threshold and then walked over, the brightest, sweetest smile on her face. "Your Royal Highness," she said as the Princess entered, followed by the guards. "Welcome to Londinium and to Lancaster House. You honour us with your visit."

She could see Morgan's eyes, wide and fearful, over the Princess's shoulder.

"I was told you are very plain," the Princess said. "More lies." She turned to the man who'd announced her. "Bring the box."

"Would you like to take tea with me in the drawing room?" Elizabeth said, doing her best to ignore the horrified expressions on the servants' faces. They were so silly—she hadn't lied about who she was, she was merely being polite.

"No," the Princess said sharply, breaking Elizabeth's flow. "I will not be here very long."

"Oh. Do you have another engagement?"

"I am returning home as soon as my business here is over."

Elizabeth smiled again, wondering why the Princess was being so cold. Had she already met Cathy? No, judging by what she had said about being plain, she couldn't have. Was there some point of etiquette she was unaware of?

"I see," Elizabeth said, hoping that her smile didn't seem too forced. "Has your tour of Albion been enjoyable?"

"It has been most enlightening," the Princess replied frostily.

"I must say, your English is very good."

The Princess drew herself up as if Elizabeth had said something rude. "Did you expect me to sound like a savage? My tutors were educated at Mumbai, Oxford, and Yale. I have had elocution lessons since the age of three. I am fluent in ten languages and English is my least favourite."

Elizabeth blinked. She was so rude! But all she could wonder about was the places other than Oxford that she mentioned with such pride. "I'm sorry, I'm not familiar with Mum—Mumbabai, nor Yale. Are they in Mundanus?"

She could see Morgan close his eyes again, as if prayer were something he had only just discovered and wanted to do again and again. Like lawn tennis, she supposed.

The Princess fixed her with a glare. "I have come to expect ignorance here. You are no exception."

Elizabeth was so shocked the words flew from her mind. As she grasped for a pithy retort, the man came back in, carrying a large ebony box inlaid with exquisite marquetry of ivory and mother-of-pearl.

"I bring a message from my father, formerly known as the Prince of Rajkot. My father, the Maharana of Gujarat, no longer recognises the authority of the Patroons of Albion. We are henceforth the independent Kingdom of Gujarat, and the Maharana and Maharani of Gujarat will serve our Fae patrons directly. The thirty-seven members of the Rajkot Court who were born in Albion or Great Britain have been expelled. Your people are no longer welcome in

Gujarat. This box," she waved a jewelled hand at it, "contains the trade contracts previously held by citizens of Albion, many of them residents of Londinium. They are declared void as the Princely State of Rajkot no longer exists. All rights to export our goods are denied. No tithes will be paid to you or any of the Patroons of Albion from this day. Our sovereign border is closed to you and should any of your agents be discovered doing business in mundane Gujarat, they will be expelled."

Elizabeth bit her lip. She had the impression that the speech had been rehearsed and was very important, but she didn't understand all of it. She knew nothing about Rajkot or Gujarat or contracts, but it was clear something had gone very wrong. People expelled from their court? No tithes? This sounded very serious.

"But…but why?" was all she could think of to say.

The Princess took a step towards her, intimidating in her regalia. "Over fifty years have passed since those in Mundanus threw off the shackles of your disgusting empire. That knowledge was hidden from my family, our Court held under Albion's thumb, our nobles Charmed and intimidated into following your Patroons and their pawns placed in our Royal Court. No more."

"Disgusting empire?" Elizabeth said, feeling her cheeks flush. "How dare you!"

"No, little Duchess, how dare *you*! How dare you profit from the wealth of our kingdom whilst taxing our royal family and denying us the right to trade our own goods? I came to Albion to see it for myself and to do the bidding of my father, the Maharana." The Princess took another step forwards, forcing Elizabeth to move back a step. It didn't seem that she was delivering a message by rote anymore. "And what do I find, Duchess? I find people who think of the world as it was hundreds of years ago. I have been treated as nothing more than a thing to be paraded at parties to demonstrate the power and influence of the ones *I* granted permission to escort me there! I have been spoken to like a child, a savage, an object to be slavered over and bargained for like a goat in a mundane market. I have had people touch my skin as if expecting it to feel different, without asking permission to approach my royal person. But that is not the worst I have found here."

She moved forwards again, Elizabeth stepping back until she nudged against a vase on a pedestal. It teetered but didn't fall.

"My father said, 'Go to this distant Albion and tell me how our people fare there. Tell me if I have been too harsh in my judgement.' *Our people. Our. People.*"

Elizabeth slipped away to the side, desperate to put some air between them, to give herself a moment to think. "I…I have no idea who you are talking about!"

"Exactly!" the Princess said, so loud the crystals tinkled in the chandeliers. "I have visited every court in Albion, attended balls and dinner parties and recitals, and not one of our people was there. Where are the two emissaries from Marwar? Where are the three wives who returned with their white husbands after they fell in love in our Court? Where are the children we were told were born to them? Where are the twin princes of the Zambian court who came to make their home here, mentioned in letters home over a hundred years ago?"

"I have no idea!"

"Precisely! They've been hidden away, pushed out of your courts and denied permission to return home by their Patroons! My father will learn that this place is everything we feared and worse. He is a kinder, more merciful ruler than any of yours have ever been. I can only hope that those exiles who crawl back to Albion in disgrace are welcomed by their own here. But I doubt it."

Princess Rani swept towards the door, pausing to turn and face Elizabeth. "You know nothing, closeted away in your ivory towers, seeing nothing but *white* faces. There is a whole world of beauty that you are denied by your ignorant, immoral Patroons. Gujarat is the first of the former Princely States to break free, but it will not be the last. Our neighbours will follow our example. Our friends in America—the *colonies*, as you so offensively call them still—are in agreement with us. Your ancient, backwards men cannot keep the influence of Mundanus a secret forever." She looked Elizabeth up and down and then her face softened. "I pity you. Duchess or not, you have as much power as that umbrella stand."

She flicked a finger towards the carriages and her man hurried out before her. Elizabeth just stood there, trembling, as the hem of the Princess's sari disappeared.

Morgan closed the door and Elizabeth's face burned under the stare of all of the servants. "Don't look at me like that!" she cried. "I didn't do anything wrong! She obviously hated us!"

"I shall put this somewhere safe until the Duke returns," Morgan said, picking up the box. "Don't just stand there!" he said to the staff, and they all hurried off, leaving Elizabeth alone in the hallway.

Elizabeth sniffled, feeling shamed and upset, even though she was sure she hadn't done anything wrong. Was this what politics was like? It was awful. Being Duchess had suddenly lost its appeal.

20

"Chief constable now?" Amesbury said, staring at the screen of Kay's computer. "Well, he's done all right."

"The crooked ones usually do, right?" Kay said, and he nodded.

"If you need to know anything about him, just ask Kay," the gargoyle said from the other side of her desk. "She's a genius on that computer."

She winked at the gargoyle. Max was sure that if it had been possible, the stone cheeks would have blushed.

"All we need to know is how to get a message to him that he won't be able to ignore," Max said.

"I can help you with that," Amesbury said. "And I know how to get it to him."

"So is this a sting operation?" Kay asked, and both Max and the gargoyle nodded.

"I'm going to set up a meeting with him, saying I have critical information on the disappearances featured in the newspaper, and that I can help him find the one behind it all."

"But that won't make any sense to him," Kay said. "The disappearances go back too far. The same person can't be responsible for them. I mean, that's what he'll think, being a mundane."

"I prefer the term 'innocent'," Max said.

"He's far from that," Amesbury muttered. "He's as crooked as they come."

"But he's also probably unaware of what exactly is going on," Max said. "It's a grey area. Either way, if I say as much in the letter, he'll know it's something his contact will want to know about.

Once he tells the Fae-touched, they'll know they have to be there to contain a potential breach."

"And that's when you'll bust them like a total badass."

The gargoyle grinned at Kay. "Yup."

"I don't want to arrest the puppet in Mundanus," Max said. "I'll watch the meeting point at a distance—with your help, Robert—and then once the puppet is identified, I can make the arrest in the Nether."

Amesbury nodded. "And then what happens to my old boss?"

"I'll have to investigate the extent of the corruption and how much they've tampered with him," Max replied.

Even though Amesbury didn't look satisfied, he accepted it. Max found him easy to work with. He was calm and methodical. He'd only needed two cups of tea and a bit of a sit-down after meeting the gargoyle for the first time. His own experience made it easier for him to accept the "weird shit," as Kay called it, and the chance that he could stop it from happening to anyone else made him highly motivated. He still wasn't an Arbiter, though, so he had to be kept away from the puppets as much as possible. In the long term, Rupert was going to have to make more. The gargoyle scowled at him when he thought that.

They'd had two puppets under surveillance since the tip-off from the Peonia boy about the Second Sons, and he couldn't have done it without Amesbury's help. At least it had been a good reason to get the gargoyle to leave the office. Max had tried to convince it to stay in the Nether as he came back and coordinated the next move, but the gargoyle had insisted. With Rupert's high-tech sensors planted all around the two family houses, there wasn't any way they could leave the Nether without them knowing.

"I'll leave it to you to set up the sting," he said to Amesbury, who nodded. "Tell him I'll go to his office at eight o'clock this evening. At least most of the staff will have gone home. Let's get back to the Nether," he said to the gargoyle.

"But the sensor thingies are—" the gargoyle began, but Max wasn't having any of it.

"Nothing beats eyes on the job," he said. "Those sensors don't cover everywhere. Come on."

• • •

Cathy shut herself in her bedroom, needing some space away from all the fussing. At least Will hadn't been home when they'd finally got back—if he'd seen the huge hole she'd blasted in the side of the carriage he never would have wanted her to leave the house again.

Carter had a concussion. They'd ended up sitting on the Nether road for a while waiting for him to be well enough to travel again. Carter had mostly held his head, looking like he was going to be sick any moment, trying to give her his resignation. Cathy spent the entire journey back telling him she wouldn't accept it. She could only hope that it had sunk in.

Once she'd explained what happened, Morgan told her about the Princess's visit and how disastrous it had been. She felt terrible. She should have checked the day's itinerary with Morgan before she left. The panicked message from Charlotte and then the attack had pushed all other thoughts from her mind. Morgan was only too happy to deliver the box containing the voided contracts to her study, leaving it to her to break it to Will.

She lay on the bed and shook for a while, knowing it was a delayed reaction to the stress of it all, then fell asleep. A hand on her shoulder woke her.

"Cathy?"

She looked up into Will's eyes. In those moments of drowsiness all she could think of was how handsome he was. Those big brown eyes, so kind, focused on her. Those lips, so soft, ready to be kissed.

"Morgan said you were attacked. Are you all right?"

"I'm fine. It's all fine. They ran away. Carter was brilliant."

"Tom is looking into it," Will said, smoothing her hair away from her face. "We'll find out who it was. I'm putting extra footmen on your carriage from now on, with the same protections as Carter."

"But those Charms cost a fortune; how will you—"

"Shh, don't worry about that." He kissed her forehead. "I'll do anything to keep you safe."

"You're not going to say some bobbins about me not being able to go out again, are you?"

Will frowned. "No, of course not. I pledged to make those roads safe. If you changed your behaviour and news of that attack got out, it would look very poor indeed."

Cathy nodded. At least Will's political ambition and her desire to be as independent as possible aligned for once.

"There's someone who wants to speak to you downstairs. Are you up to it?"

"Give me a few minutes to freshen up. I'll be right down." They kissed and she did her best to ignore the way her traitorous body wanted more. He slid his hand down behind her neck and lifted her to him for a deeper, more passionate kiss.

"Tonight," he whispered, kissing her neck. "There are a few things I need to attend to first, then we'll have the rest of the evening together."

She kissed him back and it was only when he left that she remembered what she'd learned about the marriages he was arranging. "Shit." She pressed her fists into her forehead. When he kissed her like that it was hard to remember anything.

She got up, washed her face, and tried not to think about how those kisses had felt. She had more important things to do than become some simpering thing pining for her husband to return and ravish her. She had to check in on Wilhelmina, whom she'd neglected terribly over the day. She also needed to work out the best way to prevent pregnancy without Lord Iris—or Will, for that matter—finding out. She should have done that already but there were never enough hours in the day and sneaking to a mundane pharmacy was so hard.

She went down the stairs and Morgan guided her towards the drawing room. "Who's waiting to see me?" she asked.

"Dame Iris, your Grace."

Cathy missed a step. "What?"

"She doesn't look like the one who…the one who used to visit," Morgan said in a whisper. "I think she's new."

Cathy readied herself as best as she could and went in. A lady stood waiting for her near the window, her presence somehow filling the entire room. Cathy found herself bobbing a curtsy when she turned from gazing over the gardens to look at her.

"Cathy," she smiled. "A pleasure to see you again."

Cathy took in the glossy black hair, the porcelain skin, the large, dark blue eyes. Something about her face was familiar. "...Eleanor?"

"The very same," Eleanor said with a dazzling smile. "You're the first person to recognise me other than my husband."

"Holy shit," Cathy gasped.

Eleanor raised an eyebrow. "I know it's rather a shock, but really, must one resort to such language?"

"I..." Cathy went over to her. "How?"

"A combination of your husband's swift thinking and the kindness of our patron."

Cathy snorted. "There's no kindness in him."

"There is if one has earned it," Eleanor replied sternly.

A sinking dread settled in Cathy's stomach. After everything she'd been through, Eleanor seemed incredibly pro-Iris. But then, what did she expect? Lord Iris wasn't going to restore a woman's youth unless she was of use to him.

"I'm not very good at earning his kindness," Cathy said. "And you know I'm not...you know I don't fit in."

Eleanor nodded and smiled, coming over and taking her hands. "My dear girl, I know how this life chafes at you. I'm not going to try and force you into being the opposite of what you are. We've both seen how unsuccessful that is. Don't look so fearful, my dear. You have a handsome, clever husband, a bright mind, and a passionate heart. I am certain that together we will find a way to align your happiness with the goals of our family."

Cathy managed a smile and pulled away as Morgan brought in the afternoon tea. "There's something I want to talk to you about. As Dame but also, I hope, as my friend."

Dame Iris sat down and gestured for Cathy to do the same. "Tell me what concerns you so."

Cathy poured the tea, buying some time to think of a way to put it. By the time both cups were full, she was no closer. She sighed at the ceiling. "Look, there's no way I can dress this up. Bertrand Viola is planning to marry his daughter off to Nathaniel Iris."

"I know," Eleanor replied, stirring her tea.

"Oh." Eleanor looked at her expectantly. "Well, the thing is… he's just a…well, Charlotte and I…"

"Just say it, Cathy."

"He's a total arsehole and Emmeline is so sweet and he'll just be the most awful husband and we can't let it go ahead."

Eleanor's eyes were impressively large. "You do have a peculiar eloquence, Cathy. We simply need to find a way to make it more palatable for Society. As for your opinion on your brother-in-law, I suggest you keep that to yourself in future."

"But Eleanor, he's a thug!"

"Nathaniel is a passionate young man. He'll calm down as he matures. As for this marriage, I see no reason to oppose it. The Viola girl is sweet, by all accounts, and comes from a respected and wealthy family. A family that will have political ambitions now that that idiot Frederick Viola is no longer with us. Those ambitions need to be kept in check and that's exactly what this match achieves, along with the one between your sister and Bertie's cousin. The Violas will be kept close where we can keep an eye on them and Bertie will need to keep Will happy to keep his daughter happy and safe. It's all very neat and tidy. Just the way Lord Iris likes things to be."

Cathy's heart fell when she heard her call him "Bertie." Of course, they probably knew each other before Eleanor was spirited away. "But it will be such an unhappy marriage. And Emmeline's mother—" She stopped herself just in time. "Her mother is a dear friend and I know what Nathaniel is really like, and I can't in all conscience tell her that her daughter will be happy."

Eleanor finished her tea and placed the cup and saucer back on the table. "Cathy, dear, I am very fond of you. And it's clear that you've never had a woman help you navigate life in Society. You have such potential and I'd hate to see it wasted. I have no intention of forcing you to be anything other than yourself, but you have to let go of some childish notions. Marriage is not arranged for happiness; it's arranged for the mutual benefit of the families involved. If the couple discovers happiness, then it is their good fortune. I suggest you reassure your friend as best you can and leave matters to take their course."

"But—"

Eleanor stood. "And you need to learn which battles are worth fighting." She smiled sweetly and kissed Cathy's cheek. "This isn't one of them, dear. Now, I will take your leave as I have a great deal to catch up on and a husband I need to get back into order."

Cathy stood and watched her leave. "Shit and bollocks," she whispered beneath her breath once the Dame was gone. She picked up a slice of angel cake and shoved it into her mouth, trying to decide if Eleanor was an ally or simply a kinder jailer.

The sound of a carriage arriving drew her to the window. Thinking it had come to pick Eleanor up, she stood and watched, churning over her options. There was no one in the Iris family who would oppose the marriage. The only thing she could do to stop the wedding was take down Bertrand Viola, and thereby make a marriage with his daughter a less attractive proposition. But she had no idea how to do that without it being catastrophic for Charlotte and her children. It would be so much easier if Charlotte were willing to escape into Mundanus, but Cathy could understand her fear. She didn't have the right to bully her into anything, no matter how much she thought it would be preferable to living with that monster.

The carriage stopped and Mr Lutea-Digitalis climbed out. Choking on the angel cake, Cathy dashed from the room to warn Wilhelmina, only to find her coming down the stairs with her bag, Will beside her. Dame Iris was nowhere to be seen.

Cathy pointed at the door and shook her head at Wilhelmina as she desperately tried to swallow the mouthful of cake.

"I'm going home, your Grace," Wilhelmina said with a smile. "I wanted to thank you for your hospitality."

Cathy finally gulped the last of it down. "What? Wait, nothing has changed!"

"On the contrary," Wilhelmina said. "The Duke has intervened—he listened, as you promised he would—and has seen to it that my husband will take better care of me."

"But that isn't enough!"

"It is for me," Wilhelmina said, reaching her. "Your Grace, I have no intention of causing a scandal. I don't want to cause any trouble. I just want to live my life without being afraid."

"But how can you be sure he won't just be like he was before? How can you be safe?"

Wilhelmina smiled shyly at Will. "I trust my Duke when he says it will never happen again. That's enough for me."

The knock at the front door brought Morgan into the hall as Will kissed Wilhelmina's hand, making her blush crimson. "Remember what I said, Mrs Digitalis. The moment you feel unsafe, you send word to me. It won't happen, but if it does, you know I will intervene."

"Thank you, your Grace," she replied breathlessly, and then picked up her bag as her husband was admitted.

"There you are, my dear," he said to Wilhelmina as if they'd simply been separated during a crowded ball. He bowed deeply to Will and inclined his head to Cathy.

Cathy watched as he kissed his wife's cheek, balling her fists up as Will came to her side, probably to hold her back if needed.

"I'll see you at Black's," Will said to him, and Digitalis gave him a nervous smile.

"I look forward to it, your Grace," he said, unconvincingly, and the couple left.

"What the hell was that?" Cathy asked once the door was firmly shut.

"Now, don't start," Will said. "Let me explain first. Is there any tea left from the Dame's visit?"

She nodded and marched to the drawing room. Will followed and closed the door behind them.

"Oh, angel cake," he said cheerfully. "I do like that."

"Will!" Cathy folded her arms as he went to the table and broke a chunk off a slice and ate it, as if nothing had happened. "How can you protect her?"

Will grinned, looking rather smug. "Remember me telling you that there's often a quieter, alternative way to solve problems? Well, there was the proof. Tea?"

"I wanted to see a change in the law."

"I know, my love, but there was no way that could happen. The Patroons would never allow it, and that poor woman couldn't stay here for much longer without the gossip starting. It really had to be solved swiftly, before Digitalis took it higher."

"There you go again, putting the men first."

"Oh, Cathy. Come and sit down, my love, and let me explain."

She hesitated, torn between wanting to yell at him and wanting to know how safe Wilhelmina could possibly be. His hand patted the sofa next to him and she wanted to be close to him again, no matter how angry she was. She sat beside him as he poured more tea.

"This is rather stewed," he said. "Shall I call for more?"

"Just tell me what you did."

He twisted round so their knees were touching, something she found remarkably distracting. "I obtained some information on Mr Digitalis and learned he has a secret that he has managed to keep hidden thus far. I made him aware that I know of it now and that if he treats his wife with anything less than the highest respect and affection, I'll destroy his reputation and his standing within his family."

Cathy stared at him.

"I know," Will smiled. "I was rather shocked by how simple it was too."

Sickened, Cathy realised Will assumed she was speechless with admiration. "You think that blackmail is the best solution to this?"

"I think that Wilhelmina is safe and her husband won't cause any trouble, now or in the future."

"What if he loses his temper and pushes her down the stairs?"

"My love, a change in the rights of the woman within marriage wouldn't prevent that. A man's temper is not something that can be reined in by such things."

Cathy wanted to bang her head against a wall. He'd not only undermined everything she had done to keep Wilhelmina safe, but also cut off the motivation for anyone to change the law. "But men mistreating their wives is all but sanctioned when the women are seen as property."

"Darling, please can't you see that you're talking about things that simply aren't going to change? I have found a way to keep her safe, and if you discover any other mistreatment, I can help to protect the ladies in those marriages too. Quietly. Without earning the wrath of the Patroons."

"Oh, for fuck's sake!" Cathy yelled, unable to hold it in any longer. "Digging up dirt on all the men in Londinium and blackmailing them is not a solution!"

"Then give me a better one. One that doesn't endanger us."

"We need to have some bloody guts and make the change and weather the storm."

Will rested his head in his hands. "This damn wish," he muttered. "It makes you say the most ridiculous things."

That was what Will thought drove her? How could he have such an opinion of her? "This isn't Poppy's wish magic! This is me! I stayed to change Society and fuck all is changing!"

She expected him to shout back but instead he looked hurt. "Is it the only reason you stayed?"

"I didn't know you enough to stay for you back then."

"But you know me now." His hand reached for hers, rested on top of it. "You said you love me. Isn't that enough for you to stay?"

His eyes looked so sad. His hand held hers tenderly and he smelt so good. She shook her head, feeling derailed. "That…that isn't the point. The point is that I'm getting nowhere. Worse than nowhere! Now people are shooting at my carriage and—"

Will paled. "Shooting? No one mentioned that!"

"It doesn't matter."

"Of course it does!"

Cathy squeezed her eyes shut, feeling like she was trying to keep her balance on a beam as Will kept trying to pull her off. "All that matters is the work," she said, more to herself than him. "And Margritte hasn't replied to my letters and this bloody Ladies' Court is a crap idea and isn't happening by the look of things. Charlotte is wasting away and she hasn't heard from Margritte either. We're starting to worry about her."

When she opened her eyes, Will looked serious. "I have some news about Margritte, my love."

The way he said it made her shiver. "Did Nathaniel find her?"

"Yes. The Patroons were putting on the pressure and he pulled out all the stops. I did all I could, but it wasn't enough."

"When?"

"A day or so ago—but I only just found out myself."

Cathy's throat tightened. "What will happen to her?"

"The Patroons discovered that she collaborated with a Sorcerer to capture me. They've exiled her to New Amsterdam. She's forbidden from making any contact with anyone in Albion for the next hundred years. It could have been much worse."

Cathy slumped, pulling her hand from his, tears falling freely.

"I'm so sorry, my love. I did all I could."

She nodded. "I know."

There was a knock on the door and Will called, "Come in," as Cathy wiped away the tears.

"The Marquis of Westminster is here," Morgan said. "Shall I show him in?"

Will nodded. "Maybe he's found out something about the attack," he said to Cathy.

Tom entered, having followed Morgan to the drawing room. "I'm still working on that, your Grace," he said. "I'm here to see Cathy. It's a personal matter."

Cathy felt the tension return to her stomach as she saw the look in Tom's eyes. This was bad.

"Can't it wait?" Will snapped.

Tom, as surprised as her by his reaction, blushed. "I'm afraid not, your Grace."

Cathy kissed Will's cheek and went over to Tom. "I'm sure it won't take long," she said to Will, and left with her brother.

"We'll be taking a carriage," he said. "Will you want a cape or wrap?"

"What's going on?"

Tom sighed. "I've just had to arrest our former governess, Cathy. Natasha Rainer is in my custody."

21

When Sam's car pulled up outside his house that evening there was a minibus outside, just as his security team at the gatehouse had warned him on the way in. The housekeeper was standing on the front steps, looking very stressed.

He got out, saw that there were two people sitting in the front of the minibus, and went straight over to Mrs Morrison. "Who are they?"

"I told security at the gatehouse to let them through because the woman said she's Eleanor but that's rubbish," she said in her broad Lancashire accent. "I told her to wait in that there bus till you got back. She said she wants to take your guests home, but I thought they didn't have a home, Mr Ferran. I thought that was why they was 'ere."

"Okay. Go inside, Mrs M, I'll take care of it."

She gave a last glare at the minibus and went inside. As Sam approached, the driver got out, nipped round, and opened the door for the passenger. A very beautiful woman, who looked for all the world like one of the princesses from his childhood books, climbed out.

"Sam," she smiled. "Mrs Morrison didn't recognise me. I really am Eleanor. Don't you see it?"

"Jesus," he whispered. "What fuckery is this?"

She pursed her lips in a very Eleanor way but didn't comment on his language. "I've been restored to my rightful place at the head of my family. I now have the resources to care for the other people rescued from the asylum. I've come to take them to their new home."

"But they don't want to go back to the Nether."

"I know, I won't force them into it, but I'll house them in a property that has a reflection. Then I can visit them easily and it will be easier to find staff who understand the delicacy of the situation. It's the only way. I wouldn't have chosen to travel in such a ridiculous vehicle unless it were absolutely necessary."

Sam folded his arms. "Does Cathy know about this?"

"No, Cathy has enough to deal with. Besides, as I'm now Dame of her family, she would have to agree with me. You've been very kind, Lord Iron, but we don't need your help anymore."

Sam didn't feel he had the right to decide for those people—and besides, without Eleanor there to bridge the gap between them and life in Mundanus, things would fall apart. None of them would speak to him, for one thing. "If they want to go with you, I won't stand in the way. But I want you to make it clear that they have a choice."

Eleanor raised an eyebrow but then inclined her head in agreement.

He stood aside as she and the driver went into the house and kept out of the way in his study whilst things were sorted out. He hoped it would all be done before the representative from the Sorcerer of Essex arrived.

Finally, there was a knock on the door. He let Eleanor in. "All done?"

She nodded. "They all elected to come with me and pass on their gratitude for your hospitality, as do I. We may come from opposite worlds, Lord Iron, but you will always be dear to me."

He smiled, trying to adjust to her youthful face. It wasn't just that, though, it was her bearing. Before, she'd seemed quietly matriarchal, someone who could humiliate with just a look or bolster confidence with a few words. Now it was like trying to have a conversation with a queen. "Any time you need me, Eleanor, I'm here."

"It's Dame Iris now, dear. We mustn't let our standards slip just because of the extraordinary circumstances."

"Can I ask you something, before you go?" At her nod, he said,

"I don't understand. Why would you want to go back? From what Cathy says, life in the Nether sounds like hell."

Dame Iris gave a sad smile. "Cathy sees life in the Nether as suffering under tyrannical rule. It's her way. But I can assure you, the tyranny of ageing is far crueler than that of the Fae. She's too young to understand that and I hope she never will. Oh, don't look so worried, dear. She's going to be absolutely fine. I will look after her and soon she'll be far too excited and busy to get herself all worked up about silly things."

"Why? What's she doing?"

"She's going to have a baby," Dame Iris replied brightly. "And with that dashing husband of hers and all that comfort and wealth, she'll soon forget about Mundanus. I wish you good health and a happy life, Lord Iron. I would like to say that I'll see you again, but I doubt our paths will cross in the future. Good day to you."

Sam watched her go, too shocked to reply, and then it was too late. He listened to the crunch of the gravel beneath the minibus tyres as he tried to imagine Cathy settling down in the Nether. She'd never mentioned being pregnant. He shook his head. No, he just couldn't see her wanting this. "Fuck!" He slammed his hand against the doorframe. He should have just hugged her in London, broken the magic and brought her home with him. No, that wasn't right either. It was her choice. Wasn't it?

He pulled out his phone and called her. "Cathy, Dame Iris has just taken all the people from the asylum with her. They wanted to go, and I didn't think I could stop them. Look…she said you're going to have a baby. Are you? Are you sure you're okay? I can be with you in just a couple of hours, just say the word. You don't have to stay there, even if you're pregnant, okay? Just…just call me and let me know you're all right."

Sam paced the room a few times and then decided to shower. It could be days before she picked up her messages.

Cleaned up and back into his jeans and an old fleece, he felt much better. No voicemail or texts. He sighed. Should he just go down there and see her?

The sound of a car on the drive drew him to the window of his bedroom and he saw a taxi parking up. Beatrice.

He raced down the stairs and opened the door, eager to greet her personally. The woman he assumed was Beatrice was paying the driver, so he slipped on his shoes to go and help with her bags.

She shuffled along the seat and tried to open her door but the driver was saying something and she looked confused. Through the closed doors, Sam could only hear a muffled voice, but it was enough to tell the driver was angry about something. He walked round and knocked on the window.

The driver opened it. "Look at this!" he said, thrusting a sheet of paper at Sam. "Tell this silly cow that it ain't money!"

Sam looked at the calligraphy saying something about a promise to pay the bearer…and realised it was a huge banknote from a very long time ago. He only recognised it because of a documentary he'd accidentally watched once when he had the flu and couldn't be bothered to change the channel.

Sam pulled out his wallet and gave the driver a fifty. "Here you go, mate. She's got a weird sense of humour. Keep the change."

"Cheers," the man said gruffly, and unlocked the doors.

Beatrice got out, pulling a carpetbag with her from the back seat. She had dark blonde hair coiled multiple times at the back of her head and pinned into place with some sort of decorative net that he'd never in his life seen a woman wear. She looked about forty and was wearing a loose white dress, the sort of floaty thing that Leanne used to wear as a student. In the summer. The woman looked absolutely freezing.

"Do you have any bags in the boot?" Sam asked, and she looked down at his shoes, confused. "Is that your only bag?" he asked, pointing at the one she held.

"Oh. Yes. Should I have more?"

He shook his head and she looked relieved. Sam gestured towards the house, closing her car door for her, and the taxi drove off.

Beatrice wore flimsy silk slippers and was staring down at the gravel rather than heading inside. He could see her wriggling her feet, making the stones crunch beneath them.

"Let's go inside," he said. "It's bloody cold out here."

She followed him in and when Sam shut the door he could hear her teeth chattering. He steered her towards the living room, which already had a fire blazing in it, thanks to Mrs Morrison. Beatrice went to the heat gratefully.

"It's winter," she said.

"Yes," Sam said, wondering if the Sorcerer had ever let her into Mundanus before.

"I forgot," she said. "I'm Beatrice. Oh! My credentials, yes."

Beatrice fumbled with the clasp on the carpetbag, her numb fingers clumsy with cold. She was wearing several rings, some with jewels, some plain, and when she bent over a long necklace that had been tucked beneath her dress fell down to brush the bag. He wasn't sure what it was made of, but it didn't look metallic. She tucked it away again and the bag's clasp sprang open.

She rummaged and then pulled out a small drawstring bag that looked like it was made of silk. She presented it to him on both palms, like an offering made at an altar.

He took it, surprised by how heavy it was, opened the bag, and found a disc of iron inside that he knew was pure and had been made by the first Lord Iron, even before he took it out. It was a couple of centimetres thick and ten centimetres in diameter.

Sam eased it from the bag and let it sit on his palm for a few moments, revelling in how it made him feel…connected in some inexplicable way, to something so much more than himself. It had a shield embossed on the surface, with three curved swords arranged in a column, like scimitars, but somehow he knew they weren't. As he tried to work out why he felt that way, the knowledge came to him as if he'd known all along: they were seaxes, the weapon of choice of the East Saxons. And he knew that the first Lord Iron had made some of those and they had slaughtered men and their blood had fed the earth.

Sam could feel his chest expand with a feeling of strength and pride, with a sense of his feet being rooted to the ground and an energy flowing between the earth and himself. He was aware of the huge iron slab at the centre of the house, the forge at the edge of the estate, and even, distantly, the sense of the others being out there too.

And it felt incredible. Sam wanted to roar and beat his chest like some rugby thug, to fuck ten women and then go and invade somewhere or at least go and start a fight with someone. If William Iris had walked in then, he felt like he could snap him in two and then take Cathy as his own and—

He put it back in the pouch and drew the string shut, closing his eyes and regaining his sense of self again. He gave the seal back to Beatrice, pushing away the desires that he knew were not his own.

"That's…that's the one," he said.

Beatrice stared at him, in the same way she'd stared at the gravel. He almost expected her to come and prod him to see if he was real. "And so are you," she said, and then bowed. "Well met, Lord Iron, master of the blood and star metal, brother to the binding metal and protector of the innocent. I am Beatrice, representative of the Sorcerer of Essex, King of the lands between the Lea and the Frisian Sea, the Stour and the Thames, keeper of Waltham Forest, holder of the secret of salt."

"The secret of salt?"

Beatrice nodded.

Sam wanted to ask what it was, but had the feeling she could keep secrets well. "Okay, so we're properly introduced. You said you have a commission?"

"Yes. For chains made of pure iron, four of them."

"Can I ask what they're for?"

She considered his question. "To imprison some Fae who will be problematic."

"Will be? Aren't they already?"

She looked down again. She seemed to need a long time to think of appropriate replies. Perhaps she was worried about revealing something her master would disapprove of. "Yes and no. Can you make them?"

He was certain he could make chains; he'd practised the skill. The pure iron aspect could be problematic without drawing attention to—he stopped his train of thought. That seal was made long before the high-tech furnaces his company owned even existed. Working the iron in the forge was all about removing just the right amount of impurities to maintain the strength of the metal. He'd need to practise, and he had the feeling it would take more than the forge skills Jim could teach him.

"I can make chains," he said. "But I'll level with you: I'm new to this so it might take a while to work out the purity aspect."

She nodded. "Yes. I anticipated this." She looked at his arms and shoulders. "You work the iron yourself, though, yes?"

"Yeah."

She looked pleased. "This is very good. You'll attune much faster. Your predecessor distanced himself from these things, but you, I feel, are different."

"Amir didn't like any of the esoteric stuff. Look, I know this is probably not the way this is done, but could you teach me about the history of the Elemental Court? About what all this stuff means?"

"Stuff…" she whispered. "You want knowledge?"

Perhaps English was her second language. "Yes. I met the rest of the Court and they don't know anything. But I've done things, seen things, that they don't think are even possible. I'd really appreciate some guidance, and I figure the Sorcerers are the only ones who know, but they're a weird bunch and the only one I know just died and—"

"You knew one?"

He nodded.

"Which one?"

"Ekstrand, Sorcerer of…Wessex, I think it was."

"He was a friend?"

"God, no, I couldn't stand the guy."

"Stand…could not stand. Oh, I see. Why not?"

"Because he didn't give a shit about anyone except himself."

The way she stared at him was unnerving. "And he died."

"Yeah. And there's no replacement, by the look of things, so if I could meet your master—"

Her eyes flashed with anger. "No one is my master."

Sam winced. "Sorry. I mean...your boss. The one you work for—who sent you."

"He is my brother. Not my master."

It explained why she was trusted. "Sorry. Maybe your brother could—"

"He is not a man who likes others." She put the seal back into the bag and then turned to face the fire, spreading her fingers in front of it as she stared into the flames. "I will help you," she said finally. "I have knowledge of the Elemental Court and its place in the world. Mayhap I could live in this house, while you make the chains, and it will be a trade, my knowledge for your skill, yes?"

"Yes!" Sam said, loud with exuberance and relief. She jumped and looked at him fearfully. "Sorry. I'm just so glad. It's been so frustrating."

"You are very loud," she said. "And you move so much."

Sam stopped, put his hands in his pockets, and smiled. "Sorry. I guess your brother is one of those quiet types, then."

Relaxing, Beatrice nodded and returned to the fire. "Yes. He is very quiet."

• • •

Max had spent a lot of time watching buildings. Sometimes they were in the Nether, sometimes Mundanus, but the waiting was always the same.

Concerned that the puppet would get into the building via magical means, Max had chosen a spot in a multi-storey carpark across the street on the second floor to give him a good view of the main entrance and right inside the chief constable's office. It was exposed with only a chest-high concrete barrier between him and the brutally cold, north-eastern wind.

Thankfully, the chief constable hadn't closed his blinds, and Max suspected it was for a similar reason: he wanted to look down at the street to see if someone was on the way.

Amesbury was round the back, in case the puppet took a different route inside, and the gargoyle was in the Nether, watching—

No, it wasn't. When Max focused on what the gargoyle was seeing, it wasn't the Nether at all. It was the roof of Cambridge House, en route to the office.

They needed more Arbiters. The gargoyle was becoming less reliable by the day. Max couldn't understand the gargoyle's fascination with Kay. She was skilled and intelligent, but she was both of those things even when the gargoyle wasn't there. Why did it need to spend so much time near her?

He checked his watch. It was two minutes to eight o'clock. The chief constable came to the window and looked down into the street. Max crouched, avoiding the man's gaze as it swept briefly across the carpark. When he moved away from the window, Max stood again, his leg complaining.

There was a flash of Kay's face, smiling. She was embracing the gargoyle and seemed pleased to see it. "Can you look something up on your computer?" it asked her, and she nodded. "Can you find anything out about Jane Shaw?"

His sister. Max could only recall her hair, a bright red, and how the freckles dotted her nose. She was older than he and told him off like their mother did when she wasn't around.

"Did she live in Bath?"

"Yeah. She was…Max's sister."

Kay looked at him and reached over to stroke his ears. "Your sister too, if you think about it. Maybe more so than Max's now." The gargoyle didn't reply. "So she had a brother called Max Shaw; that should make it—"

"No. He—I—we weren't called Max then. That's the name they gave the Arbiter, after dislocation."

"What was Jane's brother called?"

"Matthew."

She smiled at him. "Then that's what I'm going to call you. No one seems to call you anything. They only refer to you as 'the gargoyle,' and it seems a bit weird calling you Max."

"Seems a bit weird calling me Matthew," the gargoyle said. Max agreed.

"I think you're more a Matt anyway," Kay said. "How about only I call you that? Then you can see if you like it. Now, Jane Shaw..."

Max focused on the street when she starting typing. The gargoyle found it far more exciting to watch than he ever could.

A man was walking down the street, collar turned up, hands in his pockets. Max recognised him instantly. George Reticulata-Iris, head of the Aquae Sulis Irises and Cathy's father-in-law. Interesting.

"Jane Shaw, maiden name, married in 1930 and became Jane Perry, died 1985. She had two children. You're an uncle. They're still alive, by the look of things. Hang on, this looks like something interesting..."

Max forced himself to concentrate on the view below rather than on what the gargoyle could see. George Iris looked up and down the street and then went into the police headquarters. Max shook his head. So brazen. The Irises had grown too powerful in Bath.

"There are benches in the park that people buy as memorials for loved ones," Kay said, pulling him away again. "She bought one in memory of Matthew Shaw. It might still be in Victoria Park."

There was a pull, one he hadn't felt before, a desire to go to the gargoyle. Max shrugged it off. He had to see if the Iris went into the office. If he did, then that, coupled with the Iris magic detected on the journalist and outside the foundry on the night his father disappeared, was enough to justify an arrest. George Reticulata-Iris was over three hundred years old and had always lived in Aquae Sulis, so he could easily be responsible for all of the disappearances listed in the article, and the others Amesbury had uncovered.

Max nodded with satisfaction when he saw the chief constable open his office door and admit the Iris. They shook hands. He would collect Amesbury, see to the gargoyle, and then arrest George Iris in the Nether. If Max was right, this was the sort of arrest that would be called the breakthrough of his generation. If there had been a Chapter left to care about such things.

He called Amesbury's mobile. "I've got a positive ID."

"He's in there now?"

Max could hear the emotion in the usually calm voice. "Amesbury, you're going to go back to Cambridge House and wait for me there. Do you understand?" There was a pause. "If you go in there now, you will be at risk. He will Charm you again, and you will make the arrest very difficult. Keep control of yourself. I will bring the one responsible to justice, but only if you don't interfere."

"I understand," Amesbury replied, sounding more like himself. "I'll call you when I'm back at Cambridge House."

Max ended the call and kept watching the office. Now it wasn't just a matter of observing the relationship between the Iris and the police chief, it was also to check that Amesbury hadn't lost his reason and gone storming in. This was why he needed another Arbiter on his team.

Twenty minutes later there was no sign of anyone else in the office and then he got the call confirming that Amesbury had indeed done what he'd promised. When Max tried to confirm through the gargoyle's eyes, he discovered it wasn't in the office anymore and was sniffing around Victoria Park. Probably looking for the bench Kay was talking about. Max couldn't fathom why; it bore no relevance to either of his investigations and a dedication on a piece of public furniture was hardly anything of note. When he was done with the Iris, he would have to have a conversation with it. He couldn't afford to have the gargoyle wandering off whenever it felt like it. No wonder the Chapter used to keep the souls in jars.

At half past eight, the chief constable and Mr Iris parted ways, the police chief locking up the office after himself. Mr Iris left the building and walked back down the street he had come from earlier. Once the police chief left the building, Max abandoned his position, stretching out his leg which ached from being cold and still for so long.

He left the carpark, heading for an alleyway to cut through to the centre of town along a different route from the Iris. No doubt they had the same intention: to get to a place that was reflected into Aquae Sulis and open a Way to get to the Nether city.

Max took his time, giving his leg a chance to loosen up, as he knew exactly where Mr Iris lived. He hobbled to the top of Lansdown Road until he reached one of the Peonia properties. He used their garden wall to access the Nether, left their garden as quickly as he'd arrived, and then walked down the hill in Aquae Sulis, believing it was no bad thing for any puppets out strolling that evening to see an Arbiter keeping an eye on things.

A few couples were out, walking arm in arm towards Lunn's or some restaurant, or other puppet's houses. He didn't care, ignoring them as he steadily made his way to the Royal Crescent. People crossed the road to avoid him, looking anywhere but at him. Carriages passed, either with faces pressed to the windows, staring fearfully, or with curtains rapidly drawn to block the sight of him from those with delicate dispositions.

Reaching the edge of the Crescent, he paused to identify the correct door and then headed towards it. The building's sandstone was dull beneath the silver sky; behind him was the landscaped hill that dropped down away from the Crescent, giving views over greenery for the innocents of Mundanus, which simply gave way to the silvery mists as if the place were in an island of permanent fog.

He knocked on the door of number one. The Iris residence took up half of the Crescent, with the other half rented to the Lavandulas so that they might house guests to the city in one of its most admired locations.

A butler answered the door, pausing very briefly as he took in the sight of an Arbiter on the doorstep before bowing. "Good evening, Mr Arbiter. How may I help you?"

"I'm here to see Mr George Reticulata-Iris."

"I see, sir. Please come in. May I take your coat and hat?"

"No." Max stepped into the entrance hall and the door was shut behind him. It was the typical Georgian decor he had expected, along with the predictable vase of iris flowers arranged in a prominent place for all to see as soon as they arrived.

"If you'd like to follow me, you can wait in the drawing room whilst I inform Mr Iris that you are here."

"I'll wait here." He had no interest in a sofa and drink as he waited.

The butler nodded and left, going up the stairs at a brisk pace. There was the usual sound of the news passing through the household, resulting in the running of feet upstairs—probably a maid who'd never seen an Arbiter before—and a few doors slamming. Sure enough, the face of a young woman peered over the balustrade at the top of the stairs, a lace maid's cap framing her round face. She gasped when he looked up at her, and pulled back, then he heard the same footsteps running back in the direction they'd come from.

More footsteps, and then Mrs Reticulata-Iris arrived at the top of the stairs, dressed in a gold evening gown. "Good evening, Mr Arbiter. I'm sorry for the delay, but my husband was dressing for an engagement when you arrived. He's just making himself presentable."

Max nodded. At least he wasn't trying to climb out of a window, as had happened on a few occasions during his career. He didn't expect anything like that from someone so prominent in the city, however. Even though he had more to lose, Mr Iris undoubtedly had more arrogance.

Mrs Iris came down the stairs, smiling at him all the way, as if he were a tradesman waiting to be paid who didn't have the manners to wait in the servants' wing. She paused next to a mirror at the foot of the stairs, checked the position of her necklace, and then adjusted one of the irises in the vase.

"Have you been offered refreshments?"

"No, but I'm not in need of any."

"I do apologise; I imagine poor Jones was caught off balance by your arrival. Ah, I think that's my husband now."

Mr Iris arrived at the top of the stairs, dressed in white tie, adjusting a cufflink. "Good evening, Mr Arbiter," he said as he came down the stairs. "How may I help you?"

Max was about to launch into his arrest, but as he'd waited, he'd considered his next move more carefully. Someone so high-profile would have the favour of his Patroon, and he needed to be able to present irrefutable evidence to push for a harsher punishment than might be given in the event of doubt.

"Mr Iris, I need you to show me your arms."

"I beg your pardon, sir?"

"Take off your tailcoat and roll up your sleeves."

He noted how the man's lips paled.

"What is the meaning of this?" Mrs Iris asked.

"If you do not cooperate, I shall be forced to take you into custody," Max said.

"Do it, George!" she said. "There must have been a silly mistake. There's nothing wrong with your arms! Are you looking for a birthmark? He doesn't have any!"

"Anna-Marie," Iris hissed. "Do be quiet, woman!" He shrugged off his tailcoat, gave it to his wife, and then undid the left-hand cufflink to roll up the sleeve of his shirt. He held out his arm, turning it to show the underside, and looked at Max. "There, nothing to see."

"And the other one."

"This is so humiliating," Mrs Iris whispered. "Can't we at least do this in the drawing room, Mr Arbiter?"

"No."

Mr Iris fumbled with the other cufflink, either stalling or too nervous to remove it quickly, but eventually he pulled the sleeve up, his face now very pale.

A lurid purple scar ran from his wrist, up his forearm, and stopped near his elbow. It had been stitched, judging from the marks either side of it, and it matched the location mentioned in Lord Iron's file. As Max suspected, no Charms of the Fae could perfectly heal a wound made by Lord Iron's blade.

"See! Nothing at all!" Mrs Iris said, rather shrill. "Now can we please be left alone. We're going to be late."

Mr Iris stared at Max, seeing that the glamour hadn't worked on the Arbiter. He closed his eyes, a sheen of sweat covering his brow. Slowly, he let the sleeve drop and replaced the cufflink.

"George Reticulata-Iris, in accordance with the Split Worlds Treaty and with the sanction of the Sorcerer Guardian of the Kingdom of Wessex, I'm taking you into custody."

"But whatever for?" Mrs Iris shrieked. "There was nothing on his arm!"

Mr Iris took the tailcoat from her and shrugged it on, tugging the ends of his sleeves into place. "Now, don't make a fuss," he said to his wife. "Tell the Lavandulas I've been called to help the Arbiter with his enquiries and regrettably, we won't be able to attend this evening." Seeing the tears in her eyes, he held up a finger. "Now, now. No silliness. Go and send the note. I will be back as soon as I can."

She hurried off, bursting into tears once she was out of sight, as Mr Iris smoothed his waistcoat and checked his cravat in the mirror. Satisfied that he looked presentable, he turned to Max. "Well then, Mr Arbiter. Time to go, I believe."

22

Tom watched Cathy stare out of the window into the mists. She looked shaken and occasionally tearful, but was quieter than he'd expected.

"Don't you want to know what I've arrested her for?"

Cathy looked at him. "Does it matter?"

What an odd response. "She's the one behind those awful pamphlets. I thought it was you."

Cathy smirked. "That's why you were investigating it? To get one over on me?"

How did she do that? How did she make him furious with so few words? "Blast it all, Cat, you really are insufferable. I wanted to get it squared away before the Patroons came after you. They were getting close when I found Rainer."

"Incredible, the things men do to protect women," she muttered. "I'm sure it wasn't all altruistic."

"Why are you being like this? You must have seen one of those disgusting things. They were being read by young ladies, Cat."

"I did see one of them, yes," Cathy said, fiery again. "And I thought it was bloody brilliant. There's nothing disgusting about educating a woman about her own body."

"It wasn't just biology, as if that weren't distasteful enough!"

"Oh, Tom! You're such a bloody prude. That pamphlet was empowering. Girls get married off without having a clue about what's going to happen to them. If I hadn't gone to university, I'd have been the same. Mother didn't tell me a thing—she just drugged me and shoved me in a carriage! Girls have the right to be informed!"

"It was seditious material."

"Seditious? Bollocks!"

"Catherine, I simply cannot bear it when you talk like a common mundane. You're the Duchess of Londinium, for goodness' sake! Why must you cling to their way of speech? It's such a crude affectation."

She was stunned into silence. He savoured it.

"How was that material seditious?"

"It encouraged young women to question the wisdom of accepting their natural place in Society. It contained information on birth control! Encouraging unnatural behaviour threatens the peace and stability of Society."

"Unnatural behaviour? Is that what you call a woman having the right to choose when to—"

"I am not going to have an argument with you about this. I simply cannot bear any more of it."

"More? We've never talked about it." She peered at him. "Did Lucy read one of those pamphlets?"

He looked out of the other window.

"Shit! That's why you're so upset about it! How dare your wife be educated, eh?"

"Be quiet!"

"Did she start to ask difficult questions? Not so keen to just accept it all without complaint?"

"Cat, I'm warning you—"

"Is it harder to keep her happy now she knows what—"

"God damn it, Catherine, she knew it all already!" He tried not to blush at the memory of the night he'd found the pamphlet. "They do things differently in the colonies," he added.

"No wonder they want to declare independence," Cathy said. "They must think we're a bunch of backward idiots!"

He frowned at her. "Independence?"

Cathy pressed her lips together. Under the pressure of his stare, she sighed. "The Princess of Rajkot delivered a message to our household when I was…indisposed. They've declared independence from Albion. Rajkot is no more. It's Gujarat now."

Tom closed his mouth, realising it had dropped open. "And did she mention the American colonies?"

Cathy nodded. "According to Morgan. But it's all secondhand information." She waved a hand, trying to fool him into thinking it was unimportant. "Anyway, that's for Will to worry about."

He raised an eyebrow at her bluff. "Happy to pass it on to your husband when it suits you, eh?"

She blushed at that. "Shut up."

Tom made a mental note to raise the issue with the Duke. And his wife, for that matter. Though whether Lucy would tell him of any plans within her family to break away from Albion's rule was another matter entirely. Surely they wouldn't have married their daughter into a prominent Albion family if they planned to break away.

"How did you find her?" he asked after a while.

Cat, still guarded, had the wherewithal to look innocent. "Who?"

"I'm not a complete buffoon, Cat. We hear nothing of Miss Rainer for years and then, mere weeks after you became Duchess, I find her at the centre of a network distributing dangerous material that bears an uncanny resemblance to some of the opinions you've expressed to me. She says she's been acting alone but someone is funding her. It's you, isn't it?"

"Where are we going?" she said, evading the question with one of her own.

"The Tower. She's in one of the cells there."

Her pained expression touched something in him too. It had been hard putting his former governess into that cold stone room and locking the door. She'd been nothing but kind to him as a child.

"She hasn't been mistreated," he said. "I'm not a monster, Cat."

"But we both know you're prepared to do terrible things when you have to."

"Bringing you home was far from terrible! You shouldn't have run away in the first place!"

Cathy glared at him but didn't talk back. Was she learning restraint at last? "What will happen to her?"

"It depends."

"On what?"

"On whether she cooperates. I have to root out the funding, Cat. I have to. If I leave any loose ends it's my and the Duke's necks on the line. She was operating from a London printer. It's on our patch."

Cathy closed her eyes and sighed. "Sod it. Look, I'm behind it all. You'll only Truth Charm her, or worse, and I'd rather she not be put through anything more awful than she has been already."

The knot of tension that had been at the centre of his back for days started to ease. "I knew it. Good, at least you've been decent enough to own up."

"I accept all responsibility. I put her up to it, and I funded all of it too. So there's no need to do anything to her, all right?"

He could see how desperate she was to protect her. "Cat, I have to exile her."

"Why? *I* did it! I wrote the bloody thing!"

"I have to demonstrate that I've identified the culprit and taken action should the Patroons catch up. She's not a member of the Great Families, she's not Agency staff…they could do anything they want with her. I'm going to exile her to keep her safe. And you safe too."

"Me?"

"She's not good for you, Cat. She encourages you, I'm sure. And I can't risk the connection between the two of you being uncovered. If the Patroons traced her, got hold of her, forced her to talk…it would be all they need to attack you."

She stuck her chin out. "Let those bastards try."

He tutted at her childish stubbornness. "You have no idea…. At least you have me to protect you from yourself in this. And don't bother trying to think a way around this, Cat, I've already filed my report and judgement with the Tower. I left your name out of it."

"Then why bother to come and get me?!"

"Because I needed to know if you were behind it. And I thought you would want a chance to say goodbye." Her brow crinkled as the attack she was about to launch was quashed by the thought of being given one last meeting with Rainer. "It could have been a lot worse for her if someone else had found out," he said. "What were you thinking?"

"I wanted the women in Society to know what they should. No one else was going to tell them."

"It's one thing to educate, it's another to incite. Cat, you told them that most women in mundane England choose who they're going to marry and when to have children. Why do that?"

"Because it's the truth!"

"But what can it possibly achieve, other than making them unhappy? Don't you see? The ones who might have been scared or reluctant to marry, for whatever reason, now know things have changed for other people but not for them, and it never will. Why tell them there's another way when they can never benefit from it themselves?"

Cathy's eyes shone with tears. "Because when I wrote it, I believed I could achieve that for them. I thought that if they knew it was possible for women to have more rights, they would start to push for it themselves. If daughters talked to fathers who loved them, furnished with the arguments and words from that pamphlet, maybe they could have started something quietly, a sea change from the bottom up, as I worked on change from the top down." Tears broke free and she started to weep, openly. "But everything I've tried has failed. Short of burning it all down and starting over, I can't see how anything is going to change."

Tom reached across and took her hands. "God's teeth, Cat, never say anything about burning everything down ever again. Never! You understand?" When she didn't reply, he edged forwards, resting his head against hers, feeling her tears dripping onto his hands. "I don't think you realise how many enemies you have. They tried to kill you, Cat!"

"They were just trying to scare me."

"They had a modern pistol!"

"They could have used it, too. They just wanted to frighten

me into shutting up." She pulled back from him, freeing her hands to wipe at her cheeks. "All I did was voice an opinion, Tom! That's all! And they shot at my bodyguard. Disproportionate is an understatement. Am I supposed to be quiet, to hide away, just because some twats have tried to bully me? I'll show them! I'll—"

"You'll get yourself killed. Or worse. Silenced. The Patroons are already talking about you in worrying ways, Cat. Will and I can't keep you safe forever if you insist upon being so difficult."

"But how will things ever change if I don't force them to?"

He sighed. "More people should study history. Don't you remember any of your lessons with Miss Rainer? I heard the ones she gave you after I left were all about the suffragists and the suffragettes!"

"A lot of them were."

"She couldn't have taught you about them without the wider picture. There were other factors, Cat, other forces operating in the world. In *Mundanus*. The Nether is stagnant. It will never change because it is literally incapable of change."

"No, you're wrong! What about Gujarat? That's the kind of change the Patroons will never admit is possible, but it's already happened!"

"But that's a world away from what you're fighting for. They had genuine grievances. The Patroons here have done what all imperialists do—taken more than they've given back. There are no grievances at the heart of Albion. There are no reasons for the changes in Mundanus to have any impact upon us. England is as it ever was, stable. We're not being oppressed, here or there."

"The women in the Nether are!"

"No they're not, Cat. They are cherished and protected. The vast majority are comfortable, cared for, and want for nothing. You forget that you're an exception. You were corrupted at a very impressionable age and I know you're very…vocal, but one or two voices amount to nothing. There are no economic factors or world wars to force men to see women differently here. Yes, the young men go off on the Grand Tour, but only the wealthiest of our families, not all. And the wealthiest are the ones most likely to toe the line with the Patroons because they want to keep what they have." From the way she was staring at him, tears still rolling down her cheeks, he felt he was finally getting through to her at last. "Cat, I love you, but you are a complete idiot if you think you can bring about change in Society when it comes to the rights of women. Even your own husband, who's a decent enough chap and has been incredibly lenient with you, knows this is true. Haven't you noticed how he's been stalling the Ladies' Court? He's been in meetings with the men of Londinium for hours and hours, every day, trying to hold everything together because of you."

The carriage rolled through an archway and he saw the Tower come into view. It seemed to snap Cathy out of her shock. She wiped her face again, sniffing loudly.

"Will and I just want you to be safe," Tom said. "And for you to accept things as they are. Like Lucy. She's found a way to be happy. Can't you find a way too?"

The carriage rolled to a stop. "I'd rather die than eat this shit and pretend it tastes good," she said, and opened the door, jumping out before the footman had even lowered the step.

• • •

Max was glad that he'd had the foresight to ask Rupert to make a box in the Nether for him, just in case. It was good to be able to just thrust the door handle and pin into the Iris hallway wall and open a door straight into it.

As Rupert had instructed, when Max said "Light," the entire ceiling glowed white, exposing the confines of a plain black box. There was nothing inside except a table and two chairs, cuffs attached to the top of the table. He locked Iris's wrists in them and left without a word, using the same door handle but twisting in the opposite direction to exit into the office at Cambridge House.

He ate alone and went to bed, Kay having left, Amesbury back at his hostel and the gargoyle still sniffing about the park. At least it had the sense to stay hidden whenever anyone came close.

It returned in the small hours and curled up at the foot of the camp bed, waking Max. It was four in the morning. Good. The Iris would be tired and at his least alert.

"Are you going to beat him up?" the gargoyle asked as Max drank some coffee, wanting to be more alert than his prisoner.

"It wasn't what I was planning to start with."

"Because I am more than happy to do that for you."

"I don't want you anywhere near that man. You know why."

The gargoyle nodded. "I found the bench."

"Did it make you feel better?"

The gargoyle frowned at him. "You think I'm stupid, wanting to find it."

"I don't think you're stupid. I just don't see the point. It won't bring her back. And before you ask, we are not going to find her children. Nothing good would come of it."

The gargoyle sniffed. "Go beat that bastard up for me."

Max drained the cup and pulled the file containing all the pictures they had of the people who'd disappeared. Then he went to the darkest empty corner of the office and used the door handle again.

George Iris was slumped forwards, his head resting on one arm. Max could see from the red skin on his wrists that he'd tried to free himself. He jolted upright at the sound of the door closing, blinking away the disorientation as best he could.

"I'm going to ask you some questions. The way you answer them will affect the case I present to your Patroon. If I think you're lying or holding anything back, I'll go and get some tools and ask the questions again."

"I'm sure there's a clause regarding the use of torture in the Split Worlds Treaty," Iris said, swallowing hard.

"There is. It says that Arbiters are allowed to use it on puppets who kidnap innocents." Max dropped the file on the table and sat down opposite Iris. "You probably made plans before you fell asleep," Max said, "but there's nothing you can say here that will convince me you're innocent. I have enough evidence to push for your immediate expulsion from Society."

"So why bother with the questions?"

I want to know whether I need to ask for your legs to be broken first. That was what gargoyle wanted him to say. Max ignored it. "I like to be thorough."

Iris sighed. "There's barely any point to this. I'm the head of a powerful family and my Patroon will be very motivated to protect me."

"Your Patroon can't protect you from my boss." He opened the file and spread the photos out on the table. "These are the one hundred and twenty-three people who have gone missing from the city of Bath and surrounds over the past one hundred and sixteen years. I know there are more, but let's start with these."

Iris scanned the images, his face impassive.

"How many of these people did you steal to order for your patron?"

"That's a rather bold assumption."

"If you're going to fight me on every question, you'll be chained to that table for a very long time. I can go and sleep, eat, drink. Go to the bathroom. You can't." He tapped the table. "How many?"

Iris sighed. "I'd much rather discuss a deal."

"I'm an Arbiter. I can't be bribed."

"I know that, but you're not without sense either."

He tapped the table again. "How many."

Iris looked away.

Max stood up. "I'll come back in a few hours. I'll bring a Truth Mask with me. The one with the extra-sharp spikes."

"About half of them. I think. I don't recall exactly."

"Do they all just blur into one over the years?" Max said, sitting back down.

"Something like that. You have to understand, Mr Arbiter, it wasn't my choice to do this. I didn't wake up one morning and decide it would be a jolly jape to go into Mundanus and destroy people's lives."

"But you went and did it anyway."

"I had no choice. My patron expects his requests to be carried out immediately and without question. If I had disobeyed, I would have been replaced and another would have done his bidding."

"I have no interest in the pressure he put on you. You're a puppet, I know that already. I'm going to point to each picture, you say yes if you took them, no if you did not."

The photos were sorted and the ones he denied taking were put back in the file. All of the pictures from the newspaper article were included among those left on the table.

"Why did Lord Iris want these people?"

"I have no idea. It's not my place to question why."

"Let me rephrase that. Did he ask for these people specifically?"

"No. He asked for people with particular qualities. That one, on the edge there, I took him because my Lord asked for a skilled musician. And that girl there, the same reason." He paused, frowning to himself. "I didn't want to. I knew their families would—"

"What other qualities?"

Iris sighed. "That one in the red shirt, he was taken because he had committed a crime, a violent one. The same for that one with the awful hair, yes, him, and that one with the appalling teeth. They were easier to take, I confess. I think I did some good removing them from Mundanus."

Max noted the reason on the back of each picture and placed them back in the file. When they were done, he scanned the remainder. Over forty photos remained, including that of his father. "Which quality did these people have?"

"They were rebellious, in a variety of ways, but that was the quality he wanted."

Max pointed to the picture of his father and the other foundry workers. "Tell me about those."

Iris frowned. "That was a difficult night."

"That's when you got your scar."

Iris nodded. "I'd already taken about half of them the previous night. They were a common lot, but they were some of the first to unionise in the city and were very vocal about it too. They were planning to strike and force the owner to increase pay. It was rather controversial at the time."

"And how did you take them?"

"A very simple Persuasion Charm. Nothing violent. I invited them to my house for dinner, just like all the others. Once they were in the Nether, I simply told them to step through a mirror into Exilium."

"And what happened the second night?"

"The owner of the factory was waiting for me and attacked. That's how I got the scar. I never went back there again."

"The people taken for being rebellious. What happened to them?"

"I have no idea. They were certainly never returned from Exilium."

"Could they still be alive?"

"One can live indefinitely in Exilium, but only with the favour and care of one of the Lords or Ladies. Lord Iris is not one for keeping pets."

"At least, not in Exilium," Max said, and Iris bristled but said nothing.

"I should think he took whatever he wanted, or used them for whatever purpose he had in mind, and if they survived, well, it would be mere speculation."

"Speculate."

"I imagine they would have starved to death. I've heard tell of such things. Once the Fae lose interest in a mortal that's trapped in Exilium, it's very easy for them to forget about them altogether. The nature of the place is such that if they have no interest in an individual, they will never see them."

"I know how Exilium works."

"Quite. That's all I know. Now I know you have no interest in a deal, but what if I could help with another investigation of yours? Would it make your report to my Patroon more favourable?"

Max called the Aquae Sulis Reticulata-Iris family tree to mind. George was the firstborn. No leverage there for the Second Sons. But perhaps he knew something that could bear fruit later on.

"What do you know of the Second Sons?"

Iris brightened. "I've had dealings with them."

"But you're the firstborn in your branch of the family."

"My younger brother fell in with them some years ago. He was bereaved and wasn't coping very well, truth be told. They approached him when he was at a low ebb and convinced him that joining them would be very beneficial for him."

"And was it?"

Iris snorted. "Hardly. They encouraged him to take dreadful risks, drink far too much, and do the bidding of the ringleader. Nasty piece of work."

"When a man who's kidnapped over fifty innocents and led them to their deaths says that, 'nasty' may be an understatement."

Iris stared at him. "I did not choose to do that, sir."

"Did this 'nasty piece of work' make your brother commit any crimes?"

"No, but only because I intervened and pulled Vincent out when I found out what was happening. He was too weak and lost in grief to realise he was being groomed to be nothing more than Bertrand Viola's bully boy."

The ability to feel a sense of triumph had been taken from Max a long time ago, but not the ability to feel an easing of the tension as another, critical piece of the puzzle fell into place.

"Now, I've been very generous with my information; I trust you will be generous when you present to my Patroon."

"I don't know what gave you that idea, Mr Iris," Max said, gathering up the photos and putting them back into the file. "I'll present the facts, as I always do."

Iris laughed, though it was less convincing this time. "You

would be excellent at poker, sir. But no matter, I have every faith in my Patroon. He understands the pressure we are put under."

"Yes," Max said, tucking the file under his arm and standing up. "He'll have learnt it from being put under pressure by the Sorcerers to punish criminals such as yourself as harshly as possible." He pushed the door handle into the wall. "I'll be back for you soon, Mr Iris."

23

Cathy didn't open her eyes when she first heard the knocking.

"Go away."

There was a pause, and the sound of a hushed conversation, then more knocking.

Cathy groaned. She was at the Tower, now she remembered, and had somehow thought it was a good idea to lie down, fully dressed, and fall asleep in her corset.

"Give me a minute," Cathy called, sitting up. In the small hours of the morning, raw from a prolonged and tearful goodbye, she'd been too exhausted to even contemplate going home. She wanted to be alone, to think things through. From every angle, it had looked hopeless. Both Margritte and Natasha were gone now, leaving only Charlotte as her trusted ally, and she was falling apart.

Tom had been right. Will had been stalling the Ladies' Court. She didn't want to go back home and tell him what had happened and be angry with him and devastated by Natasha and Margritte's exile at the same time. It was simply too much. So she'd sent a note, flopped into one of the many guest rooms set aside for travelling dignitaries, and slept poorly. Now all she was left with was the desire to free Charlotte from Bertrand, Charlotte's daughter from the marriage to Nathaniel, and herself from this corset.

"Don't give up," Natasha had whispered in her ear. "Withdraw and reconsider, but don't let them destroy you."

"They haven't," she said to herself, trying to pat her hair into some sort of order. "It'll take more than this." Cathy tried to smooth the wrinkles from her gown but soon realised the futility of trying to make herself look anything but a woman who'd cried for hours and then got a couple of hours sleep. "Come in."

A page opened the door. "Your Grace, there's a visitor for you, and she says it's urgent."

"Who?"

"Your mother," said her mother, pushing past the page. "You may leave now," she said to the man, who bowed and left without even a glance at Cathy. "They've been keeping me waiting for over half an hour. Good grief, Catherine, you look absolutely dreadful."

"Thanks. What do you want?"

"I need you to sign my request for the Oak. As it's such short notice I need to have a second signatory of significant rank and I can't get hold of the Patroon because he is a useless man with an excess of ears and little between them."

Cathy smirked at the description, then blinked at the scroll thrust beneath her nose. "I haven't even had a cup of tea yet."

"Well, call for breakfast, we have a lot to do."

Cathy pushed the scroll away. "This is really not the best time."

"Elizabeth is to be married tomorrow, Catherine. It is the only time. I need you to put your rank to good use and help me to make all the arrangements today."

"Wait, what? Tomorrow? That's insane."

"No, it isn't. They met yesterday, the contract was signed last night, and this is going to happen the way I say it is or the entirety of this family will come to know the true extent of my wrath and believe me, Catherine, you have only seen a sliver of it before now."

"Is this what Elizabeth wants?"

"Yes. She's overjoyed. She's with the dressmaker now, having a fabulous time making the most unreasonable demands and making as many of the servants cry as she can. Now, are you going to call for breakfast or must I do absolutely everything today?"

"I've got other plans for today."

"They're cancelled. I've already told William. You'll have to deal with his sulking tomorrow, he isn't best pleased that you'll be with me tonight. It's the only way we are going to have a chance of getting everything ready."

"Who did you bully before *my* wedding?"

"I had more time to arrange that one, despite the Irises changing the date."

"Time enough to keep me drugged and locked up and—"

Her mother took off her hat and for a moment Cathy wondered if she was going to beat her with it. "Catherine. I have no regrets about that whatsoever. Look at all you have now. You're Duchess, you have more power and wealth than, frankly, you deserve, and all because I had the good sense to make sure you made it to the Oak without any more silliness. Please sign this and give it your seal!"

"Go find someone else to do your dirty work," Cathy said, batting the scroll away when it was thrust towards her again.

Her mother looked like she was going to cry, just for the briefest moment, but then schooled her face to hide it swiftly enough. She looked up at the ceiling, down at the flagstones, across to the window, as if the solution were a thimble to be found somewhere nearby.

"Is this room private?"

"What?"

"Could we be overheard here?"

Cathy shrugged. "I've never been in this room before now. The best place to talk is in the gardens, if you're worried about that."

"I want to talk to you there."

"Can't I at least have a cup of—"

"No. It has to be now. If I wait I may lose the courage to tell you what I must and that would never do."

Cathy stood, tried her best to ignore her aching ribs, and led her mother out of the Tower, eliciting many curious glances along the way. As they passed the door to the kitchens she spotted a man carrying a tray of pastries and called him over so she could take a couple of them. She ate one on the way into the garden and was glad when her mother declined the other one.

Once they were among the greenery, her mother led Cathy to the point farthest away from the Tower and most shaded by ornamental trees. Cathy didn't mind too much, seeing as it gave her the chance to eat the second pastry, but she could have murdered a coffee to go with it.

Her mother clutched her hat, a dramatic wide-brimmed affair in black and red to match her dress, over her stomach. She bit her lip and fiddled with the edge of the straw brim, looking more nervous than Cathy had ever seen her.

Cathy folded her arms, trying to be patient, even though she felt like crap and had more important things to do than—

"I'm leaving your father."

Cathy blinked.

"Once Elizabeth is married. I'm leaving him then, when I know all my children are in good places and what I do can't harm them."

"Bloody hell," Cathy said. "I wasn't expecting that."

"There's more." Mother looked up again, down again, her fingers pulling a strand of straw from its place. "I'm leaving him to be with my lover. My former lover. The one I loved before I had to marry that man."

Cathy felt as if she'd slipped into another Nether whilst she'd slept. A lover? What was more surprising, that her mother had one or that she was even capable of love? "Oh. Okay. Who's he?"

Her mother looked up from her hat. "She, Catherine. The one I love most in the worlds is a woman."

"Okay." Cathy tried to imagine her father alone, and found it quite easy. There had never been any affection between them.

Her mother gawped at her. "'Okay'? Is that really all you have to say about it?"

"I'm sorry—you're right. I mean: Yay! Congratulations?"

"What?"

Cathy reflected the confusion on her mother's face. "What do you want me to say?"

"Aren't you...appalled with me? Disgusted?"

"No. Why would I be?" Then Cathy realised what her mother feared. "Oh, Mother, I'm not like that. In Mundanus, I marched in the Manchester Pride when I was a student." At her mother's blank expression, she added, "It's a big parade that celebrates love. I had a friend who—look, it doesn't matter. What matters is that you love her, and that she loves you, right?"

Her mother nodded. At least the urgency of this wedding made sense now.

Then Cathy started to see her own experience of being drugged and forced into marriage in a different light. Now she understood it wasn't just because of what Society expected; she had merely been an obstacle to her mother's future happiness.

Wrestling the new insight into place, Cathy felt too many emotions all at once for it to settle into anything comfortable within her. The anger was still there, butting up against a fragile sympathy for a mother who had always been cruel and unloving. Now that there was another reason for her mother's emotional distance, Cathy felt an empathy she'd never believed possible. But it didn't change the fact that her mother had treated her like a tree to be hacked down to form a path out of the woods.

Her mother's bottom lip was trembling. "I've never told another soul. I think you're the only person in the whole of the Nether who would be so good about it."

"Lucy would probably be cool with it too," Cathy said with a shrug. "Really, you loving a woman is not a big deal for me. Treating me like crap…not defending me when Father got violent…those are still problems."

"That's perfectly reasonable," her mother said, straightening up. "I'm not going to expect you to treat me differently because of this. It doesn't excuse me for being an awful mother."

Cathy struggled to imagine her mother in love, not only with someone she wasn't supposed to marry, but with a person she wasn't even supposed to be attracted to. Perhaps that cruelty in her was drawn from the same well as passion and love that couldn't be expressed.

"I suppose you didn't want any of it—the marriage, kids…" Cathy's belief that having a child of her own would be a terrible mistake was getting stronger by the minute.

"I didn't." Her mother sighed. "I wasn't as brave as you, Catherine. And I hated you for that. For showing me what I wasn't." She breathed in, blinking rapidly. "But not anymore. I've done my time. My lover and I have borne children and done everything as we should for our patrons. We've been dutiful to our parents and now it's *our* time. It's harder for her; she's fond of her husband and regrets having to hurt him."

"While you're champing at the bit."

Her mother's eyes darkened. "You know what he's like, Catherine, you more than most."

Cathy nodded, remembering his temper but also the way he'd talked to her in the carriage on the way to her wedding. There was a more thoughtful man there, beneath the rage. He wasn't going to take being abandoned by his wife well, but she wasn't going to stand in her mother's way, either. Her mother had the right to love who she wanted and her father would get over it, eventually. "But how will the two of you survive? Where will you go? Won't Lord Poppy go mental?"

"We've made very careful plans," her mother said. "The one I love is very resourceful."

"Why didn't you just tell me all this before? I wouldn't have been such a dick about Elizabeth staying and all that."

Her mother shrugged. "It's always easy with hindsight. I should have known you would understand. You've never fitted in." She tilted her head. "Are you more like me than I thought?"

"I'm straight," Cathy said. "It's just in all the other ways I don't fit in." She drew in a deep breath, trying her best to put her own hurts aside. Her mother was trying to escape and regardless of what had passed between them, Cathy felt that helping her was fundamentally the right thing to do. She didn't want to be the kind of person who'd keep another woman trapped out of spite. "Listen, I'll help you get the wedding sorted, but you have to tell me the truth: is Elizabeth really happy about it?"

"Catherine, he's rich and not particularly bright. She knows she'll have everything she wants and rule the roost, too. She couldn't be happier."

Satisfied, Cathy nodded. "Come on, then. Coffee first and then we'll sort everything out. But I'm not going to put up with any bobbins from Elizabeth, I'm telling you that now."

• • •

A day in the forge was definitely the best way to handle the fallout from exposing Copper's ugly secrets. As Des fielded threatening calls from the rest of the Court, he crafted chain links and thought about the strange woman who'd come from the Sorcerer.

When he went back to the house for lunch, Des ran through the messages, each one full of expletives and read in a deadpan monotone. Sam listened as he chewed his sandwich, knowing that at least half of the threats were just grandstanding. They couldn't afford to cut him out entirely.

"Anything from Nickel?"

"No, sir."

"And where's Beatrice?"

"She said she was going for a walk. She made it clear she'd find her own food when she returned."

"She's a strange one," Mrs Morrison said, returning from the pantry with a selection of spices. "I told her I were making a curry for tonight, and she just looked at me like I'd spoken bloody French at her. Didn't have a clue."

Sam chuckled. "I don't think she's very well travelled, Mrs M."

"I lent her m'wellies and me coat too. Does she live in Australia or something? Did she not know how cold it is here at this time of year?"

"Something like that."

"How long is she staying for?"

He shrugged. "I don't know. A few days at least."

"It's no trouble," Mrs Morrison said. "I just thought a curry would make a nice change. Them guests you had before were a bit set in their ways. Fussy eaters. Can't you have someone normal to stay for once?"

Des looked at her, wide-eyed, but Sam didn't mind. Having someone around who was willing to speak to him like he was a normal person wasn't just nice, it was necessary. "Sorry, Mrs M. Should I find a nice wife to settle with?"

She nodded. "Not some stuck-up fancy woman neither. Someone with a bit of sense."

"I'll bear that in mind. I'll be in the forge if anyone needs me."

He worked for the rest of the day, pausing only for the odd cup of tea on the doorstep into the forge, enjoying the heat on his back and the freshness of the air on his face. Here, a world away from corporate bollocks, with the breeze in the trees and the robins digging for worms nearby, he felt at ease. He thought of Leanne in the early days at university and smiled without a choking grief for the first time. He worried about Cathy and whether he should drive down to check if she was okay but felt that would be crossing a line. She knew where he was. But what if she couldn't phone? What if they'd done something to her?

"Are you making the chains?"

Beatrice was heading over to him, the lower half of her dress spattered with mud. Mrs Morrison's wellies and coat looked odd, but at least she was warm.

"I've been practising the technique," Sam said, chucking the dregs of tea onto the grass as he stood up. "Not the pure iron bit, though. Not quite sure how to approach that."

"There are two ways," she said, almost at the door. "One is to remove the impurities from yourself so you might better recognise those in the metal and remove them."

"Errr…"

"But that will take too long. The other is to use the old way."

"The only way I know about is hitting it. Or using tech."

"Did he teach you nothing at all?"

Sam shook his head. "Amir—the one who was Lord Iron before me—was a bit screwed up about this stuff. And the rest of the Court, too. They don't know anything about the Fae or anything that isn't totally normal."

"They are inferior," she stated. "Iron is the blood metal, the foundation of all earthly magic."

"Isn't copper important too?"

"It only obstructs the flow of Fae magic. It does not break it. Only when in concert with iron does it reach its full potential."

"Can the other people in the court do…you know…magic?"

"If properly trained. But they are ignorant now. The Sorcerers saw to that." There was a curl to her lip as she said that.

"They wanted the Court to forget what it was."

"Of course. Less of a threat, that way. The language of sorcery doesn't require the Court's cooperation."

"But your Sorcerer wants me to make something for him. Why not use sorcery to make these chains?"

She tilted her head at him, studying each of his features in turn. "Iron needs something of you in it, to be at its most powerful. No matter what the Sorcerers said, iron forged by its Elemental Lord has a quality unlike any other. The Fae feel it."

"And copper?"

"Less so, but yes."

"So, what have you been up to?" Sam said, indicating the mud on her dress with his empty tea mug. "Getting the lay of the land?"

"I've been warding your property against intruders. If I am going to stay here, it needs to be secure."

Sam was surprised, briefly, before remembering that she worked for a Sorcerer. She must have picked up some stuff along the way. Maybe she was an apprentice. Somehow, he didn't think she would welcome a question about it. "I've got security and cameras covering the perimeter."

"They may be sufficient for the mundane threats that approach, but not all of the threats out there." She reflected his frown. "You don't know about the ones coming to kill you?"

"What?"

"You have many enemies, Lord Iron. They want you to die."

"What? Seriously?" When she nodded, he paled. "Um...look, I've got some stuff going on with Copper at the moment, but killing me? That's just crazy."

"Intention does not always manifest in action; perhaps you are correct." She looked past him into the forge, disinterested. "That is a place of great power. Do you feel it when you work there?"

He thought of the way to Exilium he'd found beneath the anvil and how the iron road had stretched away from it impossibly. "Yeah, I know it's a special place."

"There are stories of Lord Iron's forges. Seven places of power, seven keys to his potential."

"Oh." He thought of the slab at the heart of the house, of the seven markers showing the other forges, and probably the other points that joined Exilium to Mundanus via those twisting iron and copper roads.

"Do you know where they are?"

"I have a fair idea." He scratched the back of his head, uncomfortable with the way she stared at him. "So...this 'old way' you mentioned before, for the pure iron chains. Could you teach me?"

She nodded. "Yes. You're strong and more attuned than you realise. Do you have a knife?"

"No. What for?"

She looked at him as if he were a stupid child. "To cut you. We'll need your blood, Lord Iron. Purity always has a cost."

24

Of all the times Tom could have chosen to whisk Cathy away, why did it have to be last night? Even now, after a restless night's sleep, Will was still angry. Angry that Tom didn't run it by him first, angry that Cathy had dropped everything to go and then decided to stay at the Tower, angry that she still wasn't back.

He'd sworn when he received her note telling him she wouldn't be home that night.

> *Will, Tom is going to exile Natasha. I'm devastated. He gave us a few hours together at least. Don't wait up; I'm going to stay here. I'm exhausted. I'll tell you all about it tomorrow.*
>
> *C xx*

Tom must have found out Natasha was helping Cathy with her feminist agenda. He understood why she wanted to stay, and she'd hardly be in the mood for his affections in the state she was in, but it still angered him. But as he lay there, his breakfast tray getting cold, he knew the real reason for the anger.

He'd just wanted to get it over and done with. This morning she was supposed to wake in his arms, their child forming within her. Lord Iris would be pleased. She would be safe. Dame Iris would be, too, satisfied that her plan had secured the family and removed the pressure on her as well as him.

"You will stay for lunch, of course," she'd said to him after Lord Iris had released them all from Exilium. He'd been surprised that she asked, thinking that after so long apart she and her husband would only want to be with each other. But Sir Iris had things to do, as did she, and the most pressing issue for Eleanor was how to make sure Cathy was brought into line. Otherwise Lord Iris's favour would go the same way as it had for her usurper, and that would never do.

She'd led him into one of the many receiving rooms in the wing of the Patroon's house that Will had seen far too much of lately. "Now, this is what we're going to do about Cathy," she'd said, outlining how he was to take the potions that would influence Cathy's behaviour, and also guarantee conception after their next coupling.

"That way you don't have to worry about such silliness as making sure she has consumed them," Dame Iris said with a smile. "You'll have to put up with all the women you speak to fawning over you, but I imagine that isn't a new experience for you, and hardly an unpleasant side effect to deal with."

He couldn't bring himself to admit he'd Charmed Cathy into sleeping with him already. It felt so low, so sordid. Was this any better?

"Why the scowl, William?"

"I don't feel comfortable with this."

"Oh, William, everyone uses Charms of attraction! Heavens, there would be no children in the entirety of the Buttercup family without them!"

"It just doesn't seem…very sporting." It sounded so feeble. At her raised eyebrow he lowered his eyes. "When I found out that a Rosa had made me love her, I felt like such a fool. I'm no better than her if I do that to Cathy."

"Nonsense," Dame Iris said. "The Rosa did it to you for her own gain, did she not? Well, that is why you were so wounded by it. You wouldn't have chosen to act the way you did to benefit her when your goals were incompatible. It is the opposite situation with Cathy. You're doing this to protect her. And she already loves you. It's a world away from what was done to you."

Will remained unconvinced. Would she have fallen in love with him without that first Charm? Was it really love? He couldn't bear to think about it. "But Dame Iris, she says she doesn't want to have a child."

"Cathy is a dear girl, but she does have an unfortunate way

of rushing into things she should consider more carefully and overthinking the things she need not. Take the asylum. She seemed to be making it all up as she went along. I doubt she considered the full ramifications of her actions when she really should have. Having a child requires no thought whatsoever, but for some reason she's considered it far too much and simply tangled herself in a knot about it. All we are doing is freeing her from her own worst enemy. Herself."

Will kept his eyes averted, knowing she had made up her mind.

"Just like you will with the jewel our patron made for her. I take it you have that in hand?"

"Yes, Dame Iris, the jewellery will be ready for me to collect first thing tomorrow."

"Excellent." She stood, smiling broadly. "Wait there whilst I collect what we need. The potions I have in mind are powerful enough to last a few days, just in case your other duties get in the way."

And so you can watch me drink them before I leave, he'd thought, but he couldn't blame her for wanting to see it all done properly.

He'd left her house with two potions settling in his stomach and what felt like a rock in his chest. But in the carriage on the way home he realised the Dame was right. There was nothing else to be done. And he and Cathy had made love before, and she'd enjoyed it. The potions would simply make it harder for her overthinking to get in the way, and simply make sure that their lovemaking created the desired outcome. It wasn't as if he was going to hurt her, or abuse her.

As for the choker and her previous insistence that she wanted to preserve the effect of Poppy's magic, well, that was another example of her not knowing what was best for her. Besides, surely it was better for her to act in accordance with her true self, rather than something influenced by magic? When the hypocrisy of that stung, he shifted in his seat and returned to the thought that justified all of it: she would be safe.

When she left with Tom before he'd been able to lure her to

bed, he'd paced, then decided to make better use of his time. He summoned Bennet and spoke at length with him about the Agency and the way it was run. If he had to take away something Cathy thought she wanted, the least he could do was give her something else in return. By the time Bennet had left, he had a plan that he knew would make Cathy melt, no matter how angry she'd been with him. The thought of it had enabled him to get to sleep as he waited for her to come home.

And now, the morning creeping into the sociable hours of the day, she was still not home. When he sent an enquiry after her to the Tower, he received a message from one of the pages that her mother had come and they'd left in a carriage together.

"Damn it, Cathy!" he'd shouted at the note, crushing it in his fist before tossing it into the fire. Half an hour later he received a message from her by Letterboxer.

> *Will, my mother needs me to help with arranging Elizabeth's wedding. It has to be tomorrow. I won't be home tonight, but I will come back in the morning to get changed. Can you come? It will be at 11 a.m. Elizabeth is driving me insane.*
>
> *C xx*

At least that part of his plan was going well. Soon the contract between Nathaniel and Bertie's daughter would be signed and both of their positions would be safer for it. He penned a quick note back.

> *My love,*
> *Come back tonight if you can. I miss you. I'll clear my diary for the wedding, then we can be together.*
>
> *I love you,*
> *Will x*

He paused, added another *x* to match what she'd sent him, and sent it. He could put the day to good use. He would collect the choker—then he could at least give that to Cathy before the wedding, reducing the chance of her saying anything incendiary at such a public event. Then the rest of the day he'd work on the figures that emerged from his conversation with Bennet. Even though putting that choker on Cathy was the right thing to do, he still felt he had to give her something she wanted. Something that would make her smile. Something that would make him feel less monstrous.

• • •

Sam felt a hand on his shoulder, shaking him awake. His room was dark save for a shaft of light pouring in from the hallway.

"Mr Ferran. Wake up, sir."

It was Ben, the head of his security team. "What's going on?"

"Sir, there's been an attack on the—"

Sam sat up, instantly awake. "Is Mrs M okay? Beatrice?"

Ben nodded. "Something strange happened. The cameras on the perimeter went down, that was the first sign something was going on. John—one of the men patrolling the grounds—was knocked out and the door to the conservatory was broken into."

"What?"

"But the intruders stopped and gave themselves up."

"Who?"

"Three men, sir. They…" He swallowed and Sam noticed the sheen of sweat on his upper lip. "They came to kill you. They wouldn't have got to you, sir, there's motion sensors—"

"They broke in, though!" Sam said, getting out of bed. "Shit, what were you lot doing?"

"We were on the way in," Ben said. "There's a reinforced door between the conservatory and the rest of the house—they would still be there, trying to get through, by the time we got there if they hadn't given themselves up already."

Sam turned on the light and put on his dressing gown. It was three thirty in the morning. The fact that Ben—a huge black man almost seven feet tall—looked freaked out was the most frightening thing.

"I've never seen anything like it," he said as Sam found his slippers. "They were just kneeling there, hands on their heads like we'd already busted them."

"Where are they now?"

"In the gatehouse, sir. We didn't want them anywhere near the house just in case it was a ploy to do something worse. We've checked and double-checked the perimeter for others, and the house too. My men are just giving it all a second sweep."

"It's the first time you checked this room."

Ben straightened. "The second, sir. I move quietly, when I need to." He tapped the goggles resting on top of his head. "And I don't need any light either. Yours was the first room I checked."

"Sorry," Sam said. "I'm just a bit freaked out. Have you called the police?"

"Not yet, sir. Given the circumstances, I thought I should check with you first."

"Yeah, maybe hold off on that for a bit. Are Mrs M and Beatrice okay?"

Ben nodded. "Mrs Morrison is fine. She checked the silverware and the safe and then went back to bed. Beatrice is fine too. She wants to speak to you. I'd like to stay in the house for a while, keep an eye on things. My second has everything in hand at the gatehouse."

"That's fine," Sam said, and they went out into the hallway together before heading in different directions. Sam went to Beatrice's door at the end of the hallway and knocked.

"Come in."

She was sitting on the bed, dressed as if she'd never been to bed. Her dress was clean, though, and she looked calm.

"You okay? You wanted to see me."

"I wanted to ask you a question."

"Okay. They didn't make it into the house. You're safe here."

"I know. I stopped them. Sit down. You are quite pale."

Sam perched on the stool that went with the dressing table. "You made them give themselves up?"

She nodded. "I knew they were coming. I could have killed them, but I thought it might...upset you."

Sam gawped at her. "Um, yeah, that was the right thing to do."

"I want to know why they were sent here to kill you."

"You're sure they were?"

"Yes. They were going to come into the house, find your room, and shoot you in your bed with silent guns. They could have done that. They were very skilled. They have killed lots of people, some of them very important. Lord Copper sent them. Why?"

"How do you know all this?"

The corner of her mouth twitched. "Magic."

He rested his head in his hands. He was shaking. Copper sending someone to kill him just seemed…ridiculous. "But if this was a hit, why not do it somewhere I'm not so well protected?"

"They had a key to the house, and they knew the movements of your men. Someone helped them. A woman who is angry with you called Susan."

"Jesus." Now it made more sense. She was helping Copper, to rid him of a problem and to clear a way for her to take what she saw as rightfully hers.

"I want to know why Copper wants to kill you. This is not natural."

"No shit!"

"I mean, within the order of the Elemental Court, Copper should ally with you. It was always thus."

Sam told her about the mining scandal, the threats he'd made to Copper and the rest of the Court and the reasons why. Then he told her about going to the caves with Nickel.

"And even though you felt the way she expected you to, it made you more eager to fight Copper?" Beatrice said, and Sam nodded. "Even though you wanted to do just the same as he does?"

"Yes, *because* I felt that! I knew that if there was some…*other* reason for the Court being the way they are, there's no use asking them to stop. I have to force them. Just like I have to force myself to not be like them too."

"Do you know why they are this way?"

Sam heart quickened. "No."

"Because it is all out of balance. The Elemental Court. The Fae. They are both victims. It wasn't always this way."

"Is this something to do with the Sorcerers?"

Beatrice smiled. "It is everything to do with the Sorcerers. It is what they did. They sundered the world and pushed the pieces apart." She held her hands together and then moved them apart as she spoke. She raised her left hand. "The Fae, imprisoned by the Sorcerers, driven mad by the severance from humanity." She raised her right hand. "The Elemental Court. Yoked by the Sorcerers, divorced from self-knowledge, left unchecked as their hunger devours the world."

"But they had to split the worlds, right? I mean, those Fae, they're evil bastards. They had to keep them away from people!"

Beatrice let her hands fall to rest on her lap. "That is what they told everyone, and themselves, right until the end."

"The end?"

Beatrice opened her mouth and then closed it again, tilting her head. She seemed to be considering something as she looked at Sam. "You are not happy with the Court as it is," she finally said.

"No. They're doing far more harm than good."

"And you are not happy with the way the Fae behave."

"No. I don't like the way they use the people in the Nether, either."

"I feel the same." She looked away, frowning to herself. "This is very hard for me. I have spent a lot of my life alone, and I have never had a friend."

"What about your brother, the Sorcerer? Don't you get along?"

"We did, once. We were very close. So close that we said we were one soul split into two bodies." A pained expression crossed her face. "I find myself wanting to tell you things. Secrets. My soul is burdened, it seems, in a way I did not appreciate until now." She fixed her eyes on him once more. "I have never felt the desire to share this with another person. But then, all people before you have disappointed me. You have exceeded my expectations, and it is a strangely pleasant feeling."

"What did you expect me to be like?"

"The rest. I thought you would be nothing more than a greedy man, obsessed with nothing more than iron and money. Like your predecessor, and his before him. For six generations I have come to meet Lord Iron and commission a piece from him. Every time, I left disappointed."

Six generations? Sam didn't want to think about how old she was. There was enough to take in already. "So that's why you came? To see if I was like all the others?"

"Partly." She stared at the floor again and he had the impression that a great number of calculations were being made behind those eyes. "I came to measure your skill, to see if the recent changes had affected your power and to find information I need. I also planned to manipulate you into doing something for me. I hope that is not needed now."

"Oh. Okay. Listen, Beatrice, I'm feeling kind of out of my depth here. What you showed me today was awesome. I never thought I'd be able to do anything like that." He looked at the palm of his hand and the faint line of healing skin that looked as if it had been cut over a week ago, rather than a matter of hours before. He thought of her standing next to him in the forge, coaching him to believe things about himself, his blood, and the iron in his hand that sounded ridiculous to most of his mind but utterly true and immutable to the rest of it. He'd watched the impurities bubble out of the iron and drip to the floor, at first unable to understand that it was really him doing it. He'd thought it was some sorcery on her part until he did it again and again, long after she'd left him to go back to the house. "But," he continued, "I get the feeling you're holding stuff back that's…big."

"I will tell you the truth if you make a pact with me, Lord Iron, one that binds. You to me and me to you. In truth alone, no more than that."

"With more magic?"

"Yes. Something simple."

"But how do I know it isn't doing something more than what you say?"

"You have met the Fae," she said with certainty. "Caution serves you well. It will simply be a promise, witnessed by these walls, heard by our hearts, honoured by our souls. If one of us seeks to betray the other, the betrayed will know and will have the right to destroy the other."

"I don't want to destroy anyone!"

"Good. I have no intention of betraying your trust. Do you have intention of learning from me to use the knowledge against me?"

Sam paused. "No," he said, feeling three steps behind and not liking it at all.

"Then let us begin." She reached over and pressed her hand over his heart. She felt hot—too hot, almost. "You do the same."

He rested his hand over her heart, feeling it pound beneath his palm.

"When I speak a secret to you, you will know it for what it is and its worth. When you speak it to another against my wishes, you will know if you are about to betray me, and in betraying me, yourself. The same for any secret you share with me. Now, Lord Iron, you say the same to me, and mean it."

She led him through the words. He didn't feel any different when he was done, but she smiled and withdrew. Perhaps it was too subtle to be felt, perhaps she was just making him feel he was about to learn something special. Either way, he felt that learning more about what he was and how everything fit together was never going to do him any harm.

"I have lied to you," Beatrice began.

A shudder went through Sam, every hair on his body standing on end as she spoke. He knew, without a mote of doubt, that she was speaking a truth that was something precious, something that had its own worth and something he would have to keep secret too.

"I lied to you to protect myself because I did not trust you and I apologise, Lord Iron. I see your worth now. I told you that I was sent here by the Sorcerer of Essex, but the man bearing that title is dead. I came of my own volition, acting of my own free will, as I have for many hundreds of years.

"Over those years I have studied and I have made deals and I have looked for answers and I have seen the way of the worlds. I have mastered the magic of the soul and the magic of the mind, and I have woven them together in a way that men cannot fathom and Fae cannot conceive. I have listened to the Earth and read forbidden texts and scraped away the truth that was hidden from us all. The worlds were not split to protect mankind. They were sundered to give the Sorcerers dominion over all. But they were mere mortal men, so terrified that others would take their stolen knowledge that they withdrew from the world and slowly went mad. They cared more about what they had forgotten than whether their knowledge benefitted anyone but themselves.

"Lord Iron, I confess to you that I killed all the Sorcerers that plagued the mundane plane. I hunted them down and I ended their lives and those of the creatures they had enslaved and manipulated."

Sam shuddered. He was certain that no one should ever kill another, but the way she spoke sounded weird, almost mythical. Did she really mean it? "You killed Ekstrand?"

"Yes. It was necessary."

"Wait, all of them? Even your brother?"

"He was the first. But that was different. He had come to kill me, with smiles and soft words and a keen blade. That's what the Sorcerers had to do, to be recognised as such; they had to finish their training, have their knowledge tested, and then, when they had proven themselves, they had to kill the one they loved most in the world to be seen as complete. I thought my brother loved me more than he cared about becoming one of the Heptarchy. He was my first teacher. I learned sorcery from him, even though it was forbidden to teach those arts to a woman. And I learned that love is nothing compared to the lure of power.

"Every sorcerer that I killed was already a murderer, many times over. They wrenched souls from bodies and enslaved them. They took children from their parents, parents from their children, all to grease the wheels of their power. I have worked for over five hundred years to cleanse Mundanus of them, and now that it is done, I have only one task left to complete."

Sam's mouth went dry. "It isn't to kill me, is it?"

She laughed. "You would already be dead."

"You might be waiting for me to finish those chains."

"Ah, true, but I have no intention of killing you. I have ended so many lives, I have no desire for more death. Each one takes a little more from me. Yours would take too much."

"So what's the thing you have left to do?"

"I have removed the Sorcerers, but not their legacy. I want you to tell me where the other six forges are, Lord Iron. I want to know where the iron roads begin in our world."

"So you can go to Exilium and kill the Fae too?"

She shook her head. "No, Lord Iron." She held up her hands as she had before and slowly drew them back together. "So I can undo the damage that the Sorcerers wrought."

25

The clock was striking ten in the morning when Will heard Cathy's footsteps on the stairs. His valet was presenting a tray of cufflinks for him to choose from as he listened to her lady's maid say that an outfit had been prepared and the bath already run before the door to her private chamber slammed shut. Morgan came to find him in the dressing room.

"Her Grace has returned home somewhat later than anticipated, your Grace," he said. "I understand that she is to dress for the wedding immediately." After the briefest pause, he added, "Her Grace conveys her apologies that she has not had the opportunity to greet you in person."

Will smirked at Morgan's attempt to cover Cathy's flustered arrival. "Thank you, Morgan. Is the carriage ready?"

"Yes, your Grace. It's been fully repaired and is waiting outside."

Will chose a pair of cufflinks set with lapis lazuli with golden fleur-de-lis at their centre. He waited as his valet attached them for him and then helped him into his frock coat before giving it one final brush down. Inspecting himself in the mirror, Will was satisfied that his clothing and hair were perfect. His close shave followed by a hot towel had left his skin radiant and he'd slept better that night, thankfully, so there was no need to disguise any dark circles under his eyes. He nodded with satisfaction to his valet and dismissed him.

He went to the chest of drawers and opened the long velvet box that rested upon it. The choker that Tate had fashioned was exquisite. There were dozens of tiny diamonds strung on filigree strands that were barely visible, each with a delicate setting that hardly weighed them down. The sapphire at the centre was set into a band of silver made of dozens of the strands woven together, no wider than one of Sophia's little fingers, framing the gem and running the length of the choker. It was backed with something as soft as moleskin, with an adjustable clasp, strong enough to support the weight of the gem and hold enough structure for the diamonds to remain light around it, giving the impression of tiny stars. Tate had shown him how the gem would be in contact with Cathy's skin as she'd formed the threads around the back of it. It was a striking design, more modern than many ladies in the Nether would ever wear, but he had the feeling it would appeal to Cathy for that very reason.

He ran his fingers over it. It was the right thing to do. He'd shown it to Cathy's lady's maid, telling her to choose a dress to go well with it for the wedding. "Oh, her Grace is so lucky," she'd sighed, but she wasn't looking at the choker as she said it.

She'd been delighted to plot the happy scheme with him, thinking she was facilitating a romantic gesture between a couple in love. As promised, she sent another maid to tell him that the time was right.

He went to Cathy's dressing room, pausing to listen to her talking to her maid about Elizabeth's ridiculous demands and laughing about what her mother had said in response to one of them. She sounded happier than he expected, considering she wasn't one for family gatherings—or marriages, for that matter.

He closed his eyes, remembering the way the men of the Court had looked at him as she'd spoke. He recalled the sour faces at Black's, the reluctant bows, the way practically every man of the city had come to express his "private concerns" about the Duchess to him. The way Sir Iris had roasted him in his study, the threat of the Parisian Court. No more. He couldn't let Cathy put them at risk again.

It was the right thing to do.

He knocked once and entered, making Cathy yelp and grab her dressing gown too late to cover her corset and the stocking tops he could glimpse through the fine silk of her chemise. Her hair was pinned up in the Regency style he liked on her—as he'd instructed her maid to suggest—her face framed by gentle curls and, more importantly, her neck bare. Her skin was still flushed from the bath and the fragrance of her bathing oil filled the air.

"Will!" she laughed, blushing. "I'm not dressed!"

He nodded to the maid who scurried away as Cathy frantically tried to put on the dressing gown when half of it was turned inside out. "I've seen you in greater states of undress, my love," he said, watching the flush spread down her throat as she glanced at him.

"Shoo! I have to get ready; we're leaving in ten minutes and I haven't even got my dress on."

"Stockings and suspenders? How very modern of you."

He grinned at the deepening blush. "Those stupid bloomers and garters do my head in. These are for convenience, not for you!"

He went to stand behind her, seeing himself reflected in the glass she stood in front of. Holding the box behind his back, he kissed the nape of her neck and gently pulled the dressing gown from her hands, letting it drop on the floor beside them. Peeping over her shoulder to look at her eyes via the reflection in the mirror, he ran a fingertip over her shoulder, down over the swell of her breast to finger the edge of her chemise peeping out from under the top of the corset. "I'd like to unlace this," he murmured, kissing her again.

He listened to her breath catch in her throat and saw how her eyes darkened in the mirror as her lips reddened. "I…Will, I have to dress."

"I missed you, my love," he said against her skin, tickling it with his breath, as his hand moved up from the lace, brushing the top of her breast again to skim the base of her throat.

"I'm sorry I had to go. Mother needed me, and I don't know if I'll see her again after today."

He paused, looking at her reflection again. "Are your parents planning to travel once Elizabeth is married?"

She shook her head, biting her lip, twisting her head slightly to brush her cheek against his hair. "If I tell you, you mustn't tell another soul, Will."

"Of course, darling." Another kiss, another swell of her chest. He was tempted to have her there, against the dressing table, and be late for the wedding.

"Mother is leaving my father. That's why she wanted to marry Elizabeth off so quickly. She couldn't wait any longer to be with her lover."

Will pressed his lips against her shoulder, wondering who that could be. "You aren't going to warn your father?"

She looked horrified. "No, Will! And you must swear to me that you won't say a word to anyone at the wedding. I shouldn't have told you."

He smiled at her in the mirror, skimming over her skin with his lips, back to the nape of her neck. "I promise. You're so soft."

"Will," she breathed, clasping her hands together after starting to reach back, as if she were trying to stop herself from touching him. "Stop it; I have to get ready, not…"

"I have a gift for you," he said, sliding his hand away from her chest slowly, enjoying the way she responded to his touch.

"Can't it wait until Elizabeth is married?"

"No," he said, bringing the box round with his right hand, circling her with his left to open it in front of her from the centre of a loose embrace. "I hope you like it."

He watched her eyes widen, her mouth open. "Oh! Will, it's beautiful. Too fancy for me, surely."

"Nonsense," he said, easing it from the strips of velvet that held it in place. "I commissioned it especially for you. I thought you might like something more…modern than most."

Cathy smiled at him. "It isn't my birthday or anything."

"I don't need a reason or anything," he mimicked her tone, tossing the box aside and holding it up in front of her so she could see it glitter beneath the sprite light. "You're my wife. I love you. I wanted to give you something special to wear to your sister's wedding. I'm just glad I commissioned it as soon as she came to stay!" He kissed the back of her neck again, ran his lips around to her other shoulder. "Will you let me put it on you? I confess I asked your maid to pick out a dress to go with it. I'd love to see you wear it today."

"It isn't more for a ball or dance or…?"

"No, it can be worn in the day." He forced himself to be patient, running a line of kisses up to her neck again, peeping over her shoulder to lock eyes with hers in the reflection. "I'd much rather see you wearing this and nothing else. But if we must go to this wedding, I suppose I will have to live with you wearing the dress with it. Until we get back."

She looked back at him, hungry, her hands pulled apart by her lust to reach back and hold his hips against her. "I'll wear it—with the dress—but put it on before I make us late."

With a smile that she reflected back to him in the glass, he pressed the sapphire against her throat, wrapped the band around her neck, and fastened it shut.

He felt her shudder, as if she were cold, and a slight frown replaced her smile. She looked distant for a moment, lost even, and he spun her around and kissed her deeply, coaxing her attention back to him. He held her close, feeling her respond more passionately. It seemed that breaking Poppy's wish magic also meant that nothing else was acting against the Charm working on her now.

Will ran his hands down her back, his fingertips brushing the lacing of the corset until he felt the swell of her buttocks and the silk covering them. He had just got the slippery fabric pinched between finger and thumb to pull the chemise up when there was a knock at the door.

"Not now," he growled.

"Your Grace," came the voice of the lady's maid. "You'll be late if I don't dress you now."

Will loved the way Cathy was pushing him back towards one of the wardrobes in her passion. "Hang the wedding," he said.

"The wedding!" she gasped. "No, Will, we can't be late." She moved away, putting her hands on his chest and holding him at arm's length. "Wait downstairs, for God's sake."

"Do you like my gift?"

She reached up to trace it with her fingertips. "I love it. And I love you. And I want to tear those very fine clothes off you, so go downstairs before you end up being just as undressed as I am!"

He laughed. "Only if you promise to come home afterwards and spend the night with me."

"Fine, fine, I promise, now shoo!"

He left her to dress and waited for her in the carriage, unable to stop smiling with relief. He would make sure he distracted her just enough through the day to keep her mind on him and nothing else, then they would come home and he would make love to her and… he sighed. It was all going to be fine. He'd tell her about his plans for the Agency afterwards, when it was all done and he could properly relax. Besides, he didn't want to raise any topics that might remind her of anything other than him.

He smiled as she burst from the house, the sapphire of the choker matching the trim of her gown and her opera gloves perfectly. She paused at the bottom of the steps, spun around, and headed back up them, only to meet her maid rushing out of the house to press a reticule into her hand. Cathy dashed down the steps, allowed the footman to help into the carriage, and sat opposite him, panting.

"You nearly made us late," she said.

"That was you," he said, leaning across to take her hands. "How could I help but kiss you when you were standing there, all soft and sweet-scented in your underclothes."

"Stop it," she whispered, beaming at him.

"Carter's on the back, he can't hear us. Now," he moved across the gap to sit next to her, "let's see if I can find a way to keep us occupied until we reach the Oak…"

• • •

As weddings went, it was by far the most enjoyable Cathy had ever attended. Considering she'd only been to three in her entire life—one when she was a child and too young to really understand what was happening and the other her own—it wasn't much of an achievement. She'd expected it to be far worse, especially when they arrived to a rather tearful Elizabeth, who was upset that Lord Poppy hadn't turned up.

"He came for your wedding!" she pouted at Cathy as she went over. "Why not mine?"

Cathy shrugged. "He probably knows you're willing. He doesn't have to make sure it happens."

She hadn't meant it to be a comfort, but somehow it brightened her sister. "Yes, that must be it. I wish he was here to see me at my best, though."

"Count yourself lucky," Cathy said, and Elizabeth scowled at her.

"Oh stop that!"

"What?"

"That thing you do, that…dismissing everything I think is important and making me feel silly for wanting things."

Cathy met Will's eyes across the distance between them, her mind only partially on Elizabeth. He was waiting at a discreet distance with Tom, ready to accompany the party up the aisle at the appropriate time. "It's not my fault you always want silly things."

"You're doing it again! On my wedding day, and I tried so hard to be nice to you on yours! You ended up being Duchess and you even ended up being our patron's favourite, even after the despicable things you did! And you don't even try! It's so unfair!"

"What's all this noise about?" their father said, coming over from greeting other guests. "Catherine, are you upsetting your sister on today of all days?"

"I hardly have to try," Cathy said with a shrug. "I think she's allergic to me." But her sister's words had penetrated, no matter how much she tried to hide the fact. She'd always dismissed Elizabeth for being the very epitome of what Society wanted from their young ladies, without even considering any effort her sister might have put into it. Seeing her life through Elizabeth's eyes was a revelation. And all this time she'd been raging against so much, when really, she was blessed.

She was drawn back to Will again. He was saying something to Tom that made her brother laugh. Elizabeth was right. With no effort at all she was married to one of the most handsome men in Albion, a man who beyond all expectations loved her too. How he could find something loveable in her, plain and difficult as she was, was a miracle.

Cathy felt tired, yet happy. It had been such a wildly emotional time of late. She'd lost two of her friends and closest allies, was soon to lose her mother—though that was for a happier reason—and she was still desperately worried about Charlotte. But the tension beneath it all, the constant sense of not doing enough, of not changing anything, had eased. She was simply withdrawing and reconsidering, as Natasha had said, taking a moment to breathe in all the madness. Eventually Margritte and Natasha would return and they would resume their efforts. There was no need to rush. She would work something out, some way forward that would keep Will smiling at her that way. It was so blissful when they didn't fight.

Will glanced over at her, gave the smile he reserved just for her, and she simply melted. Cathy smiled back, planning to have one drink at the reception, just to be seen, before racing back home with him in the carriage. She had to have him. Even though there was the tiniest hint of worry at the back of her mind that she shouldn't, Cathy couldn't for the life of her remember why she had worried about being intimate with him. Something about…

"Catherine!" Elizabeth's shrill voice cut through her. "Stop staring at William and arrange my train!"

As she fussed with Elizabeth's dress under their mother's watchful eye, a carriage arrived bearing the Iris crest. Cathy looked up, expecting to see Will's parents emerge with Imogen, but only his mother stepped out, and she looked dreadfully pale.

"Where's George Iris?" her father said, but her mother pretended not to hear, disinterested.

Will went over to his mother, who broke down as he got to

her. Startled, he guided her away, out of sight round the corner of the building.

"Something's wrong," Cathy said, wondering if she should go and help.

"Is there a stain?" Elizabeth squeaked, thinking she was referring to the train of the dress.

Just as she was about to find Will, he came back into sight, looking grave. Cathy abandoned the hem of Elizabeth's gown and went to him, tuning out her protestations.

"What's happened?" she asked him.

"I have to go, my love; there's a family emergency and I'm needed at home."

Cathy saw her mother-in-law being guided back to her carriage by one of the footmen. "Is it Imogen?"

Will kissed her hands. "Please give my sincerest apologies to your family. I don't know how long I'll be gone." He started to go, then turned and gently stroked her cheek with his thumb. "Go home after the wedding and wait for me, my love. I'm so sorry I can't be with you."

Wanting to go with him, but knowing she had to stay, Cathy watched Will climb into the carriage and give her a worried smile as it pulled away.

Elizabeth's bottom lip was trembling when she returned. "Don't tell me the Irises are going to snub my wedding too!"

"Something terrible has happened," Cathy said, looking at her father. "I don't know what, but Will's mother was so upset. I've never seen her that way."

"I can't believe it!" Elizabeth moaned. "Surely this is a bad omen!"

"Hush now," their father said. "Your groom is waiting inside, that's the most important thing. The Irises wouldn't miss this unless something extraordinary happened, which it evidently has and there's nothing to be done about it. Now chin up, Elizabeth. Let's see that beautiful smile. You're about to become a Viola!"

Elizabeth smiled right on cue, no doubt thinking about how she was about to become a very wealthy young lady too.

Cathy started to head towards the wedding party but was held back by her mother, who judged it better to have Cathy drop out than there be an unbalanced group. Instead, they went inside to sit with the rest of the guests, Cathy feeling a guilty thankfulness that with Will absent, she didn't have to walk up the aisle as part of the ceremony.

Being back in the huge building that surrounded the Oak brought back memories of her unhappiness on her wedding day, and her anger, but it seemed so distant now. She didn't know then how happy she'd be with Will. If she had, would she have been less reluctant to marry? There were other reasons to strain against the bonds made that day, after all. Not that she could recall them easily now. Perhaps she had simply grown up, or rather grown into herself now.

Everyone else in the rows of seats nodded to her, though Cathy saw how many of them did it without any real warmth. All of them were respectful, at least. She saw her aunt, the Censor of Aquae Sulis, and gave her a polite nod, which earned the slightest one back. At least she had a beaming smile and merry wave from her Uncle Lavandula. He smiled at the scowl his sister gave him and winked at Cathy before turning to face front again.

The groom waited at the front, a fair-haired man who looked twice Elizabeth's age and rather bemused by it all. Beside him stood Bertrand Viola and no matter how much she knew she must, Cathy couldn't muster a smile for him. Charlotte sat in the front row, bolt upright, facing front. Oh, how she wanted to go over there and punch Bertrand in the face!

"That's a beautiful choker, Catherine," her mother whispered as the last guests took their places. "I've never seen a design quite like it."

"Will gave it to me this morning," she said, tracing the outline of the sapphire as she spoke.

Her mother reached across and squeezed her hand. "I do hope you find happiness with him, Catherine."

The earnest words made tears prick in Cathy's eyes. She leaned over. "I hope you find it too," she whispered, and they shared a smile both sad and hopeful.

The wedding went smoothly without any drama, which was quite remarkable, considering Elizabeth was involved. Then again, Elizabeth was at the centre of attention, where she most liked to be, so she could be happy and even seem quite sweet without having to be shrill at any point.

Cathy tried to get to Charlotte during the reception, just to give her a smile or a whisper of reassurance that she hadn't forgotten about her, but Bertrand kept steering her away. He wasn't even trying to hide what he was doing. She resolved to go and visit her again soon.

After the tenth person enquired after Will's health and the well-being of the Irises, Cathy had had enough. She made her goodbyes, kissed Elizabeth as she genuinely wished her well, and then climbed into the carriage with relief. She saw Bertrand escorting Charlotte out as the carriage pulled away and her heart ached to see how pale and thin she looked.

All the way home, Carter inside the carriage instead of on the back, Cathy chewed her thumbnail, trying to work out a way to free Charlotte from her odious husband. If only divorce were a possibility—but there was no way to make that permissible fast enough. With a sigh, she doubted any changes would happen to the law anytime soon. It all seemed so hopeless. She needed to talk to Will about the Ladies' Court and about Gujarat and couldn't believe they had slipped her mind. She was tired, that was all, and Will had been so affectionate that morning, it was hard to keep a thought in her head when he was like that. Keeping her mind on anything seemed—

"We're home, your Grace," Carter said, opening the carriage door for her.

She hadn't even noticed. As she climbed down the step, Morgan opened the door, looking worried. "Is it Will? Is he back?" she asked, hurrying up the steps to him.

"No, your Grace. Is he not with you?"

"He was called away. What's wrong?"

Morgan lowered his voice. "The Arbiter is here, your Grace, the one who visited before. He said he needs to speak with you on a matter of great importance and refused to leave until he saw you."

Max? She realised she hadn't checked her phone for a few days. "Is he in the drawing room?" At Morgan's nod, she went straight to it and found Max waiting for her.

"Hi!" she said. "Long time no see. No tea for us, thanks," she said to Morgan, who had trailed after her nervously. Carter took up his position outside the door, having had time to eye Max warily before Cathy shut it.

Max inserted something into the keyhole. "So we can't be overheard," he said.

"Is the gargoyle with you?"

"He's nearby. I tried to reach you by using the mobile telephone but you never responded."

"Sorry, I haven't been able to get into Mundanus for a few days. What's up?"

"You didn't get my warning, then?"

Her first thought was of Will and how his mother had looked. "About what?"

"I had reason to believe you were going to be attacked."

"Oh! I was. I mean, my carriage was. They ran away. How did you know that was going to happen?"

"It came up in an investigation," Max said. "I take it you know a Mr Bertrand Persificola-Viola? He's a resident of Londinium."

"I do," she said, not bothering to hide her feelings about him.

"I have intelligence that indicates he's the head of a secret society called the Second Sons. They're responsible for several breaches of the Split Worlds Treaty and the attack on your carriage. There's evidence to suggest they're targeting you specifically, and I have reason to believe they're a threat to your person."

Cathy's heart felt as if it had jumped into her throat to pound there instead. "Bertrand Viola sent those men? Wait, you said 'second sons'...is Will...?"

Max shook his head. "I have no reason to believe your husband is involved with them, and I'm confident I know all the members of the group now. I doubt he even knows they exist."

Cathy breathed a sigh of relief, feeling terrible that she'd even contemplated his involvement. Of course Will wouldn't be involved with anything like that. "Bertrand Viola? Shit, I bet his bloody goons were behind those letters, too!"

"Letters?"

"Hate mail, threats...nasty stuff. Are you sure?"

"As sure as I can be without interrogating him myself."

"Take a seat," Cathy said, gesturing to the sofa. "I need all the details."

26

Will paced in the waiting room, desperately hoping Sir Iris hadn't passed his judgement yet. He'd left his mother with Imogen, who was just as distraught, after coaxing out a garbled account of his father being arrested for no reason. Will knew enough about Arbiters to know they didn't arrest men as powerful as his father without good cause.

At first he considered contacting Faulkner and asking him to look into it. But Faulkner and the rest of the Arbiters who were willing to do his bidding were based in London; they wouldn't have anything to do with events in Aquae Sulis. Besides, it would take time to arrange a meeting, time he felt would be put to better use trying to get an audience with the Patroon and working on a plan of his own.

After what felt like hours, he was finally collected and escorted to the Patroon's study. Sir Iris was seated at his desk, as before, only younger-looking than the last time Will had sat in this chair.

"You're here about your father, no doubt."

"In part, Sir Iris. Have you passed your judgement on him?"

Sir Iris leaned back. "No. But I won't lie to you, William. It's very serious. Are you aware of the case against him?"

Will shook his head. "Whatever he has done, I am certain he did it for the family and our patron and that is enough for me."

"Bold words, young man. The Arbiter has pushed for his expulsion from Society and exile into Mundanus, where he'd be kept under close surveillance until his death."

The thought of his father's ageing and death in Mundanus made

Will feel nauseous. "Sir Iris, it is not my place to interfere in any of this, and please don't think that I don't trust your judgement…"

Sir Iris straightened. "Any other son and I would throw him out of my office now. I haven't the time or inclination to listen to anyone pleading for their loved one."

"Please don't think so little of me, Sir Iris. I wouldn't dream of wasting your time so. I come with critical information that I fear may not have reached your office. I simply ask that you hear me out before making your final decision."

Sir Iris smiled, and this time, Will believed it. Perhaps having Eleanor returned to him had dusted off his heart. "You've certainly pulled rabbits out of hats in the past. Speak—I'm eager to see if you can impress me twice in one week."

"My father was arrested at home, by an Arbiter claiming to work with the sanction of the Sorcerer of Wessex. Sir, I have good reason to believe that the Sorcerer of Wessex is dead and has not been replaced."

Sir Iris looked genuinely shocked. "How could you possibly have come to know this?"

"I overheard a conversation between two Arbiters, sir, discussing the crisis." Will kept his eyes fixed on Sir Iris and his breath as even as he possibly could. It was a hell of a risk he was taking, but he had to try to save his father and stretching the truth was a necessity. He could never say it was a conversation he'd received thirdhand between an Arbiter and his wife, but he could report the pertinent information from it.

"And you are certain of this?"

"As far as I can be, Sir Iris. My initial enquiries have confirmed this." Sir Iris didn't need to know that those were reports from the Agency staff, who were far from reliable. "It seems to me that this is a rogue Arbiter, acting without the support of a superior. If you were to be lenient with my father, I am confident"—his heart banged as he said it—"that there would be no further action taken. There is no Sorcerer watching over Aquae Sulis to press for a harsher punishment should yours be considered unsatisfactory."

Sir Iris was staring at him, lips pressed tight together.

Will decided to make the most of the silence. "It isn't just my filial devotion that drives this, Sir Iris, though of course as a loving son I want to see my father safe and well. There's another factor, one I learned of only this morning, that makes my father's survival more pressing." He paused, but Sir Iris just waited, so he continued. "I've learned that Isabella Rhoeas-Papaver intends to leave her husband very soon, possibly within days. No doubt Charles would try to keep this hidden, fearing that if the news were to emerge that his marriage had failed, his patron would be displeased and he would lose the support of the Lavandulas as well as the other minor families who pay their tithes to him in Aquae Sulis. If you were to stand by my father, give him nothing more than a slapped wrist and send him home, he'd be able to maximise our gains from the Papaver family's collapse in Aquae Sulis and tip the balance of the Council. We could take the city, Sir Iris, leaving the Lavandulas in place as figureheads if we chose."

"If *we* chose?"

Will coughed. "I mean, the family, Sir Iris. It would of course be the decision of you and my father. If he were still able to profit from this intelligence."

Sir Iris maintained his stare for a few seconds longer and then smiled broadly as he clapped. "Bravo, William, bravo. I see now why our patron favours you so, and why my dear wife speaks so fondly of you."

Will dared to breathe normally again, giving a smile but not letting his guard down for a moment. "So you agree that it's worth the risk to call the Arbiter's bluff?"

"I do, William, I do." Sir Iris stood. "Your father will be home for dinner and nothing will be said of this unfortunate incident. I will discuss your insights regarding the Papavers' marriage with him, so he will ensure we emerge from their crisis with Aquae Sulis under the full control of the Irises."

Will stood too, and accepted Sir Iris's handshake. "Thank you for taking the time to see me, Sir Iris."

"My door is always open to you, William. And give my regards to your wife. I trust she is better behaved now?"

"Indeed, Sir Iris. If you'll excuse me, she's waiting for me now and I am eager to return to her."

• • •

"I'm sorry, your Grace, Mrs Persificola-Viola is resting after the wedding and isn't receiving visitors."

Cathy smiled at the butler, hoping he didn't notice how she was shaking. "I'm actually here to see Mr Viola. It's a matter of some importance."

The butler stepped aside and gestured for her to enter. "He's in the drawing room, your Grace. If you'd like to follow me?"

It felt strange seeing Bertrand get up from the sofa when she entered, rather than Charlotte. It was the room in which they usually took tea together.

"Your Grace," he said with a bow. "I'm afraid the wedding has quite worn Charlotte out. Would you like me to pass on a message to her?"

"As I explained to your butler, I'm here to see you. No tea, thank you," she said to the butler, who waited near the door. "I won't be staying for very long."

The butler nodded, gave Bertrand a last glance, and, dismissed, closed the door.

"How can I help you, your Grace?"

Cathy had rehearsed the words over and over in her head in the carriage, but now, about to say them, she hesitated. Will wouldn't be happy about what she planned to do.

"Has whatever it was slipped your mind?" He checked his pocket watch. "I was about to go out. If you'd prefer to send a letter, that would be far more agreeable than standing there looking like a lost child."

His tone made her bristle. No wonder Charlotte was wasting away. It was far more important that she be helped than a bloody marriage take place—one that none of the women involved even wanted. "I'm here to ask that you destroy the contract between yourself and Nathaniel regarding his marriage to your daughter."

Bertrand's nostrils flared and his cheeks flushed the same red as Freddy's did when he'd drunk too much. "I beg your pardon, madam?"

Cathy ignored the racing of her heart, determined to see this through. "Destroy the contract, sir; otherwise I will destroy you."

A vein at the side of Bertrand's forehead pulsed and then he laughed at her. "You have simply no idea how the world works, do you, you silly little girl?"

Any worry about what Will might think flew from her mind as he laughed again. She stormed forwards into the room until the sofa was between them. "Listen to me, you misogynistic twat. I know you stole your wife from Mundanus. She was a suffragette, and you kidnapped her on the way home from a rally. If you had any idea of how the *real* world works, you might have taken the trouble to ensure that any pictures of her at that rally were destroyed. But you didn't. I have the proof of your crime, and don't give me any bullshit about how she'll deny it, because an Arbiter's Truth Mask can cut through any gagging Charm of yours faster than you can say 'shut up, dear'."

Bertrand stopped laughing.

"Oh, taking me seriously now?" she continued, thrilled by the fear in his eyes. "And before you even think about cursing or gagging me, know that the Duke of Londinium protects his family very well. The Irises care for their wives more than any of the Great Families and," she held up her left hand, indicating the bump of her wedding ring beneath her glove, "he would know the moment you did anything to me."

"You wouldn't dare report me," Bertrand said, gathering his wits. "You're too fond of Charlotte. You wouldn't want to see her carted away by the Arbiters to be brainwashed into slavery or thrown back into Mundanus."

"I would rather see her thrown into Mundanus or even held by the Arbiters than watch her waste away. Being with you is simply a slow death. You are a hateful, toxic, cowardly little man. Your elder brother was an arse, but I'd rather spend a year in his company than a minute longer in yours!" She headed for the door. "If I don't hear from Will by six o'clock this evening that your daughter's wedding is off, I'll go straight to the Arbiters. I will bust your sorry arse, and I will wave you off when they drag you away."

"If you do this to me," Bertrand said, his voice low and quiet. "I will seek out every single person you love and destroy them before I come for you."

"Yeah, yeah. Whatever. Good day, Mr Viola. I trust you'll be contacting Nathaniel Iris the moment I leave."

Reaching for the handle, Cathy felt a movement behind her. She twisted as Bertrand stormed towards her, fist pulled back. "Do it!" she yelled. "Hit me like a real man. The Irises would tear you apart and piss on your grave."

Bertrand's hand stopped, inches away from her face. He spat on her instead. "You're disgusting."

Cathy wiped the spittle from her cheek. "I think you mean 'your Grace'," she said, finding the door handle behind her back and twisting it. For a dreadful moment, she feared he wasn't going to move and let her open the door, but he turned away, moving towards the mantelpiece. Was he going for the poker? She didn't wait to find out.

As she ran from the room, Cathy almost collided with the butler. "I'm going," she said, and didn't wait for him to open the front door for her as the sound of smashing crockery came from the drawing room. "Right now," she added, and ran out of the house.

• • •

"Something wasn't right with Cathy," the gargoyle said, pacing. "You should have let me in."

Max kept his eyes on the West London street below. It was cold on top of the fire escape and his leg was aching. "There he is."

The gargoyle hunkered down next to him, staring at the man

walking towards the pub. "I'm going to enjoy this." Its grin bared every single one of its stone teeth.

"I'll move into position," he told the gargoyle, and climbed back through the window they'd been standing next to. He went from that room into the hallway, down a set of stairs, and into a cleaning cupboard he'd scoped out beforehand. Max put the earpiece into place as Kay had shown him and made sure the little microphone symbol showing on his mobile phone was green. Through the tiny piece of plastic in his ear he could hear the sound of Oliver Peonia pacing back and forth in the room next door, muttering to himself nervously.

Through the gargoyle's eyes, Max watched as Bertrand Viola went into the pub behind a group of mundanes. Less than a minute later, Max could hear the creak of the stairs leading up from the public bar below up to the private room in which the Peonia waited. Max pressed a second button on the phone below the microphone, which was large and red. The word *recording* flashed up at the bottom of the screen, as had happened in Kay's demonstration. He was faintly aware of the gargoyle's relief that it worked just as she said it would.

"Good evening, Oli," Bertrand said.

"Good evening, Mr Viola. Awfully cold out there, what?"

"Indeed. Where are the others?"

"I thought I was early," Oliver said, a slight tremor in his voice.

"No, they're late."

"W-whilst I have the opportunity, sir, I'd like to say thank you. For bringing me into the fold, so to speak."

"We second sons have to look after one another," Bertrand said warmly.

"I was wondering if I could suggest a new member for consideration," Oli said. "He's a chum of mine and a jolly decent chap. He's the Duke of Londinium now, but he's been a second son for a lot longer than that."

There was a pause. Was Viola suspicious? "I did plan to ask

him, but his wife interferes too much in his affairs. What the deuce is holding up the others? I told them it was urgent."

"I could always take a message for you and tell them when they arrive, if you're expected somewhere else," Oliver offered.

"I don't have time...and you're green and untested..."

"I might be new, sir, but I'm jolly reliable. Why, I travelled the world with William Iris and got us out of all sorts of scrapes. Are you...are you in a bind, sir? You do seem rather flustered, if you don't mind me saying so. If there's any way I can help..."

"How close are you to William's wife?"

"The Duchess? Oh, not at all. Barely know her. Heard some rum things about her, mind you. Bit of a harridan, so I've been told. She has a sharp tongue and strange ideas about women and chaps and—"

"I need your help dealing with her. She's blackmailing me and I need to...to teach her a lesson."

"Blackmailing you? Gosh! Why not tell Will? He'll soon sort it all out."

"That fool has no spine when it comes to that whore. Londinium would be better off without her. He needs a decent woman at his side. If you help me to solve this problem, I'll set you up in a Londinium house in one of the finest squares."

Max checked to see that the phone screen still said "recording." The gargoyle was gouging chunks of stone from the cornice outside as its claws clenched.

"Gosh...that sounds rather splendid. Will does deserve a better wife, it's true. It's the least I could do as his friend, what?"

Bertrand chuckled along with Oli's nervous laugh. "I need you to send a note to her via Letterboxer, asking her to see you, at once. Tell her...tell her that you've discovered something about William that you feel she should know, and that it's most sensitive. Tell her to meet you at Bathurst Stables. I'll take care of the rest."

Max had heard enough. Any doubts he'd had were long gone, and he'd recorded enough to make a case to the Duke of Londinium should he become obstructive when someone from his city was arrested by an Aquae Sulis Arbiter. None of the Londinium Arbiters could be trusted, after all.

He dropped the phone into one pocket and pulled the special door handle out of another. Leaving the cupboard, he checked that the gargoyle was alert at the window and then entered the private room.

Oliver leapt away from the Viola as if the man were on fire and shrank into the corner of the room as Bertrand took in Max's face.

"That damn whore," he whispered. "She planned this all along, didn't she?"

"Bertrand Persificola-Viola, with the sanction of the Duchess of Londinium, I am taking you into custody." He took hold of the man's arm.

"Whatever she told you about me, it's a lie. I can prove it."

"I just listened to you plotting to harm her," Max said. "I also heard you accept thanks for membership into your secret society, one that has been responsible for several critical breaches of the Split Worlds Treaty, the attempted assault of the Duchess of Londinium, and the blackmail of several prominent members of Nether Society."

"What do you care about them?" Bertrand scoffed.

"Nothing at all. But I do care about the babies you pressurise young men into stealing from innocents and the Charms you encourage them to use in Mundanus." Max thrust the pin of the door handle into the wall, opened the Way to the same box that had held George Iris only hours before, and locked Bertrand into the cuffs fixed to the table.

"If I'm going to be thrown out of Society," Bertrand said, red with anger, "then I'll take my wife with me. I stole her, Arbiter, from Mundanus. So you'd better go and clap some irons on her too."

"I know about your wife already," Max said. "I made a deal with the Duchess about her, in fact. She helped me to trap you in West London, and in return, I'll overlook your wife if she wants to stay in the Nether. She's no longer an innocent and her family are long dead. I see no reason to press for her expulsion from a place willing to keep her. She isn't a risk to anyone else. Unlike you."

Bertrand tried to launch himself at Max but the cuffs held fast and he kicked the chair instead. "I'll see you hanged!" he yelled as Max put the pin of the door handle into the wall. "I'm a *Viola*, damn you! I'm not common filth! You can't treat me this way!"

Max left the man to shout alone. By the time he was back in the room above the mundane pub, Cathy was coming up the stairs after seeing the all-clear signal from the gargoyle.

A very sweaty Oliver waited nervously where Max had left him. "Gosh! That was dreadfully thrilling. I felt like one of those spies I saw in a mundane film on my Grand Tour. I thought I did rather well."

Max pulled the bug off the Peonia's jacket and dropped it into a pocket. "The Second Sons are over. You're off the hook."

"Oh, that is splendid news. I…I don't suppose you could put in a good word with the Duchess? Let her know how I helped?"

"I already know," Cathy said from the doorway. "Thanks, Oli. That was brave of you."

The Peonia beamed at her and then bowed. "I am your servant, your Grace. Now, if you don't mind, I'd very much like to drink the best whisky they have in that bar downstairs until I stop shaking."

Cathy moved aside for him. Once he was gone, Max went over to her. "Your husband wasn't one of the Second Sons. And Bertrand was planning to kill you. Whatever you said to him worked. He was desperate."

"Thanks, Max," Cathy smiled. "That's a massive weight off my mind. There's no way Nathaniel will marry the daughter of a disgraced criminal. He's too proud for that." She looked at the floor, frowning a little. "I hope Charlotte meant it when she said this would be the best-case scenario. It's the only one I could come up with."

Max nodded and opened the window to let the gargoyle in. It went straight to Cathy, who embraced it. She let it go and took a deep breath. "Well, I should get back home before Carter has an aneurysm. With any luck, Will won't be home yet, and he won't know I've been gallivanting all over London with you."

The gargoyle sniffed at her and the space around her. "Don't go yet," it said. "Something's not right with you."

Max pulled the Sniffer from his pocket, agreeing with the gargoyle. "Do you feel any different to normal?"

"I've got a headache, but that's stress."

The Sniffer's light glowed green and Max flipped it over. "There's Iris magic active on you."

She frowned. "But I haven't…" Cathy brushed the choker at her throat with her fingertips. She was still wearing it and her Nether clothing beneath her cloak. She paled. "What kind of magic? Could it be my wedding ring?"

"I don't like the look of that necklace," the gargoyle said. "You should take it off."

"But Will gave this to me this morning."

"Feel any different afterwards?"

Cathy shrugged. She was usually more certain of herself.

Max rummaged in his pockets for one of the new gadgets Rupert had given him as a low growl started in the back of the gargoyle's throat. "How's your husband?" it asked her.

"Oh, he's fine," she said brightly. "Wonderful, actually."

The gargoyle's growl got louder and Max looked at what was upsetting it—her eyes. The pupils were far too dilated. Her cheeks flushed at the mere mention of Will. His fingers closed around an unfamiliar shape and he pulled it from his pocket.

"I want to test you," he said. "I think you've been Charmed, and I assume that, seeing as you don't know how, you want to know what it's doing to you?"

"It's obvious," the gargoyle snarled.

Cathy looked from it to the gadget nervously. "Will it hurt?"

"No. Stand still."

When he reached for her hair she flinched away. "No! The Irises will know if you touch me. Tell me what to do with it."

Back when Rupert had demonstrated what to do with it on

Kay's hair, she'd said it was like mini hair-straighteners, but he wasn't certain if Cathy would understand the reference. He certainly didn't. Max directed Cathy to separate out a lock of her hair and then run it between the two little arms of the detector, pinching them closed and then pulling it down the length of her hair. After it beeped, his phone buzzed and he checked the screen. The results were displayed on it.

"You've been exposed to two massive doses," he read. "One in mid-November and a second one that started a couple of days ago. Both have the same signature, and by the look of you now, I reckon both were Charms designed to make you feel strongly attracted to someone."

Cathy's face drained of colour. "What?" she whispered.

"I suspect that choker is Charmed too," Max said. "There's a background reading here that's definitely Iris, very strong, and different from the attraction Charms. You should take it off."

She fumbled with the clasp, shaking. It finally came free and as soon as it was away from her throat the gargoyle hooked it with a claw and whipped it away from her, sniffing at the sapphire. "It's this. It's first-gen, I just know it."

"From Iris himself," Max said to Cathy, who by now was so ashen-faced he thought she might pass out. "I can confirm that if I take it with me for testing."

"Mid-November?" she whispered. "Attraction? Are you sure?"

Max nodded. "Positive. It's all stored in the hair, like some mundane drugs. That's why Ekstrand took your hair to test when he first met you. He wanted to know what Charms were active on you. There were none then. Now you are being magically influenced to find someone attractive to the extent that it will impede your judgement, make you susceptible to their suggestions, especially if those are leading to intimate contact with them, and—"

Cathy staggered away, turned around, and vomited into a waste bin. She drew in a rasping breath and then vomited again. "Oh God," she groaned. "Oh God, I thought that was real. That night…

that night with the strawberries—" she vomited again, heaving until there was nothing left.

The gargoyle dropped the choker in Max's palm and went over to her. "Are you okay?"

Cathy went to a nearby chair and leaned against its back, shivering. "No. I am very not okay."

"Want me to go and break his face? I can do that. Just say the word."

"No," Max said. "No one is breaking anyone's face without the permission of the Sorcerer."

She looked at Max. "What about Poppy's wish magic? Is that in my hair too?"

"Wishes granted directly by the Fae are different," he replied. "They're not something inhaled or digested. They influence the soul directly, without any physical component. You either drank or ate something that contained these Charms, or inhaled them, in a perfume or cologne, or made skin contact with something holding the magic."

Cathy squeezed her eyes shut. "I thought he was different. I believed him. Oh God, I still feel like I want to go home to him!" She retched again, even though her body had expelled everything it could.

"It's the Charm," Max said. "Your husband, I take it?" At her nod, he said, "And you saw him this morning?" She nodded again. "And he said he would see you tonight, intimating—"

"We've got the bloody idea!" the gargoyle said. "No need to rub it in, for heaven's sake!"

"I'm simply trying to help Cathy understand that the desire to return home is seated within the Charm's effect and shouldn't be trusted. He has implanted a suggestion that when they are reunited, the lust created by the Charm will be sated, therefore—"

"Enough!" Cathy yelled. "That's enough," she said again, more quietly. "I understand." She stood up, straightening herself, her hand on her stomach, her face still grey. "I see the truth of it now. Thank you. For opening my eyes."

The gargoyle padded after her as she headed for the door. "Where are you going? You're not going back to him, are you? Cathy?"

She stopped, kissed the top of its head, and sniffed as tears started to fall. "No. I know what I have to do now. And it doesn't involve that bastard." Her voice cracked as she said it, but Cathy pulled the cloak tighter around herself, gave him and the gargoyle one last look, and walked out.

27

Will bounded up the steps to the front door two at a time and smiled at Morgan as the door opened. "Morgan! Good evening! Has the Duchess dined? I'm famished. If she's already eaten I'd like something quick, cold cuts perhaps, and wine for both of us. We are not to be disturbed until the morning."

It was only when he handed his cane to Morgan that Will noticed the look on his face. "I'm afraid her Grace isn't at home, sir. An Arbiter was waiting for her when she returned from the wedding. They had a conversation in the drawing room, and then the Arbiter insisted she leave with him. Alone."

Will tore off his cape, furious. Why was it so damn hard to spend time with his own bloody wife? Then he stopped, chilled. "Insisted she leave? He didn't arrest her, did he?"

"No, your Grace! Nothing as terrible as that. But when Carter pressed to accompany her, the Arbiter wouldn't permit it. She seemed concerned about something, nervous perhaps, but not under duress."

"How long ago was this?"

Morgan checked the grandfather clock behind him. "Over four hours, your Grace. The Duchess said she would be back by seven at the latest, but…"

It was almost nine. He'd been waiting to see the Patroon for hours, then once everything was resolved he'd gone to his mother and sister to give them the good news. They were in such a state, he'd stayed until their nerves had settled and his father returned home. He'd never seen him look so haggard. Then his father had insisted Will debrief him and they'd got into a rather involved discussion about Aquae Sulis and then Jorvic. Will had elected to use a Way to Bathurst Stables and return on the last leg by carriage, seeing as he'd left the city via the stables and didn't want there to be any gossip about his not having returned home.

Even if he'd stepped straight through a glass into his study, Cathy would have been long gone. "Which Arbiter? Faulkner?"

"No, your Grace, the one who visited before. His name is Max. My impression is that her Grace has known him for some time. I understand he was involved in the recovery of her uncle. Not that I attend to gossip, your Grace, but—"

"From Aquae Sulis!" Will's teeth clenched. The same one who'd arrested his father? Was this some personal vendetta against his family? No. The Arbiters were incapable of such things.

"Inform me the moment she comes home," he said, and went to his study.

He poured a brandy, unable to shake the feeling that something terribly important was happening and he knew nothing about it. He downed the glass and poured another, running through options in his mind, discarding each one as soon as it was considered. He could contact Faulkner, but the same problem as before stayed his hand: a London Arbiter would have little idea of what Max was investigating. Surely visiting the Duchess was way out of his jurisdiction? Perhaps a formal complaint would be in order. He doubted it would bring Cathy home any faster, and he didn't relish the thought of having to tell Faulkner that his wife was tangled up in something he had no awareness of. It would be too humiliating.

There was no one else to ask for help. Tom wouldn't have any idea what an Aquae Sulis Arbiter was up to either, and Will didn't want anyone else to know that he had no idea what she was doing or where she was. He heard the clock strike nine. Was he overreacting? Surely any moment she would walk back through the door and tell him all about it. And then they would make love. He scowled. He should have done it that morning and made themselves late. It was only Elizabeth's wedding, after all.

A parlourmaid knocked and asked if he wanted a fire. At his

nod, she did her work at the grate before drawing the curtains to give a semblance of nighttime. She curtsied, lingering a little longer than necessary to look at him with barely disguised lust before leaving reluctantly.

Will shut his eyes. This damn Charm was being wasted; the one person it was designed for wasn't there. He went over to the fire, warming himself, willing Cathy to come home. He twisted the ring on his finger, imagining its twin on hers and then, out of nowhere, he remembered Elizabeth coming to his study and telling him about the conversation she'd overheard between Cathy and the Arbiter. On a phone. In the nursery wing.

He abandoned his glass on the mantelpiece and raced up the stairs, heading straight for the nursery wing. If he could find her phone, he could call the Arbiter, demand to know where his wife was and that she be brought home immediately.

After whispering the Charm at the green baize door, Will stepped through. He saw the warm glow of Sophia's night light down the corridor and heard Uncle Vincent moving around in the bedroom across the hall from hers. Will slowed, walking quietly, having no desire to explain himself to his uncle.

He went to the schoolroom, closed the door, and switched on the light. Dismayed, he took in the hundreds of places a mobile phone could be hidden away, and there wasn't even any guarantee she kept it in here. He paused. She wouldn't keep it in the main house, as that would mean every time she used it she would have to smuggle it into the nursery wing. That wasn't impossible, but hardly practical.

Assuming she kept it in the room Elizabeth had heard her speaking in, it would have to be somewhere that wasn't used in everyday teaching. That eliminated the dozens of drawers and boxes that were easily accessible to both Vincent and Sophia.

There was a Charm for finding things that had been hidden, but Will couldn't bear the thought of going to Tate and asking her for one. He went to the walk-in cupboard in the corner, one that he'd never seen Vincent or Sophia go into, and switched on the lamp inside it. There were several shelves, filled with books and paper mostly, but deep enough to hide things behind what was on view. He grabbed one of Sophia's little chairs, stood on it, and began to rifle through the topmost shelf.

It didn't take long to find. Will focused on the two shelves out of Sophia's reach and sure enough, there was a mobile phone wrapped in a square of felt. At first glance it looked like a random piece of crafting material that had simply fallen out of the box next to it.

As soon as he switched it on Will checked that the ringtone was set to silent, glad that his Grand Tour had been so recent; he knew how the mechanism worked. His father—his brother, even— wouldn't have had a clue. It took him a minute to work out the interface and where the call logs were stored, but he was soon skimming a list of calls received and calls made. There were more of the latter, presumably because she had to keep it switched off so it didn't make any noise during the day, but there were only two numbers that had been called, listed as "Max" and "Sam."

Why was his wife phoning them in the first place? Then the screen lit up with an incoming call from "voicemail." Will accepted it and listened.

The first was from Max, a few days old, warning her that she was likely to be attacked. If only she'd picked that one up. He grudgingly admitted to himself that perhaps a direct line to an Arbiter looking out for her wasn't entirely a bad thing. He saved the message and listened to the second that had been left a couple of days ago, bristling at the sound of that man's voice. Sam. Lord Iron now. Whatever he called himself, Will hated the worry in the man's voice.

"Cathy, Dame Iris has just taken all the people from the asylum with her. They wanted to go, and I didn't think I could stop them. Look…she said you're going to have a baby. Are you? Are you sure you're okay? I can be with you in just a couple of hours, just say the word. You don't have to stay there, even if you're pregnant, okay? Just…just call me and let me know you're all right."

Will stabbed the end call button, seething. What business was it of that man's to call his wife and say such things? And why would

Eleanor say Cathy was pregnant before she was? Was it simply confidence, having made the plan with him already? Or was it because Eleanor wanted Lord Iron to know that Cathy was pregnant by her husband, so that he would stop hankering for her? What better way to put a man off another's wife?

He should have run that man through when he had the chance, before he was changed into...whatever he was now. Yet again, a moment of patience and mercy was coming back to haunt him. He should have made Cathy pregnant and killed the man who clearly wanted to be her lover, and none of this would matter now. Will breathed in and out slowly, resting his forehead against the doorframe, getting a grip on his rage at Lord Iron and at himself. At least he understood now why Cathy was keeping in touch with him; she'd used him to care for the people she'd rescued from the asylum. His trust in her remained intact.

He wanted her home. He wanted to hold her close and shut everyone else out and just be with her, make her his completely. He found Max's number in the contacts and called him.

A standard network voicemail message played after a few rings. Damn! He ended the call, not having planned a message. He could always leave one later. He switched off the phone and put it back where he'd found it. There was nothing to do but go back into the Nether and wait.

• • •

The cemetery was not where Max had planned to spend the rest of his evening. He'd delivered the Viola to his Patroon with a full and damning report of his crimes, gone back to Bath, and filed his report. As he dropped it onto the tray on Kay's desk he felt a sense of completion, the closest thing he could relate to satisfaction. He knew the Second Sons were gone and that no more innocents would be at risk from them. He had found the man responsible for his father's death and that of many others and done all he could to see him punished. George Iris would age and die in Mundanus, and Max would make sure he never took another person ever again.

Max hunted for any messages from Kay that might have come via Rupert, but there were none. He planned to go to the Iris Patroon in the morning to ensure the judgement was correct and establish the arrangements for George Iris's monitored residence in Mundanus. The innocents of Bath were safer that night than they had been in a long time.

Whilst he'd been dealing with the Viola, the gargoyle had gone back to Kay when it realised it had to let Cathy go and do whatever she chose to do. There was no Chapter to give her sanctuary from the Irises, after all. It had waited patiently in the office as Max wrote his report and then came over to him to tell him what Kay had found for them.

His father's grave.

Kay had bought a potted fern for them before she'd gone home for the evening, and had left it in the sink of the kitchen area for Max to collect if he wanted it.

"I know you think this is a waste of time," the gargoyle had said to him when it showed him the modest plant. "But it isn't a waste for me. And given our job, I didn't feel like putting flowers on his grave."

Max looked at the plant, trying to understand why taking it from the sink to the other side of town, finding a plot of empty earth, and leaving it on top wasn't a waste of time. "But there aren't any remains in the grave. He died in Exilium. The Patroon confirmed it."

The gargoyle rested its chin on the sink edge. "Can't you do it for me? I want you to be there. I want to be…whole, when I put these there for him."

"What about my mother's grave? Do we have to do the same for hers?"

"She was buried up north. She moved away to be near Jane when she was old. One day I want to go there. She fought for that grave for Dad, when he was declared dead. Kay found a thing on the

Google about it. No one's been to it for years. It doesn't feel right. We got the bastard that killed him. We did the job. Now I want…I want to tell Dad."

"But—" Max began, and then stopped. The gargoyle knew as well as he did that there was no one there to tell. He shrugged. "I don't have anything better to do, I suppose."

So he found himself standing in front of a neglected grave in a forgotten corner of the cemetery, overgrown and strewn with the last clumps of rotting leaves remaining from the autumn. The gargoyle held the potted plant, staring at the stone covered in holly.

It put the pot down and began ripping the holly away, its stone paws immune to the prickles. Max kept a watchful eye as the gargoyle cleared the detritus, ripped out weeds growing at the edges of the gravestone, and then began to gouge the dirt and moss from the engraving on the stone itself with its claws.

"That's better," it said, moving back. For the first time, Max could read the words.

JOHN SHAW

1879–1920

LOVING FATHER, HUSBAND, SON

LOVED AND REMEMBERED

The gargoyle put the plant at the base of the stone. "We got him, Dad," it said, resting its head against the gravestone with a soft clunk. Max took off his hat and rested it over his heart as he waited. After a few minutes the gargoyle turned and saw what he'd done. It nodded at him.

Max remembered the day they'd found Axon, the way the grief had torn through him. He didn't know if he should invite that back in. The gargoyle reached a paw towards his arm.

"It's okay," it said, and at its touch, Max was flooded with a profound sense of peace. Where there had been the most horrific grief at the thought of his mother, there was now a sense of duty done. The sadness was still there, omnipresent, but something had eased. A question that had always gnawed at a deep part of himself, one normally locked away, had been answered.

"Goodbye, Dad," he whispered.

• • •

Sam heard the crunch of the gravel and a car pulling up to the house as he finished the call with the gatehouse. Looking out of the window, he saw the London black cab they'd allowed in at his request and dashed to the front door before the bell had even been rung.

When he opened it, the cab was parked, its passenger door just opening. Cathy was getting out, promising the driver she was going to find someone to pay, dressed in a black cape over a very fine Nether gown.

"Cathy!" he said, going down the steps in his socks, pausing before he reached the gravel. "I'll pay the driver, it's fine."

She turned to look at him, her hair hanging in strands around her face, which was blotched from crying. Her eyes were red-rimmed and puffy but she smiled at the sight of him. She crossed the gravel between them, tears streaming down her cheeks. "Please hold me, Sam. Please."

He didn't hesitate. Sam wrapped his arms around her and felt her jolt, as if there'd been a build-up of static that discharged between them. Then Cathy sagged into his embrace, and he held her tight as she wept. "It's okay. You're here. They can't touch you now. No one can hurt you now."

"I tried," she said into his shoulder. "I did everything I could, but it wasn't enough. And Will—" She broke down.

"What did that fuck do?"

"He made me love him. It wasn't real, none of it was." The words dissolved and she sobbed and sobbed. He wrapped his arms tighter, imagining the Earth itself reaching up through him to hold her firm, to be her strength as hers faltered.

"Eleanor…" He paused, wondering if he should bring it up, considering the state she was in. But he had to know what they were going to be dealing with. "Eleanor said you were going to have a baby. Are you…"

"Eleanor said that? They were in it together, then. No, I'm not pregnant. I found out what he was doing to me before that could happen." She crumpled in his arms. "I ran away, Sam. I said I wouldn't, but I have and I hate myself."

"Shush, shush. How could you fight them if they were fucking with you like that? You did the right thing."

Over her shoulder, he saw the driver winding down his window, about to call. He held up a hand and then a finger, silently telling him he'd be just a minute.

"I'm not giving up," she said after a few moments. She pulled away just enough to look at his face, still enclosed in the circle of his arms. "I'm going to take them down. I'm going to find a way. I don't care how hard it is, those bastards can't carry on treating people this way."

Sam nodded. "Good. Listen, I need to pay that driver, and then I'm going to introduce you to a new friend of mine. I have the feeling you're going to find her very interesting."

"Can I stay, Sam? Just for a little while. Just until I'm on my feet again?"

Sam kissed her on the forehead. "You can stay as long as you like. It's going to be okay now, Cathy. You're safe."

• • •

Will woke with a jolt, the glass slipping from his hand to smash on the hearth. He listened for another knock on the door, thinking that must have been what woke him, but there was nothing.

Something felt wrong. He felt a hollowness inside, an absence he couldn't explain. His heart was racing. He got up and saw that it was after ten. Cathy still wasn't back?

He felt the wedding ring with his thumb absentmindedly as he headed for the door. Perhaps she'd just returned and he was woken by the sound of the front door. He stopped, realising that the wedding ring didn't feel right.

Raising his left hand, Will saw a loose band of wood where his wedding ring had been. The sense of loss sharpened within him and he knew, without doubt, that she was gone. Panicked, he imagined her lying on a Nether road, dead at the hands of the ones who'd attacked her carriage before.

No. Will quashed the fear. It made no sense. She was with the Arbiter, the one who'd warned her, who seemed to care about her well-being. He wouldn't have just abandoned her to—Will froze, remembering the message from Lord Iron. *I can be with you in a couple of hours, just say the word. You don't have to stay there...*Iron broke Fae magic—he recalled how she hadn't let him touch her when he came to the house before, to preserve the magic held in their wedding bands. What if the Arbiter had been a cover, to smuggle her out of the Nether? Into Lord Iron's arms.

He took a breath to shout for Carter, when his stomach lurched. Lord Iris. He was being summoned.

Will leaned against the arm of the sofa, steadying himself. Of course. He must know something had happened.

Despite the terrible nausea, Will forced himself to walk to the mirror. He pulled the silk from it and looked at himself, pale, distraught, before taking a breath.

"Lord Iris, Lord Iris, Lord Iris."

The mirror rippled, but instead of revealing a path through Exilium, it showed Lord Iris already there on the other side of the glass. "Speak!" he commanded as Will bowed.

"An Arbiter took my wife from the house whilst I was with the Patroon, my Lord. I've been waiting for her to return home, but just now..."

"She disappeared from the reach of my senses," Lord Iris said. "The link was severed by means other than death."

Will nodded with relief. "The Arbiter who took Catherine has gone rogue, my Lord. He tried to destroy my father only yesterday on false authority. I suspect Lord Iron is behind both of these attacks on our family, and that's why your protection was broken. He has my wife, I know it."

Lord Iris stepped through the mirror, making Will move back in surprise. He took hold of Will's shoulders, his eyes seizing him just as hard with their intense stare. "She was taken from you and you must get her back. You must tear Albion and England apart until she is in your arms again. For if you don't, it will drive you mad with longing, consume what is left of your heart, and leave you ghost-like without her. I know this better than any other truth."

Will heard the pain in his voice and suspected he was speaking of someone else, someone *he'd* lost. "I'll find her, my Lord. I won't rest until Catherine is safe by my side, with child, an Iris once more. I swear it."

acknowledgments

I cannot tell you how happy I am to be able to write this, because it means that this book is finally making it out into the world. This is no small thing. This series has suffered practically everything you could throw at it, including serious bereavement, changes in publisher, family illness and two rounds of surgery (on myself, rather than the books!). There was a time when I feared I would never be able to get this book out of my head, let alone into the hands of dear people such as your good self. If there's anything to be taken away from the past two years, it is this: tea makes everything better. No, wait, I mean: don't give up.

If thanks could be baked, the following would form a cake about ten miles high: thank you to Jennifer Udden, who has steered this little ship through such stormy and dangerous waters with skill, grace and a magnificent sense of humour.

I would like to thank Laura Duane, previously of Diversion Books, for giving the series safe harbour. Big thanks to Jaime Levine, my new editor at Diversion Books, for being so massively enthusiastic about the series and sending me emails that made me grin. Thanks to the production and publicity team at Diversion Books, including Nita Basu and Christopher Mahon, for giving the series such a splendid new look, smashing the champagne against the side of it and sending it back off into the world again with much fanfare.

Even though he's not my editor for this series any more, I would still like to thank Lee Harris, without whom the first three books wouldn't have found such a fantastic and dedicated group of readers.

Of course, this wouldn't be an acknowledgements without thanks going to my wonderful husband, Peter, and the Bean, both of whom have been very understanding and supportive and generally wonderful. Thank you, my darlings.

A huge thank you to the readers of the first three books who have waited so long for the next part of the story. Your tweets, emails, posts, blogs and gifts have meant the world to me. Thank you so much. And don't worry, there won't be such a long wait for the fifth and final book of the series!

And Kate. Still miss you, darling. It was hard sending this out into the world without having read it to you first. But as I wrote, I could still hear you shouting at Will, laughing at Rupert, and commiserating with Cathy. This book is for you, too. I love you. I always will.

EMMA NEWMAN writes dark short stories and science fiction and urban fantasy novels. She won the British Fantasy Society Best Short Story Award 2015 and *Between Two Thorns*, the first book in Emma's Split Worlds urban fantasy series, was shortlisted for the BFS Best Novel and Best Newcomer 2014 awards. Emma is an audiobook narrator and also co-writes and hosts the Hugo-nominated podcast 'Tea and Jeopardy' which involves tea, cake, mild peril and singing chickens. Her hobbies include dressmaking and playing RPGs. She blogs at **www.enewman.co.uk** and can be found as **@emapocalyptic** on Twitter.

If you want to go deeper into the Split Worlds, go to **www.splitworlds.com** where you can sign up to a newsletter and find over fifty short stories set in the Split Worlds!